SINGING
to the LIONS

REPUBLIC OF
VIETNAM
SERVICE

A Vietnam War novel by
ROBERT A. GISCLAIR

Singing to the Lions

A Vietnam War novel by Robert A. Gisclair

ISBN 978-0692496480

Library of Congress Control Number: 2013943416

This book is also available in an eBook.

Cover art by
Fabio and Andre Hirata
www.fabiohirata.com   www.andrehirata.com

Layout by Kelly Doucet Alario

Second edition published in the United States of America 2015 by

MorumbiPublishingHouse

morumbipublishing@gmail.com
www.singingtothelions.com
(985) 291-3204

TESTIMONIALS

Bobby Gisclair is a truth-teller. With raw, muscular prose, he pens a story that plants you in the war-drenched jungles of Vietnam and in minds and hearts of the men cast there by destiny. War IS hell but Gisclair's unwavering eye and deep knowledge of the physical and psychological terrain makes this journey a mesmerizing read.
-- Ken Wells - author of Meely LaBauve

"This is the most deeply touching book I have read in a long time. Bobby Gisclair's Singing to the Lions plunged me into war and kept me experiencing what a new soldier feels, hears, and sees. What a testament to those who go into service for the rest of us. Thank you, Bobby, and all who give of yourselves for the good of our country!"
-- June Shaw - author of The Killer Cousins

Gisclair's ability to make his readers think with the mind of a soldier and experience what he is feeling is eye opening for those of us who have not been to war and rewarding for those who have. Few writers about the military have done this as compellingly.
--Mary Gehman - author of The Free People of Color of New Orleans

Gisclair's powerful novel stands aside Oliver Stone's Platoon and Tim O'Brien's The Things They Carried as an essential chronicle of the life of the grunt in Vietnam. Released by a small, regional house in Louisiana this book deserves much wider attention.
--Mark Folse – Goodreads

Mr. Gisclair has written the All Quiet on the Western Front of the Vietnam genre. The story is well written, gripping, and a true page turner. It is truly realistic of infantry grunt conditions during this conflict in history.
--Doyle - Goodreads

… A great story that will resonate with anyone that has ever worn a uniform for this country.
--Irish_Times (Chicago, Illinois)

…I have read many books about Vietnam but before reading "Singing to the Lions" only three novels really stood out; "Matterhorn", "Fields of Fire" and "13th Valley" and this stands tall among these. I was shocked at the literary quality of what I assume is a first novel. It was like reading Hemingway for the first time. The writing was simply beautiful as the deepest chambers of a mind were unfolded for the reader so naturally. I sincerely hope Mr. Gisclair has more in the works and I hope he realizes how good a writer he really is. I have been waiting for this book for years and finally someone with the talent to write it did so and I thank Mr. Gisclair for his willingness to again live with all those ghosts to tell their story; a brave thing indeed.
--Steve – Amazon.com

Fiction sometimes teaches the greatest lessons. May we all go forth singing to the lions. A tribute to the tenacity of the human spirit.
--laurel e thomas - Amazon

This is a great book that is well written and will touch you deep, in your heart, your mind, your very soul. Like any great book, regardless of subject or genre, this one had me laughing, crying, thinking, feeling, wondering and dreading arrival of that final page, the last sentence, knowing my wonderful literary journey had ended. Well done Mr. Gisclair, please give me more!
--Russell - Amazon

After years of hearing several vets give small descriptions mixed with gaps of deep silence as they struggled to relate what it was like to fight in Vietnam, this book paints the picture of its gruesome reality. It not only reveals the resilience of the human body but its fragility. The book displays the broad but detailed scope of human observation possible when survival is threatened. It exposes the dynamics of relationships with others and with himself when life itself is constantly at risk. For those who never experienced but often wondered what "boots on the ground" really means, this author reaches deep inside of himself and gives you that answer.
--Armadilloz - Amazon

Best book we have read since Pillars of the Earth. We hope there is a sequel...
--lukeandro – Amazon

Singing to the Lions

Has received 2014 Honorable Mention in:

The New York Book Festival

The Hollywood Book Festival

The San Francisco Book Festival

The Paris Book Festival

and a member of the 2014 New York Table of Honor

PFC Robert A. Gisclair
Alpha Co./501st Infantry
101st ABN DIV

This book is dedicated to Nguyen Van Sai.
A great educator, friend, and human being. Hope you're
still alive, friend, and your beard is five feet long.

Acknowledgements

First on my list to thank is my wife Cida. She not only typed the manuscript, all its revisions, and gave good, sound advice on the story itself, but also put up with my bouts of irritability, and silly mood swings. My sons Ulysses and Diego share first position with her for their patience and understanding.

Next are Dr. Mary Morton and Professor Jackie Jackson of Nicholls State University. Their influence goes beyond writing techniques and I wonder if such people realize how they sometimes affect students in ways that stay with them forever...

Curtis Eller, a friend and fellow veteran, has helped me to remember many things that I had somehow forgotten.

My sister-in-law Debbie Gisclair has helped tremendously with grammar, and shown such understanding that I think she must have a bit of saint in her.

I wish to thank my late agent and friend John Ware, whose professionalism helped to bring my writing to where it is now.

I also wish to thank my friends Davis Kieff and his wife Stephanie Kieff, Woody Falgoux—author, and Mary Gehman—publisher.

Prologue

He loved his blindness. Just as he loved his hearing and his sight, he loved the complete dark that came with the night. He turned his head slowly from side to side to try to catch any sign of light from the hill in front of him. But the darkness was complete, and he saw only the deepest black.

He had never seen any light on these nights while he sat on the earth and waited. The sudden thought that he could someday see a light sent him a message of caution.

In a quick reflex his right hand went to the ground at his side and touched the small stick he had put there before the pitch-black set in. A thrill of joy came to him when his forefinger contacted the knot on the stick. Perfect: his finger safely touched the knot just as he had planned. He knew his senses were working well.

He loved the silence and the calm that came with the dark. All the citizens of the great forest were either sleeping or waiting patiently for any sound which could produce either breakfast… or the great enemy. Every creature was extremely alert. Even in sleep their instincts waited to react to anything disturbing the night's stillness. He listened unconsciously for these sounds while exploring quiet corners in his mind.

For a fraction of a second, his peace was interrupted by a slight stirring before him. But at almost the same instant, he heard the "click". His brain—working faster than any computer—identified it as a leaf being overturned by a prowling ant. His hearing, also, was working well.

Still, he reacted to the sound. He reached to the ground with his left hand and gently touched the stick on the other side. As with the first finger, it went faultlessly to the tiny fork of the branch, and again he felt reassured and happy. He knew exactly where he was. He picked up a stone the size of a lemon, calculated the direction of the nearest tree, and catapulted the stone into the dark. Sweeter than any music came the sound of a dull "thump," as the stone hit its target five yards away. Everything was set. He could, for a few more precious moments, relax.

Content with himself, he slowly raised his head. His eyes turned upward toward the three-canopy forest top that admitted no light. He knew that beyond the thick leaves and branches above him was a starry sky stretching to eternity, and everywhere in this eternity was a presence filled with calm and peace and purpose...and his mind drifted to its limit.

Part I

CHAPTER I

His name was White, and for long seconds now he had been bewildered. His mind swirled in that halfway world between sleep and consciousness, which tugged against each other for dominance. The sleep pulled him down into a numb void where there was no pain, and for a moment he gave in. But stronger and more insistent, his conscious mind stubbornly jabbed at him to awaken. It had already begun to stir as his nerves and muscles sent painful messages to his awakening self. Slowly and direly, he was forgetting the oblivion in a sleep brought on by extreme fatigue.

Suddenly, realizing completely where he was, a depressing verity came to him. There was no time for an easy awakening. A harsh day awaited him and he knew he must move now. Turning his head to one side he saw, scattered through the brush on the forest floor, the other soldiers in the company. He hated them. But even more, he feared them. There was something about them that was foreign and indescribable, not wholly human, and he instinctively knew they were very dangerous.

They sat on the ground, their rucksacks already packed. In front of each of them was the small, hand-made stove that heated the water to make their chocolate or coffee. They had already eaten, and most were now smoking, waiting for the water to boil. White's eyes rested too long on one of them. His heart jumped as the man turned his head slowly to him. As if he could feel White looking at him his fixed stare bore deeply into White.

The look White received shocked him. Nothing in his life had prepared him for the expression of the man staring at him. It was completely calm. Not a muscle twitched; there was neither squinting of the eyes nor snarling lips, nothing that usually showed anger or violence. But something in that face was much more terrifying.

It was not the face and eyes of a rage-filled, angry death, but a cold, passionless, sure death. It seemed to White that the man seated on his haunches looking at him was some terrible, mad Buddha who viewed the surrounding universe of violence, and the stench of death, without interest. It was that detachment which frightened him the most.

To White's shock, the man reached out with his right hand and grasped his rifle. With the smooth motion of a cat, the soldier rose and lightly walked the five yards separating them. Not a pebble turned nor leaf crackled as his smooth, easy stride brought him to White's side. Gripped by a wild fear, White stared up at the man's dead, shark-like eyes. His heart beat rapidly as the man squatted down by his side. He imagined everyone in the world could hear its frantic pounding.

In a strong Spanish accent, with a voice like a deep, loud drum, but carrying only to White, he said, "I know ess rough, Blanco. But we movin' out soon, an' you better get ready *pronto*."

Being a replacement, he had expected he would be somewhat ignored, but he had never imagined he would be so totally overlooked. Before the Mexican, the only person to have spoken to him since arriving into the company was his pale squad leader, Smith. But when White remembered the hostile, evil blue eyes of the eighteen-year-old sergeant, he wished he would never speak to him again.

The quiet voice of this man, however, and the unexpected concern—even with that frightening stare—had a calming effect on White. He slowly nodded his head, and the veteran walked noiselessly back to his place near his pack. In one graceful movement he sat back cross-legged on the ground. In another moment he was back into his Buddha-like trance.

White sat up, forcing his aching back to straighten. He had a startling thought. From the veteran who had just come to him and the others around him, he had not heard a single sound. Totally quiet, they were packing or drinking chocolate and smoking, but he could not hear anything from them. The full realization of their ability to act without making any noise overcame him; with it came the determination that he, too, must become soundless. He began to roll his poncho and poncho

2

liner. A bit pleased with himself now, he didn't know until later that the veterans around him, seemingly lost in their own private world, could hear every move he made and were patiently waiting for him to learn.

He shivered slightly from time to time in the altitude of the cool morning. Except for where he had slept, the forest floor and surrounding plants were covered with dew. Everything he touched caused the dew to soak through his jungle clothes. Occasionally, huge drops of water would fall on him from the leaves above. He trembled when the cold water ran slowly from his neck down his back. He sat on the ground in silent suffering and waited for the order to again shoulder the heavy backpack, which would begin his third day in the company.

The pain in his legs had eased to a dull ache when, from some signal far in the rear of the line, the old timers began rising and putting on their packs. He watched a few of them as they effortlessly swung the fifty-plus pound packs onto their shoulders. White tried his best to copy them. On the third try he succeeded.

He slipped his arms through the straps, shifted the weight high onto his shoulders, and tightened the straps so much they threatened to cut off his circulation. Straightening his body, bent only slightly forward, he let the weight of his pack settle into its riding position. Still, he winced when the straps rubbed on his sore, blistered shoulders.

Then, instantly, the pain was gone. What he now saw drove everything else from his mind. From a few yards up the line, he could see Smith's pale face as he walked toward him. Effortlessly under the heavy pack, without a glance or word to the other veterans around him, the three-striped buck sergeant made his way to White's side.

The acne-scarred teenager, almost an albino white, had a look of authority about him White had never seen in anyone else before. Neither high-ranking officers nor any civilian he had ever encountered had shown such assuredness and strength. Smith's cold blue eyes looked deeply into White's. In a low, all-but-inaudible voice, he said, "You're walking slack behind Lopez this afternoon after chow." He then turned and walked back to his position toward the front of the squad.

White stood as if mesmerized. Green as he was, he knew what that simple sentence meant: the slack man was the second man in the line of march, just three paces behind the point—and the point was the most dangerous place in the line. These two positions were almost always the first to make contact with the enemy and, when walking into an ambush, most often fatal. Even without any experience, White knew that what Smith had just told him was that if they ran into the enemy, he could very likely die that afternoon.

The fear and apprehension of seeing his squad leader walk up to him a few seconds before had taken away the ache in his shoulders. But a jolt of pain in his back, plus the burning of his blistered feet, took away some of his fear as the soldiers fell into file to begin the slow, quiet climb up the face of the jungle-covered mountain.

His feet ached unbelievably inside his tightly-laced jungle boots. Every step sent the weight of the heavy pack straight to his soles, while the canvas boots rubbed raw the sides and tops of his feet. The pain climbed into his calves, which seemed knotted in cramps. His knees creaked with each step. His thighs seemed to want to give way at any moment. His back and stomach cramped with the constant strain of holding the backpack while bent slightly forward. His arms hung numb at his sides, his right hand clutching his rifle. His neck strained as it bore the weight of his steel helmet.

Just standing with the pack had caused him to sweat profusely. Now, walking, sweat flowed down his face and neck. But he managed to keep the three-pace interval between himself and the man in front of him while they ploughed through the undergrowth on the forest floor. So began the day's march.

Standing above everything in the jungle were the giant trees. Like monster sentinels, the two-hundred-foot-tall trees towered over the green mass below. From a fifteen-foot or more diameter base they rose until their tops drank in sunshine. Yet unnamed species of insects and reptiles lived out their lives in this, the third canopy, the brightest part of the forest.

One hundred feet down was the beginning of the second canopy. These hundred-foot-tall adolescent trees had residents of other species. Groups of monkeys fed there in the shaded light. Ferns, flowers, and mosses grew in the hollows where the trunk and branches met. Exotic birds of blue, green, red, and yellow flew from the second canopy to the third in search of nuts, fruits, lizards, and insects, competing with the monkeys for their meals.

Another fifty feet down, deeper into the dark shadows below, were the smaller trees of the first canopy. In the dark of this canopy, a false tranquility reigned, the silence as thick as the jungle itself. From there to the ground was the home of the larger apes, the giant snakes, and the tree cats. Every living thing in this part of the jungle moved with caution, using the branches, mosses, and ferns for cover.

Forty feet further down, ten feet off the ground, in an unbelievable chaos, were the tops of giant ferns, palmettos, knife-edged grasses, occasional bamboo, and smaller, thorn-covered vines. Scattered among these were the saplings of the upper terrace trees, waiting for a fallen giant to create an opening in the forest, to allow shafts of light to reach them.

The very bottom, called "ground level," was covered with a thick layer of dead branches and leaves. Huge moss-covered boulders, half hidden with dead leaves, were scattered on the forest's floor. Ancient vines of incredible size twisted themselves around the bases of trees, climbing their way upward toward the sun.

A dark, gloomy light barely penetrated to ground level and, with the dense vegetation, made it impossible to see beyond a few feet in any direction. The air, with never a breeze, was heavy and damp. An intense ammonia smell of rotting wood and leaves assaulted the nose. The trapped heat, humidity, and odors gave the effect of living in a greenhouse in summer. The ground was the most dangerous level of the forest because it was home to the two most deadly citizens of the jungle: tiger and man.

Through the merciless thorns and creepers, the long line of soldiers sweated and strained. Single file, they made their way through, holding a course almost parallel with the mountain but with a gradual, climbing curve.

Sweat had accumulated in White's boots and made a sloshing sound with each step he took. Small, thorn-covered vines, called "wait-a-minutes" by the veterans, grabbed and tore at his pack, clothes, and flesh. His lungs ached and pulled for more of the heavy air. He feared he would pass out in the intense heat. He sweated so heavily that he couldn't figure how he hadn't already passed out. Straining for every step and breath, he knew he was near his limit. But, just when he thought he couldn't possibly go another foot, some force from deep within pushed him onward.

In another hour he felt near his breaking point again. His legs shaking uncontrollably, he fell to his knees. Panting and struggling for air, sides and chest pierced with stabbing pain, he turned to look back at the other men. The first thing he saw was the veteran who had been walking directly behind him. The man had stopped, his shining green eyes focused on White. And his stare was the same dead-like, penetrating look as the Mexican's.

Two or three soldiers passed him, but the men in his own squad had stopped. They all stared at him. Behind the green-eyed soldier were Smith and the Mexican. They seemed to him human machines, more like mildly curious than caring whether he could get up once more. White saw that he would get neither pity nor help from any of them.

Behind the Mexican, panting desperately was one of the replacements that had come to the company with White. If anything he seemed to White more pitiful than what he, himself, actually felt.

Immediately behind the replacement was the squad's machine-gunner. Of all the stares looking at White, his was the strangest. His was not the blank, unreadable eyes that White had seen in the others. Looking for words to describe what he saw in the machine-gunner, the only thing White could think was…what? He didn't know what. But he felt a sudden relief of fear.

And it was the machine gunner's eyes that helped to bring White to his feet once more, giving him another ounce of strength. He grunted, strained, and, with a supreme effort, managed to get back on his feet. Still fighting for breath, he awkwardly moved on behind the man in front of him.

Within another half an hour, he was again at the point of collapsing. He knew he could not last much longer when, incredibly, the long line of soldiers suddenly stopped and began removing their packs.

It was time for the noon break. While the veterans began to unpack food and water, White only managed to slip his pack off his shoulders, letting it fall. He went limp and crumbled, falling outstretched on his back to the jungle floor.

CHAPTER II

Taking great gulps of air, White lay sprawled out on his back. After a few minutes, when breathing finally became steadier, he slowly turned his head to one side. He could see that the long file of soldiers had broken up. Either individually or in pairs, they were sitting on the earth preparing a meal.

Twenty feet from where he lay, the Mexican who had marched behind him that morning and a blond-haired soldier from another platoon were seated together, talking in whispers. He had seen the blond-haired soldier before. He seemed friendly with the men in White's platoon but was most often with a black soldier in his own platoon and squad. White watched them in fear and fascination as they seemed to communicate on a high level with a minimum of words.

Suddenly, they stopped talking. As if both could physically feel his stare, their heads turned at the same time and met his eyes.

It jolted him when he realized that the two soldiers he saw were no longer teenagers. They had somehow been transformed into something wild—something not human. Instead, they seemed full-grown wolves, expectant of fierce action, ready at any moment to kill. Their eyes also revealed in looking at him that they were not seeing a fellow wolf but, instead, some inferior thing not belonging to the pack.

White knew this was true. These two soldiers were reading him as if he was an open book with large print. His insides quaked and his mind spun as their stare made him realize how inadequate and unreliable he was; yet, he still could not release his eyes from locked contact with them. Like a snake hypnotizing a bird, their eyes bore deeply into him, and, like the bird, he lay there and couldn't break eye contact.

Simultaneously, as if synchronized, they turned their hypnotic gaze from him to each other. White had never experienced anything other than the normal, ordinary, daily events of his community in the Mid-West. Every day of his life had been rational, plain, and easily explained. Small-town Nebraska held few secrets and fewer mysteries. But as he looked at the two veterans, something foreign injected itself into his consciousness. He sensed that they had not seen him only with their eyes... but with their minds.

Now it seemed they were communicating with each other far more effectively than with mere words. For seconds their eyes locked. Then, as if both had reached a mutual conclusion, as if on cue, the tall blond reached to his side, picked up his rifle, rose, and walked away. He weaved silently to his own position and sat opposite the black soldier he was often with.

The Mexican turned his head once more. Focusing on White, he reached to the ground and unerringly grabbed his rifle by the pistol grip, forefinger automatically on the trigger and thumb on the selector switch.

He rose and in a few graceful strides stood above White. His hard face stared down at him. Then his mouth began to move. In his strong accent, almost inaudibly, he said, "Get your t'in's and follow me." He began to turn away but stopped before taking a step. Turning again and with the same quiet voice, he said, "Grab you' rifle first, and 'den you' pack."

Then, a sudden change appeared on his face. His stone-like, cold expression was replaced by an expression that White could not describe. In an instant he lost that savage, intense air and was very human. Looking puzzled, and talking more to himself than to White, he said, "You got to eat sometin.'"

Just as quick was his transformation back into the perplexing void and savage look that had been there a few moments before. His eyes bored deeply into White. After what seemed to White a lifetime, the Mexican turned, returned to his own position, and sat back on the ground.

White's mind raced ahead of him while his hand fumbled for the rifle at his side. Fear of the short soldier clashed with the sudden hope springing from this seemingly friendly encounter. He got to his feet.

Ignoring the pain in his tortured body brought on by every move he made, he grabbed the top part of the aluminum frame of his pack. Half carrying it, half dragging it, he began walking toward the Mexican.

Two paces from the veteran, he sat down and lowered his rifle to the ground. The Mexican was stirring a dry powder into the hot water of his canteen cup. He had not yet looked at White but with a quiet voice said, "Get a box of 'C's' out of you' pack an' a canteen cup an' some water. Some heat tabs, too, an' matches." He sipped his chocolate as White scrambled to do what he was told.

White brought out the first box he came to. Pointing to the small can on the ground in front of him, the Mexican said, "You can use my stove." The stove was an empty, burnt, prune cake can. The lid had been removed, and there were ventilation holes cut into the side on the top and bottom. "Fill half you' canteen cup wit' water, pop a heat tab in 'de stove, an' let it get hot," he said, still not looking at him.

White scurried to comply. As he did, he knew again that something eerie was happening to him. The same strange feeling he had when the two veterans were staring at each other, when he sensed they had been talking without words, attacked him again. He saw his hands moving, but it was as if they had a mind of their own. His thinking seemed separated, detached from his body, as he moved automatically to obey the Mexican. He watched, as if seeing himself in a dream, while his hands deftly searched inside his pack.

Oddly the strangeness started to seem natural. He saw how efficiently and smoothly he was moving, and for a moment he let his mind wander from what he was doing. He was drifting to an easier place, a place different from the misery of the physical abuse of the last few days.

A hard voice brought him back. "Open w'atever you got an' eat it," said the Mexican. His face was stern…threatening…frightening. White knew that for a second he had let himself be too distracted from where he truly was. And he sensed that the Mexican knew it, too.

White opened a can of beans and franks. Unexpectedly, the smell and sight of the food made him sick, and he said, "I'm not hungry."

"Eat it anyway, even if it make' you sick," said the veteran.

White would have eaten anything rather than dispute an order from this man, so he took a spoonful of beans and placed it in his mouth. At first, he thought he would vomit. But as he chewed, the sickness left him. He realized how hungry he was and how desperately he needed food. He began wolfing down the beans and franks.

"Slow down," said the Mexican.

Every nerve in his body called out to him to eat as fast and as much as he could. But the two words from the Mexican made him slow his eating frenzy to an almost normal pace.

When White had finished off the can, the Mexican said, "Now look in 'de box an' eat everytin' you find."

White rummaged through the box of C-rations. The first thing he found was a waterproof packet. Inside it was a candy bar. He ate it ravenously.

He was about to open a pack of cocoa when the Mexican said, "Save 'dat for later."

Next was a can of peaches. In seconds they were gone.

Again the Mexican said, "Slow down."

White got a grip on himself and slowly, but eagerly, drank every drop of the sweet syrup.

He found a can of crackers and ate them all. Then he found a tin of cheddar cheese, which he scooped up hungrily with his fingers. When all the cheese was gone, he licked his fingers until they were clean. Finally, he ate a can of pound cake.

"O.K.," said the veteran. "'De water's hot. Put in 'de chocolate and all 'de sugar."

White mixed the hot brew as instructed and began taking sips of the steaming chocolate.

The Mexican looked at him and said, "I'm walking point 'dis afternoon. Stay behind me an' I try to take it easy on you". But he had said it without a sign of emphasis, without feeling, like a zombie. Almost as an afterthought, but still without feeling, he then said, "Keep 'de empty can from 'de pound cake for you' stove."

Taking the last sip, White glanced toward the man before him. The Mexican's eyes were closed. He seemed in a trance, at peace, as he sat erect on the earth, taking in and letting out deep, even volumes of air.

"So," thought White. "This is Lopez."

White's taut, overworked nerves began to ease as he took quick peeks at Lopez. "He looks so calm," thought White. Half a minute before, he had seemed a zombie—a killer zombie—but now he seemed the most composed person White had ever seen.

For the first time since he arrived in the company, White felt it might be possible to survive this hated jungle and war. While the food gurgled pleasantly in his stomach, he continued to study the calm detachment of Lopez's face in that totally relaxed position. He wiggled his buttocks, straightened his spine, and tried to copy the slow, even breathing and serene expression of the man in front of him.

"Rest," the face opposite him seemed to say. "Rest and regain your strength." White closed his eyes and breathed deeply, forcing himself to be calm. He tried to block out any stress. He deliberately rejected wild images he had of lying dead on the forest floor. Finally, after taking a dozen deep breaths, his thoughts began to drift. He found that, like minutes before, he could partially detach himself from the aches in his body. But this was different. Now he was never really away from his body. He was still here. He was only resting...breathing. Seconds, and minutes, went by.

Then something tugged at his calm. He opened his eyes to find Lopez looking at him. There on his face was a human, relaxed look that eased the sudden tension in White's mind. In that moment Lopez looked so young. White could see that Lopez was perhaps younger than he was. He watched his face, fascinated.

Lopez's mouth began to move and, no longer like a zombie, said, "Take everytin' out of you' pack."

White immediately opened the drawstring of the pack and dumped its contents on the ground.

"Take you' canteens an' ammo off, too," he said.

White again quickly complied.

With graceful ease Lopez rose up, rifle in hand. Squatting near White's empty pack, he began separating its contents into two piles. When he had finished, he looked at White and pointed to one of the piles saying, "Don' need 'dat stuff. Jus' added weight." It contained extra socks, extra underwear, an extra shirt, pants, a one-man mosquito net, a fold-down entrenching tool, shaving kit, pen, paper, a fold-up mess kit with fork, knife, and spoon, and an air mattress.

"'Dat stuff's O.K. if you' in 'de sticks for jus' a few days, but we could be here another mont'. We gon' higher every day an' 'dat stuff drag you down," he said.

White looked at the things on the ground and could picture possible uses for them later. But when he remembered the terrible climb that morning, he knew the veteran was right.

Lopez turned to the other pile and said, "Light stuff goes on 'de bottom, heavy stuff on top. LRRP (Long Range Reconnaissance Patrol) ration' firs', 'den 'de poncho liner, 'den 'de C-rations an' 'de poncho. When you finish, close it up an' strap it."

White followed the instructions both as quickly and as quietly as he could.

When White had finished, the Mexican got to his knees, saying, "I show you how to fix you' canteens an' ammo bandoleer." He spaced all six canteen pouches evenly around the belt, then adjusted it so that it fit tightly around the upper part of the pack. He brought the ends of the belt around behind the frame and attached them in the inside center of the backrest. His hands worked like magic, evenly spacing the canteens along the belt, with one on each side of the pack. "Now you can reach back an' get a drink an' not take off you' pack," he said.

With ten pouches side by side, each holding a twenty-round clip of ammunition, the cloth bandoleer had two long laces on each end. Lopez stretched the bandoleer tightly across the pack, tying a bow where the laces met at the back of the frame.

Finally finished, he reached for his rifle, rose to his feet, pointed to the pile of extra gear, and said, "Get 'dat an' come on." He then turned and walked out into the jungle.

White stuffed all he could into his shirt and pants pockets. The rest he scooped up with his left arm. Picking up his rifle, he entered the slight opening in the forest that Lopez had made. For fifty yards he followed as silently as he could, until they came to an area where there was a large boulder, half covered with dead leaves.

"Don' make a big mess," said Lopez, "but dig through 'de leaves 'til you get to 'de groun'. Put 'dat junk in an' 'den cover everytin' back up."

White did what he was told. He then looked up to see Lopez

standing alertly above him.

Looking down at White, he dug into his front left pants pocket, taking out a small packet of toilet paper. He tossed it down to White and with a grin said, "Now sheet on top of 'de pile. When you finish, cover it up light an' come back to our 'spot.'" With this he turned, and in a few steps, disappeared into the jungle.

White rushed to comply. While he squatted there, fear overtook him. He was alone in the middle of a hostile forest. Hurrying to empty his bowels and bladder and to clean himself, his mind imagined an enemy behind every tree. He lightly scattered leaves over his feces.

His heart was pounding furiously as he pulled up his pants. He turned to face the area where Lopez had entered the underbrush. But exactly where was it? He looked frantically for any sign of a trail that would lead back to his own previous position and equipment. But on every side an unbroken green mass stood before him. The fifty yards separating him from his spot seemed like fifty miles. He knew he must not yell out, and he knew that he had to act quickly. He took the general direction Lopez had taken but was lost in a minute. Panic-stricken, he moved on.

A sudden thought occurred to him. Suppose that while searching for his pack he came onto the company, surprising them. No one but Lopez knew where he was, and the other soldiers were likely to shoot anything moving. He began sweating heavily. Then a soft voice said, "Hey, man! Right over 'der."

White turned sharply toward the voice. The green-eyed soldier from his squad was sitting on the ground, smoking and sipping chocolate. Totally detached and calm, the man pointed with his rifle toward a thick cluster of brush.

"What kind of man is he?" thought White as he looked down at the mesmeric face. Strange to him was how, in his exhausted, near breathless condition, he could even be curious about it.

Since being drafted he had seen many different ethnic types. But this man was different from all of them. Straight, jet-black hair, olive complexion, and thick, black eyebrows made him look as foreign as his unfamiliar accent made him sound when he again began to speak.

"Ah t'ink you gonna be all right, Blanc. But you got a lot ta learn.

Jus' listen good ta w'at Lopez say." He paused for a moment and then said, "An' don't get loss."

"That accent," thought White. "What is it? Greek? Italian?" It wasn't like anything he had ever heard. But whatever accent it was, and whatever else he was, he was definitely a veteran. And somewhere in his mind White knew that the man wanted to help him.

White followed the direction, passing four more men before coming to his pack. Not one had so much as raised his head. Again he realized how further skilled than he were the veterans, and he knew without doubt a stranger could never have approached them as he just had.

"They all knew it was me. They all knew," he thought.

He sat on the earth near his pack, looking inquiringly at Lopez. The veteran looked up at him and said, "Clean you' canteen cup an' put it away. When you finish, get a little res' before we start again."

The two men sat on the ground, resting. White's body still ached, but his spirit felt much relieved by the show of friendliness. His pain lessened while he sat in the same position as Lopez. Occasionally, White would look up at the dark face across from him, but Lopez seemed lost in thought.

White sat perfectly still, listening to the intense silence. His mind began leading to new, unfamiliar channels when some vague change alerted him. He looked up to see Lopez's protruding, black eyes and impassive face now looking at him. An instant of panic swept over him, but the unshaken look of the veteran quickly calmed him. Rising to his feet, and to White's complete surprise, Lopez winked and said, "O.K. Blanco. Lez' go."

White watched closely as he swung his pack onto his back. He copied the move as best he could, suddenly finding his own pack in place. He tightened the straps.

Slowly and quietly, he, Lopez, and the other soldiers of their squad began moving to the front of the line. White looked at the other members of the company as he walked past them. Representatives of every people on earth were in the ranks of the American Army. White, black, brown, red, yellow—and every combination of them—were there in the line. And they all had in common the same vacant, dangerous look.

There had been, however, one exception. Humped over and looking wildly panic-stricken, was the replacement in his squad who had come to the company with him three days before. He dully took his position at the rear of the squad.

White looked searchingly at him for some sign of recognition. But he only glanced blankly White's way, not recognizing him and, indeed, seeming not to see or understand anything.

White's tortured body was nothing to him compared to the sudden heart-shattering feeling he had at the sight of this soldier. But another change was taking place in his thinking. He felt a slight dizziness as something new entered his mind. Before now, he would never have believed in anything so strange, but he knew that what he felt was true. It was almost overpowering when, looking at his fellow replacement, he knew that he was seeing a dead man.

The shock of this revelation stunned him. Then something else became clear. A few minutes before, when he had been drifting too far, Lopez's voice had brought him back. Now, he himself had to choose. He could shut it all out, deny it all, and refuse the harsh reality he now faced, or he could try to live. He hurt for the short, soon-to-be-extinguished life of the replacement, but he resolutely set his eyes forward to Lopez and moved on.

Standing ahead of the line of soldiers was the unbroken, virgin jungle. Lopez looked back at White, then turned and walked into the underbrush. Weaving and bobbing, Lopez was soon more than three paces in front of him. White hurried to catch up but was instantly ensnared by the thorn-covered wait-a-minute vines. Not knowing how to disentangle himself, he ripped his way through one vine only to be trapped by another.

Lopez stopped and waited for him to catch up. With a voice even lower than before, barely audible, he said, "Look for 'de holes in 'de jungle. Don' fight it. Flow easy." Then he turned and began again.

This time White studied the jungle in front of him intently, squinting his eyes in an effort to see better. He blinked, then tightly shut and opened them. Gradually, like a focusing camera, the blurred jungle began taking on a different form. Now he was starting to see it. It was not so much actual holes in the brush that were to be looked for but, rather, areas in the tangled vegetation that offered the least resistance—almost secret paths—through the thick undergrowth.

White focused again on Lopez, who had come into a patch of the small vines. He walked, chest out, directly into them and then stopped to look back at White. With the vines clinging to his shirt and pants, he twisted his body sideways while he stepped slowly forward. As he twisted, the vines unclung from his clothes and made a slight opening for White to enter. "He's teaching me," thought White, surprised by the obvious lesson.

Lopez then veered to the left, ducking under a low branch. As soon as his pack had cleared the branch, he quickly changed direction to the right. Zigzagging, dipping and stepping, Lopez flowed through the bush. White managed to make his way behind him, breaking a trail for the rest of the men to follow.

White noticed immediately that his pack was much easier to carry. His concentration on Lopez took his mind off of the extreme fatigue he felt from the last three days.

Lopez glided effortlessly through the vines and underbrush, rarely disturbing a leaf. His rifle, always pointed ahead of him, seemed a part of his arm. He held it one-handed, like a pistol, with index finger on the trigger, thumb on the selector switch. This left his other hand free to push aside vines and branches, helping to make a path through which he could pass.

His large, black eyes, slightly protruding, sat above a generous Mayan nose. His thick, wide lips rarely opened to reveal the teeth behind them. Under his short, military-cut black hair were two wide ears that jutted outward from his head. A thick, short neck led downward to slightly drooping, almost narrow shoulders and then to a compact, muscular body that White knew must indeed have great stamina.

As White walked along, more at ease, his thoughts now turned toward the unseen enemy. Logic told him that, with the amount of vegetation around them, they could walk directly into enemy soldiers waiting in ambush. That was the real danger.

Now, for the first time, came a realistic picture of what his real chances of completing a year's tour would be.

CHAPTER III

Without warning, the hair on the back of White's neck stood up like that of a cat. Something extraordinary was happening to him; some extreme new sensation was digging its way into his consciousness. He tried to stop it, afraid of what was coming. But it wouldn't stop. It was too powerful, too insistent. He felt an odd sensation as though he was being watched, like the surrounding jungle had thousands of eyes—all looking at him. His scalp tightened and his muscles tensed. His mind raced and his pulse quickened. He felt a strange tingling. Then came the real shock.

The change was as physical and as immediate as when a person takes drugs, one minute being normal, the next seeing everything in a different light. Colors and movement became tangible. Odors and sounds became physical things, as dense as the surrounding trees. It was as if his conscious mind had suddenly changed places with his subconscious, or as if the milky, cloudy images of a dream had become solid.

Reality, as he had never seen before, unfolded itself around him. Instantly and with great clarity, he saw the jungle in a new perspective. The trees, the thorns, the smell—life and death—were all intensely real.

Everything had been horribly, physically transformed. Before this moment his life had been filled with uncertainties. This, now, was the true world. Looking around, he felt small and frail, not able to deal with this new reality. All he had ever known before this moment was nothing compared to what he now knew. Death was sure. There was no escape. Rotting, stinking death awaited him and everybody else.

He walked onward like an automaton, his eyes locked on Lopez's back. The pain was gone from his body and he was no longer tired. But now he felt a new qualm of nothingness, as if nothing he or anyone else could do would mean or change anything. His existence, and the existence of everything else, was meaningless, an empty void. For a moment he wondered if he was going mad but then realized—it wasn't madness. It was reality. And when he fully understood it, he wished he would go mad.

He was very close to the point of mental collapse when Lopez abruptly stopped. He slowly turned and looked at White. There was such a strange look in his eyes that White felt a quick relief from the mental struggle raging in his head.

Staring deeply into Lopez's eyes, White could see a change coming into them. He knew instantly that this man understood what was happening to him. For a brief moment there was a look of compassion in his face, and then he did the completely unexpected. He smiled. There was no longer compassion in his face but a joyful, pleased look. It was the most beautiful smile White had ever seen.

With three paces Lopez was at his side. "Don' thin' 'bout 'dat now," he said softly. He paused and then said, "You doin' good, Blanco. You' not gon' *loco*. You' waking up."

For a moment more he looked at White. Then his smile disappeared, and the same cold, vacant expression that White had first seen in him took its place. For seconds that seemed like forever, he drilled White with that stare. He then turned and again began walking through the underbrush.

It was a new White now following Lopez. He could plainly see the holes before the veteran entered them. His ears were alive to the tiny crackles when his feet crushed the leaves beneath him. His nose began to distinguish different, subtle smells in the heavy air. His skin felt the slightest touch of leaf or branch.

In gentle degrees the world opened before him, and, because the revelations were now coming slowly, he had time to study them and then admire them. Every measure that came to him was consumed, digested, and—after another half hour on the march—began to be savored. Exploring his new world, he lost track of time.

In the late afternoon Lopez began looking for a suitable place to camp for the night. He by-passed the most obvious, comfortable ones until he spotted a thickly overgrown knoll. He veered off toward it, stopping in a clump of brush near its base. Removing his pack and helmet, he sat on the ground.

White set his pack down ten feet from where Lopez sat cross-legged on the earth. He watched while the other members of his squad settled in on either side of him and removed their packs. Other members of his platoon began arriving.

The captain, first sergeant, their radio men, the forward observer team from artillery, and the chief medic arrived. They climbed to the ten-foot crest of the knoll, choosing places for themselves in the bushes inside the perimeter. The other platoons began to arrive until the company had completely encircled the knoll.

With his back to the center of the perimeter, Lopez sat behind a fallen clump of branches, intently studying the terrain in front of his position. Nothing moved but his eyes as he memorized every tree, rock, and shrub. Centering himself directly behind the largest of the fallen branches, he placed two egg-sized stones on the ground near him.

White knew that he had marked his place for when the total darkness set in. He chose a six-inch deep depression for himself near a knee-high rock. He laid two marking sticks on each side of him and then began to memorize every object within twenty yards. When he was done, he unpacked his poncho and liner and spread them on the ground in the depression. Removing the bandoleer from the pack, he hung it over his right shoulder and under his left arm, as Lopez had done.

He took out a box of rations, removed a canteen cup from its pouch, and set them on the ground. From a side pocket on his pack, he pulled out the empty can of pound cake. Taking out his bayonet, he pierced several ventilation holes in the can.

He began opening a can of spaghetti and meatballs when a slight movement in the far corner of his eyes caught his attention. Lopez was walking toward him, and White was relieved that he could now look at him without fear.

Lopez's dispassionate look was gone. Replacing it was a tranquil expression that contradicted his usual rigid appearance. When he reached White, he squatted down to his heels, saying, "You was t'inking sometin' earlier. 'Das good. It's good to t'ink." He paused for several seconds, and then continued. "Now you got to t'ink 'bout water. We don' know when we run into some, an' we won' get supplied for four or five more days—maybe more."

White nodded his understanding, glad that no words of response seemed expected. He wasn't sure he could have talked. And if he could, how could he express to the veteran the gratitude he felt for saving him earlier from mental collapse?

Rising, Lopez looked down once more. Talking slowly, as if speaking to a child, trying not to frighten him but at the same time making him understand the importance, he said, "We gon' get you ready for 'A Shau.'"

He had spoken as if he really didn't expect White to understand. But White knew that he had heard something very important. His eyes followed Lopez as he went back to his position on the perimeter.

"What, or who, was A Shau?" he asked himself as he finished preparing his meal. His gut twisted not knowing. In his imagination he saw a blurry something—a killing something—clawing at his belly.

Something told him not to ask Lopez about A Shau. Whatever it was, he would be finding out soon enough. Too soon, he suspected. Also, he realized that it was something the veterans would not like to talk about.

All at once he realized that the clawing was really a churning in his stomach. He could hear it now as well as feel it, a growling protest, and an urgent appeal from his body. Then the smell of the food turned his attention from the terrible words. "A Shau."

He had finished eating and was drinking a half canteen cup of very hot chocolate when he saw his squad leader appear several yards behind Lopez. Smith came intently through the bush his eyes locked on Lopez. His every nerve and all his concentration seemed focused on reaching Lopez without a sound. Unblinking, careful not to crack a leaf, he patiently inched forward until he was two feet from Lopez.

Lopez sat there, seemingly unaware that anyone was staring intently at the back of his head. An evil smile fastened itself on Smith's face as he triumphantly took another step.

"Got you," said the jeering squad leader. "I snuck up on the great Lopez."

"Impossible," thought White, disappointed that anyone could

sneak up on the Mexican. The desperate confidence that had built up in him concerning Lopez seemed to sink. But then he knew. He knew beyond any doubt that Lopez was aware of everything happening around him. White waited anxiously for his response.

Then it came. "Sure you did," said Lopez, never blinking an eye. "Wit' all 'dat focking noise you make, you couldn't even sneak up on 'hem," he said, pointing his head toward White. "Not only 'dat," he said, "but you stink."

Now a sour frown appeared on Smith's pale face. He walked around and sat next to Lopez. With eyes cold as blue ice, albino-blonde hair plastered to the side of his head with sweat, and a grimace, he whispered something to Lopez. The two soldiers began a conversation that White could not hear.

White had watched and listened to the encounter between the two veterans. His former self would have seen the exchange as a hostile, threatening move on the squad leader's part. But his new mind realized Smith's rigid expression and challenging words were signs of respect, and saw clearly that Smith knew he had not been successful in surprising Lopez.

It occurred to White that because he had heard and seen it, the scene had been intended for him. And with this new idea came the suspicion that maybe the veterans weren't as callous as he had first thought.

Practicing an emotionless face, he finished his chocolate. After the last sip, he took his canteen and poured an ounce of water into the cup, dirty from the chocolate. He cleaned the inside of the cup with his finger. When he looked up, he saw Smith staring at him. He then brought the cup up to his lips and drank the water. Smith kept staring at him, and he stared back.

For half a minute, they measured each other while Lopez sat looking out toward the jungle. Smith suddenly rose, rifle in hand. He turned to Lopez and said, "Your friend is sassy."

Never turning his head, Lopez said, "I don' have no fren's."

"Sure," said Smith with a small smile. "You're a real hard ass, Lopez. A real fucking hard ass". Then, to White's complete surprise, like they were really friends, the two veterans grinned broadly at each other.

Smith turned back to White. Smith's eyes never blinked as he went to him and squatted down. White looked into his intent, cold face. He saw plainly that the squad leader was indeed a hard man. But with an abrupt change, his features softened. Eyes still locked on White, he said, "You have guard from eleven to one. Jackson from second platoon will wake you". Getting to his feet, he turned and walked away.

White's head veered to Lopez, who still looked out toward the jungle as if oblivious to what had just happened. But White knew he had seen and understood everything.

In the best conditions there was but a shadowy, dim light in the lowest level of the three-canopy forest. By mid-afternoon the shadows became deeper, and the already bleak light started to fade. Objects began to lose their shape as their outlines mingled with the surrounding landscape.

In the flatlands and the cities it was still afternoon, but in the jungle it was twilight. As if a switch had been thrown, normal animal sounds that could sometimes be heard during the day abruptly stopped, and a tense silence enveloped the jungle.

White sat immobile with his rifle on his knees. Not knowing why or how, he sensed an instant warning that made him turn his head to see an obscure shape at his side. Lopez's voice, barely perceptible, said to him, "After you pull you' two hours on guard, don' get up to wake you' replacement. Throw a small stone at me an' I get him up." Before White could respond, the shadow was gone. After another minute there were no shadows. The pitch black had arrived.

White unlaced his boots and crawled into his poncho and liner. He lay there with his right hand gripping his rifle, his eyes staring unseeingly into the trees above him. His ears listened for any sound while he lost himself in thought. Ideas swirled and chased each other as his exhausted body begged for rest.

Then it came back to him. "A Shau". The word echoed through the darkness around him. But even that evil word couldn't keep his focus as he began to lose consciousness. Eventually, he fell into a light, uneasy, exhausted sleep.

Something touched him lightly on the shoulder, and he awoke instantly. A soft, Negro voice said, "Your watch."

White was able to put a face to the voice of the lineman from second platoon. As quietly as he could, White answered, "O.K.".

White's hand reached for his rifle. He sat up, staring into the dark. Feeling the ground on both sides, he found the two marking sticks. He vividly pictured the location of everything before him.

He listened intently while his mind traveled from rock to tree to shrub, looking for any passage that would allow an enemy a silent approach to his position. Minutes dragged by. He began to lose some of the fear of N.V.A. (North Vietnamese Army) crawling to him to cut his throat. All he heard was the intense quiet of the forest. His mind drifted, and he soon lost sense of time.

A pain in his buttocks brought him back to his body. He shifted his weight, reaching into his pocket for his watch. Getting under his poncho and liner, he struck a match and cupped it in his hands. Looking at the watch he saw that his two hours on guard had passed.

He blew out the match and got out from under the cover of his bed. For an instant he thought about crawling to the next man on guard to wake him, but then he remembered Lopez's last words. He felt on the ground until he had found a small pebble. He was about to pitch it out toward Lopez when something struck him on the chest. He heard a tiny click as the pebble that hit him fell to the ground.

He knew the pitched pebble was a message from Lopez. He knew it was to let him know not to move.

"He's awake," thought White. "He heard me."

He strained to catch any sound of Lopez crawling to wake the next man for guard. He listened in vain. There was no sound. He then lay back down and looked out into nothing.

23

CHAPTER IV

It had been six days since White's rebirth—six long days of marches, trees, and thorns. For almost two weeks he had been in the murky dimness of a three-canopy jungle. But now something in the forest was different. It took him some time to realize that it was the light which had changed. His surroundings had become much brighter.

Gradually, he began seeing shafts of golden-green sun rays descending to the forest floor. These beams of energy, like a limelight, caused the dewdrops on the giant leaves of the elephant ears to sparkle like diamonds. Tiny particles of dust and vapor floated and spiraled like ghosts through the shafts of light, only to disappear as they drifted into the shade.

He walked into one of these shafts while looking upward through the leaves. At first, his eyes were almost blinded by the brightness. After stepping out of the direct rays, he saw a patch of blue through a hole in the green canopy above.

He noticed that he now only occasionally saw the hundred-foot trees. But he was still too new to the jungle to know he had entered into a stretch of two-canopy woods, and that accounted for the change in the light.

For another hour he followed the black soldier in front of him. White now knew his name was Williams, and he had been with the company for two months. White could tell by Williams's style of walking that he was not on the same standing in the company as Lopez, the green-eyed veteran, or Smith. But he also knew the man was not as green as he was.

At mid-morning the long file of soldiers began to slow down. He didn't know what that meant. It was much too early for the noon break. He didn't think it was because they had found water, since they had run across a small stream the day before and had filled their canteens.

He turned his head toward the rear of the line. Four men back he saw Lopez and Smith walking side by side. The squad leader was whispering something while Lopez nodded his understanding.

When White turned back toward the front, he was again nearly blinded by the brightness. He felt a surge of heat like when opening an oven. But the air was so fresh. The ammonia stink of rotting plants was gone, and a breeze lightly ruffled the leaves of the trees.

He stopped and stood there dumbfounded, scanning the half-acre clearing into which he had arrived. Several of the soldiers from behind brushed against him while they walked by, but he hardly noticed. He relished the blue sky and the sun that shone down hard on his face. Its warmth burned its way through his sweat-soaked clothes, and he almost laughed with pleasure.

Suddenly Smith was before him, his pale eyes hot with anger. "Form perimeter," he said and turned away. He stopped after his first step and again faced White. "You better stop dreaming, dude. You're gonna get zapped, anyway, and that don't matter. But if you get somebody else killed with your dreaming, I'll kill you myself."

White knew instinctively that Smith, like all the other veterans, didn't bluff.

White walked toward Williams, selected a position next to him, and sat, ten yards from the opening of the clearing.

He noticed, confused, that the veterans were no longer trying to be quiet. Ten feet to his right he could see Lopez. Two places further down from Williams was the green-eyed veteran. White wondered again about him. Was he Greek or Italian? What was his name?

Williams lay back and rested, but Lopez and the other old timers were busy making chocolate or coffee. Copying them, White dug into his pack and began heating water in his canteen cup. He could hear sounds coming from the clearing. Again he asked himself why the veterans were so lax despite their uncanny ability to be silent. But he knew there was a reason for it. He heard a rustling of leaves and looked behind him to see Smith.

The sternness had left his face when he knelt next to White. "Look, man," said Smith. "You think this nice clearing and this nice sunshine is great, don't you?"

White did not answer but looked steadily at his canteen cup.

"Do you know what kind of clearing this is?" continued Smith. "It's a clearing made by our bombs. That means there's been North Vietnamese activity here. Yeah, N.V.A. That's those bad mutha-fuckers from above the D.M.Z. (Demilitarized Zone). They're not hit and run like the V.C. (Viet Cong). They're hard-core muthas that come down south to kill us all."

He let several seconds go by before continuing. "We'll use this clearing to get supplied by chopper, and what do you think the Gooks will do when they know we're here? Every fucking N.V.A. for miles will be coming after us."

White lifted his eyes to look into those of the veteran.

"Now do you understand?" asked Smith.

White nodded his head.

Smith rose and said, "When you finish your chocolate, join me in the clearing."

White leaned back against the tree. Looking around as his water began to boil, he thought about what he had just heard. The force of the bombs that blasted away the trees and shrubs to make the clearing had also thinned out the vegetation for a few yards outside of its initial impact zone. Because of this, he could see several seated figures even at the opposite side of the perimeter.

On his far left he saw where his platoon merged with another. The first man in second platoon was Jackson. He whispered something to the tall blond sitting with him. The last man he could see on the right was the same recruit in his squad that had arrived to the company with him and had failed to recognize him a few days before. The youngster was panting horribly on the ground, oblivious to everything around him. Next to him knelt the chief medic, wiping the perspiration from the recruit's brow. White watched as the medic lifted the recruit's head enough to give him a drink from his own canteen. The medic's intent Indian face looked down at the recruit as he talked to him in words White couldn't hear.

White sat on the earth sipping his chocolate, studying the men he could see, when the first explosion shook the ground and trees around him. Quick as his racing heart, he flung his body onto his stomach, flat against the trembling earth. While he lay there, the sudden realization that he was defenseless startled him. He snatched his rifle and bandoleer. Then he faced outward from the perimeter and waited fearfully for the attack.

The whole episode had taken five seconds. He looked to the side and was instantly confused. He could see four men at once, and all their reactions to the explosion had been different from his.

The green replacement lay on his stomach with his back to the perimeter, hands on top of his head and face to the ground. Williams had sat up and clutched his rifle but was now lying back again. Lopez and the "Greek" were sitting cross-legged and motionless, looking intently at White.

He knew he had reacted for nothing. The calmness of the veterans told him that whatever the explosion, it was not a threat. Looking into the serious faces of the two veterans, he felt total embarrassment. At first, he took their stares to be a reproach for his panic. But looking deeper, he saw something else. Bewildered, he sensed their approval.

He got to his feet and placed the bandoleer around his neck and shoulder. Reaching down to the ground, he picked up his spilled canteen cup and placed it near his pack. He took a final look at the two veterans. Both were now staring vacantly outward from the perimeter. Turning, he began walking toward the bomb-blasted hole in the jungle.

The scene from inside the clearing was truly beautiful. They were on the top of a mountain that had been blasted clean enough of trees to give a view in every direction. All around were other mountains, ridges, knolls, and ravines stretching as far as the eye could see. Many shades of green mingled in the trees and vines that covered almost every space in the surrounding forest.

Occasional pockmarked clearings showed where American bombs had torn through the canopies. Far in the distance, two mountains away, was a brilliant waterfall a hundred feet tall.

In the exact center of the clearing was a hole ten feet in diameter that held a green slime. Rain had filled the bomb crater. The water had turned green as it stagnated and now stank.

Scattered around the clearing, several men of the company were preparing a large enough area for a helicopter to land. Some were heaving together to move a shattered log from the clearing's center. Others were moving and dragging branches, limbs, and shrubs to the outside of the landing area. Two men from the forward observer group were shooting angles with their compasses, coordinating and confirming the company's position on their maps.

White was not sure which group he should join and was about to go over to the men moving the log when he heard Smith's voice behind him.

"You know anything about explosives?"

White shook his head to answer no.

"Come with me," said Smith and led White to a group of four men who were huddled next to the only tree left standing in the clearing.

Two of the soldiers were molding a white, clay-like substance around the tree. "That stuff is plastic explosives. We call it C-4. We use it to blast trees clear so a helicopter can land," said Smith. "That's the explosion that made you jump," he went on with a grin. "If you make this trip without getting zapped you'll be carrying some of this stuff next time we come out to the sticks."

White watched as the men molded the clay-like bars to the bark on one side of the trunk. One of the men dug into a plastic pack and pulled out a long, folded wire. At one end was a metal probe that he set down near the base of the tree.

"Watch this shit carefully, Dude," said Smith. "You've just been promoted. You're now the squad's explosives expert."

White stuttered back, "I don't know anything about explosives."

"Then you better guess right," said Smith with a twisted smile, "cause from now on you're the man."

White responded with a weak, "But…"

"Ain't no buts," said Smith angrily. "You can't refuse a promotion in the field. You're the man and that's it. Now shut the fuck up and learn."

The man unstrung the wire, and the group followed until they were all in the forest outside of the clearing. At the end of the wire was a hand-held lever detonator. "All right, everybody out!" shouted Smith. They all melted into the protection of the jungle. Smith turned to White and said, "Come on, Dude. You're gonna make the connection for us and blow this tree."

White and Smith went back into the clearing. When they got to the tree, Smith said, "Now, take that probe on the end of the wire and stick it into the C-4."

White did what he was told. The sergeant squatted down and broke off a piece of the plastic explosive from the last bar. Handing the palm-sized chunk of clay to White, he said, "Now stick this over the fuse and let's go."

White pressed the C-4 over the fuse. He and Smith then followed the wire back to its end in the safety of the trees.

White lay flat on the ground with the plunger in his hand. "Now," said Smith, "yell out 'Fire in the hole,' loud as you can."

White picked up his head and at the top of his lungs called out, "Fire in the hole!"

"O.K.," said Smith. "As fast as you can, squeeze the plunger three times."

When he did, a deafening noise and a sudden flash filled the clearing and the surrounding perimeter. The earth shook and the trees trembled for the first seconds after the explosion. White and Smith picked up their heads to see the tree crumble to the ground on the outward side of the clearing.

"Now we got to clean up, so the chopper can land," said Smith.

Forty men came into the clearing, sweating in the hundred-degree heat as they worked to clear a landing zone. When the L.Z. (Landing Zone) was clear of debris, White went back to his position on the perimeter.

The only thing left in his supply of rations was the instant coffee that came in every box. His stomach growled as he sat cross-legged on the perimeter and drank the bitter brew. He had used all of the sugar and cream in making chocolate, so now he contented himself the best he could with the dark liquid in his cup.

As he sipped, his head turned toward the right, and he saw the pitiful view of the replacement. He lay on his back, his glassy eyes staring into the tree tops.

White was haunted by the sight. Just as he was ready to go to him and make him eat, a startling thought came to him. Why had Lopez and the others so completely ignored his fellow replacement? Why had they helped him and so disregarded the other?

His head turned again, and he saw Lopez looking at the replacement. On Lopez's face was a strange sadness. Then Lopez turned to look at him. White began to see a change in his expression. From incredible sadness it went to one of resignation for the inevitable. Slowly, he turned outward. As he scanned the trees beyond the perimeter, his expression went completely blank.

White sat back, stunned. How could Lopez say so much without any words? But it was plain language. Nothing could save the replacement from getting killed or hurt. Trying would only hurt oneself.

Then, out of the silence, came the clop, clop, clopping of a helicopter. It grew steadily louder until it roared above the trees. A sudden gust of wind shook the leaves and branches. The whining of the engine mingled with the deep sound of the blades as the gun ship landed.

White rushed to the clearing, where several men had already gathered. He walked, head bent to the wind, toward the helicopter. The acting first sergeant was already supervising the unloading of supplies. White heard the deep, loud bellowing of the thirty-year-old, bald, black, five-striped E-7 yelling, "Get that stuff out fast. Pile all rations according to platoons and the water and ammunition in the center."

White hurried to help unload the bird. He turned to lay a box of rations in his platoon's pile, and, when he glanced to the side, he froze. Instant suspicion flooded him. Stacking boxes for third platoon were two Orientals. They brushed against other soldiers as they helped unload supplies.

He hadn't seen them or anyone else from third platoon before. When the company went on the march, one platoon separated from the main body. They "ranged," sometimes a half mile or more to the front, back, or sides of the company, scouting for enemy. If the main body made contact, that platoon could come to their aid from the enemy's side or rear.

Third platoon had been ranging and had just joined the company for re-supply. The two Orientals were among the group stacking their rations. To White they seemed so foreign, so like what he thought the enemy should look like.

Part of his training after basic had been the political aspect of the war. He knew the Viet Cong were South Vietnamese who sided with the communist government of the North. They fought a covert, hit-and-run war against the Americans and South Vietnamese government. Every hamlet, village, town, and city had V.C. fighters and sympathizers living in them. It was believed that the V.C. had spies everywhere, even in American units, and that you couldn't tell them apart from the other southerners.

He had heard so many stories about how you couldn't trust any Vietnamese. But none of the other soldiers around them seemed suspicious of the two from third platoon. They rubbed shoulders and bumped against the other soldiers and were so obviously a part of the company that White realized he indeed had a lot to learn. Still, even if they were accepted by the other veterans, how could they not have been, in the heat of battle, accidentally killed by their own troops?

Then, as if they, too, could feel his thoughts, both looked up at him. The pairs of slanted eyes instantly told White much about the two men, but the most important thing he saw was that both were veterans.

A dizzy feeling came to him as he stared at the two men. Their intent black eyes bore into him, and he visibly shook. He was brought back to the job at hand by the loud voice of the first shirt.

At the top of his lungs, the sergeant shouted, "All right, let's get this shit finished, so we can get the fuck out of here!" When everything was unloaded, the helicopter revved up, and, as suddenly as it had appeared, roared off into the sky.

"Let's go, let's go!" shouted the first shirt. "Every Gook in the country will be on our ass. Get that shit unpacked and distributed. Let's go, let's go!"

Food, water, and ammo had been divided among the company. Everything they would not need but that might be useful to the enemy had been smashed, buried, or burned. The company moved out with second platoon broken up into squads on flanks and point, a quarter mile from the main body.

The order of march found White again toward the front of the long file of soldiers. Williams was walking point. Walking slack was the green-eyed veteran. Next in line, and right before White, was the replacement. Behind White were Lopez, Smith, then the squad's machine gunner. Stretching behind and out of sight was the rest of his squad and company.

Within a minute of starting, they were again into the tangle of the two-canopy forest. For a quarter of an hour, they ploughed along. At times, White could see up to the point, and he studied Williams as he broke trail ahead of the slack. Following awkwardly behind them, the replacement looked to neither right nor left, struggling pitifully to keep up.

White looked back over his shoulder to see Lopez. In an instantaneous change, Lopez's expression went from vigilance to something else. Startled, White read on Lopez's face extreme danger. Panicked, he turned back to the front and saw the flesh on the point man's jaw explode from his face. At the same instant the green-eyed slack man went down like a rag doll, holes being punched out of the back of his shirt and pants, canteens bursting.

The sound came simultaneously. On his dive to the ground, White could see the stunned replacement stare helplessly while the bullets went through his body. He seemed confused and afraid as the last second of life left him on his fall to the ground.

His heart racing, nausea gripping his gut, White looked behind him. Lopez lay flat on the earth, staring at him. He removed his pack and placed the bandoleer around his neck.

White hurried to do the same. The move brought another burst of machine-gun fire that threw up dirt and leaves inches from him. He pressed his face into the leaves. He strained to push his body deeper into the ground. He wanted to lie still, unmoving, until the shooting stopped. But something pricked him. Something assaulted his consciousness, and he knew he had to act. He slowly turned his head until he could see Lopez. Lopez, too, lay flat and unmoving. Then his hand began to move. He pointed a finger to himself and then pointed to the right. Then he pointed to White and motioned a swing to the left.

White could never have imagined he could be so completely flat against the ground. He crawled on his belly to the left. He could feel his heart beat frantically against the earth. He skinned his nose on a buried twig in the leaves. He imagined bullets tearing his flesh with every inch, but he went on.

Suddenly, there was a single shot. For a minute there was deadly quiet. Then a voice called out, "It's O.K. I got him." White looked back to Smith. He signaled to continue to the left. White went on for another minute until he heard footsteps. Behind him, moving forward, were other members of the company.

From where the shooting had come, someone yelled for a medic. White picked up his head and was shocked to see the green-eyed slack man kneeling near the downed point. White had seen the bullets rip through his clothes and pack. He had seen him crumble to the ground. But the green-eyed veteran was very much alive. Lopez had moved up to them. A shout from the rear told them to form perimeter.

White got shakily to his feet and reached Williams at the same time as the medic. Bone protruded from the lower left side of his jaw. The medic began working on him as if his own life depended on it. As he worked, he asked the slack, "How about you, Frenchie? You hit?"

"Ah don' know," said the green eyed veteran. "Don' t'ink so. I'll check."

He began to unbutton his shirt as the captain and his radioman walked up to them. "Call for a chopper," said the captain. "O.K., Frenchie, what happened?" he asked the slack as he opened his shirt and looked for blood.

The veteran pointed down to the dead Vietnamese ten feet away. "He was alone," he said. "T'ought he got me wit' 'de firs' burs'. But all he got was mah shirt an' canteens. Lopez an' 'dis dude here," he said, pointing to White, "pull his attention off me, an' w'en he turned to Lopez again, I got him."

The captain spoke to the medic who worked rapidly on Williams, and asked, "How's he doing?"

"He'll—make it— I think. I stopped the bleeding and gave him morphine, but we need to get him out of here."

"Chopper will be here in a few minutes," said the radio man.

The captain pulled out his map, studied it for a few seconds, and said to a lieutenant, "Take a squad. Get them back to the clearing." He took another look at the map and said, "If you can't catch up with us in an hour, meet us tonight at coordinates 690-094."

He turned to his radio operator and said, "Call in new night location to the elements in second platoon." He faced the platoon and squad leaders. "All right, let's move out before any more of these young hotshots show up."

White walked over to a group of three veterans kneeling at the dead enemy's side. They had rummaged through his pockets and had found his wallet. They all looked down at a picture of a young girl. The dead soldier could not have been more than sixteen years old and could not have weighed a hundred and twenty pounds.

White looked at the dead man's face. It seemed so strange, so impossible, that he could be dead. Minutes before, he had been full of life. How could he so suddenly be so completely dead?

One of the veterans tucked the wallet and the picture into the dead man's shirt pocket. Almost affectionately, he tapped the N.V.A. on the pocket holding the picture. He picked up the dead man's rifle and said, "Wasn't much meat on this one. Just about a hundred pounds of balls."

Then it dawned on White why the veterans around the N.V.A. so clearly expressed their respect for the dead enemy. The youth had come alone to attack the company. He had not fled after the first shots. If he had, he would probably still be alive. But he had come to fight, and he had come to die. He had come alone…knowing he would die alone.

As the file of soldiers began to enter the jungle, White turned back to see the lifeless recruit who had arrived with him a little over a week before. The twisted body lay sprawled out on the jungle floor. Lopez was right. He never had a chance. So far as White knew, no one ever even asked his name.

CHAPTER V

The company moved out fast, trying to put as much ground between them and the clearing as possible before night set in. In the late afternoon they were joined by the men who had stayed behind to load the dead and wounded.

Just before nightfall they reached the top of a mountain and set perimeter. Exhausted, White curled up in his poncho liner and was almost instantly asleep. But two hours later the torture began. He lay flat on the ground with his eyes staring blindly upward. He tried to quietly stretch in an effort to relieve the sharp, throbbing pain in the middle of his back. Frantically, he held his breath to keep from groaning when an intense spasm shot up his spine.

The pain increased. He sweated with the strain of not crying out from the impression that his back muscles were being torn from his body. He tensed to the point that only his heels, elbows, and head touched the earth. The veins of his neck and head bulged as he withstood the agony.

Still the pain increased. Heavy tears flowed as he shook. His jaws and teeth throbbed from the violent pressure he had locked them into. The thought that he would soon lose control of his bladder and his bowels held no shame for him. It reached its zenith, and his tortured body held against it.

His equally tortured mind came to his rescue. He knew the hurt had reached its maximum, and he had withstood it without a sound. Some inner sense told him this was the point that physical agony could not go beyond—it could only either lessen or stay the same. That in itself was a relief and helped to calm him. He knew he had endured successfully and that he had in some way conquered something very powerful.

With the throbbing still at its strongest, he began to force his body to relax. In small degrees his muscles released the tension until his body was again flat on the earth. The torment began to ease.

With each degree that it dropped, his frantic breathing became deeper and more regular. Second by second, it decreased until he lay loose on the jungle floor. Only the involuntary muscles and the brain worked while he sank deeper into a relaxed state.

Finally, it reached the level where it had been before the terrible spasms began. He could have almost laughed with relief. He thought he could endure this level of discomfort forever, but it gradually continued to fade. When it became only a dull ache, his mind and body continued relaxing until he lay totally limp.

From the haze of half consciousness he was brutally, fully awakened. At first he thought he had been dreaming. Then he realized he hadn't been. The noise was real. He had heard a pebble hit the leaves on the ground six feet from him. He lay quietly clutching his rifle, dripping with sweat.

After a minute of intense quiet, he heard something else. Almost imperceptible, a rotten twig snapped three feet to his left. Then he heard a whispered voice that he recognized.

"What is it, Frenchie?" asked his squad leader.

"It's 'de new kid," said the other's voice. "He's had a bad time wit' his back tonight."

White recognized the accent. It was the green-eyed veteran that Smith and the others called Frenchie.

"Yeah. I know," said Smith.

"He comes on guard in twenny minutes," continued Frenchie's voice. "I'm on afta him, so I'll take his watch, too."

For several moments neither man spoke. Then Smith said, "That's all right, Frenchie, we'll split it up. I'll call you in an hour."

"O.K.," said Frenchie and noiselessly returned to his position.

A part of White's character called for him to protest, to let them know that he was as tough as they were. He could pull his guard. But another part, a grateful part, thanked the two veterans for taking his guard.

Now the weight of exhaustion and the struggle he had just had with pain pressed him further into the leaves. Then, as if a switch had been thrown, he sank into a deep sleep.

An insistent force tugged at White. In a second he went from sleep to full consciousness. When his eyes opened to the pale morning mist, his hand flew to his side to grasp his rifle.

A look around assured him that everything was all right. He wondered how he could be so sure that there was nothing to fear. Then he knew that the veterans around him would have known immediately of any danger in their area.

With a sense of relief, he realized that he was beginning to trust more than just their uncanny abilities at life in the jungle. He understood that there was no danger until he saw some sign of alarm from them.

Something struck him. A pebble bounced off his leg, and he quickly turned his head toward the direction from which it had come. Sitting on the ground and looking at his steaming canteen cup was the green-eyed veteran.

White sat upright. He reached for his pack and dug out a ration, his stove, and his last canteen of water. Putting everything he needed to make breakfast between his spread legs, he looked around him and was pleased to see that this time he was not the last one up.

In another minute the heat tab was lit, and a half canteen cup of water sat on the stove. He got to his knees and folded his poncho and liner into a neat square and placed both into the pack.

After eating, he sipped the hot chocolate and watched as Frenchie walked out of the thick brush. In one quick motion he was again sitting on the earth, smoking a long, unfiltered cigarette.

White picked up his rifle and got to his feet. He walked to the veteran and squatted at his side.

"No one called me for guard duty last night," he said, as he looked into the shining green eyes of the veteran.

"You was hurtin', so me an' Smitty took your watch," he answered.

That threw White back. In his mind he could still clearly see the wild, killer look on the faces of the veterans. But then he remembered that this man had been the second man in the company to help him. Now even Sergeant Smith, cold and stern as White knew he was, had stood his guard.

White was beginning to understand. In their own guarded way they were befriending him and teaching him. His mind searched wildly for words to express himself and his thanks to the man before him. In his mad effort at any kind of response, he finally blurted out, "Thanks."

White had been left almost speechless by the man's words. Now the man shocked him even more. He looked at White and with a small smile said, "Mah name's Boudreaux but not many folks 'round here can pronounce 'dat. Everybody jus' call me Pierre or Frenchie, or Cajun." He paused and then asked, "W'at's your full name?"

The haunting vision of the replacement lying dead on the ground had filled White with terror. But now that numbing fear was lifted from him. It was not going to happen to him. Now he could be killed, but someone would know his name.

"White. Curtis White," was the only thing he could get out.

"Dat's good," said Boudreaux. "But I'll call you Blanc. Dat means White."

Days passed. White had drunk the last of his water the day before. His pack was much lighter without food and water, and this made it easier to follow behind Smith. But he would have gladly carried double the weight of a full pack for a canteen of water.

He no longer thought of cool, clear water. Any kind of water would have done. Dirty, warm—even hot—and he would drink it. In his mind he pictured muddy pond water and knew he could drink that, too. He didn't know that before the next twenty hours passed, he would drink much worse.

He could now almost match the squad leader's sure movements as he twisted, turned, and dipped his way behind him. He knew now when to unfold the thorn-covered vines trapping him and when to plough ahead and rip them off his clothes and pack, ignoring the pain.

The long line of soldiers slowed and then stopped. Something toward the front of the column had halted the march, and each soldier took this opportunity to rest and catch his breath.

White shuffled the pack higher onto his shoulders, leaned forward, and let the weight of it rest directly on his back and off the tightened straps. He rested his rifle across one bended knee, turned sideways, and looked back toward the rear.

Four feet behind and below him he saw the sweating face of the machine gunner. Huge drops of fluid oozed out of his jet-black skin. They streaked their way down his heavy cheeks and jaws and onto the dull green bath towel around his neck. From his chin they fell to his chest and mixed with the sweat that soaked his pants and shirt.

The nostrils of his broad, flat nose quivered as the machine gunner sucked in great volumes of air. The whites of his eyes were actually light brownish-yellow, and in the center of them were the black, shiny pupils that searched his surroundings.

White watched the veteran in fascination. Before he entered the army, he had seen few Negroes and had never spoken to any. During his training he had seen many instances of racial tension. He had thought many of the blacks were like the New Yorkers—obscene, loud, and pushy. In private clusters he had heard a few whites calling the blacks "monkeys," saying they were not human.

White knew the man he watched was not a monkey. He was as human as anyone White had ever seen. More important was the recognition of the machine-gunner as a veteran ranking high in the company.

His head turned upward toward White, instant suspicion showing on his face. But then something was different. The blank, cold look White had seen in the others was truly missing in this veteran. The two men looked deeply at each other. White felt a great surge of freedom as he found he could hold the veteran's eyes. In an instant the suspicious stare of the machine-gunner was completely gone.

Replacing it was a look that struck White to his core. What he now saw in the eyes of the man was more than compassion and goodness. It seemed to White that there was no meanness or cruelty at all in this man. What showed most on his face was kindness.

A minute noise brought White out of a near-hypnotic state, and he turned his head to the front of the column. The long line of soldiers was again moving upward on the mountain, and he again began his pace behind the squad leader.

He was instantly alert to the problems of the march, but before he took his second step, he had a comforting, lasting thought. White had heard others in the squad calling the machine gunner "Louis." He didn't know if it was the guy's first or last name, but he did know that he felt safe with the machine gunner at his back. He could focus his attention to the front and sides and not worry about any danger from the rear.

White and the company sat on the ground and rested. It was the noon meal break, but few of the soldiers had any food left. Many were completely out of water, too. Only the most experienced veterans had a swallow or two left in their canteens.

White was completely out. He sat on the ground leaning on his pack and endured the extreme dryness in his mouth and throat. Occasionally, he would dab his face with the slightly damp bath towel around his neck. He breathed deeply, trying to will away the pain in his parched throat—and failed.

He glanced to his right and saw two men approaching his position. Smith and the chief medic made their way silently to his side. Reaching him, they squatted down on their haunches. After studying him for a few seconds, the medic said, "White, my name is Cloud." He jerked his thumb toward the sergeant and said, "Smith here seems to think I should check you out for dehydration. I can see he's right."

The Indian, by the standards of the company, was an old man at what looked to be twenty-one or twenty-two. He reached over and felt White's hands, face, and neck. He felt his towel and asked, "You're not sweating very much, are you?"

"No," was White's raspy voice.

"How long have you been out?" asked Cloud.

"Since yesterday," said White.

"Yeah," said Cloud, "almost everybody's out."

"We're getting re-supplied today," Smith broke in. "Third platoon's up ahead about a click (one kilometer). They found a clearing. We've just got to blast a few trees, so the birds can land."

"Can't never tell about re-supply," said Cloud. "They might not make it here." From the canteen hanging on his belt, he poured a quarter of a cup of water. "Here. Drink this. Sorry it can't be more," he said while White painfully gulped down the water.

Before the sound of the fourth round in the burst of machine-gun fire had reached them, Cloud, White, and Smith were hugging the jungle floor, eyes searching around them. It had happened so fast. White was amazed at them. They were so quick. Then he read Cloud's lips as he said, "It's far away. Third platoon."

Bursts of Russian AK-47's and American M-16's could be heard a half a mile away. Minutes passed as they anxiously waited for news from third platoon. They had been ranging a half mile ahead of the main body of the company. The platoon lieutenant's R.T.O. (Radio Telephone Operator) came running up to Smith and lay next to him. "They've got heavy contact near the clearing. We're saddling up to go there. Pass the word down," said the radioman.

"How many hit?" asked Smith.

Looking uneasy and nervous, as if afraid to answer, he said, "Four."

White was beginning to read these men. Two weeks before, he would never have understood how concerned they were about their comrades. He would only have seen a cold detachment, a vacant stare. Now he could see the tension in the faces of the men around him when the squad leader asked, "Who's hit?"

"Max and Jones got scratched. A cherry that came in with White got fucked up, but he's still alive." Then the freckled face R.T.O. looked at Smith and said gently, "Poncho's dead."

The R.T.O. and Cloud stared anxiously at Smith. White could see the strain as they waited for his reaction. But Smith could not say anything, as if he couldn't hear the word being passed along the line, "Poncho's dead." He stared blankly out into the jungle.

White was struck hard by Smith's extreme reaction to Poncho's death. He had seen a spark of sympathy in Smith but could not have imagined that anything could so completely affect him. Looking around him, White could see other members of the platoon as they, too, fearfully watched Smith.

White sensed that this was a critical moment for the company. He found himself losing concentration on everything else as he stared at Smith. He realized that what would happen in the next few moments would mean something vital to the squad.

Tense moments passed as the men around Smith cast fearful glances at him. When the twisted agony of his features began to change, something vexatious took its place. White could see it coming into him. A determination and coldness appeared on the sergeant's face when he rose to his feet and said, "O.K. He's dead. We'll be dead, too, in a little while. Who gives a fuck?" He seemed to withdraw even more into his arctic self. He looked around him at his men, shrugged his shoulders, and said, "Who gives a good fuck?" He nodded to the R.T.O. and Cloud, turned toward the front of the line, and said, "All right. Saddle up. We're moving out."

White got to his feet and took hold of the straps of his pack. He knew the soldiers had been struck hard at the news of Poncho's death. He also knew that, like them, Poncho must have been a veteran. But it shook him to his core when he realized how easily it could happen that someone could lose control of himself. He saw clearly that if it could happen to Smith, it could happen to anybody. It could happen to…him.

He realized something else, too. Another one of the replacements who had come to the company with him was gone. One had been killed, the other badly wounded. The full reality of his chance of going a year without being hurt fell on him. He knew that chance was slight.

CHAPTER VI

White's stomach turned and cramped as he walked toward the sporadic gunfire from the next hill. With each step he took, his eyes searched his surroundings for the closest hole, tree, or rock he could hide behind to keep the bullets from tearing through him. He practiced in his mind every desperate dive for cover, every swing of his M-16, every short burst of fire at an unseen enemy that could buy him an extra second to reach shelter.

With each yard, the sharp sound of gunfire became louder. The pace of the march had increased to the point where they were now nearly running to the fight. Thorns, brushes, and fallen logs slowed them only a little as they plunged through the jungle.

The quick pace, however, could not match the succession of thoughts flashing through White's mind while they raced onward. Nearly paralyzed with fear, he knew that most of the men were more aware than he of what they madly scrambled toward.

In his near-dehydrated state, his thinking seemed clearer than ever before. He knew that no amount of orders from any officer of any rank, no high official in Washington or anywhere, could have induced these men to go so swiftly forward into the firefight. Their fanatic struggle was due to a better reason than any order issued by a mere general or president. No amount of money could have spurred them to such a desperate pace. Then, instantly, he understood. They rushed to the aid of their comrades.

A heavy weight struck him when he saw that another question was whether he could measure up to this new standard. Fear of the flesh-tearing lead and steel, fear that instinct could override duty to one's comrades, pounded against a thin wall of will as he followed the veterans on a direct course to their fellow soldiers.

They nearly halted as a silence filled the air. Within a hundred yards of the fighting, the sound of gunfire and exploding grenades had stopped. In another instant the company again surged forward. Without orders, the line of march was being broken at the front, and the squads broke either left or right, surrounding the battleground. When the hill had been completely surrounded, the men cautiously moved toward the center of the bomb-blasted area.

An acre-sized patch of trees was torn from the forest. The only green left in the clearing was the slime and algae growing on the surface of the rain-filled bomb crater.

It seemed more like dragons than butterflies fluttering in White's stomach. Chills raced down his spine as he dreaded what seemed about to happen. But, through all the anxiety, he continued moving forward.

In his nervous state he was afraid he might shoot at anything moving in front of him. So it was a relief when he saw two men in a clump of brush and, recognizing they were American, had not panicked and shot wildly.

The first members of the third platoon he saw were a pair of privates dragging the bodies of two North Vietnamese. Each was pulling a dead N.V.A. by the heels toward a group of American soldiers. When his platoon reached the two privates, one of them said aloud, "Lend a hand. Grab a foot." Boudreaux and Jackson each grabbed an ankle. With four men now dragging the corpses, they quickly made their way toward the center of the hill.

White followed behind the men dragging the body of one of the dead enemy. Emotions ran through him so quickly that he was in awe that his thinking could be so clear. He watched in fascination the bobbing and twisting of the dead enemy soldier's head as it dragged along the ground. The eyes were closed, but the tongue protruded and hung to one side.

White had killed a deer once whose tongue hung out for the half mile he had dragged him. As with the deer, the hanging tongue made the dead man seem not quite human. He seemed more like a highly intelligent animal—some sort of skinny, ivory-colored, animal.

A trail of dark red smeared the leaves and ground as the hardening blood oozed from the gaping hole on the back of the dead man's head. A sickly sweet smell mingled with the rotten odor of the disturbed leaves as the body of the Vietnamese teenager dragged through them. Another smell crept upward to assault White's nose. The sphincter muscles of the dead man had relaxed upon his death and released the waste from his bowels. Piss and shit now mingled with blood to mark a rank-smelling trail behind the body.

Thirty yards to his front he could see a group of Americans looking down at something on the ground. He could see a look of anxiety on the men dragging the body as they neared the group. The men standing, too, seemed nervous as they saw Smith approaching.

Smith seemed oblivious to being watched, oblivious to the wounded Americans on the ground ten feet away. He seemed not to see the moving men around him while they formed a defense perimeter in the brush. He seemed unconscious of everything around him but one of the dead who lay on the jungle floor.

The four soldiers laid the dead Vietnamese next to their own dead comrades twenty feet from where Smith stood looking down on Poncho. An eerie silence penetrated everything as all eyes focused on Smith.

At first, he just stared down at the body without any sign of emotion. Then his face began to change into a look of extreme confusion, as when a child is frightened and doesn't understand what is happening to him. More moments passed and hurt set in.

White had never dreamed a face could show such pain. A low groan began to come out of Smith's tortured body that made the hair on the back of White's neck stand up. When Smith dropped his rifle and began to crumble, many quick hands and arms were there to grab him.

White looked down at the dead American. There on the ground below him was a picture negative of Smith himself. A young black man, acne-faced, very lean, thin lips almost smiling, lay dead on the forest floor. Bullets had riddled him, but his face and head were mercifully untouched. Someone had straightened his body and crossed his hands. He seemed almost asleep as he lay there.

Louis came to stand next to White. Looking down at Poncho he said, "He's Puerto Rican." His sorrowful black eyes turned to White as he went on. "Him and Smitty came to the company together with ten other guys. Later him and Smitty got split up to become squad leaders."

He shifted his weight to look down at Poncho and said, "They were the last two of that bunch."

No one said a word while deep, hollow sobs came pouring out of Smith. The men around him seemed helpless, like lost children themselves. They looked from one to another, hoping to find a way to help their squad leader. They were instantly set more at ease when they saw the platoon leader approach.

The lieutenant seemed well liked by his men. Even White, who had only spoken to him once, liked him. In his early twenties, he was one of the oldest men in the company and one of the few old men that the younger veterans liked. Very pale, blonde haired, blue-eyed, short but solid Lieutenant Woods was known to his men only as Sir.

Sir understood immediately that every man in the circle surrounding Smith was anxious about the sergeant. He bent down and looked into Smith's tortured face. After a few moments, he rose and said to Boudreaux and Jackson, "Take him to the farthest end of our line on the perimeter and watch him." As they began to turn away, he said, "Give him a little water if you can."

Jackson, even if from another platoon, bent down and whispered to Smith as he gently lifted him by an arm, "Come on, Sarge. We're going over there."

The rest of the company was constantly arriving. As each man appeared, he formed a circle with his squad and platoon, until the hill was completely surrounded.

At the center of the perimeter the captain radioed Headquarters and asked for evacuation. "Golden Eagle, this is Zulu One. Golden Eagle, this is Zulu One. Come in Golden Eagle."

After a pause, a voice came on the line. "Zulu One, this is Golden Eagle. Go ahead."

"Got KIA's (Killed in Action) and WIA's (Wounded in Action) at 960-094. Everyone out of water for the last two days. Situation getting critical. Request immediate evacuation by chopper. Over."

Another voice, tense, apologetic, answered, "Zulu One, this is Golden Eagle. No can do. Heavy contact in A Shau. Full evacuation impossible. Can send one bird immediately for killed in action and wounded in action only. Recommend finding L.Z (Landing Zone). in brush country to the east for withdrawal."

The captain took in a deep breath and slowly let it out before he said, "Roger Golden Eagle. There will be a platoon waiting for bird. Rest of company moving out now. Will advise location later."

"Sorry," said the voice on the other end. "But there's nothing we can do now. Good luck. We'll be standing by. Out."

White sat in a small depression on the jungle floor. Behind him he had heard the captain and the base camp talking. There was that word again. "A Shau". It was the way it was said. Lopez had said it in a way that had caused his imagination to see monsters. Now the captain had said it as if it was his worse nightmare. But at least now he knew that A Shau was a place and not a blood thirsty "thing".

On his left, he could see Boudreaux, the tall blond-haired soldier, and Jackson sitting on each side of Smith. The squad leader was breathing deeper now, and White could tell he was regaining control of himself. On his right were other members of his squad. Lopez and Louis sat near each other whispering. Every so often one of them would shift his eyes to see that Smith was recuperating.

Sir left the group in the center and walked to the men in his platoon. He paced up and down along the line and spoke in his high-pitched, North Carolina drawl. "They can't chopper us out, men," he said. "They can only send one bird, and that's for the dead and wounded. They're coming now. No time to load a chopper. No supplies, no water. I've got to tell you that you shouldn't drink that green water in the crater, but if you do, drop in lots of tabs."

Sir walked to the crater and filled a canteen with the foul-smelling, rotten muck. He opened a small bottle that held a couple of dozen water purification pills. He added the pills into his canteen and returned it to his pouch.

In groups of two or three, the men of the company got up and walked to the crater. Soon everyone who wanted to have one had a full canteen.

White had filled a canteen and was wondering how many tablets to put in when Lopez walked over to him. He sniffed at the open cap. His Mayan nose twitched, as he smelled the water. "We get sick for sure," he said. White had twenty tablets left. "Put 'dem all in," said Lopez. " 'Den let 'dem melt. W'en it's all melted drink 'bout half a canteen no matter how bad it taste. We'll be moving fas' to get out of here, and we need water bad."

One platoon had been left behind to secure the perimeter and to help load the helicopter. White and the rest of the company formed their lines of march, beginning the trek eastward toward the foothills and towns.

After two hours, a halt was called for a thirty-minute rest. White took out his canteen, filled half of his cup with water and brought it to a boil on his stove. All he had left from his supplies were three packs of instant coffee. He poured the brown powder into the green water and mixed them together until the liquid was a sickly yellowish-brown. He waited for it to cool enough for him to take large swallows.

If anything could have been worse than the smell of the rotten water, it was the taste. He nearly gagged, forcefully gulping it down. It was almost a relief when they put on their backpacks and began again to force their way through the jungle.

Within minutes, he felt a new surge of energy. The life-giving slime had given him and the others a vital lift when they badly needed it. The horrible taste in his mouth was forgotten as he shot ahead, rejuvenated, into the tangled growth.

That afternoon, he began seeing fewer of the great trees and more of the scrub trees and brush that marked the beginning of the hills and the end of the forest. White could tell by the looks of his fellow company men that they were much relieved. Though he could not tell why, he, too, felt as though a heavy weight had been lifted.

Later, he realized why. Now they could have air support. Helicopters and jets could only fire blind into a double or triple canopy, but in the brush country, when able to see, they were very effective.

In the late afternoon the stomach pains started. It began as a light twitch in his abdomen and quickly grew into an intense, wrenching ache. Microscopic organisms in the stagnant water had attacked White and the other exhausted soldiers.

The captain sent word that they had gone far enough and they halted for the night. Some of them hollowed out spots and arranged brush, logs and rocks forming a defense; others slipped away into the brush to temporarily ease the pain in their stomachs. White hurried, despite the ache in his belly, to set himself up.

Throughout the night he and the other soldiers crawled off to relieve themselves. Many were again in danger of dehydration when another reprieve was given to the company. It began to rain.

Sick soldiers quickly set up poncho roofs to catch the rainwater. Copying them, gulping the most wonderful drink in the world, White guided the fluid from the dripping poncho into his mouth and canteens.

Now he and the veterans were not worried about losing bodily fluid with their diarrhea. Now they could drink and shit and wash at the same time. Some took off their clothes completely as they freely emptied their bowels standing up. Others wallowed on the ground in the cool mud and leaves.

The rain stopped, and the stars came out. Everyone White could see seemed happy. Then more dark clouds drifted in and covered the stars. Now he was again nearly blind in the darkness before the dawn. He wrapped himself in his poncho liner and lay on the wet leaves. A sudden warning flashed in his mind, and he remembered Lopez's words: "we gon' get you ready for A Shau".

In the last two fights the company had men killed and wounded. If "A Shau" was worse, he knew it must surely be terrible. But even the dread of what lay ahead couldn't keep his exhausted body awake. Huddled in a fetal position, he fell asleep.

CHAPTER VII

The unexpected rain had stopped as suddenly as it began, and the first rays of the rising sun glimpsed the soldiers of the company sprawled out on the earth. Heavy brush partially concealed sleeping, exhausted soldiers, as well as those who sat guard, facing outward from their near-perfect circle.

From where he sat on guard White could see and hear, in the center of the perimeter, Sir, the captain, and the platoon lieutenants and sergeants. It had been decided to helicopter the company from there to a base camp near the coast. At ten that morning, waves of choppers would arrive until everyone had been evacuated.

Some of the higher brush would have to be removed to allow the Hueys to land. The captain had estimated an hour's work to clear an L.Z. big enough for five Hueys to land simultaneously. But for now he let the men sleep. While they rested, he and the others in the command group continued to make plans for the company's removal.

Except at the higher elevation, there was a muggy heat which quickly sweat-soaked the ragged clothes of White and the other soldiers. The stale, rotten odor of the fallen trees and leaves seemed to add to the thick, hot air they forced into their lungs.

Now, a different kind of heat began to show itself among the men. The sun's morning rays rushed through the cloudless sky and fell onto a shadeless hill. Wet clothes were drying on the bodies of the soldiers, and the damp earth began giving up its moisture in the glaring sunlight.

Men who had been asleep began to stir. Curvy heat waves and tiny puffs of steam radiated from clothes exposed to the sun. Then the blinding glare became too strong and awakened the rest of the men in the company.

But White had been awake for some time. He sat on guard, looking at the men around him. From the core of the perimeter, platoon leaders and squad leaders made their way to their men in the ring of soldiers. Orders were handed down that every man not on perimeter guard was to help clear an L.Z.

Forgetting the heat, men jumped to the job of cutting down the brush. Some had machetes, some had entrenching tools, and others had large knives. Those that didn't have a cutting tool hauled away brush. White's turn on guard ended, and he joined to help clear the L.Z. In less than an hour, a landing zone had been cleared large enough to land several Hueys.

With the L.Z. cleared, the exhausted soldiers searched out shady spots below the brush remaining outside the clearing. At intervals, the company changed the guards who were posted a few yards beyond the perimeter. But, apart from that, the soldiers remained as still as possible.

Then the hardest part of the morning began. It was neither the suffocating air nor heat that oppressed White, nor his cramped stomach and intestines. Neither was it because he hadn't eaten in days, nor that he knew himself to be near his end with exhaustion. What now oppressed him was the wait. He looked out at the others and could see that they felt it, too. They were so close to getting out to the rear areas where it was safe. But if they had not lost their pursuers, then a fight would take place, and the airlift would be postponed.

Now, there would be no avoiding a fight if attacked. In their sick condition they would have to fight. "If's" and "what if's" went through White's mind while he waited…and waited…and waited.

He lay on his side, curled up under a bush that partially shaded him. The only sound around him was an occasional insect flying near enough to his ear that he could hear the beat of the tiny wings. He welcomed the drone of the tiny flyer darting back and forth around the bush.

Time passed slowly. Occasionally, he heard someone stir enough to find a place to empty his bowels, bladder, or both. But, otherwise, the only sound was the tiny flying bug.

White had not been able to squeeze his whole body into the shade of the bush. From the knees down he was exposed to the sun. He watched hypnotically as steam vapor rose off his rain-soaked pants and boots.

More minutes passed. Then, without consciously hearing anything, he picked up his head and listened. Other members of the company begin sitting. After a few more seconds, the veterans packed their drying poncho liners and prepared to leave. White quickly followed suit. In another moment, he was ready to go.

He listened intently. Then, he heard it. Far off in the distance was the deep, bass-like clopping of helicopters.

The nervous excitement of the company was electrifying. Men who seemed like zombies only moments before now came to vibrant life. Faces which had looked empty were now expectant, relieved, but also terrified. Soldiers who appeared detached and fearless under fire now showed stress.

White understood that emotion. He, too, felt at once a great relief at knowing they would soon be safe. But he also felt a deep dread. In what remained of his fading optimism, he felt, in a simple, childish way, that it was not fair they could be made to stay if a fight started, now that they were so close to getting out.

The approaching squad leader drove that youthful, innocent idea out of him. Smith advanced toward White and the others in his squad. He seemed uninterested, cold, as he announced. "First platoon's on the third wave. Our squad will be on the last two birds on the right." He took one quick glance at White and knelt on the ground next to a low shrub. With a stern voice he turned again to White and said, "Gotta be fast on this one, Dude. No fucking around. Just get on that bird as fast as you can."

A loud moan gradually took the place of the clopping sound of the blades as the helicopters came closer. Keen eyes watched the five choppers approach the L.Z. White waited for any sign of the enemy trying to shoot down the incoming helicopters. Through bloodshot eyes he watched the choppers, half expecting at any moment to see them blow up in a fiery blaze.

Then a piercing whine and a great gust of wind assaulted everyone surrounding the L.Z. The helicopters seemed to be living and breathing things as the superb pilots brought all five birds to a landing almost simultaneously. Synchronized swimmers could not better coordinate movements as close or as graceful as the landing helicopters.

Within seconds, soldiers sat three to a side in the doorway of each bird. With legs hanging outside, feet on the landing skid, and hands clutching anything to hold on to, thirty soldiers boarded the first wave of helicopters. In less than twenty seconds from touchdown, the birds were ready to leave. Another high-pitched revving of motors and the helicopters zoomed away.

The first wave had not reached a height safe from small arms fire when the second landed and filled. As the second wave revved up for takeoff, the first could be seen at a safe height, heading east toward the coast and the safety of the American base camps.

The second wave lifted off, and the third approached at what seemed an uncontrollable speed. But these pilots, too, were expert and made a pickup look easy.

White had been prepared, backpack on and kneeling on one knee, since the first wave. Before his wave touched down, he and other men in his squad were running, hunched over, to the last two birds on the right.

He was quick for a newcomer but not quick enough to beat the machine gunner and the Cajun to the sides of the doorway. Both veterans had quickly seated themselves on each side and had strong grips on the edges of the doors. White scrambled between them and sat as they did, with legs hanging out, feet on the landing skid.

Another roar and the third wave was airborne. The goal of a helicopter in leaving an L.Z. was to get beyond the range of small arms fire as soon as possible. White could see in an instant that these experienced combat pilots knew exactly what they and their machines could do. In moments, they were high enough not to have to worry about rifle fire.

White was now experiencing a danger as frightening as bullets and bombs. He realized he had made a serious mistake in taking the middle. The force of one-hundred-mile-an-hour winds created by the flying helicopter sucked at his legs. Sitting in an open doorway without a safety belt, with wind threatening to suck him out and then a thousand-foot fall to the ground below, seemed to him the height of danger. He looked into Boudreaux's green eyes and Louis's dark face as they held on tightly to the inside edges of the doorway. Almost in panic, White yelled out, "You guys better hold on because if I go, I'm taking you both with me."

To the credit of the seasoned soldiers, they realized he was desperate and was not making idle threats. Both grabbed at him with their free hands and supported him the best they could. Almost gently, but in a voice heard clearly above the roar of the helicopter, Louis said, "Don't be afraid. We got you."

"Yeah," said Boudreaux. "We got it made from here. Jus' hang on tight, an' we'll be all right."

With their grips on him, he felt reassured. More seconds went by. He realized his comrades were not going to let him go, and he began relaxing. His fingers eased their clutch on Boudreaux and Louis, and he began to breathe more calmly.

When the helicopters had reached a height safe from small arms fire, the pilots reduced their speed and began an easy, even flight. At that point White knew, if nothing unexpected happened, he would finish the wild ride and land safely at a base camp.

He began studying the ground below him. The more he concentrated on the topography, the more confident he became, and he began enjoying the ride over the brush country below.

Occasional dead trees dotted the hilly, brush-covered landscape. They stood like dry skeletons, their rotting arms and fingers pointing accusingly upward to the Americans as if saying, "You did this to me."

He knew something had killed that part of the forest but could not imagine what could have so completely destroyed the trees. In what had once been healthy, live jungle, only dead trunks and brush remained. Something besides bombs had killed them.

But not all vegetation in the woods was dead. Bamboo and banana groves sprang up in hidden cracks and ravines. Small islands of new growth, first-canopy trees, appeared in scattered clusters in the desolate scene below.

At one point they flew near a dense area of two-canopy woods stubbornly clinging to the bare hills around. The pilots veered away from these clumps of jungle. Even green as he was, White could understand why. The brushy hillsides were much harder to hide enemy soldiers and camps, but the thick jungle could—and did—hide armies.

More miles went by, and again the topography began to change. One-and two- canopy forests sprang up, and the hills were again alive with many shades of green. High peaks, tops in the clouds, jutted out toward the sky. Streams appeared and disappeared from view, winding their way, ribbon-like, through the mountains.

The first signs of human habitation were small, man-made clearings. Inside these clearings, or on their edges, were grass and bamboo dwellings. Many of them were on stilts, several feet off the ground. They perched on gently rounded mountaintops near flowing streams.

Before coming in-country White had seen all the required films and attended many classes on Viet Nam. Besides that, he had read many books on his own about the country's history, customs, and different peoples. So, as he looked down at the houses he realized what he was seeing.

Below were the homes, hamlets, and villages of the mountain tribes known as the Montagnards. They were an ancient people. Probably the first inhabitants in that part of the world, they had in common what most indigenous people all over the world shared. Holding on to ancient customs, they resisted the Vietnamese invaders of their territory, constantly retreating further into the mountains.

Like the Indians in the Americas, the Dravidians, the Aborigines, and others of what were once primitive peoples, the Montagnards had been hunted and driven from their homelands. The Vietnamese had special names for them. They called them savages and wild people. Some didn't think of the mountain people as human but as wild animals that would be best exterminated.

But the Montagnards were not easy to exterminate. They were also not easy to assimilate. They had been living in their country for thousands of years and had no inferiority complex because of their treatment by the Vietnamese.

Many of the mountain villages had joined with the Americans in the struggle against the communists. Special Forces teams lived in some of their villages, training the natives in the use of small arms and tactics, while being taught the art of jungle survival.

Each house in the hamlet had a stand of bamboo, a vegetable garden, and a banana patch. Rusty-red and pale-yellow dirt showed where garden plots, suited to the thin mountain soil, had been hacked out of the surrounding jungle.

Red and yellow trails wound their way through the mountains, connecting the scattered hamlets and villages of the mountain tribes, and finally led to the first Vietnamese villages in the highlands.

Differences in the style of houses showed distinctly at the Vietnamese villages. There were still many houses of bamboo and grass, but mingled with them were cinderblock homes and buildings with tile or tin roofs.

There were other signs of civilization. Radio towers poked upward and connected the towns to the more modern world to the east. Occasional trucks ran along the widening dirt roads that eventually turned to asphalt.

Then the intense green began. A valley encircled by jungle-covered mountains appeared as if by magic. Mile after mile of flat farmland stretched eastward. Dozens of rice paddies were separated by man-made dikes two feet high. Every few hundred yards a half-dozen bamboo and grass houses, each with a small vegetable garden, made up an independent hamlet.

Waves of new rice plants blew in the light breeze. Their sparkling reflections in the water of the paddies and the shifting, intense green of the rice plants reminded him of a picture he had seen in one of his history books: Van Gogh with his swaying, hypnotic trees and fields of grass and grain. The scene below seemed a fit subject for the crazy Dutchman. Added to the effect was the occasional farmer and his water buffalo, knee deep in mud, endlessly plowing the paddies.

White shook himself to concentrate. He had drifted too far. "What did he know about art?" he thought. "Better to think about what was up ahead."

Like a great scar on the landscape and cutting the scene in two, was a modern highway. On the other side of the highway were small rice paddy hamlets. Two-foot-wide diked, irrigation canals, and man-operated water wheels seemed distributed perfectly. Family plots were separated by larger dike boundaries from each other. Beyond the hamlets stretched more miles of paddies.

White looked sideways to Louis just as the machine gunner turned his head toward Boudreaux. The tranquil scene passing below him had taken some of the dread out of his conscious mind, but that quick, cautious glance between the two veterans woke White again to where he was. He didn't know what the curious look meant, but he understood it had to do with something dangerous.

A mile ahead, void of any trees, grass, or any kind of vegetation, was what had to be the entrance to an American base camp. Vegetation halted at the wire barricade surrounding the camp. Like an island suddenly appearing on the surface of the ocean, the barren, colorless camp stuck out of the sea of green that surrounded it.

Near the entrance of the camp was a small village. A tree-lined creek separated the village from the camp. A couple of two-foot-high and two-foot-wide coils of barbed, concertina wire, with another strand on top of them, surrounded the base. At random intervals in the wire were empty cans, half-filled with rocks. Anything touching the wire would rattle the rocks, giving an alarm to the soldiers on guard.

Following the creek and winding along with it was the village's only street. Occasional mango trees, banana patches, wild sugar cane, bamboo, tall grasses, and weeds of all kinds lined the roadside.

Middle-aged and older men and women worked under the shade of the mango trees. Old women in baggy black clothes and cylindrical rice hats wove grass and bamboo mats and baskets. The men, dressed only in gym shorts, sandals, and rice hats, mended ploughs and harnesses, put new handles to hoes, and cut and stripped bamboo for the basket frames.

Being from a farm himself, White could understand the hardness of a poor farmer's life. But these people were much poorer than anyone he had ever seen, and he suddenly understood. Having broken their bodies in their younger years in the never-ending toil of the rice paddies, a few older people could now enjoy their golden years working in the shade of the mango trees. For them there would never be a true retirement.

A skinny, timid dog sniffed at a garbage pile on the street. He continuously and suspiciously looked behind him at the three naked boys, seeming to be four or five years old, who hunted him with pretend bows and arrows.

Near the center of the village was the market. Opposite the market and across a very stout wooden bridge was the entrance to the American base camp.

A wood-framed gate, laced with more barbed wire, could be

opened inwardly by the American guards at the main gate. On the left side of the entrance, ten yards into the camp, was the first bunker. It was made entirely of dirt-filled sandbags and steel plates. The walls of the structure were six feet high, fifteen feet long, and ten feet wide. Walls three-sandbags-thick were topped with perforated steel planking called PSP's. On top of the PSP's was a three-layer-thick sandbag roof. A three-foot-high sandbag wall on the roof protected the two American soldiers standing guard. A poncho had been set up for shade, and two shirtless soldiers, one white and one black, watched the helicopters fly past.

As they zoomed by the bunker, White looked up to see Louis and Boudreaux smiling at each other. He knew then that he was safe.

White's helicopter gradually slowed and then gracefully landed with the rest of the third wave. He smiled along with Boudreaux and Louis as he ran, hunched over, away from the helicopter. All three had a look of great relief on their dirty, young faces. White did feel relieved, but something gnawed at him. He had survived his first trip into the sticks, but a sudden gloom came upon him. Today was exactly one month that he had been "in country," and he grimly remembered that he had eleven months to go.

CHAPTER VIII

Boudreaux, Louis, and White jumped down from the helicopter, made their way around its nose, and joined the other soldiers of their wave. The group walked toward where the first arrivals of the company sat on the ground and waited.

Within a minute, they could see the last five helicopters of the fourth wave approaching the L.Z. When they landed, those men joined their comrades, and together the company began walking toward a huge tent, fifty yards away.

Several base camp soldiers walked in and out of the tent. It was the first time since coming to the field that White had seen anyone, apart from the pilots and crews of supply helicopters and dead N.V.A., not of the company. White watched them as they shifted their gaze toward him. When they saw the ragged, dragging infantrymen approaching, White could see their expressions switch from almost bored when leaving the tent, to something very different.

He didn't understand the difference in their faces until the strange clarity that he had begun experiencing in the jungle descended on him. What he saw in the base camp soldiers was suspicion, fear, and a sort of disgust. It was as if they were looking at wild animals.

They tried to hide what they felt by quickly looking away from the grunts, but it was too late. That look could not be taken back. White knew he and his fellow company men were savage killers in the other soldiers' eyes.

White realized it was the same look which must have been on his face when he had first seen the line veterans. He also knew he was seeing these rear area soldiers in a similar way that he had first seen Lopez and the others. Before the sticks he would have seen these base camp soldiers as normal American soldiers. Now they seemed so strange, so ignorant of the real world.

There was another big difference between the two groups of soldiers. The base camp soldiers were so clean. It was only then White realized how dirty he and his comrades were. He had been wearing the same clothes for a month. The only times he had washed them, and himself, were once when they crossed a stream and the night before when it had rained. His clothes were ripped at many places by the "wait-a-minutes." His boots were beginning to come apart on his feet. His body's sweat had soaked and dried on his clothes so many times that white streaks of body salt blended in with ground-in dirt.

White continued looking at them as they walked further away from the tent, trying to see more; but they quickly left without making further eye contact. The tent was sixteen feet wide by thirty-two feet long and made of heavy canvas. The sidewalls were six feet high and the center ridge, ten. Its sides had been rolled up for air circulation, exposing the interior to view. Surrounding the tent, except at the front and back entrances, was a chest-high, triple-layer sandbag wall.

The company, captain and first sergeant leading, lined up at the entrance. One at a time they entered while White and the rest of the company waited in the now-stifling heat of the sun. But it wasn't a long wait. With usual army efficiency at processing large numbers of men, the line flowed steadily through the doorway. When White's turn came, he stepped in. Two long tables, the length of the tent, were stacked high with pants, shirts, towels, socks, boots, soap, and underwear.

An E-6 in his thirties looked him over carefully and yelled out to the men beside him at the table. "Thirty short, nine double E's." White moved down to where a private handed him pants, shirt, and underwear. Next, in a paper bag, were the toiletries. Further down the line, he was handed a pair of boots and socks. At the end of the line was the exit. He was in and out in less than a minute.

Outside, he found himself in a group heading for another set of tents, fifty yards further into the interior of the camp. With him were Louis, Boudreaux, Smith, and Lopez. Walking side by side, fitting in, but in some obscure way apart from the group, were the two Orientals from third platoon he had seen in the first re-supply.

White studied them as they walked. They looked so different from Americans. The larger of the two didn't seem as foreign as the short one. Even his walk and carriage were somehow familiar; he seemed to be about White's own age. But the little one, whose entire look and every move, even his smell, were alien, didn't look older than fourteen or fifteen.

It still seemed strange to White, and almost careless, that the veterans had so completely accepted the two. He could hear them talking but could not understand a word. Even their language seemed so strange. All the words sounded the same. "Ching, chang, chong chung, ding, dang, dong, dung," was all he heard. All seemed the same.

Smith drifted to the two Orientals. He set his pace to match the larger of the two and said, "Guess you and Hahn will be leaving?"

"Yeah," said the soldier in perfect American. "We'll be going to Hahn's village for a day and see the folks." Then he smiled at Smith and in his West Coast accent said, "Don't worry, Smithy, we'll be back in two days." Hahn was looking at Smith with such a boyish, good-natured smile on his face that White was struck with an instant liking for him. Smith just shook his head resignedly.

Then White understood. The larger of the two, Hong, was American; the other, Vietnamese. They were talking about leaving the camp, AWOL (Absent Without Leave), and they were telling Smith about it.

But before White had time to fully absorb what was happening, he was in for another surprise. Boudreaux joined the group. Smith saw him and frowned, "You, too, Frenchie? You guys know you can't get away with this shit forever." He shook his head and said, "I'm not covering for any of you again."

All three veterans neared Smith. Boudreaux was the first to say it.

"Look, Sarge. Don' hang for me. Do w'at you got to, but I'm going out."

Then Jimmy Hong said, "Yeah, Sarge. Don't worry about us. If you got to burn us, do it, but me and Hahn's going to the *ville*."

Then, in a thick-as-molasses Southern Vietnamese accent, Hahn said, "You ver' good man, sergeant. Ver' good man. T'anke you."

Smith looked them all over, frowned resignedly, and said, "Fuck all of you."

White had heard everything. So had anyone else who wanted to listen. Three men were going AWOL, and Smith knew it. He looked carefully at Smith. He had respected him and even feared him, but now his admiration grew as he realized this was not the first time these men were going AWOL. He knew that Smith must have covered for them before. He also knew that Smith, no matter what he had just said, would cover for them again.

Evenly spaced, with twenty yards separating them, were more tents and a twenty-man outdoor shower. White sat with his squad and others in his platoon while they waited their turn to wash.

Boudreaux, Hong, and Hahn stripped and anxiously waited for their turn. When it came, they hurried to scrub themselves. When done, they dressed and disappeared into the next tent.

The other members of the company were not in any hurry to finish their showers. It did not take keen jungle ears to hear the moans of pleasure as the soldiers let gallons of the cold water fall on them. The heat and sweat were forgotten as the cool water revived them and sent delicious shivers of pleasure throughout their bodies. Giant goose bumps covered their skins.

They turned their mouths upward, drinking as they showered, until it seemed they would bust. They laughed with happiness, lathering themselves until every pore was covered with white foam. When their hands got tired of scrubbing, they let the cold water rinse them. Then they would lather up again and rinse again. No one rushed them. They stayed in the falling water until their skin wrinkled. Then, one by one, they dried off and put on new clothes and boots.

Finally, it was White's turn. He had never had a shower like that one. It was the most wonderful experience of his life. It was like the cold water was giving him a new vitality. He scrubbed and rinsed and drank. He stalled. He drank. He soaped and rinsed again.

When he was wrinkled like a prune, he stepped out of the shower. His skin felt the exquisite light itching of cleanness after being dirty for so long. As he dried off, he began to feel physically drained. He lazily put on his new outfit, picked up his rifle, and walked with a group toward the first tent.

Doctors assaulted him the moment he entered. He felt like he was on an assembly line. Robot-like soldiers moved from one robot-like doctor to the next. The only words being said by the machine-like medical staff were, "Next... Pull down your pants... spread 'em... cough... Next."

One doctor listened to his heart, another his lungs. "O.K.," they called back to a clerk taking notes. Then, "Next." He was ordered to again pull off his shirt and pull down his pants. An expert with needles and syringes jabbed him twice in each arm. In what seemed like magic, a medic had stabbed him with a needle as large as on a basketball pump, injected what looked like a horse syringe into his right and left buttocks, and told him to move on.

He moved with the line. He swallowed pills. One doctor looked into his eyes as another, looking tired, asked questions about cramps, diarrhea, sores—anything unusual. He continued asking questions, peering down White's throat. At the end of the line, he was told to come back the next day if the diarrhea and cramps hadn't stopped.

The next tent he entered was a marvel. Hot steam plates full of food were on a long table at the back. Four servers in white ladled out food to the slow-moving file of soldiers. White picked up a large plastic tray and got in line.

The smell in the tent nauseated him. He had been three days without any food, and the sight and smell sickened him. He had lost all craving for food, and his belly was drum tight with the water that he had swallowed. But even sick as he felt, he knew he had to eat.

The first tray he came to held what was either spinach or mustard greens. He took a ladleful from a freckled youth and moved to the next server, whose tray was piled high with a lump of some kind of partially-burnt roasted meat. A smiling Filipino mess sergeant hacked off a generous piece from the lump of roast and put it in his plate. "Eat, please. You eat," he begged each man in line.

Next was a great bowl filled with mashed potatoes. A bucktoothed, sandy-haired teenager with fear-filled eyes scooped a large spoonful into White's plate. With his other hand, he ladled out a helping of weak gravy.

White skipped the peas and carrots that a black private waited to put in his plate. With his other hand the soldier handed White two pieces of bread and two full helpings of butter. He then scooped up a four-inch by four-inch piece of chocolate cake and put it in the last empty section of White's tray. Off to the side were dispensers holding milk, Kool-Aid, and lemonade. White took two glasses of milk.

He turned toward the tables and saw Lopez sitting alone in a corner of the tent; he went to the table and sat opposite him. Lopez was eating like a wolf. He paused long enough to look at White, gave him a nod of recognition, and then went back to his feasting.

White liked spinach, but after his first bite, he knew he would be in a bad way before he would ever try army spinach again. He sipped one of the glasses of milk. The mashed potatoes were a little better than the spinach, and he managed several bites. The meat was tasteless, and, because of that, he managed to eat almost half of it. All he could stand of the chocolate cake was one bite.

That left the bread and the other glass of milk. He tore off small pieces of the bread and let them sit in his mouth before chewing. He then washed down each bite with a swallow of milk.

All the while he had been watching Lopez as he took in spoonfuls with gusto. He had piled his plate high with some of everything on the serving table, and White sat fascinated as he watched each pile disappear under the Mexican's attack.

A soldier from second platoon joined them. There was an amused, knowing smile on his face as he sat. He winked at White and gave a small nod of recognition. He turned to Lopez and said, "Damn, Lopez! How can you eat that shit?"

White recognized the voice as the soldier who had woken him for guard duty many days before. He had seen him talking to Lopez a few times and remembered his name was Jackson.

Turning to White, Jackson said, "What ya think of your first trip to the sticks? Bitch ain't it?" White could not answer. He didn't have the words to describe how he felt about his first month in country.

"Gets easier as it goes along," said Jackson, grinning. He looked at White's full plate and said, "Not hungry, huh? Wait till tomorrow. You're gonna think this slop is the best shit on earth." He smiled as he went on, "Yeah, tomorrow your stomach is gonna think your throat's been cut. You gonna jump into that chow like you're a dog."

That seemed impossible. White just couldn't imagine he could ever feel anything but disgust for the food on his plate. He looked from Jackson to Lopez. The Mexican didn't seem to notice or care that White and Jackson were there.

Jackson jerked his thumb toward Lopez and said, "Not everybody here is a dog like Lopez, though. He can smell a Gook from half a mile." He paused as he and White stared at the quickly disappearing mound of food in Lopez's plate. "The only thing that bothers Lopez," he went on, "is that he can't carry enough chow to fill that hole in his stomach."

Jackson laughed as Lopez turned to him, grinned from ear to ear, and said, "Fuck you."

Lopez wiped the bottom of his tray with the last piece of bread. Jackson and White stared at him as he popped the bread in his mouth and slowly chewed the last bite. Lopez looked contentedly at them as he finished off his lemonade.

He pushed away from the table and turned to Jackson. "Where Cook?" he said.

"Gone to the *ville*," said Jackson.

"Why you not go'n?" asked Lopez.

"I'm a little tired. Gonna go tomorrow. Got to let the *baby-sans* see me at my best."

Then, there was an eerie silence. The three soldiers sat there. Tiredness crept into White like he had never felt before. As if the last few minutes were the last reserves of his strength, he began to sag in his chair.

Even in the sticks he had never felt so tired. He had hurt more, struggled for breath, but never felt this tired. It was like his life force was being drained. It was an effort to just lift his head to look at the two veterans.

Lopez's blood-shot eyes looked back at him; he, too, seemed heavy with weariness. But there was something else. In him White could see a reserve of nerve and stamina that had never been touched, and he sensed that of all the soldiers in the company, Lopez was perhaps the best.

Lopez looked from Jackson to White. "Almos' finished now," he said as he got to his feet. He jerked his head towards the door of the tent and said, "Lez go."

White, not understanding what "Almos' finish now," meant, followed them. They began walking heavily toward three tents a hundred yards away.

Canvas cots filled the interiors of the tents. Each cot had an inflatable air mattress on it. Lopez stripped down to his shorts, made a pillow of his clothes, set his rifle under the air mattress near his right hand, and stretched out. Jackson and White took the time to set their equipment under their cots. They then stripped to their shorts and lay down. Before they could realize how comfortable they were and how good it felt to lie there without clothes and boots on, they looked to see that Lopez was already asleep.

White lay listening to the quiet, trying to sleep. Sparks of light flashed before his closed eyes. His nerves twitched. He thought he would never fully sleep again. He breathed deeply for a long time.

At one o'clock an orderly came into the tent and handed out letters to anyone still awake. As he handed several letters to White, he said, "Whoever wants their mail when they wake up will have to go to headquarters."

White counted ten letters, almost all from his mother. But anxious as he was to get news from home, he just didn't have any energy left to read them. He placed the letters under his air mattress and tried to sleep.

By two o'clock that afternoon, every bunk was taken. By two-thirty, everyone but White was asleep. The afternoon wore on, and he still couldn't sleep. Evening came, and the other men slept on. After midnight someone turned silently, without waking. Sometime after that White lost consciousness. At eight o'clock he opened his eyes. Some of the soldiers began stirring in the heat. For almost twenty hours there had not been any sound from the three tents. He had learned another hard lesson. In an active infantry company, no one snores.

CHAPTER IX

Hunger—more of a desperate need than an ache—woke White with a start. His body craved food as a vampire craves blood. He jumped up and looked around. Lopez and Jackson were gone, and the few soldiers left in the tent were still asleep.

He shuffled under his mattress for his shirt and found the letters. He was about to open the first one when something stopped him. As much as he longed to read his mother's news in her own handwriting, to hear the news of his father and brothers, he froze in place.

When he was in basic and advanced training it had been so good to get letters from home. He would read each one over and over again until they were stained by sweat and grime. In a way the letters seemed a bridge that kept him connected to home. But now he felt as if he was being warned not to think too much about home; that an undefined danger lurked in the pages, something which could take his mind off what he now must become if he was to survive.

After putting the letters in the order they had been mailed, he stared at the first one for a long time. It became clear that he must learn to separate and keep balanced the two totally different worlds--the one from a past that was becoming more blurred with the passing weeks, and the one whispering about a hard present and future.

An insistent groan in his stomach pointed to something more immediate. Food. He must get food. Another look at the letters and he shoved them back under his mattress.

He dressed, slung the bandoleer on his shoulder, and picked up his rifle. Blinding sunlight greeted him as he stepped out of the tent. As shocking as the sunlight was the sudden weariness that came upon him. Like the day before, an indescribable tiredness battled his equally urgent need for food. Every muscle in his body seemed drained. He had lost several pounds in the field, but now he felt like he weighed a ton. A part of him wanted to go back into the shade of the tent, but his growling stomach forced his body forward.

His pace slowed but steadied as he walked the remaining yards to the mess. By the time he reached the door of the tent, he felt, except for the hunger pangs, almost normal. He didn't see any members of his squad, but many of the men from his company were there. After filling his plate with powdered eggs, sausage, toast, and two glasses of milk, he went and sat near Jackson and the tall blond he was always with.

Both looked up and nodded. They began to smile understandingly at each other as they saw White wolf down the pile of eggs. He ate as if he had never eaten before. He never would have thought army food could be so good. The odor, too, was delicious. Every mouthful was savored. Each swallow of milk seemed incredibly sweet. Slowly, the pile went down.

When he had finished eating, he looked at the two men and asked, "Do you know where my squad is?"

"Yeah," said Jackson. "Some of them are out on the bunker line near the *ville*."

"Thanks," said White. "My name's White," he said to the blond next to Jackson.

"Yeah, I know," said the veteran. "Smithy told us about you. I'm Sam Cook," he said with a grin.

"Don't let his name fool you," said Jackson with a mischievous gleam in his eyes. "His name's Sam Cook all right, but he can't sing for shit." He paused for a moment and then smiled and said, "But he's got a lotta soul."

"Fuck you," said Sam Cook pleasantly.

Winking at White, Jackson said, "Real romantic, ain't he? Always talking about love. Just like those hippies in the states."

"Yeah," said Cook, as he grinned at White. "But what I really love is Joe."

"Joe who?" said Jackson, knowing and ready for his comeback.

"Joe momma," said Cook, and began laughing loud enough to get everyone at the near table's attention.

"How about Joe sista?" said Jackson.

"Joe joking," said Cook. "That bitch don't love nothing."

"Joe right about that," said Jackson. "But she sure like to play hide the big black snake."

Cook, Jackson, and a few men at the other tables laughed until they almost choked. Only White didn't laugh. He was still in awe of the change in these men from the killers in the field to these veterans he knew were his own age. He stared unbelievingly at the two men in front of him.

When the laughter subsided, Cook turned to White and said, "What ya think about your squad leader? A real sweetheart, ain't he?"

White's thoughts went to Smith, and he could see him in his mind's eye. Like almost everything else that had happened to him in the last month, he was not sure what he felt about his squad leader.

"I'm not sure," said White. "He seems to know what he's doing, but he's not very friendly."

"Not very friendly," laughed Cook. "He a mudderfucker."

"Yeah," said Jackson, grinning at White. "He's a real asshole." He thought a moment and then said, "But you right. He sure knows what he's doing."

"The bitch know he's an asshole, too." said Cook. "Look here, White." he went on, "You don't have to like him, but he's a good mudder in the bush. You're lucky he even paid any attention to you. So do what he says."

"Yeah," said Jackson. "Just don't be like he is."

"Yeah," said Cook.

All the while, as they talked, other grunts from other companies had been coming in and out of the tent. In a four-man group at a far table came a sting of softly-spoken words. White had only heard one of the words clearly, but the reaction it brought was instant quiet in the rest of the tent. It seared its way thought him as he watched the change it brought in his fellow company men.

Silence. Instant, eerie silence. The suddenness of the quiet sent a jolt of alarm. Everyone within hearing of the word "A Shau" went from a youthful elation back to an intense vigilance.

Before the words were completely out of his mouth, the soldier who had spoken looked around him and quickly regretted having said it. He fidgeted in his chair and looked at the tense faces around him.

"Asshole," said one of his comrades.

"Yeah," said another. "Didn't you get enough of that shit?"

"Yeah," said the first. "Why bring up A Shau now?"

"Ah wasn't thinking," said the completely defeated soldier.

"Then start fucking thinking, you dumb fucking bitch," said another. To ease the tension, he pointed with his head to other groups in the tent. "You know there's some dudes around here that are sort of sensitive how you talk about their favorite in-country play place."

His wide grin eased the tension in the room enough for someone from another company at a far table to say, "Joe momma's sensitive."

"Not as sensitive as his sister," said another as he jerked his thumb toward Cook.

White was numbed by the change in the veterans. In the field their animal stares had frightened him as much as N.V.A. bullets and bombs. Now, here, they seemed so young--his age. He listened to their light banter as they jokingly insulted each other.   He stood up and smiled weakly at Cook and Jackson. It was hard to smile because one word kept coming into his mind, one word that had changed the mood of everyone within earshot. His stomach muscles tightened as he repeated that word to himself. "A Shau." He repeated it again as he carried his empty tray to the pile of dirty dishes in a corner. Unlike the day before, when many of the returning trays had food left on them, the food left on the stack of trays to be washed would not have fed a mouse.

He went back to his tent, determined to read his letters from home. This time he wasn't stopped. The first one he read was the earliest his mother had written.

She began by saying how everyone missed him and was praying for him, and that she had already started counting the days when he would come home. She told about his father, brothers, other relations and friends, and the farm. He imagined her as she sat at the kitchen table, trying to hide her anxiety from him by telling a funny story about the family's cat trying to ride his horse.

Then came a more serious part where she almost pleaded with him to be careful. Was there a way to get any job away from the infantry?

Could he find another, more safe position? Maybe he could get a job in an office or warehouse. Didn't the army need people like that, too?

She closed sending much love and kisses from everyone, reminding him not to forget his prayers, and promising to write again soon.

Her other letters were much the same. Even so, White read them all again several times before looking at the remaining two. They were from grade school children writing to a soldier. They told how they were proud to write to a man that was defending his country from communism, keeping the world free, and helping the people of Viet Nam to gain democracy.

For the first time White felt a churning sensation as he reread the children's letters. He didn't know how he felt anymore about reasons for the war but he knew that for him it was no longer what he had thought it was.

He stared down at his mother's letters. He knew he must answer, but it was very hard to write. How could he tell her about his first month in Nam? There was no way to explain what was happening to him, especially since he didn't even understand it himself. No words could describe it; so he wrote about the weather, the camp, and about the good food, and how he missed them and loved them all. He asked a few questions, but his mind was as far from home as his body; so he closed, promising to write the next day.

The burning sun felt good on his face as he walked toward the entrance of the camp, two hundred yards away. He approached the gun battery near the main gate. Shirtless, sunburned men sweated under the blistering glare as they unloaded the 105mm shells from four parked trucks. Dust-covered deuce-and-a-half ton truck drivers lazed in the shade under their trucks.

Black and bronzed Americans unloaded the boxed rounds. They made it look easy to handle the hundreds of seventy-pound wooden crates. He saw the strange stare of the men at the gun battery when he walked by. It was almost the same look he had seen on the faces of the rear echelon soldiers when the company had arrived, yet somehow different. There was no fear in the strong, extremely fit artillerymen. Instead, he sensed that these men, closer to the front and to the enemy, felt something different for the grunts. Surprised, he knew it was sympathy.

Finally, he came to the bunker at the main gate. On the top of the bunker, facing the entrance and the village was a machine gun nest. It had a two-sandbag wide and three-sandbag high wall on top that protected the machine-gun on the front and sides. With a few sticks and some string, two ponchos had been snapped together and made into a protection from the sun, giving shade to the five men sitting under it.

White recognized three of them. He climbed the sandbag staircase leading up to the top of the bunker. He knew immediately there was something very different about Cook and Jackson. Even his squad's machine gunner, Louis, seemed different. They grinned as they sat there looking at him.

"Mind if I join you?" White asked.

"Come on up," said Louis.

"Yeah," said one of the red-faced strangers. "We're just one big happy family here."

White sat back and leaned against the sandbag wall.

"So what ya think about the mighty Nam, Dude?" asked the other stranger. "Great place to get to know about life in the Far East," said the first.

"Yeah," said Cook. "You sure can learn a lot about life all right."

"Yeah," said Jackson. "You can learn about other shit, too."

"Dude," said the first stranger. "The first thing you got to learn is how to relax after a trip to the sticks. You got to learn how to take another kind of trip."

Everyone around the bunker giggled like children when he said that. White just couldn't understand the change in Louis and the others. He was beginning to lose patience with the strangers calling him "Dude" and their stupid, red faced smiles and glassy eyes. He was going to say something about it when one of them waved a bottle of rotgut whiskey at him and said, "Hey, Dude, wanna drink?"

Everyone laughed.

"How about a smoke?" said the other, bringing his left hand from behind his back. His hand held a smoking, hand-rolled cigarette.

The red-faced stranger held the joint for him to take. Still not sure what was happening, White said, "I don't smoke."

All five men laughed and held their sides as great guffaws and shrieks came from the top of the bunker. Finally Jackson said, "Nah, man. That's not a cigarette. That's weed."

"Weed?" said White, as the others laughed even harder.

"Yeah, man. Weed. You know. Grass."

White looked out over the bare earth compound and said, "Grass?"

Another uproar from the others and Jackson said, "Yeah, man. You know. Marijuana. Grass. Dope."

Dope? White knew what that was. He looked down at the soldiers with sudden suspicion. Were they all dope heads? Where he was from, there were no dope heads. Everything he had ever heard about people who smoked dope was bad. Dope heads were all criminals. Only thieves, murderers and rapists were dope heads.

Cook must have seen the suspicion in White's face. He had stopped smiling. He looked at White and said, "Look here, White. Marijuana's not really dope. Do you think we'd be doing something that would get us hooked? No way, man."

"Look," said Jackson. "Just try a few puffs and see if you like it. If you don't, stop smoking."

White followed his instructions as the others smiled drunkenly at him. He inhaled the smoke and held it. On the third draw, tiny stars appeared behind his closed eyes. A million bells softly rang. His brain whirled.

The smoke of the burning joint made him feel similar to when he had been transformed in the jungle a few weeks before. But this was different. He couldn't move. He sat, deep into himself, lost in the extreme colors around him. From the village across the wire, he could hear sounds that seemed magnified but distorted. The sound echoed through his brain. He knew there were people around him, but he knew neither who they were nor where they all were.

When he began to come back, he realized both where he was and who he was with. But they had changed dramatically. Jackson sat cross-eyed, with a twisted grin and tongue hanging out to one side, looking at him. Sam Cook stared at him and first nodded his head yes. Then as if he had changed his mind, shook it no. He went back and forth from yes to no as if he were crazy.

One of the strangers jabbered gibberish to the other. "Eeek, yoosh, eelow, zeeka, kragga," he said, pointing a finger at White.

The other stranger looked at him and earnestly shook his head in agreement. But the stranger's face had changed into something horrible. His lips now covered from the tip of his nose to halfway past his chin.

The deformity shocked White. He shook his head to clear it, closed his eyes, and then slowly opened them again. As his eyes focused, he could see that everyone on the bunker was now normal.

He shook his head again, and everyone on the bunker began laughing. They smiled good-naturedly at him as they laughed. Then Jackson said, "We're just joking. You're O.K. now. We were just having a little fun because we knew you was spaced."

"You freaked, and we were fucking with you," said the stranger with the lips. "But now you're O.K.," he went on.

Jackson smiled and said to the others on the bunker, "Show him."

The stranger who had the enormous lips grinned at him. He pinched his bottom lip with his fingers and stretched it out and down against his chin. When he released it, the lip stayed where he had put it. Then he pulled and stretched the top lip upward and attached it directly under his nostrils. When that lip, too, stayed in position, it gave the appearance that his lips were four inches wide.

Everyone laughed. Jackson did his cross-eyed, twisted grin thing and everyone, including White, now laughed.

All that time, amused but cautious, Louis sat and watched without ever having said a word or taken part in the charade. White could see it so plainly. Louis wouldn't do anything to hurt his or anyone else's feelings.

"We were just fucking with you," said the stranger that had spoken gibberish.

"Here," said Sam Cook. He handed White another burning joint. "Have another hit."

Hours went by. Every so often someone else from the company would join them on the bunker. More joints were passed around. Someone had brought a case of C-rations and a case of warm beer. Time came for evening chow, but White could not move. He ate a can of cold beans and franks. The guard changed, but the new guards began from where the others had left off. More joints passed. Sometime during the night he fell asleep.

He felt a sharp rap on his leg. The look on the faces of the soldiers on the bunker woke White more quickly than ice water. Only eyes moved as they peered over the sandbag wall toward the village.

Seven rifles pointed at a slow-moving shadow near a clump of weeds, forty yards away. A setting quarter moon and clear sky gave too much light to the jungle-accustomed eyes of the men on the bunker.

Suddenly, a skinny brown dog emerged from the weeds. Relieved, White and four of the others went back to sleep, while two grunts sat guard near the machine gun.

At daybreak, White walked to the mess tent. After a big breakfast, the men split up into groups. Some went back to the bunker near the village. Others went to their cots and slept.

White took a quick shower, went to his cot to work on the letter to his mother. It was a long, slow process that was hard to even get started. He realized that he just had to lie. He couldn't talk about how he really felt. So he left out the danger of the sticks and omitted what he had learned on the bunker about weed. In spite of the guilt about lying, he hoped that it was working and that the people at home would never know what was really happening to him. Finally, he was able to finish it.

After lunch, he took a nap. In the afternoon he went back to the bunker at the gate, where Smith was sitting. Smith smoked a joint as he took sips from a hot beer. He looked nonchalantly at White as he handed him the joint, his eyes so bloodshot red that he looked more albino than ever. He frowned as he and White looked down on a dead-drunk and stoned Lopez.

"Great man in the field... not worth a shit in the rear." said Smith. "Been having problems at home," he went on. "Looks like his sister got knocked up by some low-life Gringo. Wouldn't want to be that fucker when Lopez gets home."

He seemed to think and then went on. "No man alive better in the bush than him. Don't know how he does it, but he always seems to know when there's Gooks around.

Looking at the drunken figure of Lopez, Smith said, "Looks like he's out, don't it? The mudderfucker will wake up quick if he's got to. But now he don't hear nothing."

He turned and took the joint from White and said, "Heard you got all fucked up last night." He took a toke from the joint, coughed and almost choked, and said, "Don't make that a habit, and don't let me catch you smoking in the field. You understand?"

White nodded that he did.

White saw Hong and Hahn strolling hand in hand down the village's main street. The villagers didn't even seem to notice them as they walked past the barbershop. They seemed so accepted, as if they belonged there. But...they were...holding hands. White had seen girls walking hand in hand but never men. His suspicions flared up.

Smith looked to where White gawked at the two men and said, "Nah. Don't believe it. That's just Gook custom. Good friends do that. Don't mean nothing."

The guards at the gate stopped the two grunts. Jimmy Hong talked to them. His California accent showed immediately that he was American, and the guards let them in. Then both walked past the bunker. They waved to their comrades on top. Even a sulking Smith waved back.

Half an hour later, Boudreaux came walking up the street. Again, the Vietnamese civilians seemed not to notice him. Just like Hahn and Hong, he seemed to belong, to fit in. He took swigs from the quart-sized bottle of Vietnamese beer he held in his left hand. Climbing up onto the bunker, he handed out joints that had been stuffed in his shirt pockets.

Smith said sternly as he took a hit from a joint, "O.K., Frenchie, you know you're not supposed to be drinking." Everyone laughed.

Then Smith turned serious. Everyone understood what came next would not be a joke. "We're going out tomorrow morning," he said, "Be gone about ten days."

"Where we goin'?" asked Boudreaux.

"Some place west of Hué," said Smith. "Beating the bush for some gun battery on some hill. They say they don't expect heavy shit, but I don't believe any of those assholes."

"Not A Shau?" said Boudreaux.

Everyone on the bunker stared anxiously at Smith.

"Nah," he said. "But you can never tell with those fuckers at headquarters. So be ready, anyway." He stood up and walked to the stairway of the bunker. As he began to descend the sandbag steps, he turned around and said, "We re-supply tomorrow at seven."

No one on the top of the bunker said a word. They eyed each other and then sat and retreated into their own thoughts.

The guards at the bunker had said they would wake Lopez at six, so White and some of the others walked back to their tents. White stripped to his shorts and lay there through the sunset until late that night. He stared up at the darkened canvas ceiling. One word kept him from being able to relax. "A Shau".

He struggled against the dread brought on by that word, but fatigue came to his rescue. Sometime after midnight, he fell asleep.

Part II

CHAPTER X

Whenever the company received information about an upcoming mission, the reality was either more time in the sticks by days, or much more violent actions, or both. But this last time out was only three days, and they had not made contact with enemy forces at all. That had never happened before. All they found was abandoned hooches and tunnels overgrown with vegetation and crumbling with a touch. Termite and ant infested logs rotted in the damp air.

Rats and scorpions scurried between the logs and brushes making up the bunkers. Spiders dashed out of hiding to investigate every vibration disturbing the web. There wasn't any sign of snakes, but there never was a sign of snakes. Even the fleas had left, not having N.V.A. or V.C. to suck on.

But rats, scorpions, snakes and spiders didn't linger long in the minds of the grunts. What did penetrate beyond the thoughts of today was what would be lacking tomorrow. Bullets, bombs, booby traps and bayonets.

They would be going in tomorrow. If everything went well, they would be at some base camp by noon. Once there, they could expect at least three days without humping the sticks. There would be all the water he could drink and all the food he could eat.

White knew that he had been very lucky. It was now three months since he had been with the company. Usually three months didn't seem like a very long time. He knew that three months of study at any school wouldn't be enough to reach the real essence of any subject. Whole generations of simple organisms can come and go in that time or less. But three months in the extreme conditions of a combat unit, and he had become very different from what he was when he had arrived. At the end of those twelve weeks, he began to be what the veterans would term "adequate".

He saw that for whatever the cause—whether twists of fate, luck, lack of experience or intelligence, God's intervention, or all of them—the first three months in combat was when most of the soldiers seemed to get hit or killed. Veterans, too—doing everything right—could be, and sometimes were, killed. But for the newcomer, his chance of survival increased dramatically if he made it through the first twelve weeks. Reasons for his getting killed after that time would not likely be due to carelessness, laziness, or stupidity.

At the end of the first three months in combat, their minds and bodies become accustomed to very harsh conditions. They become hardened. They endure. They change. And because the physical and mental exertions they have to endure are so drastic, their personalities and ways of thinking are radically changed.

They begin seeing their former life as some kind of hazy, naive dream. The only reality becomes the jungle, the company, and the enemy. Even their fellow Americans at the base camps seem foreign. As time passes and the soldiers begin understanding their ways, the Vietnamese become logical and rational. Their tenacity and resourcefulness begin to be admired. Their resilience and courage become highly respected.

When this happens, the soldiers start losing touch with the reality of life in the States. When they become lean through exertion, they begin seeing their previous life as spoiled, lazy, fat and weak. The Americans back home become the strangest of all foreigners. They learn quickly. If they make no mistakes, they watch as others get mangled or killed. Time goes by slowly...very slowly.

And somewhere in the haze of the last three months White had stopped thinking of the company as *them*. In the same way he rarely thought of himself as *I* or *me*. Everything now was the *company*. He was now numbered with them as we...they...us. We, the company. They, my comrades. Us, the grunts.

This was White's fifth time out to the sticks. None of his squad had been hit this time. Only one man in his platoon had been wounded enough to be medivac'ed by chopper. Third platoon had not been as lucky. A man had been killed and nine wounded when the company, third platoon leading, had stumbled into an N.V.A. camp deep in the mountains. In a fleeting, fatalistic way, he realized the one man killed had been the last of the replacements that had come to the company with him.

He was walking point. Dust and old pollen from the dead, waist-high grass and the dry, chest-high brush collected on his face and clothes. He tried to avoid breathing it in by blowing away quickly before taking in the heavy air. Even then, he often took in too much, allowing whiffs of the stuff to burn its way into his lungs, caking his nostrils.

The merciless sun beat down. Because the company had been lucky enough in the past few days to have lots of water, the soldiers sweated heavily. Their feet sloshed with sweat inside their boots. The salty fluid leaked down their faces and carried with it the dried pollen and dust to their chests and backs. Thick rings of dirt showed in the creases of their necks. New, floating, rust-colored particles in the air quickly attached themselves where the sweat had run, until their faces seemed striped as a tiger. The thick, chalky layers of dust accumulated in their ears, the corners of their eyes, and all over their exposed skin until the soldiers seemed like a walking, ghostly, terra cotta army.

Despite the heat and dust, White and the company were happy. They had left the jungle the day before and were now in brush country, heading to a base camp for a few days' stand down. Yet, an almost physical contradiction—a tugging yin and yang—pulled at the men as they made their way from the treeless hills toward the rice paddies and civilization. An eerie feeling of being naked—helpless to hidden snipers perhaps hundreds of yards away—strained their elation at being so close to safety.

There was so much more protection in the thick of the forest. Except in occasional places, visibility was not beyond a few feet, making it hard for the enemy to get a clean shot from any distance. The thick mass of trees and undergrowth absorbed much of the killing power of bullets and bombs.

As the weeks and months went by, White began to appreciate the jungle. The more he learned to live within it, the less he had to fight it. Each day brought new sights—magnificent sights—and new understanding.

Then, as a captive begins to love the captor, he began to love the jungle. Slowly, it became beautiful.

But the shrub country was very different. It was so open that one could see for miles. White carefully weaved through the bush, steadily moving downhill. He approached a small knoll and easily worked his way to the top.

The view rejuvenated him. Below, as far as the eye could see, was a green valley broken up into diked rice paddies. A half-mile from where he stood was the highway. Boudreaux and Smith came alongside him, and the three comrades looked down onto the scene below. They looked at each other with guarded but intense relief.

They made their way to the highway and stepped onto the hot asphalt. The company divided into two columns, one on each side of the highway, and began walking toward the coast.

Shimmering heat waves radiated off the asphalt, and the soldiers' feet burned inside their sloshing boots, the smell of asphalt stinging their eyes. But now, at least, they could breathe in the hot air without taking in pollen and dust.

Every one was traveling much lighter. All of their food was gone, and, because of the fight in the mountains, ammunition was low. Now, most of them only carried a few clips of ammo and a couple of full canteens of water. They drank as they walked, splurging on the tepid water, knowing more was close by. They walked, eyes searching the surrounding countryside, sometimes watching the dancing, hypnotic mirages on the asphalt highway ahead.

White tensed, seeing ahead of him, a quarter of a mile further on, the beginning of a village. In the jungle, things were much simplified. Any pair of slanted eyes, except for Jimmy Hong and Hahn, was enemy. No hesitation was required and no chances taken. But in the villages and hamlets, among civilians, fears burned the consciousness of the American soldiers.

He had learned that it was true almost every village had Viet Cong or sympathizers in it, but most of the people were only simple peasants. Their natural views on politics and their levels of education were limited to keeping at least something in their families' stomachs. And, even if he was too young to have put it into words, he knew that their cruel exposure to a higher level of international politics and education had been administered by way of high explosives and bullets.

He had learned much about the country by talking with Hahn and Hong. Vietnamese history always had foreign soldiers either on their soil or wanting to get onto it. For a thousand years the Vietnamese, off and on, fought the Chinese for the fertile rice fields in the South. Then it was the French, the Japanese, and then the French again. Now there were half a million American troops in the country.

All kinds of stories circulated among the American troops. Some were of suicide bombers walking into groups of Americans. Others were of patriotic whores who had purposely infected themselves with incurable gonorrhea, who then would give it to as many G.I.'s as they could.

But worse were the stories of someone who had to kill a child walking toward him with a hand grenade. V.C. would give a kid a grenade and encourage the innocent child to bring it to the Americans. Then the soldier was faced with the decision either to kill the kid or die with him. Even the most hardened hated the thought of killing someone innocent by acting too quickly. It was a dreadful thought that haunted them.

But the one great truth, the one irrefutable, solid fact, the one life-or-death lesson to the soldier, is to shoot first and kill your enemy. Only that way does he not kill you. And only that way will a soldier go on to see another day. Those are the dues he must pay if he wants to live on. It was a lesson White hoped he would never have to learn.

A quick look behind him and he could see that his comrades, too, were anxious. The company became extremely uneasy as they approached the houses, hoping to avoid a fight.

It was a small farm community surrounded by rice paddies. Cinder block walls covered with tin formed the bulk of the houses. Laced bamboo walls with grass roofs and dirt floors made up the rest of the small community in what the American soldiers in slang called "the *ville*."

This was, of course, a completely wrong term. In French, *ville* was the word for city, not village, but the only one in the company that spoke French, and knew the difference, was Boudreaux. White had learned a lot from Boudreaux. He had learned that Cajun French was a very old dialect and that to Boudreaux it was the most honest language in the world. But White knew that Pierre Boudreaux could not have cared less what words his comrades used to call anything. If *ville* was what they wanted to call the small towns, then that was what he'd call them, too. Besides, there was a nice sound to the slang, and Boudreaux liked anything with a French sound—even if it wasn't Cajun French—that reminded him of home.

He had told White about the young prostitute they would visit that day. White could almost see her in his mind as Boudreaux had explained her. The half-French blood in her veins made her a social outcast. Born to a Vietnamese prostitute and a French soldier, she made a living in the only world she knew—the world she had been educated and raised in.

Boudreaux kept a three-pace interval between himself and White. Every so often, the two soldiers neared each other enough to exchange a few quick words. A large pothole in the street forced the two comrades toward each other. Never losing his intense search of the doors, windows, and alleys as he walked, Boudreaux said to White, "So. You comin' out wit' me"?

An equally intense White answered, "Yeah."

White didn't completely understand why Boudreaux seldom let anyone go with him when he went to "the *ville*." Most of the American soldiers only ventured out of the base camps to the nearest bar and whorehouse. They would leave the security of the base camp only long enough to get stoned, drunk, and laid. Then they would return to the camp to sleep, eat, and rest.

Boudreaux's excursions to the *ville* were very different. A lack of a common language kept most of the Americans from anything but a rudimentary communication with the Vietnamese. But French had been the colonial language in Viet Nam for a hundred years, and it was through language, quite unconsciously it seemed to White, that Boudreaux became the best informed in the company—apart from Jimmy Hong and Hahn—about the Vietnamese.

The streets were nearly empty. They passed an herb store. The sidewalk outside of the tiny, faded green building was stacked with handmade, woven bamboo baskets. In the baskets were herbs, roots, and other dried plants. Some of the plants looked like withered, shrunken, brown hands. Others looked like twisted pieces of old grass rope. Some looked like dried sticks. The odors rising from the baskets were faintly disgusting but at the same time reassuring because they were the odors of civilization.

White caught the looks of the storekeeper and the old lady as they suspiciously watched the soldiers walk by. In the second it took to pass the store, assaulted by the odors in the baskets, he wondered what he must smell like to the people inside. He had been ten days without washing.

Suddenly, he saw it again. There, in the eyes of the Vietnamese storeowner and his mother, he could see that look again. Like the Americans at the base camps, the Vietnamese civilians stared at the passing grunts. It seemed to White that what he saw in these faces was a mixture of fear, rebellion, anxiety, suppressed hate, and, in some, an eager wish to see them all dead.

But overriding all of the emotions he could see was caution. Extremely war-wise, the civilians knew there was danger in the dirty, exhausted soldiers walking past. Both stayed in plain sight. Both were very careful not to make any sudden moves.

They walked past a whorehouse. The working girls would usually smile invitingly to the passersby and, wiggling their small breasts, call out to potential customers. But these girls, too, were war-wise. They knew at a glance the different look and carriage of soldiers coming out of the bush from the clean, green soldiers fresh from the States. Like the shopkeeper and the old lady, the girls followed the soldiers with their eyes. None of them moved or called out.

Further up the street was a small open market. Homemade pushcarts, their solid wooden wheels and axles worn by constant jogging down rough country roads, were piled with fruits and vegetables from the nearby farms. Small bamboo tables held cuts of pork, chicken, small fish, and dried squid. Some tables held pots and pans, farm tools, woven baskets, and assortments of simple goods. Several ducks hid under the tables, tied by their necks to the table legs with grass strings.

Village women, their teeth a clean, ebony black from constantly chewing betel nut, cooked simple food on handmade stoves. Various dishes boiled, simmered, and fried at the stoves and sent odors drifting toward the approaching soldiers. Loud haggling between the villagers and farmers, each trying to outbargain the other, hummed through the streets.

The noises and the voices stopped abruptly when the civilians saw the approaching soldiers. All movement stopped as well. Every face in the crowd had that look on it. Hands stayed in plain sight. Even the ducks, sensing a change, began an eerie, nervous quacking and pacing. The company walked past the civilians at the market. Every pair of almond eyes pierced the Americans.

Another fifty yards and they were out of the village. The road at this point was nearly straight, and White could see, a half-mile away, thick gray smoke curling upward. He knew that kind of smoke most often marked where an army camp had its dump. He took a quick look backward to Smith, who confirmed it with a nod.

New tensions mounted as the company neared the base camp. If there were any V.C. living in the village, they would not risk losing their ideal spying place close to an American camp by attacking from there. But here, far from where they must live, an attack on the company would not jeopardize losing their base.

Eyes pierced every bush and shadow. Aches and pains, blisters, heat, diarrhea, hunger and fatigue were forgotten as the soldiers pushed forward. Soon, they could see black forms with rice hats moving among the man-made heaps of smoldering trash from the camp.

Now, the smell of the dump drifted to them in a nauseating stench. Peasant women and children dug through the trash, searching for anything they could use. An old woman with a crooked stick pushed aside burnt cans, looking for what was to her loot.

White could see, across from the camp entrance, a makeshift bar and whorehouse. There were two American soldiers standing at the open-sided overhang that served as the bar. The Vietnamese bartender and the bar girl were the first to see the approaching soldiers. The haughty, saucy grimaces they reserved for green recruits disappeared. They suddenly turned rigid and guarded. Only their heads moved. Their eyes followed the oncoming company.

The two Americans at the bar, green as they were, stared intently at the passing, dust-covered, terra cotta company. On their faces was plastered that look—that distasteful, fearful look common to all the uninitiated.

Then they were at the wood and barbed wire gate. A guard came out of the bunker and opened it. The company, one by one, entered the base camp. As each walked in, a steel veil lifted from them. A swift change—startling, instant—came upon every man. A tired, cold face melted and exposed a still exhausted, but suddenly relieved, soldier. In ninety percent of the company, it revealed a soldier under twenty.

CHAPTER XI

An uneasy feeling ate at White as he stood outside of the tent waiting for Boudreaux. He had been to the *ville* before, but only to a whorehouse near a base camp. He remembered how guilty he felt as he and Lopez had walked toward the run-down house. Going to a prostitute was completely against his religion and upbringing and he knew that it really was wrong. What the church elders at home would say didn't bother him as much as what his mother would think.

Feeling miserable, he had sought any reason to excuse himself. Wasn't the Bible full of stories of good men who had gone to prostitutes? Hadn't some prostitutes been good human beings and even become saints? King David had not only given in to sexual temptations but had even committed murder.

So, he had lost his virginity in that rusted tin and bamboo shack to a much-used, middle-aged prostitute who had been the first to reach him at the door. Like a dog fighting for a bone, she had aggressively grabbed him and snapped at the other girls tugging at his sleeves, trying to take him away.

He could still see her in his mind. His gut sank when he remembered her savage challenge to the other girls and her sneer of triumph as they backed off. Her every move and expression seemed a dare.

She would have been the last of the girls in the house that he would have chosen, but something in him could not think of hurting the woman's feelings. She seemed already destroyed, as if she had lost any chance of happiness; that from this point on, it was only down. Thankfully, it had soon been over. He had felt less guilt when he realized he was then free to move on to another girl more to his taste.

His mother's recent letters had held subtle warnings about loose women and a certainty that someday he would find the perfect girl. Now, attacking him stronger than guilt, were the stirrings from his male hormones. Urges raced through him as never before and he knew he would succumb to them again.

Although he still found it difficult, it was becoming easier to lie with each letter he sent home. But they weren't really lies. He was just leaving out a few things. She didn't have to know about the danger either. Anyway, she was ten thousand miles away and would never know.

Every chance he got to talk with Hahn and Hong, White learned something new about the country and its people. With Boudreaux, too, he had spent many hours talking about Viet Nam. But Boudreaux had also talked about South Louisiana and the Cajun Country, and White had been an avid student.

Now he would be going to the city with Boudreaux. He had heard from everyone that Boudreaux's excursions were very special. Severe restrictions, guard posts, and military police were to keep the lowly GI's from going into the cities and towns. But these things barely slowed the Cajun down. He had found ways to mingle inconspicuously in the base camps and seemed as natural there as he was in the sticks.

"Round eyes" and "big noses" were some of the nicer names the Vietnamese had for Americans. Besides man-made barriers, there were invisible, social barriers that the Vietnamese used to keep big-nosed, round eyes away from some of the most respected, private places. With Boudreaux, however, White would be going out to see the real world of the Vietnamese townsmen, the world most big noses did not even imagine existed.

Boudreaux came out of the tent. With an unconscious, graceful spin, White was beside him, and the two soldiers began walking towards the main gate of the camp, a half mile away.

The Cajun led them toward one tent, veered around it, and then moved toward another nearer the gate. White saw in an instant that Boudreaux was hiding their movements from any curious eyes. In this zigzag, camouflaging course, they seemed two common privates, going about their duties. But a more careful observer would have seen that both soldiers carried their rifles one-handed by the pistol grip, thumb on the selector, finger on the trigger, ever ready, like a grunt.

The men at the gun battery nearer the main gate were experienced observers. One look at them and White knew they were seasoned veterans themselves and had seen grunts many times. The new clothes, clean-shaven faces, and scrubbed bodies could not hide from the soldiers on the guns that what approached them was tested infantry.

They were easily seen, too, by the veteran driver sitting on a sand bag in the shade of his deuce-and-a-half. He sat unmoving while groups of artillerymen unloaded the cases of shells from the back of his truck. His eyes followed the approaching vets.

White knew that by now the driver would have lost many friends and comrades to bullets, bombs, and land mines. Now he was a short timer and his nerves were frayed, but he still seemed able to hide it from most of the people around him. He sat in the shade of his truck while smoking a joint.

"Dere's our ride," said Boudreaux looking at the driver. "He's for sure to give us a lif." Boudreaux walked up to the driver and said, "Need two to ride shotgun?"

"Maybe," said the driver. "Where ya going?"

"Hué," said Boudreaux.

"I can take you to the main road. From there I'm going south."

"Fine. T'anks," said Boudreaux and then sat cross-legged on the ground near the driver.

White sat in the shade of the truck with them and watched while shirtless black, brown and bronzed artillerymen swung crate after crate of the wooden boxes from the truck to the men below.

White and Boudreaux watched in admiration as the high stacks of boxes in the truck went down and neat rows of 105mm rounds went up. When every crate had been unloaded, White, Boudreaux, and the driver climbed into the cab.

Getting on or off a military compound in a war zone is not the easiest thing to do. They would be stopped at the gates by M.P.'s checking every vehicle for I.D.'s, passes, traveling papers, etc. But a deuce-and-a-half coming from or going to a gun battery was seldom stopped. It was so usual to see an ammunition truck with driver and guards. So, as the truck reached the main gate, the M.P. at the bunker waved them through.

No one said a word until they had passed the checkpoint and were on the dirt road leading to the main highway. A light yellow dust drifted to the interior of the cab. The driver's nose began twitching, and he began taking in and letting out huge intakes of air. With each breath he let out a mighty "Ah, ah, ah…" until, finally, he sneezed.

"That's because I haven't had my asthma medicine," he said, pulling a joint out of his pocket. He lit it, took an incredibly deep toke, and held it. He offered the joint to White. When both White and Boudreaux declined, he let out the smoke and began coughing violently.

"Don't want none?" he said between breaths and coughs. "I thought you guys were from the sticks. Never heard of no boonie rats that would pass up some good shit like this."

"We just got out of the bush," said White.

"Gonna wait 'til after we get to town," said Boudreaux.

"But this is some extra good shit, man," he said, taking another toke. "Got it direct from *mamma-san* from her private stash." He paused a moment and said, "She'll never have to worry about arthritis. This shit is so good I'm not sure I've still got feet left."

He stopped talking and stared bug-eyed at his hands on the steering wheel. "And who are those two crazy guys on the wheel driving this truck?"

Boudreaux and White looked at each other, knowing the driver was seeing something they weren't. As he finished the joint, he quickly lit another. This one, however, he smoked calmly like a cigarette.

The truck bounced and swayed on the dusty trail. They passed heaps of twisted, rusted metal. American trucks had been so deformed, burnt, and shattered by mines that White knew there had probably been no survivors.

Waist-high brush on both sides of the sand and dirt trail grew to the very edge of the road, and he could see a thousand good ambush sites within a few feet. The truck slowly rambled on, a perfect target for a V.C. sniper.

He shifted his gaze to the driver. White couldn't see any trace of fear in him. The driver seemed simple-minded or crazy to be so cool, being a constant target.

He seemed to have drifted off into a safe world of his own. He never spoke another word until they came to where the sand road met the highway.

The truck stopped in the dust of the road. The driver turned to Boudreaux and White. With red eyes and a hazy, twisted, far-away grin, he said, "This is where I turn left."

"Thanks for the ride," said White.

"Yeah," said Boudreaux. "Be careful out 'dere. But why you don' have somebody ride shotgun wit' you?"

"Nobody left. Just cherries left now and they're fucking useless," said the driver. For a moment he seemed to come back to reality as he looked at the two grunts. "It's you guys that got to be careful. I got the best job in Viet Nam, The Republic Of. All I do is ride around and stay high, high," he said, lighting another joint.

White and Boudreaux got out of the truck and into the glaring sunlight. Standing on the dusty roadside, both looked up at the driver. With a resolute, stoned smile, he swung his truck onto the highway and steered left toward Da Nang.

Ideas struggled to form themselves in White's mind. Unanswered questions gnawed at him. He knew his relationship with the others in the company was something rare in the world. He sensed that their bond, their comradeship, or whatever it was, was something most people would never know.

With a deep gratitude he realized how fortunate he was. The driver was alone in a hostile, dangerous world. But he had Boudreaux. He had Louis, and Lopez, Smith and the others. He had comrades that he knew would risk their lives to try to save him and that he would risk his life to try to save, and he knew that he was truly one of them.

His eyes followed the truck for a little longer. He heard when the driver shifted gears and headed south, an easy target, alone. Then he fully understood that the driver, seemingly lost in a drug-induced haze, knew he might die at any time, all alone, and that his monument would be a rusted, twisted lump of charred metal.

White looked sideways to see that Boudreaux's eyes, too, were following the truck. "He's not crazy. He's jus' getting short an' nervous," said Boudreaux. "But he'll be home before us if he got any luck lef'."

The two soldiers turned their attention to the highway before them. Any kind of vehicle which could be put together was jockeying for a place on the asphalt highway. Deuce-and-a-half and three-quarter-ton army trucks bullied their way through a stream of smaller vehicles of all kinds.

Old black French cars zoomed along. They had once been beautiful, graceful examples of France's elegant and sometimes oppressive presence; but now they were clattering, smoking heaps held together by wire and rope.

Small French trucks of different types edged their way through the melee. Three-wheeled lambrettas, their tiny cabs filled with goods or people, whined their way toward or away from town. Small motorcycles, scooters, and mo-peds, their engines screaming, zigzagged and weaved through the traffic.

White wondered how, in all the confusion and rush, were he and Boudreaux to get anyone to stop. With the mad scramble, who would stop for them? As had always been the case, Boudreaux made it seem easy.

Five yards from where they stood was a wobbly wooden table. On the table were many different sized and colored bottles, filled with gasoline. Standing behind the table was a Vietnamese peasant, sidelining as a gas station.

The slanted eyes, partly shaded by his rice hat, stared suspiciously at the two approaching soldiers. He tried to ignore the two, turning more toward the open highway. He barely nodded an agreement when Boudreaux politely told him, "*Bonjour.*"

It was a natural thing for the Vietnamese to be cautious when dealing with grunts. The farmer backed up when Boudreaux advanced toward him. He seemed on the verge of running for his life until he understood that what the big-nosed, round-eyed thing wanted was to buy some gasoline. When greed boosted his courage, he began to aggressively bargain with Boudreaux over the price of two bottles of gasoline.

In a mixture of pigeon Vietnamese, French, and a splattering of English, Boudreaux and the farmer agreed on a price. His greed outweighing his good sense, the farmer tried to persuade Boudreaux that he didn't have change for the red bill. Boudreaux argued and then threatened to take all his gasoline. The farmer dug up the few cents change. Boudreaux put the change in his pocket, turned to White, and said, "I only pay Gook prices, an' I get my change back."

Boudreaux slung his rifle over his shoulder and grabbed a bottle in each hand. He turned toward the highway and held up the two bottles of gasoline. Almost at once, a white lambretta swerved off of the highway and came to a stop near the table.

White could not understand a word, but, after another babble of sound between the driver and Boudreaux, the two soldiers climbed into the back of the small vehicle.

From the single front wheel to the two back wheels, the conveyance was about ten feet long and four feet wide. This tricycle-type machine had a thin metal floor and was covered with a thin, box-like cab.

There were already three Vietnamese peasants in the back when Boudreaux and White squeezed into the tight compartment. The tiny wheels threw dust and pebbles onto the gasoline bottles and the farmer as they screeched onto the highway.

The odor of the Vietnamese came to White. Not unpleasant, the mild, fish-like odor penetrated the tight air of the cab. In his hunched-up position, White looked around to his fellow passengers. They seemed as if they didn't even realize he was there. Each seemed lost in his own private world, detached from the cramped vehicle and the other occupants.

Boudreaux sat cross-legged against the wall of the jolting machine. It swerved viciously from side to side, missing motorcycles, bicycles, cars, and trucks by inches. The engine screamed a protest as more speed was demanded.

Without warning, the lambretta hit a deep rut in the highway. The jolt lifted all the passengers into the air and then slammed them down hard onto the floor of the cab. Through the groans in the cab, White heard one word.

"*Merde*," came loudly out of Boudreaux's mouth.

White did not know what that meant, but it seemed the Vietnamese did. The woman and a man laughed out loud. The other man looked up disapprovingly. Then, as if unable to help himself, he laughed. They all looked at the Cajun, and he, in turn, grinned at them.

The ice had been broken. Points in common had been reached. Each of the Vietnamese now took turns eyeing the Americans. White was shaken when he saw the woman look at him and smile.

She had laughed at whatever Boudreaux had shouted out. Her smile was as friendly and good-natured as White had ever seen. Full of good cheer, her shiny, black teeth gleamed with humor.

Like all middle-aged peasant women, she constantly chewed betel nut. The mild narcotic not only dulled aches and pains caused by hard work, but also stained their teeth a glistening black. Her equally-dark eyes shone with sympathy and wisdom.

When White smiled back, a blur lifted from his eyes. He no longer saw a strange, foreign, peasant woman. Instead, she was a mother-like, pleasant-to-be-near woman. Even her rice hat and clothes seemed fitting. Everything about her appearance was perfect, in place. In that instant his memory flashed back to one day when Louis, with a distant look, said, "Gooks can steal your heart."

They veered off the highway and came to a stop. The driver said something to Boudreaux and then motioned to get out of the truck. Boudreaux and White stood to the side as the lambretta roared off. White lifted his left hand slightly in a quick goodbye and was touched to see the woman and one man lift their hands in farewell.

CHAPTER XII

Turning from the exhaust fumes of the lambretta, Boudreaux seemed boyishly excited as he patted White on the back. His grin proved infectious because White, too, began to grin.

When totally at ease, Boudreaux always reverted to primitive Cajun English.

"Ya like boil' shramp?" he asked White.

White had never had shrimp before and said so.

"Come on," said Boudreaux, smiling like a child.

They walked fifty yards to the French restaurant. The waiters recognized Boudreaux. They grinned as they shouted out to the kitchen staff in the rear of the open-sided restaurant. "*C'est l'Américain.*"

Words and handshakes went back and forth between Boudreaux and the waiters. Laughter and shouts aimed at him could be heard from the kitchen. He turned and shouted something back. Everyone laughed except White. High school French had not prepared him for so much. He had not understood a word. The continents seemed to gently collide in a mutual affection as the playful banter went on between Asia and North America.

Boudreaux and White ate boiled shrimp and drank cold beer. Every so often a cook would come out of the kitchen to have Boudreaux taste some horrible-looking, many legged, cooked sea creature. White liked the boiled shrimp but couldn't stomach the idea of eating some of the things that Boudreaux, with real appreciation, chewed and swallowed.

"*C'est bon,*" he would say. The waiters and the cooks would nod in agreement.

"*Oui, c'est bon,*" said a cook, smiling so broadly his eyes seemed like two small slits in his head.

On the table in front of Boudreaux was a pile of shrimp heads and peelings. The pile in front of White was much smaller. They had eaten several pounds of the boiled shrimp and now sat back contentedly. They pushed back from the table enough to stretch their legs and lean back.

It was usual for a low-ranked American to get looks of disapproval when in a social mixture of middle, high, and very high Vietnamese. All but the best in the country were always ready to kiss up to a rich Westerner. But being human first, curiosity and humor also played a part in their makeup. So as the mutual fondness between the soldiers and restaurant staff became more apparent, the sour faces of some of the patrons at the other tables began to melt.

White, casting secret glances at them, began to see smiles as the teasing between Boudreaux and the cooks continued. As a table would empty and the customers walked past, their eyes looked carefully at Boudreaux and White. For a flash White saw them without slanted eyes and ivory colored skin. They were regular "city folk" going back to work after a relaxing lunch.

When the restaurant had only two other customers, the waiters and cooks came to sit with the soldiers. They joked and teased even more. A waiter tried talking to White. It was no use. He couldn't understand a word. Then, with a big smile, the waiter pointed to the shrimp heads. He patted his stomach and said, "*Bon?*" After several tries White understood. He smiled back at everyone and said, "*Bon.*"

Finishing his beer, Boudreaux got to his feet. He winked at the group of Vietnamese and said something in French. Then he translated for White. "De shrimp an' de company's good, but Ah know somet'in' Ah like more dan food."

He translated their response to White. "Yeah, we know," said a waiter. "It taste a little like shrimp, too." When one of the cooks asked White something in French, he just grinned and said "*Bon.*" That started Boudreaux and the Vietnamese laughing again.

The bill for the shrimp and beer came. Boudreaux handed the waiter a five dollar note. When the change came, he left the equivalent of forty cents on the table and pocketed the rest.

The cooks and waiters patted Boudreaux on the back as he and

White left the restaurant. They all smiled at White, and one even spoke to him, but he didn't understand. All he could think of to say was "*Bon.*"

As they stood in the sun waiting for a ride, White remembered what Boudreaux had said at the gasoline table. "Thought you only paid Gook prices and always got your change," he said. He had seen the satisfied cooks and waiters as they had divided the few cents tip.

"Yeah," said Boudreaux. "Ah only pay Gook prices, an' Ah always get my change back." He turned to White, grinned and said, "Excep' dat sometime Ah leave a rich Gook's tip."

Boudreaux hailed a rickshaw, and the two soldiers climbed aboard and sat side by side on the tiny seat. Boudreaux had not stopped smiling from the minute that they had walked into the restaurant. White wondered at how calm he seemed. He knew there was no doubt that Boudreaux realized the danger of being here. Bombs killed people everyday in the bigger cities in Viet Nam. But Boudreaux looked oblivious to any worry. The question puzzled White until he finally asked.

"Pierre, don't you worry about V.C. when you come to town?"

"Worry? Why worry?" he said, still smiling. He paused for a moment and thought carefully. "Yeah," he went on. "'Dere's lots of V.C., but w'at ya gonna do? Stay in camp?"

Then the smile disappeared, and he again went on.

"Sure 'der's lots of V.C. An' N.V.A. too. If Ah was a Gook, Ah'd maybe be V.C., too. But just cause 'der's V.C., 'dat's not gonna stop me from goin' out. 'Dis is 'de only normal t'ing Ah got, and Ah'm gonna take it."

They passed stores and market places humming with haggling shoppers and merchants, mechanic shops and bars where the odor of old oil and stale beer drifted out into the streets and small cafes and restaurants where the odor of the rotten fish sauce called *nuoc mam* hung in the air. In every part of the city, the sidewalks were jammed with street vendors, shoppers, and makeshift cafes. Pedestrians made way for old men with bent backs and twisted joints shuffling through the crowd. Bicycles, motorcycles, and lambrettas filled the streets.

They entered a tree-lined boulevard leading to a quieter part of the city. The change was immediate. The stink of car exhaust was replaced with the sweet smell of the mango trees. In sharp contrast to the melee behind, the only sound came from a faint squeaking of the rickshaw's wheels as they rolled on farther into that part of town. The sidewalks and streets were free of litter. Few cars and trucks used the boulevard.

The only people to be seen were middle-aged housekeepers in traditional clothes sweeping the doorsteps and sidewalks. French-style houses with small, grass-covered front yards lined both sides of the boulevard. Around some of the houses were wrought iron fences and gates that separated them from the street and their neighbors.

From far off, White could see two-story French colonial buildings, sitting in a cluster of trees. Perfectly balanced, the arrangements of the buildings with the trees and walkways exuded an aura of harmony.

White's pulse quickened expectantly at the sight. Something different was happening. Something important. Boudreaux, understanding the look on White's face, turned to him. In a tone of admiration, he said, "'Dat's 'de University.'"

He signaled to the rickshaw driver to stop, paid the fare, got his change, and the two comrades began walking under the shaded paths of the university.

"Ya wanna meet somebody?" asked Boudreaux.

"Sure," said White.

They walked into the main building and climbed the staircase to the second floor. In the first room they came to was a wooden desk where a small Vietnamese man sat.

In a time when most of the better-educated colonial peoples of the world struggled to dress, act, and think as Westerners, the man sitting at the desk was totally traditional.

A black Chinese cap sat on a grey head of hair. A black, collarless, long-sleeved shirt trimmed in red hung rather loosely on him and fell to below his waist. His pants were loose and black and went to his ankles. On his small feet were soft, red Vietnamese slippers.

His grey hair and thin, grey, wisp of a beard were the only indications of his age. Only in a man's later years, when becoming an elder, would a Vietnamese grow such a beard. White knew that some men, being pretentious, began to grow an elder's beard before reaching certain maturity. But he knew instinctively this man was not that type. The man was indeed at the perfect age to have such a beard.

But even with the beard, to judge his age would have been very difficult. His wrinkle-free face and curious, eager expression made him look much younger than he could have actually been. His full concentration seemed pasted to the stack of papers on the desk before him.

White had a flash of warning that it was going to happen again. As the man lifted his head, he had another experience of *déjà vu*. The moment before the man saw them, the eerie idea came to White that the man was almost expecting them. But the strangest thing about it was that the man looked at him first. Only after a deep, questioning stare with his hypnotic eyes did he release White and turn his attention to Boudreaux.

The old man smiled, got to his feet, and began walking toward them. Even if he couldn't understand it, White knew that he was hearing "good" French when the man began to speak. Harmonious, refined, perfect language flowed out of him.

Boudreaux, with a slight bow with his head, answered in his crude but pleasant sounding eighteenth century dialect. They exchanged handshakes, and then Boudreaux said in English, "Professor Nguyen Van Thieu, 'dis is mah fren' Curtis White."

The professor turned to White and extended a tiny hand. "How do you do, Mr. White? I am very pleased that you came," he said. Even his voice had something hypnotic about it. He had spoken with a diction and vocabulary so exact that one knew English was not his native language. Every syllable and sound had been pronounced perfectly. But what stood out was that he went through the two sentences without any change of tone. From beginning to end, there was no rise, fall, or feeling.

White was temporarily speechless, but in a few moments he gripped the man's hand, surprisingly warm, and said, "I'm fine, Professor, and I'm glad to meet you, too."

"Can ya take a walk 'round 'de school wit' us, or are ya too busy?" said Boudreaux.

"I am presently preparing a lesson plan in English grammar for some of my more advanced students. But, yes, I can walk with you a little. That is," he went on, "if Mr. White will tell me something of the region of the United States he is from." He smiled up at White as he spoke.

Looking down at the small, elderly man, White felt an acute respect and bewilderment. He looked into those eager, black eyes and saw an understanding and wisdom that he had never seen before.

"I'm from a small town in Nebraska, Professor." said White.

"Of course," said the professor. "The plains east of the Rocky Mountains, isn't it?"

"Yes, Professor," said White.

The three men slowly walked through the hallways and tree-shaded paths of the university. Then, like an approaching storm, White felt it coming on again. It began with a soft tingling sound. Then, gradually, slowly, he was again struck by an intense feeling of extreme realism. Just as it had happened months before and had happened on several occasions since, he was suddenly assaulted by a feeling of great clarity.

He looked toward Boudreaux and marveled at the easy, glide-like stride of his steps and the serene, open demeanor of his face. The Cajun had hung his rifle by the strap, muzzle down, on his shoulder and seemed almost unarmed. A peaceful expression emanated from him that denied the wild look in his eyes when in action.

White then turned his gaze to the professor. It seemed so strange to him that the professor had the same smooth glide and the same sure expression. The skin of his face and hands seemed to glow with life. The elder looked over at him, and, suddenly, in the strangest feeling of his life, White felt that the man could read his every thought. The old man smiled, reinforcing that idea.

Light air currents lifted and then let fall the long gray hairs on his chin. His deep, black, penetrating eyes went from Boudreaux, to White, to his surroundings. His sure, toneless voice explained the university.

"This is our science department," he said when they passed an antique laboratory. "Unfortunately, biology, chemistry, physics, and geology must all share this room. At times it is most inconvenient." He paused and then, with a grin, went on. "On the other hand, it gives our students in different areas of study an opportunity to interrelate and cooperate with each other."

They passed students while they walked. Both male and female students had an intense, concentrating look about them. In a mildly frightening way, they seemed more like automatons than young adults.

Their sure, calculating faces showed an earnest, self-imposed, strict rigidity. It was as if there was no laughter or play left in them, as if the inner child had been rooted out, aborted by circumstances, killed at an early age, and forgotten.

Some of the male students recognized Boudreaux and smiled or nodded. But none of the female students would as much as look at the two Americans. All of the people they passed, however, gave a small, almost imperceptible, bow to the professor.

As they walked, the Professor asked more questions about White's hometown and region, revealing knowledge so surprising that White paused for long moments before answering.

The professor knew about the now-almost-vanished Indian tribes, their languages, and many of their customs. He knew which Europeans had first settled the area. He knew about the economy, crops, population, and major cities.

Then, as if he had been gently led to it, White began talking about his family. It had been weeks since he had let such thoughts come to him, but now, at the professor's eager smiling face, White began to talk of home.

"My father is a farmer," said White. "As far back as anyone knows, we have always been farmers." After several more steps he went on, "When we weren't in school, my brothers and I worked with my father. Then I got drafted."

A thought crossed his mind, and for a while he was silent. But a curious look from the professor urged him on.

"My mother likes to sew. She still likes to make vests for my brothers and me." He remembered something awkward and, for a moment, had a pained expression, but went on. "She embroidered things on them. Usually some kind of Indian design. We didn't like to wear them because there was always something about them that wasn't right, out of style, and I guess I was a little ashamed to wear them. She tried to copy some of the styles she saw on television and magazines, but I never liked any of them." He looked from the professor to Boudreaux and said, "But sometimes we wore them because it made her so happy."

"Yes," said the professor, smiling. "Please go on."

"There's really not much to say," said White.

"But don't you have a field of study, an interest that you would like to pursue in civilian life?"

"Well," said White, "I always did like agriculture. I suppose that, at heart, I'm a farmer, too."

"Yes," said the old man. "That is a very worthy profession, as well as a very ancient one. I congratulate you, Mr. White, on a noble choice."

He seemed in a trance. Between the soft voices, the smooth glide of the walkers, the intense faces of the students, and the feeling of calm, White realized he had fallen completely under the spell of the City and University of Hué.

An hour later they were back at the entrance of the main building. The professor stopped and faced the two soldiers. With the same monotonous, but somehow dignified drone, he said, "I regret very much that now I must return to my work." Then he turned to shake hands with Boudreaux. He didn't have the same emotionless speech in French. In a song-like, cultured voice, he said something to Boudreaux which had the Cajun laughing.

Then he turned and faced White. The tiny, ivory-colored hand extended to the American. His smile was so strong it caused creases in the corners of his eyes. Then he said, "Thank you for a very pleasant and informative hour. Please feel free," he went on, "to visit me here at the university whenever you come to town." Now, because of his wide grin, he seemed almost a boy.

White wanted to express his gratitude to the professor. He struggled to find the right words to explain how wonderful it was to have escaped, even for a short time, the tension of the bush. But he was more thankful for the brief look back, even in a melancholy way, to his home and family. He looked into the shiny, black eyes of the professor and knew that words were cheap things, something used for a last resort.

He stood before the little old man facing him and groped for something to say. Then, with what he hoped was sufficient humility, and a slight bow, he said, "Thank you, sir." He paused for a moment and then said, "It's been very nice for me, too."

White had been watching everything closely. He knew, without knowing how he knew, what most Westerners would scarcely guess at. The bow was something very special. It was better not to bow at all than to bow wrongly. He realized that to the Orientals in general, and to the

Vietnamese in particular, nothing seemed more ridiculous and even insulting, than a round-eyed, big nose and his stupid, overdone bow.

CHAPTER XIII

The university had been something special. White had not imagined anything like it existed in the whole country. After any trip to the sticks, a few days at a base helped him in the sense that it gave him a chance to rest and renew his strength. But the tour of the university had given him a badly needed psychological boost.

The deep bonding with his fellow soldiers and the extreme clarity that sometimes came upon him gave him a certain sense of pride in becoming a proficient soldier. But there was also an equally strong depression brought on by every contact with the enemy, and a growing helplessness when anyone in the company was hurt or killed. And he was afraid that there was more, and worse, to come.

At home he had been content in a world he felt he understood. He had not been the best student in his class, but he had felt at least average. Actually, he had been average in everything–football, basketball, and all the other school sports. Physically, though not as strong as some, he still had energy left when others were spent.

Book wise, too, he had been average. Only in geography and history had he excelled, collecting books on different cultures and climates. He still liked both, but found that now he valued them more from a practical perspective.

He felt almost as he used to as he stood in the shade of a tree, basking in the pleasant smell of the clear air. He almost shivered as chills of pleasure ran up his spine, and was almost laughing when he turned to look at Boudreaux.

Boudreaux, as always, seemed to understand everything. He looked at White and in a thick Cajun accent said, "Now we gonna go somew'ere else. Ready?"

"Yeah," said White. "I'm ready, Pierre."

Boudreaux stopped another rickshaw, and they got into the seat. A quick word to the driver, and the rickshaw started down the boulevard. They turned left at an abandoned warehouse and followed the avenue farther into the city.

That part of the city had once been almost as rich as that along the boulevard, but now the houses began to look shabby. After a quarter mile the rickshaw stopped in front of a big, single-story house.

Like all the other houses that had been built for French businessmen, the stuccoed walls had been painted white. Now they were dirty. Two wooden doors, seven feet tall, faded green and peeling, were matched by equally faded green shutters. Both the doors and shutters were closed.

A crack appeared at the door the moment the rickshaw stopped. Whoever had peered through the crack shouted something back into the interior of the house.

When the two Americans stepped onto the sidewalk, the green doors opened, and a young woman stood there. She beamed at Boudreaux as she slowly walked to him. When she reached him, she stood motionless, submissive, and waited for him to speak first. She smiled even harder when he took her hand and said something to her in French.

She was so occupied with Boudreaux that she hadn't even noticed White. But the other girls at the now-fully-opened French doors had seen him and ran to him. Both of his arms had a girl gently squeezing them. Two more girls stood in front, blocking his way. All four were talking suggestively to him in Vietnamese and jabbering angrily at one another, trying to force the others away.

They were all better looking than the one who now led Pierre toward the green doors. French blood had contributed heavily in her makeup. She had a bone and muscle structure much larger than the pure Vietnamese girls. Her skin was slightly darker than the others, with hair shorter, softer, and almost brown. Her cheeks and temples were lightly scarred by acne. She was not as tall as the others and, because of a larger frame, looked chunky.

But White could see that behind the skin of the young woman

was something very striking. Almond eyes sparkled with open joy as she looked up at Boudreaux. In a hard place and time, an era of constant struggle and dread of tomorrow, she glowed with tenderness. White looked into her hazel eyes and glowing face, charmed by her compassion.

A tugging at his arms turned his attention to the girls surrounding him. Now they jabbered at him in broken French. When they saw he didn't understand, some again tried Vietnamese. When that didn't work, one of the girls began in broken English. "Hey. You. G.I." she shouted. "Me number one girl. I lovee you too much. Me. You. Boom-boom. O.K.?"

Proud of her mastery of English, the girl pulled at White. The others, not as fluent as the first, began shouting, imitating the first, "You boom-boom. You boom-boom."

White had had enough. He grabbed the one who had spoken the best English by the waist, and pulled her to his side. The others he shooed away with a wave of his hand and said, "*di di.*"

The other girls walked off grumbling. White, his girl, Boudreaux, and his girl walked into the house.

The salon was unexpectedly cool. Its twelve-foot ceilings captured the heat. In the center of the ceiling hung a slowly turning fan, forcing the heat toward the open patio at the back. Ten wooden chairs lined the barren, faded white walls of the salon. Toward the back of the house was a high archway leading to the bedrooms, the kitchen, and the covered patio.

It was evident that twenty years earlier, the house had been an elegant example of a minor French official or businessman's home. Now it was fading and decrepit, serving as the best whorehouse in New City Hué.

Boudreaux and the girl walked through the archway toward the shaded patio. They talked quietly, almost whispering, as they walked. Behind them went White with his girl. She impatiently tugged at him and, in a high pitched squeal, asked, "You boom-boom now?"

Boudreaux turned toward White with an understanding look, saying, "We'll meet you on 'de' patio w'en you done."

The girl led White to the inner hallway that circled the sides and back of the house. Along its outer wall were other doors. She opened one of them, leading White into a large bedroom.

She was not beautiful and didn't seem overly intelligent, but she was pretty enough and a professional. It even seemed that she liked her work. At any rate, she was enthusiastic about her job. In a matter of a few minutes, they were done. She then led White to a large bathroom. They showered in cold water while she dutifully lathered and scrubbed him.

At that point, she began to smile and rattle on in Vietnamese. She giggled as she scrubbed him, watching while he revealed an asset of being nineteen years old. This time, things lasted longer.

Back in the bedroom, she constantly yakked in Vietnamese. If she wanted to stress a point, she would repeat a word a little louder. When she saw that White still didn't understand, she searched for an equivalent in her halting, heavily accented French. When that, too, didn't work, she shook her head in frustration and let out a stream of what White thought was street slang.

White watched her, his hands behind his head, as he lay on the big iron bed. He watched her and almost loved her, while he sucked in deeply the safety, the luxury, and the peace. He tried repeating words in Vietnamese. She laughed at his terrible accent.

He couldn't make her understand a word he said, so he sprang on her like a panther, held her down on the bed, and began tickling her. She protested in angry Vietnamese and fought back, all in vain. Then she surrendered and began laughing, then seemed to be begging. Finally, they both collapsed on the bed, laughing. She tried to teach him how to say her name. Xuan. But the pronunciation was too much for him. The closest he could come to it was Zahn, so he called her that. Zahn.

They went out to the patio. Boudreaux and his girl weren't there. Zahn struggled in Vietnamese, then in French, to ask White if he wanted a beer. She finally made him understand by pretending to pour something into a glass and drink. When she repeated in French, "*biere*," he finally understood and said yes.

White saw a movement in the corner of his eye. He turned toward an opening door and saw a late-middle-aged woman. She was Vietnamese, but there was something different about her. Her teeth were not stained black. Something about her dress, motion and carriage seemed less foreign. But there was no doubt of who she was.

She was the *Madame* of the house, an elite. Her word was law. Any decision she made was the right one. She seemed very sure of herself and knew what kind of world she lived in. She seemed intelligent, and was, by any standard, beautiful.

She came to the table, scarcely glancing at White, speaking rapidly and angrily to Zahn. She looked scornfully at White as Zahn let out a stream of hysterical, apologetic sounding Vietnamese.

White understood only when he heard the word "Boudreaux." The transformation was like magic. The woman's expression quickly went from an almost cold contempt to a pleased, friendly smile. She said something in French to White. She tried again when he didn't answer. Zahn explained that he didn't speak French.

The woman stood silently thinking for a moment. Then she signed him with her perfect hands to relax and drink his beer. She spoke firmly but calmly to Zahn and then walked into the kitchen connected to the patio.

A few minutes later, Boudreaux and his girl joined them at the table. Boudreaux's girl seemed to see him for the first time. She smiled. She said something in French. White understood only one thing, *Bonjour*.

Glad that he had taken French instead of Spanish in school, and in a surprisingly decent accent, he said, "*Bonjour, mademoiselle.*"

Everyone laughed but Boudreaux. He said, "Pretty good. At least ya didn't sound like ya from Texas."

Boudreaux's girl's name was Linh. White studied her while they talked. The acne scars and crow's feet lines around her eyes melted away when she laughed.

She said something to Boudreaux as she went off into the kitchen. She came out with a woven straw market basket, went to the front door and out into the afternoon heat.

Zahn stood up. Facing White, she said something in a mixture of Vietnamese and French. He didn't understand a word. Exasperated, she turned to Boudreaux. He smiled at both of them and said. "She's gonna do a little work 'round 'de' house. Says she'll see ya later."

The two soldiers sat quietly for a long time. There was no need to talk. They sipped the cool beer and eased further into the comfort of the shade and the wooden chairs.

After three months in Nam, White knew about death, and worse. But he had never known love. He loved his mother, father, and family, but love for a girl was something he had not yet experienced. He had dated several girls but nothing serious had ever come of it. He had once known "puppy love," but he was no longer a puppy. The puppy in him had died, brutally murdered.

Yet he suspected that youth is something elastic and bounces back. He knew that Boudreaux had more experience than he with girls and asked, "Pierre, do you love Linh?"

Boudreaux turned his attention to the ceiling. For a long time he sat motionless. When he turned back toward White, with a very sad and almost regrettable expression on his face, he said, "Not like 'dat. But Ah like her an' she like me, an' we good fr'ens." With that simple sentence he had reached down into the roots of what he knew of love and exposed it to White's developing mind. White sat silent for a long time. He nodded his head, looked at his friend and said, "That's good, Pierre."

The last of the quart-sized bottle of Vietnamese beer had lost all of its coolness, but the young Americans poured it into their glasses anyway. They swished the warm liquid around their teeth and tongues, savoring the taste.

"What ya t'ink?" asked Boudreaux. "'Dis is better 'dan 'de bush or w'at?"

"Yeah, Pierre, much better," said White.

But he said it with a sad, forlorn look. Something had been weighing heavily on him, pressing against even this moment of happiness. Finally, he asked Boudreaux. "But, Pierre... what about home? What do you think it will be like when we get back?"

Frowning, half turning toward White, Boudreaux said, "Don' know. I jus' know 'dat nuttin's gonna be 'de same again."

"What do you mean, Pierre?" asked White.

"Ah jus' don' feel 'de same way Ah used to 'bout nuttin'," said Boudreaux. "Nuttin' over 'dere seems real. It all seem so fake, so phony. It's like everybody back 'dere is only half alive."

Those few sentences brought White another step down because he knew exactly what Boudreaux meant.

"But, Pierre," he said. "Do you think we'll get over it?"

"Don' know," said Boudreaux. "Hope so. But in 'de meanwhile we got ta stay alive, an' 'dis is 'de place 'dat helps me t'ink 'dat maybe one day it'll be all right."

Boudreaux's simple analysis always seemed to ease some morbid thought. Then, as White remembered the university he asked, "Pierre. Why does the professor's English sound so strange?"

"Ah didn't even know he talked English so good," said Boudreaux. "Maybe he jus' learned it in a book or somethin'."

"Yeah," said White as he leaned back into his chair.

Then more minutes of silence. The quiet was so fine, so fitting and soothing. But White felt a sudden heaviness. "A Shau", whispered in his brain. He looked at Boudreaux and wondered if he should ask. Finally he said, "Pierre, what about 'A Shau'?"

When he saw the instant change in Boudreaux, White regretted having asked. A super-vigilant tenseness surged through Boudreaux as his eyes quickly surveyed the doors and hallways leading into the patio. When he saw nothing suspicious and realizing he had overreacted, Boudreaux's face turned to ice.

Physically forcing himself, he began to limber up. He took several deep breaths, held the last for a moment, and began. "A Shau Valley," he said. "Deep in de mountains. Very bad place. Full of N.V.A." He stared off into the darkening shadows of the courtyard and slowly shook his head, remembering, and said, "All of us old timers been 'der. Los' many fren's. Booby traps everyw'ere. Artillery. Everyt'ing. Worse place in de country."

The story went on and White could see it in his mind. The valley itself, surrounded by high mountains, had a pleasant looking, peaceful setting of gently rolling hills filled with elephant grass, scattered bamboo and banana groves, patches of thick forest, and streams of clear water. Compared to other stretches of jungle, the beauty of the A Shau seemed like Eden. But upsetting the tranquil scene, camouflaged by giant elephant ears and butterflies, were hidden bunkers and hooches that sheltered and supplied regiments of N.V.A.

With their usual genius and ingenuity, the N.V.A. had hidden tunnels, hospitals, supply warehouses, ammo dumps, administration offices, mess areas, reserves, and everything else needed for maintaining an army in the field, strategically scattered in the valley. Ingenious booby-traps waited for an overly curious American, thinking he was picking up a souvenir, to blow himself up. There was not a square foot of ground not coordinated on a map, sighted in, that could not be hit by N.V.A. artillery.

But surrounding the valley, among the jungle-covered mountains, were its real defenses. Hidden in the trees and scattered at strategic spots on the ground were thousands of bombs and mines. Sharpened, poisoned bamboo stakes lay hidden in the underbrush, waiting for a G.I. diving for cover to impale himself. Shallow pits with sharp bamboo spikes, lightly covered with sticks and leaves, waited for a soldier to fall in. Green trip wires, almost impossible to see in the tangle of the forest, waited for an American boot to touch them and trigger the bombs the wires led to. Hand-dug tunnels connected all parts of the battleground. Trails easily reached every part of the N.V.A. defenses from the great supply dumps in the valley. Machine gun nests, concealed and covered, overlooked every inch of ground an invader must use to climb the hill to get into the valley.

Again, the quiet grew thick as the two soldiers stared at each other. But now it was White that seemed in a state of shock. He hadn't thought anything could have caused such a strong reaction in the Cajun. Yet a simple word had shaken him to his roots. Having to know regardless of the answer, White said, "You think we'll ever go there?"

"Almos' sure," said Boudreaux, once more in control. "But don' worry too much. You ready now an' got as good a chance as anybody."

White now understood never to talk about A Shau to anyone anymore. The only thing he could think of to say was, "Thanks, Pierre."

From the back of the patio came the squeak of an opening door. Both were instantly alert. They turned to see a man emerge from the back gate. Dressed in only gym shorts and shower shoes, the middle-aged man seemed the perfection of his race and age group. His slightly graying hair was styled in a short flattop. His bronzed skin was taut over a muscular frame. Intelligent, slanted eyes looked out from a handsome clean-shaven face.

He was at first suspicious. Then his expression changed to a sign of recognition as he saw Boudreaux. He walked to the table with an outstretched hand. Boudreaux jumped up and shook the older man's hand.

"Ah, *mon vieux,*" said the man. "*Je suis très content de vous voir.*"

"*Moi aussi,*" said Boudreaux. "*Ça vais bien?*"

They joked in French, laughing together at something the man said.

White had stood up with Boudreaux. When introduced, he clasped the man's powerful hand. Hidden strength was in those fingers, and White knew that there was indeed something special about the man. He knew he was looking at a very fit, hundred-and-forty-pound, thinking human muscle.

The man and Boudreaux talked on for a few moments. Then he excused himself, nodded slightly to White, and walked into another part of the house.

Linh returned. She came through the house carrying a basket of fresh vegetables. On the patio side of the kitchen's wall was a counter top made of concrete and wood. At one end was a sunken, open wood stove. Linh gathered pots, pans, the vegetables and meat, and laid them all on the counter. She smiled as she worked, softly humming to herself a slow, sad song that pulled at the heartstrings of everyone on the patio. She used dried sticks to build a fire.

The smell of raw onions and garlic drifted to the table. Boudreaux told the story of the woman and the man. Their name was Nghia. They owned The Green Doors. They had emigrated when young, met, married, and raised a family in France. She had been a well-paid seamstress, he a well-known champion lightweight boxer.

The smell of the now frying onions and garlic filled the area while the story went on. They had had a good life in France, but always there was a gnawing loneliness. They had fit well, were part of Parisian life, and their children were now totally French. But they had come to see that deep inside, at their core, they were Vietnamese. As they got older, they realized that they ached for their homeland. Very industrious and wise with money, they found that, if they were careful with their savings, they could open a business and retire comfortably back home.

The sweet smell of fresh peas cooking took Boudreaux's attention from the story. They were assaulted by the aroma of roasting chicken. For the first time since he got in-country, White's mouth watered. He knew that whether French, Cajun, or Vietnamese, the food steaming in the pots would be something to remember. He asked Boudreaux what it was. "Cajun," said his friend. "Smells good, huh?"

They were served at the table. Linh served Boudreaux first. To White she brought a plate with a mound of white rice in the center. On top of the rice, sautéed with onions, garlic and boiled egg halves was a mound of peas. They had been cooked to such tenderness that green pea gravy oozed to soak the rice. On the side of the plate, still smoking, were a chicken thigh, a drumstick, and a neck, cooked to a golden brown in their own skin.

That night, while White and Zahn lay on the big iron bed, he looked at her sleeping form through the dim light. He knew now why Boudreaux would risk court marshal, and even death, to come here. He also knew that, if he lived, he, too, would be back.

Again, a thought made its way into his mind. The A Shau Valley was waiting. Like a viper it crept into his thinking. Then, in a great effort, he began to will it away. He closed his eyes and searched for a calmness that would cover him. He rejected everything that made him think of anything but here and now.

His breathing became deeper. Worming its way into him was a vague uneasiness that he had enjoyed tonight's meal so much. It might hurt his mother's feelings that her fried chicken was no longer the best. But that was another thing she would never know.

In another quick flash, he realized he now felt no guilt at all about going to a prostitute. Zahn was a nice girl, even if not the smartest. He could hear her breathing, already asleep, next to him.

More dim shadows and images gently passed before his closed eyes. Somewhere he heard the soft laughter of a woman and the shrill giggling of little children. He saw an ancient cottonwood tree by a creek, and then he was asleep.

CHAPTER XIV

For two days and nights, time had seemed suspended, abstract, like a dream. The last fifty hours had been so reviving that White had scarcely noticed their passing. His senses had been dulled to everything but the pleasure in the quiet and safety of the whorehouse. But now the dream had ended, and he was again back in real time. Around the corner, quickly disappearing was The Green Doors.

The rickshaw rolled through the crowded streets and stopped where the river met Highway One. White and Boudreaux paid the driver and sat in the shade of a small tree, waiting to catch a ride to the base camp and their unit. A light breeze stirred the leaves while the two soldiers sat cross-legged on the ground, rifles resting across their knees.

In his mind, White could see Zahn. She was an amazing creature. She seemed an honest girl, but she, too, wanted a steady man. She longed, in her simple mind, to have someone like Linh had. As she and White had said goodbye, she tried her best to act like Linh, nearly choking in an attempt to say something fitting, like a real lover, to her beloved. But the best that came out was, "I lovee you too much."

But White knew there was no acting on Linh's part. Boudreaux, because of his being French, was her only link to a long-dead French soldier she had truly loved. Maybe it was because of this that she felt a strong attraction to and gratitude for the Cajun. Maybe it was not love, but White felt that it was with true friendship and liking, and true fear for him, that she had said goodbye to Boudreaux.

Even Madame and Monsieur Nghia had seemed not anxious to see the two young Americans leave. Both, however, were extremely practical. In the hard world of their country at war, there were more serious events than the two soldiers leaving for the bush. So, they happily accepted the thirty dollars that Boudreaux and White paid for their two-day stay, said a cheerful "*Adieu*," and prepared for what a new day would bring.

White didn't like the feel of his starched and ironed fatigues. Zahn had washed, over-starched, and ironed his and Boudreaux's clothes. They felt stiff as cardboard as he sat on a grassy spot near the bowl of the tree. His boots, shining like black glass, reflected the swaying leaves and branches above them.

They wondered at the lack of traffic on the highway. At that time of the morning, the highway should have been filled with vehicles of all kinds. Anything that could be made to roll should be fighting for position on the highway. It was strange that now only rarely did an army truck or jeep come along.

Looking across the highway they saw a farmer and his water buffalo wading through the rice paddy. They sat in the shade of the tree like twin Buddhas searching for Nirvana, hearing only the sound of the sucking of the buffalos' hooves pulling out of the muck of the paddy.

At the junction of the highway, a dented black car came to a stop. Even from fifty yards away, Boudreaux and White recognized Jimmy Hong and Hahn as they got out of the ragged French wreck. Both White and Boudreaux smiled realizing that they, too, had been instantly seen and recognized by their approaching comrades.

"What's up?" asked Jimmy Hong in his strong California accent.

"Hey," responded White and Boudreaux.

Hahn, at twenty, served as company interpreter. Like almost all Vietnamese, he was very polite. Just his presence lifted the spirits of even the most hardened. Smith, too, always grumpy, always scowling, became milder around Hahn.

Like all Vietnamese, Hahn seemed much younger than he actually was. He looked like a boy, thirteen or so, instead of a man older than most of the men serving with him.

As White had matured in the company and began to really like Hahn, he had to fight an urge to watch over him like he was a little brother.

Another thing about the Vietnamese was their hatred of the Chinese. Since they had separated themselves from China centuries before, there had always been strife and war between them. But despite the usual animosity for the Chinese by the Vietnamese, Hahn and Hong became friends with Hahn teaching Hong the language. Now Jimmy Hong's Vietnamese had improved greatly. Hahn said he was even beginning to lose his terrible Chinese accent.

Smiling at his friends, Hahn said, "How do you do?"

Boudreaux answered, "Good, Hahn. How're you?"

"How's things in your village, Hahn?" asked White.

"Ver' fine, t'ank you, mister. Ver' fine," said Hahn.

The four comrades sat on the grass and squirmed into a comfortable position. From a burlap sack he carried, Hahn pulled out two packages wrapped in banana leaves. Inside one were a couple of dozen egg rolls and a small jar of *nuoc mam*. The other had several palm-sized packs of cooked rice wrapped in banana leaves. On the top and sides of the rice were slices of different cooked vegetables. Hahn placed everything on the ground between them.

"My mother make," he said with an eager smile. "Ver' good. Eat please."

They sat there eating the egg rolls dipped in the rotten-smelling sauce. With their fingers they pinched off chunks of rice and vegetables. If the strips of vegetable were long enough, they dipped those, too, into the *nouc mam*.

"Real good, Hahn," said Boudreaux.

"Yeah. Real good," said White.

"Yeah," said Hong. "His mom sure can cook."

Everyone in the company knew there was a special friendship between Hong and Hahn. Louis had once explained to White about their friendship. Unusual as it was for the Vietnamese to associate voluntarily with a Chinese, Hong and Hahn began talking at their first meeting. Whether it was because Hong was American born and raised or because they recognized something in each other that went beyond usual social norms, they became friends. After a few weeks had passed, Hong was invited to visit Hahn's family and village.

Hahn's mother was the first to begin to accept the American youth. His brothers and sisters came next. Then his father, reluctantly, began to soften. But the villagers were more traditional. At first, they had treated him politely but were reserved almost to the point of being rude. Slowly, however, the California teenager's natural good nature and home-taught good manners had penetrated the caution that the villagers felt toward strangers, especially Chinese. Slowly, they began to look on Hong with a certain fondness.

White knew that humor and teasing are important parts in establishing strong relationships. And, as long as it doesn't go so far as to hurt or anger someone, mutual teasing is a sure sign of friends. It was in part taking advantage of Hong's good nature and in part because of his own youthful self that Hahn prodded his friend. "My school friend ver' pretty, too," said Hahn, teasing Hong about a girl in the village. "But her *pappasan* no like American G.I. and no like Chinee," he laughed.

They all laughed except Hong. The three others watched him expectantly, waiting for the comeback they knew was coming. For many seconds he seemed lost as to what to say. His comrades knew as well as he the difficulties he faced. The girl's family didn't trust the people in the next village, much less a Chinese American foreigner.

It was a heavy problem. He knew he must show respect to her father. Without that everything else would fail. White could see the tugging in Jimmy's mind as to what he should do. His feelings for Hahn's schoolmate had gone beyond liking into a real, desperate love. The California boy in him plotted their romance, regardless of the consequences, but it all seemed so impossible.

He frowned in deep thought while the others, sitting and grinning to each other, watched him. Then White saw something else. The adolescent, confused look on his face disappeared, and a manly, completely sober expression took its place. He searched for an adequate response but could only say, "Fuck him."

"You no can fock him," said Hahn. "You no can fock her, too," he laughed.

"Little Jimmy Cherry," laughed Boudreaux.

"Poor innocent lamb," said White.

Jimmy Hong looked at the three soldiers with him and knew that every man there was his comrade. He knew, too, that he must not get angry with their teasing. He searched hard for something clever to say that would impress them, but all that he could think of was, "Fuck all you mudderfuckers."

"No fuckie-fuckie?" said Boudreaux.

"No boom-boom?" said White.

"No fock-fock?" said Hahn.

Still not able to think of anything better, Jimmy Hong said again, "Fuck all you mudderfuckers."

The three others laughed until their sides hurt. They were so busy laughing they almost missed the three-quarter ton truck stopping for them. They climbed in back and sat on the stacked crates. The truck gave them a ride to the dirt and sand road leading to the base camp and their company. From there they walked the half-mile back to the camp.

Sitting on top of the bunker at the gate were Louis and two grunt guards. Lying asleep in the shade of the poncho, stretched out on the lumpy sandbag roof, was Lopez.

"Had a good time?" Louis called down to them.

"Ver' good time, mister," said Hahn. "No boom-boom but ver' good time."

Louis was puzzled by the laughter. Then he remembered about Hong and the girl. Smiling, he climbed down from the bunker and stood next to Hong. With a sad face he looked at Jimmy Hong and said, "No boom-boom?"

Hong stared up at him and said, "Fuck you, too."

Now the five comrades walked into the interior of the camp back to their tents at the company area.

Later that night, when everything was quiet, White could hear the gentle drone of the generator, two-hundred yards away. That was the only sound he heard. He tried to think of the last two days at The Green Doors. But he couldn't hold an image of it for very long. He lay quietly, thinking of the quickly approaching morning, as he stared blindly at the ceiling.

Next to the terror of combat and the dread of possible mutilation of one's self and one's comrades, and almost as physically sickening as it is psychologically draining, is the few hours' wait before leaving to go back into the sticks.

White and the company waited gloomily. Most sat or lay quietly in any shady spot they could find. Others milled around, looking for a signal from a comrade to sit and talk. The officers, some of the higher sergeants, and the three-man "red leg" group from artillery squatted or sat in a circle, reading and studying a map. They planned routes, as best as they could, through the ridges of the mountains where they were going, plotting coordinates of major peaks and crags as reference points for themselves and supporting artillery.

White saw his comrades twitching. Their new clothes and equipment felt uncomfortable. They were too new. They had not yet been molded by constant wear to the bodies of the men. They stank of newness. The smell was fine in the rear areas, but out there any smell other than the rotting ammonia reek of the jungle was like a beacon pointing to you.

White knew the smell wouldn't last long. After a day of humping, grunting under the full weight of new, tightly loaded packs, sweat would drench them. After a few nights of sleeping in dirt and leaves and rolling through the rot of the forest floor, the new clothes and boots would lose that new smell and begin to fit.

Scattered through the platoons and squads were the replacements. White didn't like to look at them. They were like babes in the woods, terrified by what they didn't know, but guessing what had happened to the ones they were replacing.

There were no street toughs here. There were no good ole bad-ass country boys. Here, what they saw in the veterans were black, white, red, and yellow wolves--all wolves--and all equal under the new law. With an eerie, alien instinct, a replacement would soon realize that only he was not equal.

White had heard there were race riots in the States. There were ethnic, religious, and class riots and tensions all over the world. But here, on the verge of going back into the sticks, no one rioted. Most couldn't even talk.

It would take a heart of stone or no heart at all to look at the pitiful recruits and not want to protect them. But White now knew he couldn't save them and that they didn't know how to save themselves. The best most could hope for was a wound serious enough to get them out of the boonies.

Only occasionally would a veteran see something special in a replacement. Sometimes, one of them would show a certain aptitude, and the men of the company would begin to work with him. One of the comrades would adopt him first. Then others, seeing he had a mentor, would also begin teaching him.

Sadly, this only happened to about one in four. No one could do anything about the others, and the end was always the same. Better not to get involved.

Sometimes one of them would get the nerve to ask a question. But it was always before going into the jungle for the first time, and it was always the same question.

"Do you think that I can make it?"

"Sure kid, you can make it," was the dull answer. But even the green recruits could see it was a forced answer. The veterans didn't like to lie.

These dismal thoughts didn't show on White's stern face. His hard eyes scanned the recruits, looking for a possible future comrade. He looked out hopefully but saw only fear.

He was brought out of a gloomy mood when his eyes lit on Louis, strong, capable, and good. Next they rested on Boudreaux, dependable, compassionate. Lopez, exceptional instincts, unbeatable, loyal.

Then the hateful word came down, "Saddle up. Get ready to move out." The old timers jumped up and effortlessly threw on their packs. The green replacements, struggling to mount their packs, were already panting.

CHAPTER XV

It was the same every time. The first day of humping after a stand down is almost as bad as one's first day in the field. The backpack's straps grind and blister the shoulders. The sweat soaking the drab green bath towel which each soldier carries around his neck smells of heavy salt. The replacements think they'll die, but the veterans, now including White, know that in a day or two they'll be back in form. For now, though, they sweat out the poisons of ease and civilization.

At the end of the first week, White was back in top form. No contact had been made yet, and he was thankful that only the misery of humping the sticks was all they had so far faced.

When he and his brothers had been boys, they had loved to go camping by horseback near the creek a mile from his home. Camping was one of the things he really had liked, and had since he could remember.

The peacefulness he felt had only been disturbed by thoughts of some of the creatures crawling around during the night. Snakes had been the biggest concern. Rattlers and copperheads liked to crawl into something warm at night. A warm blanket or sleeping bag could hold an invitation they couldn't resist.

In the jungle there were many more dangerous creatures than in the tame countryside of Nebraska. But as the weeks had gone by, White had become immune to any serious worry from animals.

The foot-long centipedes crawling through the dead leaves at night no longer bothered them. A lucky bite might even get a grunt sent to a hospital for a few days.

Some of the many kinds of spiders and snakes were poisonous and therefore dangerous, but no one in the company had yet been bitten, so his mind had turned away from that danger. Poison plants, too, were something he no longer considered dangerous.

But apart from N.V.A., there lived in the jungle something that was truly detested by everyone. More hateful to the line of sweating, grunting soldiers than the wait-a-minute thorns, more disgusting in their minds than the ivory-colored, long-toothed, jungle rats, and with a more quiet and slithering attack than the best N.V.A., were the jungle leeches.

They lived in damp areas of the jungle and were less than an inch long. When full of blood they grew three or four times in size. They were never felt until full and ready to drop off, and trying to pull them off was useless. The maddening creatures clung so tenaciously by their sucking mouths that pulling on them would often tear them in half, leaving the head buried in the flesh.

Dabbing them with salt was a good way to make them release. A touch of salt on their slimy bodies, and they would squirm for a moment and then reluctantly let go.

But the best way was with fire. If one touched them anywhere with the tip of a lit cigarette, they let go immediately and fell, twitching violently, to the jungle floor.

To kill is something a soldier might have to do at any time to stay alive, but to torture is something completely different. Only a certain kind of personality is capable of that. But the tiny, wormlike animal was so disgusting and hated that the soldiers took a grim pleasure in burning them, torturing them, and watching them twitch violently and fall; then, as a final revenge, stomping them and grinding them into the earth with the toe of a ragged boot.

The company had just walked into a nest of the small land leeches. When one was discovered, it was certain that most of the soldiers would be infested, so they rushed to an area free of the little beasts.

When the company stopped to clean themselves of the pests, it was close to noon. The captain sent word to form perimeter and break for lunch. They separated into groups of two's and three's. Louis, Smith, and White had been together in line on the march and naturally grouped for the burning of the leeches.

First, they removed their packs and steel helmets. Next, they unbuttoned their fatigues. At the last minute, they lay down their rifles and removed their shirts. Neither White nor Louis smoked, but each accepted a cigarette from Smith. Lighting their cigarettes on the same match, they began to burn the bloodsuckers off.

Between leeches, White would glance at his two friends. He couldn't imagine a greater contrast between two human beings. Smitty was skinny and almost an albino white. Rage at the leeches and the world seemed to fill him and was expressed in his grim face and cold blue eyes. He was so thin that anyone but a veteran, on seeing him, would think there wasn't much strength in his lean body.

But such rot no longer fooled the veterans. They knew what really made a good soldier, and all of them could see it in Smith. White watched in fascination as Smith easily found the dark leeches on his white skin and, with an evil grin, burned them off.

Then White's eyes would shift to Louis. His almost-black skin glistened in the dim light and accented every curve, indent, and bulge of his magnificent physique. His natural build was another manifestation of the best physical examples of manhood developed in Africa.

But that was not what impressed White or any of the other veterans of the company. Neither was it a certain, undefined recognition which exists between the war-wise.

What was most impressive in Louis was what White always saw in him. In those deep black eyes was a core of kindness that could not be broken. As everyone else took pleasure in giving pain to the tiny beasts, Louis burned them off without malice or hate. This was true for whatever action he might take against an enemy. He could kill them but never hate them.

As he looked at Louis, White knew that a man like Louis must indeed be something rare in this world. He knew, too, that no matter on which continent or in which era Louis might have been born, he would always be a good man.

Smith turned to Louis and roughly said, "Come here and show me your head." Louis gently bowed his head to Smith, and Smith's thin, white fingers explored his wooly, short hair, searching for hidden leeches.

"Fucking blood-sucking sons of bitches," said Smith as he burned off a leech.

Next, it was Louis's turn to run his huge black fingers through the sergeant's thin, very blonde hair. When he was done, they both looked over to White and walked his way. One looked through White's scalp as the other raised his arms to reveal a hidden leech in the left armpit. With a touch of the cigarette, the filthy thing fell to the jungle floor.

Then each soldier pulled off his boots and untied the thin lines securing the cuffs of their pants to their ankles. Sure enough, there were leeches on their feet that had managed to crawl through the tightly laced pants and boots.

Each searched his own groin and legs, burning off leeches when found. When everyone was sure they had gotten all of the pests, they dressed, chose a position on the perimeter, and faced outward to scan the jungle.

White had made his way to the left of the three comrades. He set his pack in front of him and unconsciously began to memorize every tree and shrub. To his immediate right was Smith and beyond him was Louis. On his left, already with a steaming canteen cup of water on the stove, was Lopez.

Lopez grinned at him and, with a small wave of the hand, invited White to join him.

Everyone in the company knew Lopez was a chowhound. His pack bulged bigger than anyone's, with extra C's and LRRPs. To be invited to dine with him was an experience not to be missed, so White picked up his pack and moved the twenty feet to Lopez's position.

Lopez, heating water in a canteen cup, never looked up as White sat down three feet from him. He had set out several different cans and packages and now began to open some of them.

C-rations were pre-cooked meals which the U.S. Army had been using for years to feed troops in the field. Different meats and vegetables had been cooked and canned as part of the main course. Ham with lima beans, spaghetti and meatballs, beans and franks, and pork slices with potatoes were some of the high calorie meals that came as C-rations. In other cans were white bread, prune, date, and pecan breads. But the best tasting, the most valued, desserts were the cans of pound cake.

Canned peaches, pears, applesauce, and fruit cocktail were packed in a thick, sweet sauce. Wrapped in aluminum foil were a couple of three-inch by one-quarter-inch thick chocolate bars, a three-inch by one-inch can of peanut butter, jam, a three-inch by four-inch can holding four round crackers, and a small can of cheddar cheese.

Inside waterproof packets which came with each meal was a miniature pack of four cigarettes, a small pack of toilet paper, individual packs of sugar, salt, pepper, matches, a spoon, two cubes of chewing gum, and, best of all, a package of instant cocoa.

The C-rations were used mostly for troops that were nearer to the rear areas and base camps. Because they were packed naturally in their own juices or water, they were heavy, so the military had developed another kind of field food for troops ranging far away from support groups.

These were called LRRP (Long Range Reconnaissance Patrol—pronounced lurp) rations. Each package still held the toilet paper, matches, cigarettes, etc, but the main meal had been dehydrated to the point of having virtually no water left in it. They were so light that a soldier could carry many more meals in his pack.

While LRRPs assured there was less hunger from lack of food, it also meant that at times a soldier, when out of water, would have to eat very dry food or go without.

Some of the LRRP rations were rice with pork, rice with beef, and spaghetti. White liked best the pork and scalloped potatoes; the worst, chili con carne.

Lopez had everything planned. He asked White to hand him the chocolate bars. He ate one and gave the other to White, saving the aluminum wrapper. He opened a can of the cheese and crackers, spread the cheese between two of the crackers and wrapped them in the chocolate's aluminum foil. When this was done he set them aside while he opened a can of pork slices.

"Get a LRRP of spaghetti," he told White.

When both canteen cups of water were steaming, each took the water and added it to their spaghetti LRRP. They stirred the mixture, wrapped it tightly, and then set it aside to soak.

Lopez set an open can of pork slices on the blue flame. On White's stove he toasted the cheese and cracker sandwiches, one at a time.

"I've got a surprise," said White. He shuffled in his pack, coming out with a pack of pre-sweetened cherry Kool-Aid. His aunt, whenever writing a letter, always enclosed a pack of Kool-Aid.

A huge grin spread on Lopez's face. He was a man of few words in Spanish and of even fewer words in English. He seemed to think hard before he said simply, "*Bueno*."

As White fixed them each a half canteen cup of Kool-Aid, Lopez cut up the hot pork slices, dividing them into the two still-steaming LRRP spaghettis.

When the cheese and cracker sandwiches were a toasted, golden color, the two comrades began to feast. It was to be expected that in all the jungle no two people were enjoying a meal so much nor that more pleasant conversations could be held than the simple, "Good". "Hot". "Yeah."

When each mouthful had been chewed and savored, it was washed down with a sip of cherry Kool-Aid. After the main meal each soldier brought out his favorite dessert. White's was pound cake with fruit cocktail. Lopez's was pound cake with peaches.

All this time a canteen cup half-full of water heated on each stove. When both were hot and the two soldiers had finished their desserts, each added the cocoa and sugar to the water, mixed it well, then sat back and sipped hot chocolate.

White looked at a peaceful, relaxed Lopez. He looked to his left and saw Sam Cook and Jackson while they also sat quietly relaxing. He looked to his right and saw Louis as he smiled and nodded his head to Smith as they sipped their chocolate.

He was free of leeches, filled with food, satisfied with water, and drinking hot chocolate. The leaves on the ground felt like a cushion under him. The jungle was so quiet that the whole world seemed at peace, almost like being in church. Small rays of sunshine streaked through breaks in the leaves. He no longer smelled the ammonia rot of the jungle.

White looked at Lopez's serene face. He tried to remember the vacant, zombie-like stare he had seen in him when he first arrived. He remembered that he had been very afraid when forced to look at Lopez. But now, as Lopez's eyes swept his surroundings, White could only see that the Mexican had a profound understanding of the jungle. He knew nothing living that made noise to move, had a body that could be seen, and had odor could approach the Mexican unnoticed.

But in that calm exterior, White suspected something eating away at Lopez. How else could it be that he could be so proficient in the sticks and such a complete drunk on stand down? There was something bothering him beyond his sister's getting pregnant, and whatever it was stabbed at Lopez.

A part of White asked if there was anything he could do to help his friend. But another part, a wiser part, knew that there was nothing he could do for now. He could only accept Lopez as he was and appreciate him as he, himself, chose to be. Maybe some day he would try, but not now.

His mind drifted to something else. They had scarcely spoken a dozen words during the preparation and eating of the meal. No more were needed. White closed his eyes for a moment as he listened to the intense stillness and peacefulness. It was as if the whole world had regained its sanity and was now expressing it in silence.

He could barely remember how he at first had feared and hated these men. How could he have been so wrong about them? He could no longer see the killer in them or anything other than as valuable comrades. He didn't remember the agony it had cost him to reach where he now was. He could not remember that at one time he had hated the jungle.

CHAPTER XVI

The company was again on stand down. After a quick visit to the professor and a night at The Green Doors, White came back to camp. He sat on top of a guard bunker near the concertina wire. Louis, Cook, Jackson, two new guys, and Smith sat with him. A joint passed from hand to hand as each took occasional sips of warm beer. Lopez lay passed out, sprawled out on the sand bag roof, while Smith frowned at everyone as if he hated them all.

Winking at White, Jackson turned to Smith and said, "Hey Smitty. Think we gonna win the war before your tour is up?"

Smith's face twisted as if he had bitten into a lemon. "That's the stupidest thing I've ever heard," he said. "You really think those assholes want to win? Pah! Those politicians at home are all tied in with those big dogs that are making money on this shit. You think you'd want to stop it if you'd be sitting on your yacht drinking champagne with bitches in bikinis all around you?"

Seeing where Jackson, in baiting Smith was headed, Cook said, "Yeah. I guess not. But maybe the Gooks will just give up."

"Don't be so fucking green," said Smith. "When did you ever hear of the Gooks giving up on anything? Mutha fuckers got balls the size of basketballs. You guys have got to be fucking with me or you're both fucking crazy."

White had not yet said a word. Before coming to Nam he had agreed that something had to be done to stop the spread of communism. Didn't they want to take over the world? Wouldn't they, step by step, country by country, make their way west until they were finally at America's borders? Everybody said so. He shifted his weight on the sandbag he sat on and said, "But don't we have to do something to stop communism?"

Smith's head turned slowly toward him. The sneer on his face was gone. Very patiently, conscious that White listened to every word, he said, "Maybe. But first you got to show me who's the biggest enemy: the communists that want to control your life, or the big shots at home that already do? The commies that want to turn the world red, or the slick dicks at home that are stacking up the green?"

Cook and Jackson's demeanors had changed with those last words. White could see they were no longer joking. Finally Jackson said, "Yeah Smitty. I see what you mean. But what about freedom? Ain't that worth something?"

The sneer came back into Smith's face as he said, "Yeah. You look fucking free. Did you come here because you're free? You're free to come to Nam and bleed for those mother fuckers in New York and here in Nam that are all in this shit together to make big bucks. Those rich mothers in Chicago and Washington are really free too. And we're the ones that make them free."

A death-like silence filled the air as White and the others looked at each other. Suddenly Cook's head popped up and he said, "O.K., Smitty. You're right about all that. But don't you think the generals and army big shots want to win the war?"

"You think all the supplies and guns in A Shau grow on the fucking trees there? All that shit comes from China and Russia. Everything comes from them to North Viet Nam and then down here. And N.V.A. soldiers come from the north too. If we got to fight them, why do it down here? Why not fight in the north where we might win? The generals know that. But they ain't got the nuts it takes to tell the fucking politicians shit."

More silence. Then, unable to remain silent, White said, "Then you think the whole thing is just to make money?"

"Not for the Gooks," said Smith. "But ninety percent of them don't know nothing about democracy or communism. Those simple fuckers grow rice. Dumb fucks don't even know they're communists. Their water buffalos know more about politics than them."

"Then why are they fighting us so hard?" said Jackson.

"Because we're here," said Smith. "Just like the Chinese, Japs, and the fucking Frogs were here before us. And we're here for the same reason. We want something too.

"But what could we want?" asked White.

"Arms, construction, etc. Big money in arms. More than in drugs. And who's the big civilian construction outfit in Nam? And who owns Bell Helicopter? And doesn't the Hué bridge get bombed every night, then fixed the next day?" answered Smith.

Thinking, Cook lit another joint and handed it to White. As it passed to Jackson Smith said, "O.K. That's it. Enough of that political shit. Now tell Blanc what happened before he came to us…when we had stand-down at that beach, and you two guys were the richest muther fuckers in the Republic."

All this time Louis had been sitting quietly, listening to everything. White felt a sinking in his belly as he looked into Louis's sorrowful expression, knowing that he understood perfectly what Smith had said. But Louis's eyes brightened and a captivating smile flashed back into his face at the mention of the story to come.

Somehow Louis's smile made White sadder than he ever had been. Louis was one of those extremely rare people that radiate goodness of soul, and White felt a vague guilt for somebody like that to be on the front line.

Clearing his throat Jackson began the story. Looking relieved that the tension was gone, he said. "We came out of the sticks and began stand down. It was the best base camp we was ever in. Had good cots with air mattresses, hot chow, and all the cold beer you could steal. Didn't have to pull guard, K.P., none of that shit.

"Had live shows by Vietnamese or Filipino bands. Every night we boogied to the club and watched the *baby-sans* in mini skirts dancing and singing American songs."

White could imagine that he saw the scene as if he had been there with them, as the story jumped from Smith, to Jackson, and to Cook.

Cook flung his arms as he took up the story. "The camp had this long beachfront where we could use inner tubes, surfboards, masks and flippers for swimming." He paused for dramatic effect. "At the end of the compound, across the concertina wire, was a fishing village. The boats were pulled on the shore, and nets hung drying in the sun, wind blowing in the coconut trees. Peaceful." His voice trailed off.

"Third day, us and the guard sat on the top of the bunker," interjected Jackson. "Leaning against a wall, holding a half-empty bottle of rot gut, was Lopez. We was playing a game on Lopez, fucking with him to where he was ready to take on the captain, first sergeant, or anyone else who wanted some of it," said Cook.

White caught Cook's crooked smile and a secret wink to Jackson, "Yeah, Lopez," Cook said, "I know what you mean. But the captain said we can't have more than two beers a day per man."

"I don' care w'at he say," Lopez roared. "Fuck him."

Then Jackson said. "But Lopez, what about the first shirt? He's a mean ole maw dicker."

"Fuck him, too," Lopez shouted. "He a big *pendejo* pussy. De *maricon*."

At this Smith began to tell what happened next: "Company headquarters was in a plywood and tin hooch further in the compound. The first shirt, the captain and me were studying at a map. Cloud was on the floor inventorying his medical shit.

'We'll need more bandages and other things,' Cloud says to the captain. 'Sure,' said the captain. 'Morphine?' asked Cloud." Smith stuck out his chest in imitation of the captain as he continued. " 'Just get whatever you need, Doc,' the captain answered. 'Anybody gives you any shit, you call me!' Suddenly, from toward the bunker line, came a wild roar. Every head in the building shot to attention."

Smith stared wide-eyed to illustrate before continuing. "For a long time no one moved. Then the roar became loud sputtered words."

Smith turned toward White in explanation. "The first sergeant is a salty old bird. He's a mighty salty old bird. But when he recognized the voice behind the roar, said to the captain, 'Gotta check on something, Sir,' and flew out the back door.

"The same loud voice, closer this time, shouted, 'Fuck 'de fucking firs' sergeant.'" Smith let out a loud laugh. "At this the captain turned to me and Cloud and says, 'Carry on, men,' and went out.

"I looked out of the window to see Cook and Jackson on each side of too damn drunk Lopez, all three stumbling toward their own hooch.

"I heard Jackson, still fucking with Lopez, say, 'You can't talk like that, Lopez. Suppose the Colonel hears you?' " Smith drew in a breath before going on with the story for White and the new guys.

" 'Fuck 'dat fucking bitch!' had come out so loud that I thought they heard it at the far side of camp." Smith let out a loud laugh.

" 'Fuck all 'dem mutta fucks,' Lopez shouted. Jackson and Cook led him to his cot. Had a hard time calming him. Finally they got him to lay back on his cot.

" 'Don't worry, Lopez, we'll watch for them assholes. You get some rest, and we'll call you when we see them,' Jackson told him.

" 'Yeah,' Cook was saying, 'You just get some sleep, Lopez. We'll be looking for them.'

"I watched as Cloud just fucking stood there," said Smith. "That Indian looks like he's made of wood. Never laughs, always fucking serious. But for the second time that week I saw him smile."

Jackson grabbed the moment to continue the story "Then me and Cook decided to go to town. We made our way toward the main gate. Our plan was to catch a ride to town and abuse ourselves on the whores."

White and the others watched Jackson intently point to Cook with his thumb and say, "Then see if Bro here could find a new low."

Cook answered back in his usual, "Fuck you."

"But along the way we saw the base PX (Post Exchange)," Jackson continued, warming up to his audience. "It was the biggest military store we had ever seen. We looked at each other, nodded, went in.

"Radios, cameras, tape players, watches, clothes, and all kinds of shit for civilian life filled those shelves. We walked through the aisles, looking at things we'd never use in Nam.

"Then I says to Cook; 'Holy, fucking shit, man, check out this stereo!'

" 'What ya gonna do with a stereo?' he answers, 'Hump it around the boonies til' you go home?'

" 'I'm just saying it's nice,' I told him," Jackson paused to make sure White and the new guys were following.

"It was a trip watching Cook stroking the sides of this brown leather suitcase. 'Now, if you want to see something really nice, check this out,' he says to me. 'Going on a trip?' I says to him. 'Be real, man. Ain't none of this shit we can use anymore.'

"Then, I stop at a shelf of board games and pick out one, a game of monopoly. Cook looks at me like I'm nuts. 'Now ya want to play fucking games?' he says."

Jackson glanced over at Cook sitting far behind White, and winks at him.

" 'No, no.' I told him. 'Listen up. I'm getting an idea,' When I shot him my fucking-with-ya smile, he knew I was on to something."

Jackson turned to the newer grunts to explain: "Y'all know how the military never pays us soldiers in Nam in greenback dollars? They print their own money to pay us, right? The Gooks accept it like real dollars and can buy anything in the country, right?" He checks for nods of agreement from the audience.

"So," Jackson said, drawing out the word, "I turn to Cook in that PX store and says, 'Maybe the Gooks will take monopoly money.'

"You shoulda seen how Cook's face lit up. 'We'd be millionaires,' he says. Fucking millionaires!' "

Jackson took the turn in the story to pause and let the audience absorb the idea. He picked a cigarette from the pack in his shirt pocket, lit it under a poncho and took a deep draw. Satisfied that everyone was still with him, he continued.

"So we go to the cashier to pay for the monopoly game. A pretty young *baby-san* in a light blue *ao dai*, long silky black hair, look kinda questioning at us. We knew she couldn't imagine two grunts playing a board game. But she smiles professionally and politely at us and hands Cook his fucking change."

Jackson took another quick draw from the cigarette. "After we paid for the game, guess what we did? We left for the main gate and caught us a ride. The truck stops at the turn off for Phu Bai, and we climb down and walk a few blocks to a Vietnamese restaurant, forgot the name of it, some flower. At the restaurant we saw the hate and disrespect for us GIs in the faces of those fat cat patrons at the tables that can afford to eat at a restaurant. But you shoulda seen how quick those slanted eyes widened when I took out the roll of monopoly bills from my shirt pocket!"

Smith muttered from the right side of the listening group. "They believe you?" he asked, knowing the answer from having heard the story a dozen times before. Jackson smiled as he continued.

"Their sour faces changed just like that to warm, friendly shit-faced smiles of welcome as three of them bowing, fucking waiters led Cook and me to the best table in the house!" Jackson coughed and laughed at the same time.

Cook edged into the storytelling at that moment. "I was watching one of the waiters. I saw as the look on his face changed from suspicion of the money being fake to being sure that it was. But before that fucking waiter could say anything, I took out a true five-dollar bill, showed it to him and left it under the empty plate on the table. He never blinks or opens his mouth.

"They was chattering something in French, like '*Eassy, eassy, sivuplay*' said those waiters, while greedily staring at the fifty-dollar bill Jackson slaps on the table. You shoulda seen their eyes pop! And Jackson and me are saying '*Mercy. Mercy*,' trying out our pisspoor French as we're sitting ourselves down."

Cook paused to let the audience stop laughing. "For an hour, a whole fucking hour, we drank cold beer, and hot wine, ate roast duck, fried squid, salad, French fries – you name it, anything we wanted, from those ass kissing, very friendly waiters and cooks! We tipped everyone, shaking hands, laughing with them. It was like in a fucking movie – we were the STARS!"

Laughing so hard he had to take a second to compose himself, Cook continued. " 'Love being rich,' I says, and I saw through the plate glass window all those curious faces pressed against it, looking at us from the street. That whole village knew we were rich!"

"Yeah," Jackson jumped in to join Cook in the story that was gaining momentum. "But now I'm ready for a little boom-boom."

White and several others echoed, "Yeah. Some boom-boom!"

Jackson was just putting out his cigarette. "Cooks and waiters crowded all around us when we started to pay the bill. The waiters were chattering something in French about a '*gran plaisir*' they said, bowing deeply, almost kissing their fucking shoes. Ten-dollar notes went through our fingers like water. We was LOVED!" Jackson almost shouted. "We was admired. We was fucking generous!" He threw back his head in a belly laugh that rolled onto others in the audience.

Then he turned a somber face to the group. "A waiting rickshaw driver bows deeply, waving us to the seat of his twisted, piece-of-shit, three-wheeled heap. He smiles wide when he understands where the two of us want to go, and peddles like a madman as I pass him a fifty.

"Turning in the seat in that rattle-trap, I see the angry arms waiving and fists shaking behind us at the restaurant. Shit, Cook and me knew that the monopoly money scam had gone through. 'We're busted', I tell Cook. But a fucking ten-dollar note to the driver brings more speed and in a few minutes more, brings us around a corner away from view. Five more blocks and we were at The Green Doors."

Jackson drew in a breath before continuing. " 'Here you go, my man,' I says, giving the rickshaw driver a twenty-dollar bill. You shoulda seen the look on his face. He nearly fucking cried!"

Cook couldn't resist chiming in here. " 'Yeah, Dude,' I'm saying to the driver. 'You're the finest peddler I've ever seen,' I says. 'I'm almost tempted to give you some real money. But you'd fuck me, too, if you got the chance!' " Cook was laughing and nodding his head along with others in the audience. "Good that driver couldn't understand English."

"Jackson was laughing himself sick, too," Cook continued, "and the rickshaw driver laughed with us – can you believe it? When we stopped we all shook hands, laughing and bowing like old friends."

As the long story was coming to its conclusion, Jackson reinserted himself in the telling of it.

"The girls at the whorehouse knew when they saw us Americans that something was up. But it was beyond their wildest dreams when they saw the roll of bills we carried.

"For another three hours we felt like fucking kings. Nothing was off the table for those ladies. We was rubbed, scrubbed, pampered and played with. Our slightest wish was happily and quickly granted. We had no impossible fantasies left."

Jackson reached for another cigarette but hurried to the story's end first. "Things were going real good for us until we had to pay the bill. The madam of the house arrived and her sharp eyes recognized the monopoly money as fake. Bitch. It was time to *di di* and we did. Cook and I had to hotfoot it out of there, with a madam, whores, and a very fit, but very tired, rickshaw driver on our heels."

Laughter swelled from the audience as Jackson and Cook basked in the approval.

"Still," Jackson said, "it was a fucking glorious day."

"I really like being rich," Jackson said, drawing out the last word.

"Yeah," Cook answered. "Sure beats the bush!"

"Yeah," said Jackson.

CHAPTER XVII

Early mornings were his favorite hours of daylight. The sun was just beginning to take the chill out of the night air, with its rays gently dispersing the light morning mist. Birds greedily and excitedly pounced on bugs and worms as they sang to each other their locations. Roosters crowed nearby, and some could be heard farther away, stretching back into every part of the city.

White sat on an antique French colonial bench under a mango tree. At his back was the two-hundred-year-old, algae-covered brick wall that surrounded the ancient capital of Hué. The echo of a dog's bark bounced off the twenty-foot-thick wall in a soft, vibrating harmony.

Wanting to return to camp early, he had left Boudreaux at The Green Doors at daylight. But at the river he stopped to take in the quiet of the early morning. It was his third trip to Hué, and each time seemed more exciting than the last.

He loved this place in front of the citadel. Round eyes were not allowed into the walled-in old city. His thoughts drifted as he imagined ambassadors from beyond Annam lining up for the procession into the royal courtyards and chambers inside the capitol. Colorful silk gowns and extremely graceful manners and protocol marked everyone entering to pay homage to the emperor. It was unbelievable and sinful to him that such a place could suddenly be thrown into an arena of violence and chaos, but he knew the ancient walls had seen human slaughter many times.

His gloomy revelations were interrupted and instantly replaced with curiosity when he heard approaching footsteps. On his left, between the highway and the river, was the French restaurant. Walking briskly around its corner on the highway was a lone farmer. Very lean but muscled, the middle-aged farmer was the ideal of a rustic Vietnamese peasant.

His homemade sandals were soled with worn automobile tires. Gym shorts and a thin, faded shirt were his daily clothes, with a weathered face partly shaded by his rice hat. He had come miles, pushing his homemade wheelbarrow stacked with vegetables, searching around while he walked for somewhere to sell his crop.

Coming from the opposite direction, pushing a bicycle piled high with natural, three-foot long sponges was a city man. He was hatless and wore a simple, faded blue shirt, long black trousers, and store-bought sandals. About the same age as the farmer, the merchant seemed as anxious to get wherever he was going. The two men passed each other as if they were invisible to one another.

Across the street from where White sat was the "New City." It was called new even though some of its buildings were a hundred or more years old. Colonial French, colonial Chinese, Buddhist pagodas, new concrete warehouses and apartment buildings mixed and somehow balanced themselves into the harmonious "New City," Hué

White watched excitedly as the city seemed suddenly to spring to life. Storekeepers all dressed in somewhat outdated western clothes, opened shop. Pretty girls with long black hair, dressed in the traditional outfit consisting of long split dresses over loose long pants, called *ao dai's*, floated gracefully through the streets. Vietnamese rickshaws passed, their drivers peddling fiercely. They raced, carrying college girls in soft blue and white *ao dai's* toward the university.

Middle-aged and older women with baskets walked by on their way to market. Streams of bicycles emerged from everywhere in the city. Some were piled with goods; others carried workers or students. All began mixing together with the buildup of automobiles, motorcycles, and trucks that began to fill the highway and streets.

White watched the panorama unfold around him. Every single thing he saw was amazing. Everyone he saw was beautiful. They passed each other without acknowledgement or interest. They passed him as if he, too, was invisible.

He liked being invisible. Only when you are unseen can you truly see people and their personalities. If a person knows that he is being watched, he changes his action to show a more favorable side. But when one is nonapparent, people passing by, like innocent beasts, show their true selves.

He had come to Hué for a good meal and a night at The Green Doors. But now he felt like resting completely and he couldn't do it here. Now he was going among his comrades at camp where it was safe.

Soon he would have to join the passing parade. He would have to act and interact with those around him. Very soon he must leave to join the company at the camp and sleep for a day. But he would stay for a few more private minutes. Breathing deeply, he watched the city spring into life.

Days passed. Deep in the sticks, White had been walking behind Lopez since morning. A twitch of Lopez's nose alerted White, and a wave from Lopez's hand motioned everybody to get down. He turned and signaled there was N.V.A. ahead, waiting in ambush. He could smell them. Everyone was to wait quietly as he went around and behind the N.V.A. Making no sound, he disappeared into the brush.

Tense minutes dragged by without a sound. White was on the verge of going ahead to help Lopez when a three-round burst of M-16 fire shattered the silence. It was followed almost immediately by a frantic burst of A.K., then a final burst of M-16.

White and the company surged forward toward the gunfire, stopping when they reached Lopez. Lopez was smiling at him. On the forest floor, five feet from where Lopez stood, was a clear impression in the leaves where a man had been waiting in ambush. Inches from the impression were the marks where Lopez's bullets had punched holes into the ground at the enemy's side.

The captain came up to the front. In one quick look he understood what had happened and asked, "Was he alone?"

"Yes, sir," said Lopez.

"Think you hit him?" asked the captain.

"No. I miss," said Lopez.

"He didn't hit you, did he?"

"No. He was too scare an' he miss. Jus' shot in de trees an' run like hell. I jus' gave him another burs' and he run even faster."

The captain stood there for a long time, looking at Lopez's blank expression. Sir, Smith and Louis came up and stood with White. Hearing everything, they all looked anxiously at the captain, waiting for his reaction. He seemed not able to believe what he was hearing. He finally said, "All right, Lopez. Which direction do you think we should go from here?"

Lopez pointed with his gun in the opposite direction from that which the boy enemy had taken.

Shrugging his shoulders, the captain said, "O.K., Lopez. Let's move out."

White, Louis, Smith, Sir, and Lopez cast glances at each other. Smith stood directly in front of Lopez. After looking him up and down, his eyes stopped to stare into the Mexican's. A sneer branded on his face, he asked, "He was waiting for us, huh?"

"*Si*," said Lopez.

"And you came up from behind him?"

"*Si*. I shaked de branch of de tree, and he turn 'round an' see me."

"So you shot at him and missed?"

"*Si*."

"Then he fired wild as he took off running?"

"*Si*."

"Then you missed him again?"

"*Si*. I miss again."

Smith's face twisted as if smelling rotten eggs. He thought a few seconds more and then said, "And how old you think this dude was?"

"Young. A kid. Maybe t'irteen or fourteen. Maybe younger."

"V.C?" asked Smith.

"I t'ink so," said Lopez. Smith had not stopped looking him in the eye. Then he turned to see them waiting for his judgment as the story ended. He looked once more at Lopez. For a moment his hard face softened, and he said, "Fucking idiot." Turning to everyone else, he said, "O.K. Show's over. Move out."

Standing next to Smith, Louis looked at him and smiled, nodding his head approvingly.

More days passed and the company was on stand-down. Sometime in the months he had been in country, White had learned that the soldiers had different definitions for the term "short." Basically, it meant that the time was approaching when one's term of duty of one year in Nam was nearly done.

Some groups began counting down as they set foot "in country." These groups had calendars where they x-ed out each day. They laughed about being short, almost in the first week.

Others were more conservative about what they termed short. For them the countdown began when they reached "over the hump" and had six months or less to serve.

Nearer to the front lines, short was three months or less. Artillerymen, tank crews, mortar units, truck drivers, and others of that group began counting then.

But for the grunts, ground pounders, and boonie rats, short began when one had a month or less. To count or even to contemplate days was dangerous. The grunts didn't want to think of short. If they thought of time, it was to wonder how much time before noon break or how much time before stand down. To think "short time" was asking for big trouble. Then, if a ground pounder lived long enough, came the day. After eleven months, he was short.

The nights become sleepless—or nearly so. Any sound, any rustle of leaves or bush, and the short timer jerks in anticipation of being killed. Any squeaking door or crunch of a boot or shoe on branch or gravel becomes an N.V.A. or V.C., ready to blow him to pieces.

No amount of self control can hide from the other veterans around him the nervous twitches and shakes attacking the short-timer. He cannot totally suppress the desperation on his face. It was the haunted look of every short-timer. It was the look that White, too, would have if he was lucky enough to live long enough to get it.

Boudreaux was short. No matter how he tried, he couldn't ease the tension at the table at The Green Doors. Everyone was tense because they understood that Boudreaux was short.

The sparkle, the glad green gleam in his eyes was gone. He smiled at everyone at the table, answered when spoken to, but the *joie de vivre* was gone from his voice. Replacing it was a forced, fake, cheerful reply that fooled no one.

Trying to hide from the others what he felt, Boudreaux turned to

White and said, "Don't know what's happenin' to me, Blanc. Ah t'ought ah'd be O.K. here wit' everybody, but ah'm nervous as a cat in heat."

White answered, "It's just because you're short, Pierre. You're gonna be all right. You've got to try to relax."

"Can't relax," said Boudreaux. "Can't sleep neither." Then, as if he suddenly had an answer to a vital question, he said, "Ah t'ink Ah'l be all right w'en we get back ta da company. Maybe wit' y'all Ah might be able to res'."

"Sure, Pierre," said White. "That's it. When we get back, I'll take your guard at night and let you sleep."

"Ah can't let you take mah guard, Blanc," said Boudreaux.

"Pierre," said White. "If you're my friend, you'll let me."

Boudreaux looked long into White's eyes. After a minute he nodded his head yes.

The next morning Linh brought the coffee and eggs, while Zahn set the plates and bread for the two soldiers. Elbows on the table, White and Boudreaux slowly ate. The girls wouldn't even have coffee or tea. They sat, heads bowed low, looking at the Americans.

After forcing down the eggs and bread, Boudreaux got to his feet. He and White walked to the door and out to the sidewalk. Linh, following behind, seemed made of lead. She stopped at the gate and would not look up.

White hailed a rickshaw. When it stopped, Boudreaux slowly walked to Linh. She still had not looked up as he bent forward and kissed her on the forehead.

Boudreaux and White got into the rickshaw, and she had not looked at him. She stood there as if a statue, unable to move. The rickshaw began to roll forward and Boudreaux would not look back. But before turning the corner that would take them from sight of The Green Doors, White turned and saw that Linh had lifted her head. Her eyes followed them until they were out of sight.

The company were all back from the *ville*. The ragged bar and whorehouse outside the main gate was left with only its regular customers. Grunts on stand-down were nowhere around the compound. Now White and the others sat on their bunks, quietly waiting for the word that they would be going back out into the field.

The replacements darted quick looks at the sullen grunts. In the far corner of the tent, Lopez slept untroubled. The new watch on Louis's wrist ticked away the seconds, and the morning went slowly by.

After chow, Smith walked into first platoon's tent. Ignoring the recruits, his eyes focused, one at a time, on each veteran. His thin lips formed a smirk as his head nodded up and down.

"Got some news," he said. "We're going out tomorrow." His smirk grew wider as he saw the depressed faces around him.

White just could not understand why at times Smith acted this way. "He knows," thought White, "what everyone is thinking. Was it A Shau? Was it the Valley this time out?"

An evil grin took the smirk's place, and Smith said, "Ain't going to the bush, though. Gotta clear a road to a gun battery 'bout ten clicks from here."

Then, as though bored with his macabre game, all emotion having left his face, he walked toward the tent's flap. When he reached it, he said, unemotionally, "Gonna be leaving 'bout midnight, so you dudes better be ready."

Before leaving, he turned toward Boudreaux. His face still empty of any emotion, he said, "Didn't hear nothing about your papers."

Everyone knew what he meant. Rotation papers that would send him back to the States hadn't come in yet. He'd be going out with the company at least one more time.

"Sorry, Frenchy," he said with the closest he could come to a look of compassion.

They took their positions on the road at midnight, separating into different segments. Two squads of second platoon took point a hundred yards ahead of the main body. Third platoon was split into two columns, each in a long line on either side of the highway. Spaced in different parts of these two lines were six specialists with mine detectors. As the company moved forward, these men ran the detectors from side to side, sweeping the roadsides.

Behind that group was a deuce and a half, carrying White and the other men in first platoon. In the truck with them was all of the company's equipment.

Following a quarter of a mile behind was third squad from second platoon. If the company made contact, they were to come forward and attack the enemy from the sides and rear.

White and all the veterans felt it. Even the ones with only a taste of combat felt it: that naked, helpless feeling that you're being watched by an unseen, mortal enemy. Like something evil is ready to spring out at you in the dark.

But their luck held, and they reached the battery at dawn without any sign of enemy. To make things even better, new orders came down to set perimeter around the camp. They would stay until another grunt unit came out of the bush to relieve them.

The gun battery was situated on a twenty-foot-high bluff. White's platoon was on the west side of the perimeter near its edge. They could see below them, fifty yards away, a small river winding its way into the distance. Across the river, along its banks and inland for a few yards, was a hamlet of bamboo and grass houses.

White and Lopez were sitting in their hole, looking down into the hamlet, when Boudreaux joined them. He seemed more relaxed, less tense, now that he was with his friends. For an hour they watched the farmers as they took quick, suspicious glances at the Americans. Old ladies looked up at them defiantly as they went to the river to fill a bucket of water. Then they would turn their backs insultingly to the grunts and walk back to their home.

"Not very frien'ly," said Boudreaux as he looked down into the hamlet.

"Yeah," said White. "They're sure a sour-looking bunch."

"Old people, boys, an' chil'ren," said Boudreaux. "Looks like day trying to hide de girls."

"Ain't no boom boom around here," said Lopez.

All three knew why the people below were being openly hostile. They could guess what had made the peasants so guarded. They understood that the anger and arrogance of the farmers stemmed from constant fear. No one could have said so much, so clearly, with so few words. Lopez looked down into the hamlet and said, "Day scare we gon' kill dem."

Another hour went by. Then, from around the corner of one of the houses came a group of five boys ranging from eight to ten. They strutted daringly, eyes fastened on the grunts, to the river. Looking up with a challenge, they took off all of their clothes. They looked more like little men—brave, defiant little men—as they stared up at the grunts.

Their faces softened as they jumped naked into the river. Children's yells of pleasure reached the grunts on the bluff. Laughter and small voices rang through the ears of the American teenagers.

All of the boys began to shout out something to the grunts. Shaking their fists, they dared the soldiers to "come here", showing them their fighting stances.

It was too much for the grunts. Soldiers from different points in the perimeter began hurrying down the bluff toward the river, stripping off their shirts and shoes as they went. They shook their fists back at the kids, making wild, exaggerated karate chops and kicks. Reaching the river's edge, they tumbled in.

The soldiers tried splashing water across the river, starting a water fight against the boys. Their wild thrashing made the children laugh harder as they returned splashes to the grunts. Screams and laughter from the kids and soldiers echoed through the hamlet bringing old men and old ladies from their houses. They, too, began making their way to the river, watching the game. Loosening their hard faces, they smiled toothless smiles as the grunts and the children splashed water at each other.

Other people came to the river. From doorways of the houses, first one then another of the hamlet's girls peeked out to see the commotion. The boldest led the others to the bank where they mingled with the rest of the people. Soon, it seemed as though everyone from each house was at the river.

An older boy, fourteen or so, came to the river's edge carrying a bamboo canoe. Laced together with strips of bamboo and pitched watertight, it was twelve feet long, two feet wide with eight inch sides. It looked more like a toy, something for a small child. White wondered if anyone but a child could ride in it.

The boy threw the boat into the water. In one motion he jumped in, standing, and pushed off from the bank with a long pole. He push-poled toward the Americans and maneuvered the boat in, among, and around them. Shifting his feet and weight, he went from side to side and front to back in the boat, easily escaping the grunts trying to catch him.

The people of the hamlet began to cheer the boy. The grunts on the bluff and men on the guns watching the show began laughing at the completely overmatched soldiers.

The boy came to the American side of the river and offered the soldiers a chance to try out his boat. Most would over turn the round-bottomed boat in the first step. One soldier made it a few feet until it capsized, flipping him into the river.

White looked over to Lopez and said, "How about if I go down for a swim, and then I'll replace you for you to go?"

"Sure," said Lopez. "You an' Francés go. I stay here an' watch."

He pointed to Boudreaux with his eyes as he said it. White knew what he meant. Without words, he was telling him to take Boudreaux toward the laughter below.

Halfway down the bluff they met Louis. "Going down to see the show?" he asked. "Or maybe going for a boat ride?"

"Not me," said White. "I'm just going for a swim."

"Ah'm goin' for a ride an' den Ah'm going to de *ville*," said Boudreaux. "Can't get boom-boom, but Ah bet Ah get somet'ing to eat."

White and Louis, relieved to see him normal, smiled to each other.

"Bet Ah can cross 'de river an' not get wet," he went on.

"I'm not taking that bet," said White.

"Me neither," said Louis.

They reached the edge of the river to where the boy waited with his boat and push-pole. He smirked as he handed Boudreaux the pole. The people on the other bank waited expectantly for another American to take the plunge, but the grunts watching knew that something different was sure to happen.

Looking his old self, Boudreaux turned to White and Louis and said, "Y'all ever heard of a *pirogue*?" Without another word he stepped into the boat. Still standing, he shoved the boat away from the bank. In a few careful moments he got the feel of the boat and began swishing back and forth around the kids who were now trying to catch him but couldn't.

Applause from both sides of the river escorted Boudreaux to the hamlet side. Jumping onto the bank as soon as the boat touched land, he handed the pole to a little boy. Turning to face the people of the hamlet, he dug into his shirt pockets and drew out several packs of Salem cigarettes.

He walked toward a man that looked as though he might be the leader, slightly bowing to the old people as he went. Completely ignoring the girls and the women, he smiled broadly as he handed the cigarettes to the leader and said, "*Bonjour.*"

The gun battery was too far from a main road to risk a trip into town. No one knew exactly how long they would be there or where they were going next, so everyone stayed near their holes, sleeping, standing watch or swimming in the river.

On the third day new orders came in. A deep depression swept through the company. That morning they, and the rest of the battalion, began humping west into the mountains toward A Shau.

CHAPTER XVIII

Six days of humping and the company was now in the thick of the jungle. Each new day White's fear had increased with the expectation of what was ahead. After all the anxious weeks of wondering, afraid of the mere words, there, looming ahead of them in the distance, were the peaks surrounding The A Shau Valley. All of the things Boudreaux had told him about the valley came to mind. But the one outstanding thing he remembered was about the mountains leading into the valley being its real defenses. Now each click, each yard, each step brought them closer, and into, those defenses.

It was much worse than he expected. Even a green recruit would see in an instant how the area was heavily defended. Signs of N.V.A. were everywhere. Bunkers and spider hole fighting stations littered the forest floor. How they had not yet stumbled into booby traps was a miracle. All this and they were still two miles away. White looked at his comrades and could feel their anxiety.

Each minute he was assaulted with a heavy dread. He suddenly understood very clearly that what he must now face, and how he handled it, would be critical. Everything up to now had been a rehearsal. All the fighting and danger up to now had been skirmishes, and the dead and wounded a prelude to what was now coming.

He could see it in all their faces, but what he saw in Lopez drilled into his mind. Lopez was walking point while he walked slack. He could see that every ounce of concentration, every nerve, and every fiber in Lopez's being was centered on what lay ahead and to the side of him.

He could see Lopez's every move, but the tangled underbrush he walked through never stirred. The dry twigs and leaves Lopez walked on never made a sound as they cracked under his own feet. Lopez's nose lifted and sniffed at the heavy air, searching out anything that didn't belong.

In awe, White turned to look behind and saw Smith staring at him. He knew at a glance that Smith understood what he had been seeing and thinking. In two quick steps the squad leader caught up to him and in a muffled voice said, "He's a mudder fucker, all right."

That was it, then. They were going in. The weight of the world seemed suspended above him, ready to grind him into the earth. But then, just as he seemed crushed, that strange tingling began again. In an instant he was seeing and understanding everything super clearly, and he knew without reservation that the best man in the world for the job at hand was walking point in front of him.

The stress began leaving him. In his clear state he knew that making contact was something that hadn't happened yet, and, until it did, he must not let fear override the clarity he was feeling. He must do everything he could to be ready and face the dangers of contact when they happened. But it was hard to concentrate. Panic threatened his every move.

Waves of choppers and jets flew west toward the valley. Groups of four or five had been flying over the men for the past two hours. As a wave reached the valley, muffled strings of bombs could be heard as they contacted the jungle below.

Mingling with the rumble of the bombs was the rumble of the hunger pangs growling in his stomach. He had eaten his last ration the night before and knew he could not be at his best.

But more urgent than food and the fear of contact was what suddenly entered his thinking. What about Boudreaux? All the veterans had been nervously watching him. He was so short. How could the army send out a short timer, especially to A Shau, when he was so near to getting out? And how could his comrades not be anxious for him when they had seen before what happens to a soldier getting short?

Boudreaux had changed so much in the last few weeks. His incredibly sure movements now seemed hesitant, almost clumsy. His normally sharp attention span seemed faded, slower...unsure. His appetite was gone, and he chain-smoked cigarettes.

But maybe, thought White, he was just exhausted. He hadn't been sleeping enough. One or two hours a day were all he could manage. Maybe he could do something to help his friend.

Time came to change men on point. White saw Smith and Boudreaux walking toward the front. He determined to take Boudreaux's place. As they reached Lopez, before White could say a word, Lopez signaled for everybody to get down. He focused ahead as if seeing or sensing something to their front.

Any sign from Lopez was immediately followed, but, when nothing happened, White, Smith, and Boudreaux stood expectantly next to him.

As if still not satisfied that there was no danger ahead, Lopez turned to Smith and said, "I'm gonna point some more. I feel real good, an' I wan' to walk more point."

Smith paused as if puzzled. He scratched his head as if thinking of a weighty problem. "O.K., Lopez," he said. "If that's how you want it. But don't start liking it too much because Louis told me he wanted it for a while."

"Me, too," said White. "I'm ready."

From behind White came Louis's voice, "We need a machine gun at point, Sarge."

"No," said Lopez. "I wan' to walk it."

"Ah know w'at you guys are doin'," said Boudreaux, "You t'ink Ah can let you walk point for me?"

"No, Francés," said Lopez, "I like it. I'm jus' start to feel good now, an' I wan' it till tonight." He turned back to begin again. He knew Boudreaux wasn't fooled, so he turned around and whispered over his shoulder, "O.K., Francés. If you wan' so bad, I let you take my point tomorrow."

Boudreaux knew when he was beat. He looked into Lopez's bulging eyes and said, "O.K., Lopez. But Ah'm taking your nex' point." He walked slowly back down the line to his position.

Smith understood it all. Tomorrow would be third platoon's turn to walk point. He looked at Lopez and sneered. Before he left he hissed to Lopez, "That fucking Coon Ass ain't never gonna walk point again."

White saw and heard it all. He felt the chill of goose bumps because he knew that now he was a real part of the company, a valuable player, and he would walk point or anything else to help Boudreaux. And he knew that they all would.

Then, stronger than ever, that feeling of clarity sent him a message. He didn't want it to happen. He tried to ignore it, but it was useless. He knew he shouldn't do it. He shouldn't do anything that would keep his attention off the valley. But before he could think more about it, he acted.

He had been watching the green recruit two men behind him. Something in the replacement had captured his attention. The boy had fallen to his knees in exhaustion many times. When the company stopped, he would drop and lie sprawled out on his back, panting heavily. But each time he fell, each time he lay in exhaustion, he never closed his eyes and always turned his head, trying to see everything around him.

When they started again, he tripped, falling face first to the jungle floor. But now he was falling soundlessly. White stood above him, looking down on him with a grim, deathlike stare. The boy got to his knees; looking up at the face of the veteran, he struggled to his feet. For a moment he held White's eyes. White turned to Lopez and nodded. Lopez started forward once more, followed by White. Behind him came Louis, then the recruit.

At noon they stopped for a rest. White sat next to Louis. They shared a third of a canteen cup of grape Kool-Aid. On their right were Boudreaux and Lopez. From the bottom of his pack, Lopez had pulled out his last LRRP. White and Louis could barely hear the words as Lopez turned to Boudreaux and said, "Francés, you got some water?"

Boudreaux reached for his canteen and filled the cup half full. White knew that Lopez was always two or three days out of food before he was out of water. He was pretending to be out of water. Lopez, that insatiable chowhound, was sharing his last meal with him in the only way Boudreaux would accept.

On their left was the replacement. He sat on the ground pulling in volumes of air. He stared out into the jungle. It was plain to the veterans that he wasn't staring blindly out but that he was trying to see anything coming at him.

As he looked at the replacement, White was pulled in two directions. One was the knowledge that he didn't have time or energy to spend in working with a replacement. This close to the valley, every ounce of muscle and brain power should be used to reinforce his own

154

position and save whatever strength he had.

The other pull on him was that the recruit was showing such promise. There was a definite quality in him that White recognized was worth trying to develop. It wasn't easy to fall silently, and White admired the determination it took to do it.

Another thing ate at him. All of his friends were either getting, or were, short. Boudreaux, maybe, would be going home at any time. Next, it would be Smith, Lopez, and then Louis. What would he do? It was true that he had other friends in other platoons, but they, too, were either getting hit or getting short.

Louis, too, had been watching the recruit. Now, both veterans looked at each other. There was no warning or strain. White rose to his feet. In a few silent steps he stood above the recruit. The replacement struggled for air, but forced himself to sit up straight.

White squatted next to him and said, "You're doing O.K., kid. Pretty soon, you'll get the hang of this, and things will come a lot easier. But now," he went on, "you've got a lot to learn. Your pack's O.K., but you've got to learn to save water."

The recruit answered hoarsely, "But I get so thirsty."

"I know," said White. "But you've got to control it. It might mean the difference between living and dying."

"O.K.," said the kid.

That afternoon, when the company had stopped for the night, White, Boudreaux, and Lopez sat watching the replacement. When they had seen enough, Boudreaux and Lopez went to their own positions. White waited a few moments, and then he, too, rose.

Only the newcomer's eyes had moved as he watched the three veterans. That to him they were all evil was written all over his face. Like a scared dog, he flinched as he saw White come toward him. His face twitched as White came and sat in front of him.

"Dig out your poncho," said White.

On each corner edge of the poncho, strengthening the hole pierced through it, was a metal ring. White took out his knife and pried out the rings. This left an empty, loose hole in each corner of the poncho. Next, he cut down four saplings just small enough to fit through each hole. He trimmed off the knots and branches, skinned the bark off each, sharpened one end, and cut them to three-foot lengths.

All this time, while scrambling to follow White's instructions, the recruit had been watching him. He seemed amazed of the deftness with which White moved and did everything.

White stretched out the poncho on the ground to its full length. From there, under each corner, he planted a sapling in the earth on a thirty-degree angle, facing outward from the edges. Then he stretched the poncho's holes over the sapling, showing how to adjust the height. Now each edge could be lowered or raised as needed. But the center sagged. White bent over another sapling, skinned off the knots and branches, and placed it under the canopy of the poncho. The roof instantly sprang up, holding its shape.

The recruit sat before White, his whole attention on the veteran. "This is where you'll spend the night. Mark your spot, memorize every tree, then rest," said White. The recruit nodded his head.

Before going back to his position on the line, White looked down and said, "What's your name, kid?"

The recruit sat there as if in shock. It came back to White so suddenly. He remembered the day, months before, when he was down— desperate—and Boudreaux had asked his name. He looked at the recruit and barely heard his quaking voice when he said, "Farver."

White smiled as hard as he could. Then his face went rigid, and, with an icy stare, he said, "O.K., Farver. Remember. No talking tomorrow. No noise and no tripping."

The next day, at mid-morning, they began hearing explosions to the west. The tat, tat, tat of machine guns rattled continuously over the valley. They moved on, toward the machine gun fire and the explosions.

At noon break, closer now, they began to feel vibrations of the bombs as they sat on the earth. White was sipping the last of his water. He stared at the cup as the shaking ground rippled the water. His muscles twitched as he sat and sometimes jerked in tense spasms.

Suddenly, the rattle of machine guns and the explosions stopped. Everyone waited in the dead silence. Suspenseful minutes passed. Then they heard it: the drone of B-52's high above the A Shau. The explosions started. But these explosions were not like anything White had ever heard before. Now, each bomb sent a violent shiver through the earth. It went on and on until it seemed a continuous shaking, making it hard to rest, reminding each man what he walked toward.

After what seemed only a minute's rest, they moved out again, heading toward the explosions. Walking on egg shells, eyes piercing the trees and brush, scalps tightening with each step west, they quickly crossed any N.V.A. trail they encountered, and disappeared into the jungle beyond.

Not making contact, they stopped before nightfall. Perimeter was set. White, Louis, and Lopez found Smith before dark set in.

"We wan' to take Francés's place on guard," said Lopez.

"Yeah," said Louis. "But now it's me. Lopez walked point, and now I wanna do something."

"Me, too," said White. "I gotta do something."

Smith looked at them and said, "You know if we do too much for him, he ain't gonna like it." He thought a moment and said, "O.K. I'll take care of it. Lopez, you go over and stay with him. I'll put him on first watch, you on second. That'll give him plenty time to rest. With you there he might sleep." He looked at White. "O.K.," he said. "Just hang around him and see what you can do. Don't overdo it, but stay close."

Lopez sat in the dark next to Boudreaux. A tossed pebble told him that someone was coming. White came and sat with them. A streak of moonlight reached the jungle floor. Its light was enough that White and Lopez could see Boudreaux lying there with his eyes open.

Lopez, almost angry, said, "Hey, Blanco. Tell this Francés to go to sleep. We gon' need him tomorrow, an' he need to be strong."

"Why don't you try to get some sleep, Pierre?" said White. "Me and Lopez will watch for you."

A minute passed in the dark silence. Then, in a muffled voice, Boudreaux said, "O.K."

All through the night the bombing went on. The company was close enough now to see the flashes in the sky. White watched the flickering, deadly lights. Like a summer lightning storm they streaked continuously across the mountain range. Then came the rumbling sound and the ground quivers.

Suddenly, the bombing stopped...the eerie silence more frightening than the bombs.

But as the B-52's left, the helicopters and jets started again. Now White could see flashes from the helicopters as they fired rockets and machine gun bursts into the valley. Red tracer rounds from the gun ships streamed downward in waves.

From the ground, answering green tracers from many A.K.'s went upward toward the choppers. Sometimes, a green tracer found a vital spot, there would be a burst of red light, and a helicopter would shake. Some would recover enough to stay in the air. Then, if able, the ship would limp away, trying to make it back to any American base. Some, unable to recover, spiraled down to the dark forest below, to crash among the N.V.A. and V.C.

On and on it went. Almost no one slept that night. Just before dawn the explosions and guns stopped. The first sign of light found White and many of the soldiers already up. Out of food, they sat sipping water, if they had it, and smoking, listening to the intense quiet. Looking down, Lopez and White saw that Boudreaux had fallen asleep.

CHAPTER XIX

Morning had come too soon. Those that had not already done so began preparing themselves for what was sure to come. Now they were not only worried about Boudreaux. They were all in for it now.

All the signs showed they were vastly outnumbered, that their battalion was a puny force in the middle of the great North Vietnamese stronghold. There would be no reprieve. Every veteran knew that to go on toward A Shau was beyond stupid. They knew, too, that the generals pushing little flags on a map in Washington D.C. had no real concept of what was really ahead for them, the company. What could they do even if they would understand? Push more little flags around the map?

Any chance of withdrawal by helicopter would be slim, since any bird that dropped down under two thousand feet was shot out of the sky. But there was no walking out either. And by now, a try to get out by helicopter evacuation would be more possible by one of the many clearings in the valley.

When word came down to move out, it was with a feeling of nausea that White swung on his pack and followed behind Lopez, toward A Shau. By mid morning they had come another mile. The old timers felt it first. Then White, seeing that his comrades grew tenser, felt it, too.

Suddenly, he knew what it was. The surrounding forest was much clearer than it should have been. He could see many yards ahead, and what he now saw sent his heart pounding. Twenty yards to his front was a cluster of palmettos. Four of them had been cleanly cut off at the stem. Somebody had cut them to make a roof for a hooch. Worse, he could see ahead of him faint walking paths leading farther on.

Hearts pounding, they split up into skirmish lines and went forward.

White broke out into a sweat. Ahead, the trees were thinning out, and beyond them he saw a clearing with a dozen grass and palmetto houses.

The first thing he thought at the sight of the houses was that it was an N.V.A. camp big enough for a company of enemy soldiers. But where were the bunkers? Where were the spider holes and trenches?

When nothing happened, they stopped under the trees outside of the clearing. He saw with relief that it was a hamlet and not an N.V.A. camp. Still, there was sure to be N.V.A. or V.C. living there. Nothing moved in the hamlet. Everything was in bad condition, houses, gardens… everything. Tall weeds grew around the homes. No recent footprints showed in the trails. It seemed deserted.

But as the company inched forward, White saw that one of the gardens had been freshly weeded. Looks instead of words spread rapidly through the first soldiers near the clearing. News of the hamlet flew toward the rear of the company. The captain called orders to go on.

The soldiers started forward again, expecting at any moment to hear the rattling of machine guns, and to feel the bullets tearing into them.

Then White saw him. Sitting in the shade of a banana tree, sharpening a hoe, was a very old man. The muscles on his arms and legs sagged with age. His bony, gnarled fingers twisted around the file. In the corner of his eye White saw something else. An old woman shuffled past the doorway inside the house nearest the old man.

The old man's eyes must have been really bad because even when he looked up, he didn't see White or the squad as they approached. When they got closer, he saw and recognized them as Americans. He let out a weak yell, got painfully to his feet, and limped to the house.

The old lady met him at the door. She was as old and feeble as the man. Her snow white hair twirled neatly into a bun at the back of her thin neck. They clung to each other as they rattled on hoarsely in Vietnamese. Their old eyes widened with fear as they saw the Americans spread out into the houses looking for enemy cache. Some of the soldiers searched the gardens, too, looking for any kind of food.

Louis and Smith, followed by White, were the first to reach the couple. The old man made a brave, impressive front, trying to block the door of his house from Louis. The old woman came to life. She lost her fear and began shouting toothless words at Louis, pounding him weakly on the chest with her tiny fist.

Louis pushed her gently aside as he entered the house. On the earthen stove was a tin can she had used to cook a handful of rice. Louis dipped his fingers into the rice and handed the can to White.

The old lady became hysterical as she tried to stop the American from stealing what was probably the last of their food. Others in the company had stripped every banana tree. Some were in the old man's field digging up all the peanuts and vegetables they could find.

The old man and lady began crying helplessly when they saw all of their protest would not stop the American soldiers. They sobbed pitifully, seeming to have resigned themselves to slow starvation or maybe death.

When every scrap of food had been taken, Smith called his squad together. Others in the platoon heard what he said, and word raced through the company.

"Let's pass a collection for the old dude and that old broad."

'Yeah," said someone. "Let's make them the richest old muddfuckers in the mountains."

The old lady was the first to understand. She stopped crying as she saw soldiers pull out bills of money. She tapped the old man on his shoulder. He shook his head dejectedly as he moaned, not understanding what she said. Finally, she shook him, and, as loud as she could, made him understand.

Both stood agape at what to them had to be a ghostly white soldier with ugly blue eyes handing her the money. She didn't understand when the white thing said, "Here, you cackling old bitch."

Both began to "cry for happy" when they saw how much money it was. White was sure that they had never seen so much money before and could probably not imagine what they would do with it all. For sure they were rich now and would have enough to last the rest of their lives. In the rural areas, far from the city, one hundred and one dollars was a lot of money.

The company moved on through the hamlet. When they reached the forest, they again got into single file with second platoon leading. White turned back to look one last time at the old couple. He saw as the old man and lady stood hunched over in the doorway, trying to count so much money.

Then the scene was over, obscured by walls of brush, thorns, and trees, obliterated by a probable future. His eyes strained, probing the shadows as he followed behind Smith. Far ahead, nearer and louder, the bombing and machine guns started again.

They were close now. A Shau was very close. The replacements seemed mercifully ignorant of what this meant. To them, it must all be a horror. Humping alone was enough to take all their concentration, and they had not yet made contact with the enemy. They could not know what doom might be waiting for them in the Valley, but the old timers knew. White could see it in their faces. Even with less experience than they, he knew that what he now had to face would probably be worse than anything so far.

It was like telling a resurrected Custer and his men they had to go again and again to Little Big Horn. It was like telling a soldier after June 6, 1944, that he must again cross Omaha beach. Because the superior technological advantages of the United States were brought to near nil under the trees of the great forest.

Divisions and regiments of N.V.A. and V.C., spread throughout the mountains, could be gathered together for an assault. Many miles of tunnels, thousands of bunkers, and booby traps of every type crossed and criss-crossed, covering almost every acre of the country. Of all of the strongholds in the country, the A Shau Valley was perhaps the strongest.

Each kilometer "click" brought them closer. Nerves were raw as the company entered a magnificent jungle. The treetops disappeared in the entwined leaves and vines above. They found clean, running water. White and red flowers sprang out near the brooks. Huge groves of giant bamboo were everywhere. Jungle palmetto grew to incredible size. Every material needed to build rainproof hooches was near at hand. It was the most beautiful jungle White had yet seen.

But there was always a serious problem with all nice places. Good water, bamboo, palmettos, and a place well drained and leech free was what everybody liked. They were perfect places for American grunts, and they were perfect places for N.V.A., too.

Now White and the other veterans knew it. At some point they had crossed the last ridge and were now on a downward slope leading into the valley. The company split into three columns. In first platoon White followed as slack behind Lopez.

Then it started. They began to hear gunfire and explosions from the other companies in the ridges to the right and left. Only ahead of them, where they were going, was it quiet.

Every nerve in White's body wanted to shout. "No. Not there. Not straight ahead." Then he realized that it didn't make any difference. The fighting all around was real. The quiet wasn't a trap to lure them on. And even if it was a trap, they were already in it. Either that or the N.V.A. really didn't know they were there.

They tried to avoid trails, but the whole area was full of the crossing, hidden footpaths. Supporting bunkers of every type were scattered in the trees. Fighting positions covered each other and every inch of ground.

Second platoon was to the right of first and third platoon on the left. Sam Cook was walking point for second with Jackson walking slack behind him. They found another abandoned camp and veered away. All three points had mutually agreed to choose the worst terrain, hoping to avoid N.V.A., and walked on for fifteen more minutes. Then, without warning, the first men in second platoon were in another camp.

The N.V.A. seemed as surprised as Cook and Jackson when the Americans entered the camp. Some of the N.V.A. had been cooking rice, others carrying water, some just lazying around, waiting for orders to attack the American units when called up. Suddenly, American soldiers were in their compound.

At the same instant he realized he was in an enemy camp, White saw as Cook and Jackson opened fire. White and the company sprang forward, firing at scrambling N.V.A. Grenades started going off, American grenades, being thrown by N.V.A. regulars. Now the whole company was in the camp. Both sides were firing. N.V.A. went down. American G.I's went down. Flesh was torn from bodies. Holes appeared in men, killing or crippling them. Blasts from bombs tore out chunks of meat from desperate soldiers on both sides. Arms hung by tendons, feet were ripped in half.

It all happened so fast that White had lost sight of his squad. Then it was quiet. For several moments no one moved or made a sound, knowing any move would call down fire on them. White's every nerve was tight as his belly scraped the ground. His eyes strained, waiting to see what was next.

He lay crouched behind a log and earth bunker. From his position he could see almost the whole battleground. He could see some of the company as they searched for live enemy or friends that needed help. He saw Boudreaux behind a bunker, unhurt. Then, as his gaze shifted to the left, he saw something that twisted his gut.

Jackson was down. He hugged his open side trying to hold in his intestines and stop the flow of blood, but he never lost consciousness and never made a sound. Sam Cook, crouched behind a tree stump, saw him. He screamed at the top of his lungs, "I'm coming, Jackson! I'm coming!" He sprang from his cover, dashing toward Jackson. Everyone on the mountain top was temporarily frozen by the desperate cry. For a moment even the N.V.A. paused. Like a wounded banshee, Cook screamed out again, "Jackson! Jackson! I'm coming. Hang on!"

A single shot from an A.K brought him down. The bullet hit him dead center in the chest. He fell running and crumpled in a heap at Jackson's side. Jackson's agony increased when he saw his friend. He seemed to forget his own wound, desperately trying to turn Cook onto his back. "Medic! Medic!" he shouted. "No! Please, no!"

Third Platoon medic reached them without drawing fire. He went to work on them while the rest of the company searched for the hidden sniper.

Lying as flat as he could not to draw fire, the medic poured a bag of powder on Cook's wound. "He looks bad, but he's still alive. That's all I can do for him now," he said. Crawling to Jackson's side he said, "Let me see that cut."

"No. I'm all right," said Jackson grimacing in pain. "Fix Cook."

"Can't do nothing more now. Let me see that cut."

"Why hadn't the sniper fired at the medic," thought White? "And why hadn't he fired as Jackson tried to help Cook?"

Desperate eyes searched from one possible hiding place to another, looking for the sniper. Then someone got a glimpse of an arm and part of a boot. The N.V.A. who had shot Cook lay hiding among some rice sacks. His blood had splattered the sacks, and a part of a hand lay on the top of one of them. Word was passed to the captain. He crawled to where he could see. The arm faintly moved. "Get Hong and Hahn up here quick," he said to his R.T.O.

Hong and Hahn carefully made their way to the captain. When they got to him, the captain said, "O.K. Hahn. Try to see if you can get this guy to give up. Tell him we won't kill him if he gives up."

"Yes, mister," said Hahn. He called out in Vietnamese for the N.V.A. to surrender. A loud, quick spurt of Vietnamese from the wounded N.V.A. tore the silence. Hahn shook his head and told the captain, "Him say, 'fuck you please.'"

"Try again, Hahn," said the captain. "Tell him we'll get him to a hospital."

Another scream came from the hidden N.V.A. Again, Hahn turned to the captain and said, "Him say 'come and get him.'"

A grenade flew toward the N.V.A. soldier as he let out a final, aimless burst of fire. After the explosion the company spread out in the camp, looking for dead and wounded. When White got to where the last N.V.A. had shot Cook, there wasn't enough left of his face for his mother to recognize.

The veterans began to search for their wounded comrades. Cook was still alive. He was unconscious, but his fingers weakly moved. The medic looked up at White while feeling Cook's pulse. With a strained, doubtful voice he said, "Maybe."

White and Smith carried him and then Jackson to the center of the compound. Jackson, still alert, saw Sam Cook. His agony increased. He pleaded to help Cook. That was the only sound he made.

Dead and wounded lay in the rotten leaves. Medics and comrades shuffled around them. Then, awakening from the nightmare, they heard the orders. "Form perimeter. Form perimeter." The soldiers reluctantly left their comrades, paired off, and sat facing the jungle surrounding the N.V.A. camp.

The captain called for helicopters to try to get the wounded out. It was too late to run, so the captain decided to stay where they were. There was a good field of fire all around, and the camp was open enough for air and artillery support and maybe helicopter evacuation.

Boudreaux and White sat together, facing outward from the perimeter. Grey clouds began to cover the blue sky. The two comrades sat in silence, each deep into his thoughts. Neither talked, afraid to say something that could worsen their already frayed nerves, but each was grateful for the other's company. It was always the same. After the adrenalin rush of combat, the soldiers sat exhausted and stunned, afraid to say anything.

Then the black clouds appeared. Boudreaux turned to White. Each looked at the other's drained face. A cold wind began to blow across the mountain while they stared at each other. A large drop of rain, the biggest White had ever seen, struck him on a knee. Another hit Boudreaux on his hand. Then, as if a spell had been broken, Boudreaux looked up to the darkening sky and said, "Monsoon."

They took out and put on their ponchos. They sat in the rain, staring intently outward from the perimeter. In seconds, even with ponchos on, they were soaked.

Something on their left moved through the gray downpour. They saw Smith coming to them. He seemed even paler in the dull light. He looked old as the pent-up stress began leaving him. He nearly stumbled when he reached White and Boudreaux.

"Just got word," he said. "They're gonna try to send choppers to pick up the dead and wounded. We're staying." Then he looked at Boudreaux and said,

"They're sending replacements. Yours is on it."

The three men sat quietly. No words seemed fitting. White tried to imagine what Boudreaux was thinking. He knew he couldn't understand it all. But he knew there was always a doubt in the veterans' minds that they'll make the year. They learn not to expect to make it. And he now realized that especially when very short, they hesitate to hope. Boudreaux looked stunned. He had made it, but a great emptiness seemed to have come upon him. He grabbed his stomach and looked like he would vomit.

White felt it, so easy to read in his friend's face. Guilt had pounced on Boudreaux. Soul-wrenching, naked claws raked at his self image. How could he leave his friends now? How could he abandon them? What kind of comrade was he to leave them now when they needed him the most? He sat unmoving as if crippled, paralyzed with a new, overpowering fear.

Smith was a real hard case. Everyone in the company knew he

was the coldest of them all. But something must have stirred inside him. It was as if he, too, knew and understood everything buzzing through the Cajun's mind. For a second he softened. Then he looked fiercely at Boudreaux and with a hard growl said, "Get on that chopper."

The tension was as thick as the watery air, but a moment later Smith's hard face changed into what the men of the company had never seen. He smiled gleefully and giggled. "You made it, bro," he said.

He extended his thin, white hand to a still-dazed Boudreaux. Then, with a smile wide as the Mississippi, he said, "Goodbye, Frenchie."

Boudreaux, still in shock, shook his hand. Quick as it had appeared, Smith's smile was gone. Hard, cruel eyes looked from Boudreaux to White. He turned and walked back to his position.

The two grunts sat in the mud and leaves. Rain poured down. For a long time they wouldn't look at each other. Then White, staring at his muddy boots, said, "Thanks for everything, Pierre."

Through the sound of the rain came the deep clop, clop, clopping of a helicopter. They were coming in to land, and no one had shot at them. The two soldiers turned to one another. White thought back and remembered so many times when with Boudreaux, much had been said without words. But sometimes only words will do. He saw as Boudreaux searched for the right ones but failed. As if swallowing his own tongue, he mumbled, "Say goodbye to everybody for me."

Boudreaux stood up and slowly walked through the rain to the now-landing helicopter. He walked like a condemned man going to the gallows. He sagged, depressed, and seemed to be walking to his death instead of to life.

They stood in the rain as soldiers and medics loaded the helicopter with the still unconscious but alive Sam Cook. They watched as Jackson, still conscious, was placed next to him. Three dead soldiers were placed on the floor next to the other three wounded. Then Boudreaux climbed into one of the seats.

White's eyes followed the stunned Cajun sitting inside of the helicopter with the wounded and the dead. They followed the disappearing helicopter, dreading at any time to see it burst into a ball of flame. He watched it as it climbed and vanished into the rain. Then he sat like a broken man, staring out into the jungle.

CHAPTER XX

When the helicopter with Boudreaux, Cook, Jackson, and the others had left, it seemed to have been a signal for both sides to stop fighting. Both American and N.V.A units in the ridges around A Shau hunkered down and were satisfied to hold their positions. Also, the lull could have been due to the complete misery of the heavy rain.

All that night White and the company waited for the N.V.A. charge that would likely kill them all. Everyone stayed awake in the wet doom, waiting for the N.V.A. to hurl themselves at the perimeter. But the attack didn't come. The morning brought only more rain, but now it was a cold rain, one that chilled the bones of the heartiest man there.

It was decided by headquarters to try a withdrawal by helicopter. The soldiers waited in the rain, dreading the idea of getting shot at on an exposed helicopter. But worse was the fear of staying, knowing that, at any time, the enemy could overrun their positions.

The first wave came in and was boarded. As two tired grunts from third platoon walked past White to catch the second wave, he heard one say to the other. "Man, we were lucky. I didn't think we'd ever have it so easy in A Shau."

Waiting for his turn on the last wave, White reflected on what he had just heard. "Lucky," he thought. They had lost men, killed and wounded...They had lost Jackson and Cook. If that was lucky, what would it be like if they weren't lucky?

His wave came. He boarded, and they lifted off and climbed without any of the choppers having drawn fire. In the blur of the rain, they headed east to the base camps, and for a while the company was saved.

They had spent a dry week at a base camp, but now, for the last ten days, were back in the mud and rain. In a way they were lucky. The sector they went through was far from A Shau or any other zone sure to have regiments of N.V.A. And with the lack of actual fighting, White began thinking of the misery of the constant rain.

Monsoon. For him it had only been a word for a rainy season. Now he knew there are really two monsoons. One is the dry season when it might not rain for months, when sometimes one might go days without water. The other is the wet monsoon when it could rain every day, all day long.

Hahn had told him that people in the rice country waited impatiently for the life-giving rain. The paddies and reservoirs needed replenishing. With the constant rain came nutrients and soil that had been washed out of the mountains and uplands to feed deficient fields below.

At first, they celebrated the end of the dry season. They welcomed the clean, heavenly waters and the cool days. But in only a few days the paddies and reservoirs were filled. Silt had nurtured the land. Everyone had forgotten the oppressive heat. But still it rained… and rained.

Then levees and dikes began to break. Floods washed away tons of earth to the waiting sea. Old people felt chilled to their aching bones, without the warmth of the sun. But still it rained. In the towns and cities, some now cursed the unending rain from the interiors of their dry houses or shops. In the villages and hamlets, people huddled in the shelter of their dry grass houses. Even N.V.A. deep in the mountains, accomplished in building jungle shelters as they were in everything else, cooked their rice and slept in dry hooches.

But for White and the other American infantryman, "monsoon" had a meaning all of its own. His only shelter was a five-by-seven reinforced plastic and nylon poncho. That was his home. He wore his shelter around him while he walked, wet to the skin, through the soaked jungle.

At night, he made a hooch with it and then lay in the wet mud and leaves in his wet clothes and boots, wrapped in a drenched poncho liner. He listened to the never-ending drops, pounding on his roof, until exhaustion brought him to an uneasy sleep.

In the high mountains, the temperature at night could be near freezing. During the day, White and the company were almost always moving. This kept their blood going and the chills down. But at night, they shivered.

At times the downpour was so hard the rain looked like an almost solid wall of water. The world looked distorted, hazy, like seeing it through a waterfall. Sometimes it seemed he could swim through the gray mass he walked through. If he didn't have a covering to stop the rain, it was conceivable that he could drown by simply breathing.

Even if the rain stopped for a day, the jungle leaves had absorbed so much water that the trees themselves rained all day on the miserable men below. Their skins wrinkled like prunes. They drank water collected in their ponchos. That water had percolated down through a dense canopy filled with bugs, snakes, bird and monkey shit, and countless types of fungi and bacteria. The soldiers got sick. They got fevers. Pleurisies hurt them like stabbing, twisting knives. Boils, cysts, and sores covered their bodies. Their feet turned white and the skin peeled off from being constantly wet.

Each morning, if he managed to sleep at all, the grunt awoke, trembling, soaked to the skin. Like some of the soldiers, White had two ponchos. At night he used one as a roof. The other he wrapped around himself with his poncho liner. Then he lay in the mud and leaves, wrapped like a worm in a cocoon. He was still wet, but, after a few hours, trapped body heat would warm him, and he would sleep.

White had just woken up. He had been lucky enough not to have had to stand guard that night and had moved only to switch sides or lie on his back. Choosing a mole of a hill to set his hooch above, he had dug a small trench around the hill, allowing the water to go around, not through, the floor of his hooch. When his eyes opened, the first thing he saw was that the rain had slacked off. Now it was a gentle rain, not like the downpour of the day before.

Because he had chosen so well where to sleep and because he had wrapped himself carefully in his poncho and liner, his body heat had almost dried his clothes. His boots were still soaked, but his feet were no longer cold. It felt so good—the height of luxury—just to lie there, wet but warm.

He knew that at the first stirring, the cold would come again. That was the worst part of it—the first move in the morning. He dreaded the feel of the cold that would engulf him. He shivered in anticipation of the icy fingers racing through him. But he knew he had to move.

When he was a boy, he would stand on the pebble beach of the spring-fed lake near town, dreading the first cold dive into the clear water. His brothers and friends would laugh and dare him on until, goaded by shame, he would take the plunge. Then, after the initial shock, the water would become refreshing. After a time, he would walk into the warm sunshine, dry off, and laze in the heat of the golden rays.

But there was no heat in the high mountains of Viet Nam during monsoon. The initial shock of the cold water, when first moving, would not be followed by friendly laughter. Neither would it become refreshing, nor would there be sunshine. The best a soldier could hope for was to roll up into his poncho at night and maybe be relatively warm.

He was ready. He sat up, poncho wrapped around his shoulders, and dug through his pack. The cold air swirled through any opening in the poncho, stinging him with a chill. But soon he had his stove going. He sat with his hands near the tiny blue flame as the water began to heat.

He looked to his left and saw Farver shivering under the partial shelter of his hooch. White knew the recruit would be suffering terribly, but he also knew that pity would not help him. Pity was something none of them could afford.

White reached out of his hooch, picked up a three-foot long stick, and hurled it at the trembling replacement. His aim was perfect, but even the solid jar of the stick had no effect on Farver. White then found an egg-sized stone and violently threw it, striking Farver on his left breast. He let out a subdued groan and looked out through the cover of his poncho liner. What he saw must have chilled him even more because he shook even harder.

White's face was colder than the rain, his stern features more shocking than the first stirring in the morning. Without being told, Farver sat up, shivering violently, and began to face a new, long day. He studied White's movements and signs and, following his example, soon had his hands wrapped around a warm canteen cup and the stove.

If a hooch had been made right and everything set under it in an orderly fashion, the next thing a grunt did in rising was to slide up the sides of his poncho, along the four corners. His matches, cigarettes, toilet paper, and other things that must stay dry were wrapped in plastic, waterproof bags. These were stored in his pack. Then he folded and stored his poncho and liner. When he was ready to go, all that was left was to mount the pack, slip the hooch poncho over him, get up, and begin the day's trek.

White and his platoon were far to the rear of the company. Normally, this would not be a bad place. Usually point was the worst. But now ponchos would protect the soldier at the front from the thorns of the wait-a-minutes while they broke trail for the rest of the company. Also, the un-trampled jungle floor was less slick at the front. After many men had passed through the wet leaves and mud, they churned up the ground. What was left was a slippery, gooey, muddy mess, inches deep.

Even the old timers slipped and fell as they climbed the faces of the mountains. Every fall covered them with the pale mud and would have weighed them down even more if the rain had not been constantly washing it off.

As hard as monsoon was to White, he knew it was much harder for the newcomers. He doubted that anything in their lives had prepared them for this. Even army "basic" was nothing like what they now experienced. If they had any humor or strength left, they could laugh at what, weeks before, they would have termed "tough training." Compared to this, high school football and basketball practice, cross country runs, hours stacking hay, splinters in lumber yards, shoveling snow, or anything else he could think of in civilian life, seemed pleasantries.

Some of the recruits would stumble so miserably and fight so uselessly to gain their feet that White and the other veterans were moved to desperate compassion. Even though they, too, were on the point of exhaustion, the old timers would expend some of their precious reserves of energy to help a green dude to his feet.

On through the morning, the line of soldiers fumbled through the jungle. After a meal at noon and a rest, they moved out for an afternoon that was the same exhausting, dreary, wet hump as the morning. They walked, slipped, fell, and rose, only to walk, slip and fall again.

In the afternoon the already gray jungle darkened. With the late afternoon also came colder temperatures and colder rain. The company formed a perimeter, and soldiers began to get themselves ready, as best they could, for whatever comfort they could make for themselves.

Guard duty was assigned, posts were given, and the soldiers were then free to rest. As soon as they ate, smoked, and drank hot chocolate, they sat under their elevated hooch, wrapped in their poncho liners. They marked their places, memorizing all the trees in front of them.

Then the blackness came. The ones not on guard had already lain back into their cocoons, unmoving. White sat on guard, shivering with his poncho and liner around him, staring out into the unseen rain and trees.

Farver was showing promise. Every day he improved. Of course, he was nowhere near the point of being adequate, but already he was becoming useful. At night, when left on guard, he would shake so hard that White could hear him, but he would never sleep on duty. During the day he scratched himself on "wait-a-minutes" until he looked like a wild cat had been at him, but he endured without a sound.

White and the others watched him while he stubbornly pulled his way through the jungle. They admired his determination as he struggled, unaided, to his feet, and White could tell that for every mile of misery he covered, he learned.

In the weeks since the fight in A Shau, he had gained an impressive stamina. They let him walk point, knowing that in the heavy rain there was little danger if they didn't come on to any trails. Booby traps were always a possibility, but they hadn't seen signs of N.V.A. for days. If someone found a sign, a veteran would go to the front.

In late afternoon, the company stopped. The soldiers took off their ponchos and began to make shelters. Along the edges of the ponchos were snaps. When attached, two ponchos could be joined together, making a big enough hooch for two, or even three, men.

Louis and White joined hooches. White began heating water for chocolate as soon as they were out of the rain. He and Louis cupped their hands around the tiny blue flame, looking out into the downpour. They saw Farver fumbling to make a shelter.

The two veterans looked at each other. It was too pitifully sad to watch. Louis affirmed what White had been thinking with a nod. White turned toward the recruit and shouted, "Hey, Dude. Over here. Come on in here with us."

Farver hesitated, still looking afraid of the two veterans. But then the comfort, the promise of not being constantly pelted by the rain, overcame the fear. He scrambled to walk the few yards separating them and ducked into the shelter.

He sat in a corner of the hooch with his poncho and liner wrapped around him, suspiciously eying the two veterans. They looked back at him with hard faces. Then Louis began to soften. The greater comfort of the shelter and the small blue flame of the heat tab eased the misery they had endured all day. Louis smiled as he stared at Farver.

"Little better than out there, ain't it?" he said.

The trembling recruit could only nod his head.

"It's not easy on any of us, but you sort of get used to it after a while," said White. A tremor shook him. When he stopped shaking, he said, "Wouldn't be so cold if we weren't so high up."

"Yeah," said Louis. "Or if it'd stop raining and we could get dry."

Farver stared at the two as the three pair of hands shared the blue flame.

"Be nice if we could just sit here," said Louis. "We'd be dry by tomorrow." Several more minutes went by, and he said, "Be nice if we could have a few *baby-sans* to warm us up."

"Or even some old *mamma-sans*", said White.

"Yeah," said Louis as he looked out into the rain. He saw something moving from the center of the perimeter and said, "But somebody seems to like this shit."

He jerked a thumb to the outside, and they could see a grey-green blur coming toward them. White knew at first glance that it was Smith.

Stooping low, he entered the shelter of the hooch. Shaking as he stared threateningly at Farver he said, "You got watch from one to three." The frightened replacement only nodded his head.

Smith then turned to the two veterans. He frowned as he pointed a thumb at Farver and said, "Why are you guys wasting your time with this? He ain't got a chance."

White and Louis looked from the replacement to Smith. Then White said, "Fuck you, Smitty. It's our time, and we'll do what we want with it. Go back to your own hooch if you can't be nice."

Smith's face seemed carved from ice. He studied the replacement again, cold blue eyes digging deep into him. Then a slight change, one that only White and Louis saw, came to his face.

"O.K.," he said. "Fuck both of you if you want to waste your time."

"Anyway," he went on. "Louis. You've got guard from nine to eleven. White, eleven to one." He dipped out from under the hooch. Then he squatted down, looked once more to the three men under the hooch, and said, "Hey Dude, you better listen good to what those two shit birds tell you."

That night White lay trembling on the earth, wrapped in poncho and liner. When his body heat had warmed him, he was able to sleep. But it was an uneasy sleep. Unconsciously, he knew someone would be coming later to wake him for guard, and he would leave the wet warmth.

The next day, at mid morning, the rain stopped. For another hour, however, trapped water in the leaves above unloaded onto the men below. But the higher they climbed on the face of the mountain, the less soggy was the ground.

White, like every other combat soldier, whether he will admit it or not, had the same inner, inexplicable thing that at times whispers to him. What that thing is he didn't know and couldn't name. Perhaps it was sensory information so sensitive that he wasn't aware of the feel or smell or sound of it. Perhaps the taste of it was so slight that it didn't register to the conscious mind. But something was there. And whatever it was at times called attention to itself by signaling a dim warning he instantly heeded.

This something suddenly announced itself to White and the veterans as they climbed. They could see above them a light-grey shroud obscuring the trees. Something up there pulled them upward. They went on, walking into the watery air until the shroud became heavier.

It became harder to see around them, but the light above the shroud became much stronger. Onward and upward they climbed. A light breeze caused a swirling, curling movement of the mist that, like a Siren, beckoned them onward. Now, an overpowering urge injected each man.

It grew colder but clearer with each yard. That something in them promised warmth, and they grew increasingly desperate in the expectation of it. It grew brighter. All around them, even through the mist, they began to see colors. Then, through the mist above them, they saw the golden shape of the sun.

They scrambled and slipped toward it like moths madly making for a light bulb. Warmth. Dry warmth. Sun. They became less careful as they scrambled toward the light. The haze thinned, and grey-green shades turned bright green.

It was like a miracle. White pulled himself up the next few yards and was suddenly in sunshine. Green jungle surrounded him. Blue sky showed through openings in the trees. The bright yellow sun smothered him and the others with life-giving warmth. What they had mistaken for fog had been clouds. The company had come so high in their climb they had walked above the monsoon.

The captain sent word they would stop when they reached the top. Men who had been on the verge of extreme depression now reveled in the sun. Several of the newest men began to cry. Some of the veterans, White among them, laughed. They formed a perimeter in the green light at the top of the mountain.

Ponchos and liners were spread out and allowed to dry in the sun. White rolled on the dry earth and leaves, scratching his itching back. Some seemed on the verge of yelping with relief as the rays bathed their boots, clothes, and skin.

But for the veterans in the company, the extreme joy didn't last long. White knew why. This was just an interlude, an intermission. His moment of euphoria passed faster than it had come. One by one the soldiers sat up, fully alert now. They had things to do. They set their gear to dry. They took off their boots to dry in the sun. They cleaned their rifles. They couldn't afford lost time. White knew he must be ready. He had to use wisely this short break from the wet.

CHAPTER XXI

More humping followed the luxury on the dry, sunny mountaintop. Dark, wet days and nights passed, cold nights that made White wonder how he would ever survive. Sometimes there was more of a heavy mist than actual rain. But whether rain, mist, or the accumulated water in the leaves above, the soldiers were always wet, and along with the wetness was the cold.

Sometimes, like now, it was unbelievable. It had been raining hard, without stopping, for three days. White sat on a mound of dead leaves he had piled together to avoid sitting in mud and stared out into the darkness. Wrapped in his poncho and liner, he tried to concentrate on listening. But the only sound he could hear was the hard pounding of the rain on his poncho.

There was no part of his body that wasn't wet. His clothes and boots were soaked. All of his skin was wrinkled like an old man's. The chills racing from his head to his feet made him shiver violently. His lungs felt heavy, full of the moisture he took in with each breath. They ached because of the forced coughing he used to clear them--forced, silent coughing that strained his chest and ribs. They, too, hurt to the point that he wondered if he had pneumonia or something worse.

Even with the misery of being wet and cold, he could have easily slept. It would be so good to lie flat and allow exhaustion to bring him to unconsciousness, to a place without feeling. But his turn on guard had just begun, and he knew it would be a very long two-hour's watch.

Then it got worse. The chills. The terrible chills. At times he shook so hard he was afraid he would snap his neck. He didn't think he could endure the miserable cold for two hours. He didn't think he would make it. He grew more desperate with each shiver. He knew that if he could, he would do anything to be warm and dry. He would walk away from it all, abandon his comrades, to be warm.

He thought of the enemy. They would be dry tonight. They had their permanent bunkers and shelters that kept out even the worst rain. They would have eaten rice and drunk hot tea. They would be wrapped in dry blankets, sleeping. Some would be on guard, but they too would be dry under dry palmetto roofs. In the morning they would gather and make plans for the day. They would eat steaming bowls of noodles and sip hot water, and wouldn't be moving in such a downpour. Some would do duty around the camp. Others would pull guard, watching for wandering American units hunting the jungle in all kinds of weather. But everyone who could would find a dry place, wrap themselves in a blanket, and wait out the rain.

White envied them. The fighting and killing had not made him hate the enemy, but the jealousy of knowing they were dry brought him to the point that he now despised them. He detested the rear echelon American troops, too. They would always be dry. They always had hot food and hot chocolate. If they went into the rain at all, it was to go from one dry place to another. He hated the civilians back home and the politicians in Washington who only got wet in swimming pools. He hated the farmers who wished for rain and the useless generals who sent the grunts out hunting in this miserable water world.

The grunts often found, or were found by, the enemy. They "beat the bush," wandering the mountains, searching for enemy, because those were their orders. But whenever they could, whenever the chance presented itself to avoid a clash, White and the front line grunts, whoever was walking point, steered the company away from it. In the constant rain, however, with sign, sound, and smell limited to almost nothing, the company most often could not avoid a fight. Now they stumbled into an enemy camp without warning. Then it was a fight to someone's finish.

Leading the company away from a fight, whenever possible, was easier when the company officers were green to the sticks. Because there were many men coming into and out of the company, White had experience with different kinds of officers. In some of these new officers, their ambitions called for action against the enemy. The road to promotion was through successful engagements with N.V.A. and V.C. But those green officers' senses were as dull as their thinking. Their eyes had not been opened to the sure traces of the enemy. They missed the clear signs that the veteran point led them away from, when they were lucky enough to see the point.

They had not been honed to the sharp reality of bullets and bombs. Their minds had not been cleansed of the illusion that this was an "honorable war." They didn't yet understand that, for an ever-growing number of Vietnamese, it was they, the Americans, who were the invaders. They hadn't yet seen villages leveled by American bombs to kill one or two V.C., and had not yet smelled the rotting corpses of the villagers, women, and children who were killed along with them. They didn't know, and some didn't care, that these indiscriminate bombings made new soldiers in the ranks against the Americans out of the survivors in those villages. They couldn't see that it was the enemy, the N.V.A. and V.C., who were the "patriots."

White's thoughts swirled like rain clouds in a storm. He imagined what the morning would bring, more rain and cold, more mauling and murder, more endless hours of humping the sticks.

The minutes dragged by. Then an hour passed. Slowly, ever more slowly, time stretched itself out. He needed help. He needed something, anything, to help him get through this.

Then, somewhere in the wet tangles of his mind, he gained control and began breathing more slowly. He expanded his lungs to full volume and then slowly exhaled. Just as he had a few months before learned to partly control his pain, he allowed his mind to detach itself from his suffering body. While his ears and nose still functioned, he himself, his true self, sat apart from the rain and cold.

But gaining this control was hard to do and hard to maintain. The cold crept back into him, and he would start again, a slow, deep breathing, a cautious detachment...over and over.

Another hour passed and his two hours on guard were over. He crawled off to wake Lopez for watch. He was surprised that he had to shake him twice before he heard him say, "O.K." Then he crawled back to his own position, wrapped himself into his poncho and liner, and lay on the wet leaves. He trembled for a half hour, waiting for his body to warm his clothes and poncho liner. He curled up in a ball on his side, hands under his armpits, waiting. Finally, it came: the wet, tepid warmth of his trapped body heat, wonderful beyond words.

As he lay listening to the sound of the raindrops on his poncho, the pounding became a gentle drumming. He recognized it as African, constant, discordant, but infinitely soothing. Lost in the hypnotic beat and his body warmth, he first began to drift. Then he slept.

The company had "come in" and were quartered at a base they had not been to before. In the far corner of the tent, sitting on two bunks, were Louis, Lopez, and White. They didn't talk. Only occasionally would one look up to the others and quickly drop his eyes if his comrades noticed.

Heavy, sluggish thoughts, full of uncertainty, trudged through White's mind. He was ashamed of how he had felt so many times in the jungle. How could he have even thought of deserting his friends? How could he let the rain and cold, the miserable wet, cause him to want to do anything so shameful?

He would quickly look to see either Louis or Lopez's black, guilty eyes on him, and then quickly look away. Their strange looks at each other and at him told him more of what they were feeling than could have hundreds of words.

He remembered that Lopez, mighty Lopez, had to be shaken twice before getting up. Louis, whose serene, honest face helped to keep many of his comrades from the edge, seemed on the point of breaking. Could it be that they, too, the strongest men he ever knew, felt the same way he did? Could they, too, feel the dreaded agony of going back out into the monsoon? Would they have done anything to escape the wet? It was a bad sign pointing that way to see such a forlorn expression on Louis's face. Serious, too, was seeing Lopez sitting there when he could be either sleeping or eating.

The three were jolted out of their dreary mood by a sudden noise outside the tent. They recognized it as footsteps walking in the mud. No one moved in this kind of weather unless forced to. When the tent flaps jerked open, the three soldiers turned to face the entrance.

The first sergeant walked up to them and pulled off the hood of his poncho. He looked down sullenly at White. Then his face broke out into a wide smile and he said, "You've got R&R (Rest and Relaxation)."

At first, the words didn't mean anything. Then, after a moment, it began to register. White sat and stared at the sergeant. This meant that for at least a week he wouldn't only be out of the bush but also out of Nam.

Thoughts raced through his mind as he sat there, thinking of R&R. For the common soldiers, R&R was usually in countries not too far distant from Viet Nam. The Philippines, Singapore, and Thailand were all five-day R&R's. With a day travel time to the processing center in the South, a day of travel to the country of R&R, five days in that country, and a day getting back to Nam, a soldier could figure on eight days. But sometimes, with a little luck, someone could squeeze an extra day, and maybe two, out of it.

Australia and Hawaii were seven-day R&R's, ten days with travel. But Australia was hard to get, and Hawaii was usually reserved for married men and officers.

Louis and Lopez reacted first. In an instant Lopez's sometimes boyish face was back, a smile stretching from ear to ear. Louis, too—the real Louis—, was back. There again was that brilliant smile that always seemed to convey a message of goodness.

They looked at White's uncomprehending expression. Then he began to understand and fully realize what the sergeant was saying. In a half dazed, half disbelieving voice he asked, "Where?"

"The Philippines. Manila. You leave by chopper to the air base in an hour." He began to turn away but quickly stopped. He turned to White and with a roguish grin said, "Have fun."

White could see that both Lopez and Louis were almost as happy to see him get R&R as if it were they getting it. A lump appeared in his throat while his friends patted him on the back and congratulated him.

But there was that guilty feeling again. It seared him as he watched their mouths move, unable to hear anything. Then, as if only listening to them could free him of the tension, he heard their words.

"Lucky mudderfucker," said Lopez.

"Yeah," said Louis. "No better time than now, too."

Full of sudden life, they jumped up and seized White by his arms. "Come on, lez go," said Lopez.

"Yeah," said Louis as he pulled on White's other arm. "Ya gotta get moving. Don't worry 'bout nothing," he went on. "We'll take care of your gear for you."

"Yeah," said Lopez as he laughed. "De only t'in you gon' need in Manila is another *verga*."

"Yeah," said Louis. "Whatever that means. Lopez should know."

"Yeah, Blanco," said Lopez. "Better start eatin' more chili peppers cause you gon' need it."

White was dazed. R&R. He had reached the point in his tour of duty in Nam where he could have R&R. It seemed unreal, a twisted joke, as he and his friends stood looking at each other. Louis and Lopez smiled like children as they talked. Lopez even giggled.

"R&R," said Louis, more serious now. "That's sure good news."

"Yeah," said Lopez. "You gon' have a good time now, Blanco."

"Yeah," said Louis. "That's where I went on my R&R." He chuckled as he remembered something about his stay in Manila. Turning back to White, he said, "You sure gonna like Manila."

"You got some money?" asked Lopez. "I can give you some."

"No, thanks," said White. "I should have plenty at Headquarters."

"What about smokes?" asked Louis.

"I've got enough," said White, who could now smoke in the worst rain.

Something crept back into his mind. Just days before, he had been ready to do anything to be dry and warm. He would have abandoned his friends. These same two comrades now so anxious to help him, he would have left behind to escape the misery of monsoon.

How could he leave them? How could he go and leave them behind? They were so happy for him that it caused him to feel even more guilt. He had to say something. He had to try to explain.

"But," he stammered. "What about…"

"What 'bout you take us wit' you?" said Lopez, seeming to understand White's condition.

"Yeah," said Louis, understanding White as well as Lopez did. "What about talking the general into letting us go with you?"

"Yeah, Blanco" said Lopez. "Go talk to hem. Maybe he lissen." He grinned and said, "You' gon' need a Spanish interpreter in Manila."

"I speak jive," said Louis, "and I wanna go, too."

Then all three soldiers became serious. They shifted their heads, looking first to one comrade, then the other. Lopez, the great point man and drunk, seemed to understand it so well. His black pupils and protruding eyes bore into White as they had done months before. But this time it was not with warning or anger. Now, it was with complete understanding.

"Don' worry 'bout us," he said. "You just go an' get plenty boom-boom."

As they walked toward the administration tent, White felt sick. This was what he had prayed for. He would be out of the rain for ten more days, but what about his comrades? They would be out there again soon. He would be dry and safe while they would be wet and in mortal danger.

They reached the command tent. Lopez opened the flap, and Louis gently shoved White inside. Both grinned at him as Lopez closed the flap. White stood near the doorway dripping, while listening to them walking through the mud toward their own tent.

His papers were ready. A buck sergeant explained where to catch the chopper. He counted out White's monthly wages in American dollars, explaining where to go after the chopper dropped him off.

White was to board a C-130 at the airfield, which would fly him to Tan Son Nhat air base. From there, he would process and then fly to Manila.

At the helipad were half a dozen soldiers, all strangers to him, waiting in the rain. White stood with them, waiting. A silent, cautious inspection began as he classified the others around him. They, too, seemed to be dazed, looking, searching for a common link, a comrade, someone of like mind.

More soldiers arrived. They stood in the rain with White and the ones already there. In the shuffling around, the moving to keep warm, White noticed that the soldiers had unconsciously arranged themselves into groups. Clerks, drivers, artillerymen, and grunts, without a word being spoken, had fitted themselves together, waiting.

A helicopter landed, and the soldiers climbed aboard. They were brought to the airfield where they boarded the C-130 (propeller driven troop carrier airplane). When the plane was full, the bird took off, heading south.

Tan Son Nhat was the largest air base in Southeast Asia. Waiting for the soldiers when they landed were half a dozen minor officers and sergeants. They shouted out to the debarking soldiers, "Here for Hawaii, there for Australia. Bangkok there. Manila there." White went to wait in his line.

White was beginning to trust that indefinable instinct, that definite knowledge which makes a soldier zig instead of zag, thereby saving his life. He was beginning to understand that his ability to choose correctly was not limited only to combat.

He looked around at the men waiting in line with him. Everyone had received their traveling papers and were now waiting to give up their rifles for storage until they returned.

Some had gladly, unemotionally, given up their weapons to the armory sergeant behind the desk. They joked and laughed, telling anyone who would listen of the debauchery they planned in Manila.

White had been noticing one man in the line. He was very quiet and intent as he waited to give up his gun. White smiled as he remembered that in basic training he had been punished for calling his rifle a gun. It had been hammered into the recruits to always say "rifle". But he was beyond that now. He was a grunt. Only a grunt could call a rifle a gun. He saw the reluctance in the man's stance. He saw the hesitation in the stranger's face when he released his M-16. Then it was White's turn, and he understood. When the sergeant asked for his rifle, it was as if he wanted White's right arm. He tried to act like it was nothing, but the sergeant wasn't fooled. For a moment he held White's eyes. He gave a barely perceptible nod, looked past White to the man behind him, and said, "Next."

In the next line was a staff sergeant. He took each soldier's measurements when they came up. He called out the soldier's name, rank, and measurements to the specialist behind him.

After more shots, exams, and a debriefing by an intelligence officer, the soldiers were free to have lunch. White piled his plate with meat and potatoes and found a place to sit at a corner table.

The grunt he had seen in line that had reluctantly given up his rifle came to sit next to him. They ate without words, slowly, occasionally looking up at each other.

As they finished, they lined up at the building next to the mess hall. When they entered, they were given new jungle fatigues and boots. Next was a building where some of the soldiers were changing from jungle fatigues to khaki. In the melee, White lost sight of his new comrade. He went into the fifty-man shower, scrubbed, shaved, and then put on his new clothes. He walked out into the large terminal, sat on a folding metal chair, and waited.

In a half hour it was announced that all R&R's to Manila were to board the C-141 (jet driven troop carrier airplane) outside. White climbed the ramp and walked to the plane. At the far back left, just behind the wings, was the grunt. White sat next to him. Both nodded their heads in greeting. They sat quietly, not questioning the instinct drawing them together, no longer embarrassed that they need not speak.

Soon, the plane was full. It taxied to the runway, revved its engines, roared off and climbed into the sky. Next stop: Manila—the world.

Part III

CHAPTER XXII

The sun began to set as the plane flew steadily eastward. For an hour White and his new companion had not spoken. An obvious stillness, an extreme watchfulness, and apprehensive, fatalistic eyes had shown—better than his military files could have done—the other's main function in Nam.

Stripes to mark their rank, division, and unit badges decorated most of the soldiers on the plane. Some had made special trips to tailors to get perfectly-fitting uniforms. Some had polished their boots or shoes until they shone like obsidian. Many had taken special care to show as much decoration as they could, lining up rows of colored ribbons and silver or bronze medals on their chests.

Friendly, loud banter went from one group of decorated soldiers to the next. Shouts of "hooray" vibrated through the plane as the inside lights came on with the advancing night.

Sitting quietly, not moving, plain and unpolished, void of ribbons and brass, were scattered two and three-man groups of grunts. White felt extremely uneasy when the lights came on. A sudden tension built up in him. He looked around quickly for a dark hole to crawl into. With an almost uncontrollable urge to scream out to everyone to shut up and turn off the lights, he felt as empty as when they had taken his rifle during processing. Even more strongly, he felt open, vulnerable, as if everyone was looking at him in the sudden light.

He thought maybe it was only him, but then his partner, who had not yet spoken, said, "I wish they'd turn those damn lights off." Turning to look at White he said, "Name's Walker."

White extended his hand. "White," he said as they shook. "They sure make a lot of noise," White said, casting his eyes around the plane.

"Yeah," said Walker. "It's like they don't know there's a war on."

That simple statement told White a lot about Walker. It looked as if to many of the soldiers on the plane, the war was temporarily over. They had forgotten it the minute they stepped aboard the plane. But for White it hadn't ended. It hung around his neck like an anchor. It wasn't easy to switch off the extreme alertness and caution of combat.

With a tremendous effort, he forced himself to relax. Trying to sound as normal as he could, he turned to Walker and said, "Know anything about Manila?"

"I just know it ain't Nam," said Walker, looking expectantly around him.

More time passed. The ocean below looked like black velvet. The plane's engines droned on. Strings of lightning began to flash, and then the inside lights went out. Shouts of, "Hey, where's the light? What happened?" echoed throughout the plane. But sitting quietly, hidden, safe in the dark, the grunts smiled with relief.

Single points of light, speckled gleams on the black earth, began to appear. At far intervals, lamps in lonely, isolated homes—far from the noise of civilizations—shone through the windows of huts and homes, thirty-thousand feet below. Then, in pairs or in three's, the points of light gathered closer. Now small clusters appeared, showing a village or hamlet. Towns and minor cities, street lamps glistening, encroached more and more into the blackness of the surrounding forest. The illuminated towns grew and stretched, ever expanding, pointing the way to the metropolis.

Far in the distance, a faint glow appeared on the night sky. Brighter at the bottom where it touched the earth, it spread upward, getting fainter as it rose, until it faded into the blackness of the moonless, cloudy sky. It seemed a hundred miles wide, spanning the horizon in every direction. The glow grew until, even from far away, White knew it was a major city.

Inside the roaring plane, White and Walker sat quietly while the engines slowed. Their ears popped as the plane descended. Now everyone was quiet. There was no howling or shouting, boasting of what they planned. Every soldier sat, each lost in his own expectations. White knew they had nearly made it. If nothing went wrong, they should soon land. Then they would be safe.

The plane slowed for a landing, wheels touching down with a high-pitched screech. The engines roared, slowing the plane until it stopped. After a pause they were moving again, taxiing to the terminal. The plane made several turns and stopped again.

As if to emphasize that they had arrived, the lights came back on. One hundred eighty soldiers sat frozen, dumb, and numb. A dry voice came over the P.A. "There's buses waiting for you outside. They'll take you to your hotel. That's all."

As White stepped through the doorway, the first thing he saw was how bright everything was. The whole airport blazed with lights. He felt a sudden dread. But now he understood that he wasn't crazy for feeling that way about the brightness. He had been many months without any lights at night, crouching or lying in the darkest parts of the forest. Even understanding that now, it couldn't stop the ideas flashing through his mind. How easy for the Gooks to hit them in all that light. They couldn't miss.

But another thought followed as quickly, and he knew there was no danger here. Still, he turned to Walker behind him. Walker looked steadily at him, shifted his gaze to scan the airport, and said, "Too many fucking lights."

The bus drove along the boulevards and avenues of Manila. Civilians walked hurriedly along the clean sidewalks. Bright-colored clothes, the newest summer fashions, adorned the young men and women who walked the streets or who drove the shining new cars that sped through the wide streets of downtown.

"Wow," said a soldier. "Look at that babe."

"Yeah," said another. "And check out that new Impala."

"We're in sweet smelling shit now, boys," shouted another.

"High cotton," laughed another.

Flashing neon signs advertising bars, nightclubs, and businesses boggled White's mind. Tall, clean buildings, their glass-paned windows reflecting the different colors of the night's lights, dazzled his eyes.

Car horns, truck motors, and rumbling buses attacked his ears. Too much noise, too much light. He had gotten so used to the ammonia smell of the jungle that he no longer noticed it. But exhaust of hundreds of automobiles, buses and trucks burned the inside of his nose.

Then the uneasy feeling he felt because of the lights, the irritating noise of traffic, and the burning in his throat from the carbon monoxide suddenly vanished. He realized fully that there was no war here. He could relax his vigilance. No one was coming to blow him up or shoot him or cut his throat.

He found himself smiling so hard his face hurt. He turned to Walker. Walker eyed him with a look that seemed to question White's sanity. Then, as if he, too, suddenly understood, Walker's face broke out into a huge smile. "I think I'm gonna like it here," he said.

"Not bad," said White. "If only they'd learn to douse those fricking lights."

As the bus drove through the din of the traffic, a strange sound quieted the boisterous soldiers inside. From the depths of the darkness of the bus came the eerie, ghostly, low, triumphant laughter of the grunts, scattered in pairs or alone, that had escaped death.

Fifteen stories high, modern, clean, and situated next to downtown, was the Empire Hotel. The bus stopped at the main entrance and was met by a middle-aged Filipino. He wore spotless white pants and a light yellow cotton shirt that accented his golden-brown skin. He smiled and bowed as he said, full of enthusiasm, "This way, gentlemen. This way, please."

The awed soldiers followed the man through the carpeted, air-conditioned reception hall to a large conference room. Six forty-foot long tables with folding iron chairs around them took up the middle of the room. Each soldier had a seat while the host went to a small podium.

"Please, gentlemen, please," he said. "My name is Antonio. I will be your host here at the Empire Hotel. I will explain the arrangement between the United States Army and the hotel, but first let me welcome you to the Philippines." He paused for a moment as if waiting for applause. When all the reaction he got was a stunned silence, he went on. "Your government has honored us with the pleasure of serving you for your stay in Manila. For a modest fee we hope to supply you with everything you desire to make your stay with us a very pleasant one."

"For a hundred and fifty dollars, for five days and nights, all of the hospitality of the hotel is yours. In addition to your rooms, you will get two changes of tailored civilian clothes, a chauffeur to take you anywhere in the city whenever you like, and, of course, the companionship of one of our lovely hostesses."

"You will be meeting them shortly, but first, please go to your assigned rooms. I know that perhaps you will want to shower and change before meeting your hostess."

Stunned with the glamour and such attention, White took his keys and found his room. He stood before the door for a moment and cautiously opened it. It was beyond anything he had expected. Clean, carpeted, and air conditioned, the room had a big bed, desk, inside bar, and a television. A large, plate-glass window looked out into the dazzling neon lights of downtown Manila.

He had just entered the bathroom when the doorbell rang. A very small, middle-aged Chinese man stood there. "Tailor, tailor," he said as he showed White the measuring tape. He came into the room and in less than a minute had taken White's measurements. He bowed quickly, said something that White could not understand, and hurriedly left.

Hot water. He had forgotten about hot water. Since leaving the States, the only hot water he had seen was the tepid, plastic-tasting water in his canteen, or the sun-heated green slime of the bomb craters. How delicious it was. How indescribably wonderful it was to stand in the hot water of the shower. He lost track of time as he stood there in the steamy, falling water.

The doorbell rang again. He wrapped a towel around his waist and opened the door. A bellhop stood there holding a set of civilian clothes in one hand and a pair of civilian shoes in the other. He tipped the bellhop and walked to the bed with his new clothes. Laying the shoes and clothes on the bed, he put on his socks as he gazed out of the window.

The phone rang. A pleasant, polite voice said, "Sir, when you have changed, can you please come down to the meeting room? We have many young ladies here that would like to meet you."

Downstairs, a hundred soldiers waited outside the meeting room. White saw Walker and went to stand next to him. "What's up?" said Walker.

"Picking girls, I think," said White.

They saw one of the other soldiers staring openly at them. There was a quick, mutual inspection among the three. White's first impression was that the stranger was infantry, and, when he looked down at the man's right arm and hand, he knew for sure.

The right arm was slightly more bent than the left. The wrist hung loose in a neutral position. The pinky and next two fingers curled to form a hook, while the index finger, slightly less curled, extended out beyond the rest. The thumb cupped around until the tip of it was a little behind the index finger but separated from it by two inches.

Subconsciously, the man was still clutching his gun. After so many months of carrying it that way, his hand automatically held that position. White looked at Walker's right hand and saw the same thing. Then he looked down at his own hand and saw how easily an M-16 would have fit into it.

The soldier came up next to Walker and White. The three grunts looked steadily at each other. Then the stranger said, "Mind if I hang with you guys?"

"Sure," said White, as Walker nodded his head.

"Name's Kelly," said the tall stranger. "Red leg with the O Deuce."

White knew that he meant a forward observer in a line company for the second brigade. He had been right. Kelly was a ground pounder.

Antonio came up to the group. He smiled widely, showing perfect teeth. "Now gentlemen," he said. "Please remember that you are free to choose any of the hostesses that you like, and you may keep her for as long as you are here if you wish. But if for any reason she doesn't please you, you are free at any time to choose another." He paused for a breath and then said, "There is one thing, however. The girls can stay with you all night, but in the morning they must leave at eight o'clock and not return until noon. Now gentlemen, if you please, go in and meet them."

Antonio opened the double doors and extended his hand, palm out, to usher the soldiers to the tables. Two-hundred heads turned to see the soldiers enter. Two-hundred girls, almost all pretty, but all well-dressed, and all smelling like flowers, watched as the soldiers began walking their way. Some put on a quick, practiced smile. Others seemed genuinely friendly. Some looked scared. A few looked bored.

White, Walker, and Kelly went directly to the fifth table's furthest end. There, sitting close to each other, were three young Filipino girls. The three soldiers silently chose a seat next to each one of the girls.

For almost a minute the six people eyed and studied each other. Curious glances were exchanged between the pairs. Questioning eyes explored the faces opposite them. Then Kelly's girl began to smile. Soon the other two, seeing into the depths of the grunts, also smiled.

"I'm good," said Kelly. "You guys?"

Both White and Walker, searching the chasms in the dark orbs before them, said, "Yeah. Me, too."

"I'm off," said Walker. "Let's meet for breakfast?" he asked.

"Yeah," said Kelly.

"Here at eight o'clock?" asked White.

The other two nodded as they rose. Each extended his hand to the girl sitting with him, gently helping her up. They led the girls toward the elevators, softly guiding them with a palm in the small of their back.

The girls cackled softly in Tagalog as they walked, seeming satisfied. White reasoned that in the girl's often-brutish business, it was common to find in a new group of incoming soldiers one that was mean or at least unpleasant. But sometimes things had to go well. Sometimes, like Linh, they must have to be careful to like neither their job nor the soldier too much.

White's girl giggled along with the others. She smiled up mysteriously at him as she laughed. He looked down at her with a puzzled, but pleased, expression. He knew that she knew, as he held her hand in the elevator, that it would be a good week.

CHAPTER XXIII

Her name was Maria. That's the most that White could understand. Her English was limited to only a few words, "Coca-Cola" being two of them. "Wan, too, tree, fo, fine," she counted to show off to the other girls. That was it. That was her English. White's Tagalog was even more limited. Before coming to Manila he hadn't even known the name of the local language was Tagalog.

But there are many ways to communicate, and Maria and White had found several of those ways in the last three days. She was so strong. She took pride in her strength. She seemed determined not to be the first one to become physically drained. For the first three days she left him only from eight to noon. The rest of the time they had stayed in the room, calling for room service when thirsty or hungry.

They ordered whatever they wanted. Whatever wasn't supplied by the hotel could be had from a tip-crazy bellboy. Every morning White ordered a big American breakfast, while she only took fruit and coffee. With every meal White ordered champagne. She didn't drink in the mornings, so for breakfast he had to kill the bottle alone.

When she left for the four hours every morning, White would meet with Walker and Kelly in the downstairs dining room, where they would eat again. On the morning of the fourth day, White went downstairs to where his new comrades sat quietly. He felt the new mood as soon as he saw them. He saw the building tension in their faces. Then he knew why. It dropped on him like a bomb. Today was the fourth day of R&R. Tomorrow was the last. Time was almost up.

His shoulders sagged as he looked at the two equally depressed grunts at the table. Sullen American soldiers walked by, their heads hanging low. The air in the room felt physically solid, like a heavy weight, as if something evil had come into it. Even the hotel staff, as if they had been through this many times, seemed sad but expectant. They knew there could soon be major trouble.

"This shit sucks," said Walker with a heavy face.

"What fucking time is it?" asked Kelly. "Somebody stop the clock."

"Ain't no stopping it," said White. "Nothing we can do."

Suddenly, Kelly's head popped up. White and Walker looked at him and saw the defiance in his eyes. He shook his head as if to say no and said, "Fuck this. I'm gonna get so fucked up I won't even know my own name."

His sudden change was electrifying. It was also contagious. White and Walker looked at each other, and they, too, began to brighten. Kelly had found a way out. White called out to the aged Filipino waiter. "Hey *pappa-san*," he called. "*Lại đây*," he said in Vietnamese. The old waiter didn't understand "come here", but, sensing the excitement, he shuffled to the three Americans. He, too, seemed to be infected with the new mood and smiled broadly.

"O.K., old timer," said White. "We want three bottles of champagne."

"No understand," said the aged waiter. "W'at want, preeze?"

"Champagne," said Walker. He held up three fingers and pointed to the empty bottle.

"Yes, yes," said the smiling old man as he went off.

Halfway through the first round, the soldiers put aside their glasses and began drinking from the bottles. At first they drank silently, watching each other and the movements around them.

But Kelly's pronouncement had affected other soldiers in the dining room, and the effects of the champagne made the rounds of the hotel. Boisterous laughter and deep guffaws broke out at different tables. Soon the dining room was as lively as an old Viking drinking hall.

White was thinking about Kelly. Kelly was "red leg". That term had a special meaning for the grunts. In every infantry company was a three-man "forward-observer" team. These three came to the company from artillery units. Their specialty was maps and bombs. The lieutenant of the group was the forward observer. The sergeant was the "recon sergeant." The radioman was the R.T.O.

They had to know maps so well that they could follow the company's progress in the woods by reading the topography lines on the map. They kept in constant radio contact with gun batteries of 105's, 155's, mortar crews, naval guns, helicopter gunship, and jet fighters.

The F.O. (Forward Observer) and their R.T.O. usually traveled near the center of a moving line on the march. The Recon Sergeant was usually closer to the point. But when contact with the enemy was made, all three went to the front, adjusting fire by calling in a shift of coordinates until heavy fire fell upon the enemy.

The grunts did not like to mix with any group other than the infantry. But the "red legs" lived constantly with the grunts. They slept in the same mud and humped the same mountains. And when the company made contact with superior enemy forces, many times it was only artillery rounds of high explosives or air support called in by the F.O. team that kept the company from being over-run; rounds that came ever closer to the company's own front line, sounding by the shrill whistling of the incoming artillery as if each one would land in their laps. Then the grunts felt a keen admiration for the cool nerves calling in those rounds.

Kelly was an excellent example of "red leg". So when, near the end of his second bottle of champagne, he began to get louder, it touched a button in White and Walker's reckless, youthful selves. They each ordered another bottle. They pressed extra bills into the old waiter's hand. They toasted anything that came to mind.

"Here's to the fucking Army," said Walker. "Bunch of fucking assholes."

"Yeah," White could hear from some of the soldiers around him.

"Here's to fucking Congress," shouted another. "May the sorry muthas get their heads out of their ass and send us home."

"Yeah. Yeah," responded the group.

A quietness descended on the soldiers at the last toast. White could feel the tension mount. He felt like everyone else in the room. The war was futile. Politics and money. Big money and big politics.

But the quiet was broken as Kelly jumped to his feet.

"Here's to President Lyndon "Fucking" Johnson," he shouted. "May the son of a bitch's dog get fleas."

As infectious as the gloom at the previous toast was the sudden grasping of the lifeline thrown to the group. White jumped up and said, "Here's to Ho Chi Minh. May Uncle Ho's wife never stop bitching at him."

"Yeah. Yeah," went quickly around the room.

"Here's to Filipino *baby-sans*," said Walker. "Number one boom-boom."

"Here's to General Asshole Fucking Westmoreland," shouted Kelly. "Number fucking ten."

"Here's to *pappa-san*," said White. "Hey, *pappa-san*," he shouted to the old man. "Bring us three more bottles."

Belly laughs and "yippee's" greeted Maria and the other girls when they entered the hotel. White saw that they were a little scared by the change in him and the others. Their three soldiers, who were usually calm and quiet, were now on the way to being well lit. They approached the soldiers slowly and cautiously. Their eyes widened when they heard the low growls coming out of the soldier's throats. They seemed more afraid as they got near enough to see a wild, daring look in their eyes.

But that wild, daring look quickly disappeared when White and the others smiled at the girls. The Americans quickly jumped up. They swayed drunkenly as they each went to their girls and gently took their hands.

"Maria," said White. He grinned even harder when he heard both Walker and Kelly call their girls "Maria". Three Marias. That was somehow so funny White almost choked with laughter.

The soldiers wanted to order something for the girls to eat. They pressed them if they wanted lobster, caviar, anything, but the girls refused it all. They didn't want champagne, either. They became aggravated with the attention. They frowned at the soldiers. But with a little tickling they laughed again, seemingly resigned that the three Americans would not stop until unconscious. After all, White was sure they had seen all this before.

"Hey," said White. "How about a ride around Manila?"

"Yeah," said Kelly. "Ain't that part of the deal?"

"Yeah," said Walker. "Let's take a tour." He paused a moment, seemed to have a stupendous idea, and said, "Let's take a few bottles with us."

The others looked at him as if his idea was a stroke of genius.

The '63 Chevrolet cruised around the downtown section of Manila. Walker and his Maria rode up front with the driver. Kelly, White, and their Marias rode comfortably cramped in the back. White was really enjoying the ride. He felt great. The champagne bubbled in his head as well as in his half-empty bottle. But what really felt great was Maria's warm thigh next to his. He patted her softly on the knee. She looked at him disapprovingly and shook her head no.

But then she laughed and said something to him in Tagalog. He understood. He would never remember it, but he knew he had just heard the Filipino word for "later."

In sober conditions White might have appreciated more the cleanliness, the modernisms of the city and its people. But he and the other two soldiers were now beyond being impressed with the city. They were looking for something else—something that would take their minds off what tomorrow night would bring. It would take them back to Nam.

"W'at 'bout shomting different?" slurred White.

"Yeah," said Kelly. "Lesh get away from all thish concrete."

"Yeah," said Walker, lifting his bottle for another swig. "How 'bout shomet'ing with some grass for walkin'?"

"Yes," said the Filipino driver. "I understand."

The car passed a wooded park. White began to feel at ease, at home, with the lively tropical trees and plants that dotted the park. They were back in the shade, in the quiet, away from the heat waves and noise of the steaming streets.

In the distance, shimmering white on the green grass, were endless rows of two-foot high white marble crosses, with an occasional Star of David. When the car got nearer, the soldiers inside could see the markers on the graves that seemed to multiply from the hundreds to the thousands.

"Schtop here," said Walker.

The driver pulled to the side of the drive. He turned to the three Americans and said, "This is cemetery where Filipino and Americans die in World War," He paused and then went on, "Many thousands. Many, many."

The three Americans and the three Maria's got out of the car. At first, the girls seemed bored, but as they saw the changed expression of the American soldiers—their intense, hard stare at the thousands of crosses—it was as if the girls saw the place for the first time. It was like they really saw how severe and terrible the slaughter must have been in their country a few decades earlier.

White, Walker, and Kelly had partially gone back to their "sticks" mode, and White recognized when the girls got a good look at what the civilians in Nam saw in every grunt. The girls walked quietly and in awe, next to each of their soldiers.

White was first in line with Maria at his right side. Next was Walker with his girl. Following behind, walking drag, were Kelly and his girl. Every so often, one of the soldiers would take a drink from his bottle. They began to sway and stagger even more. Openly impressed with the thousands of headstones but not very good in history, Kelly said, "Fucking Germans."

They came to a tall hedgerow that paralleled the headstones. White followed the hedgerow, walking silently three feet from its edge. A minute before they had walked past a small hill where a Filipino honor guard had stood. Next to them a flag flew at half-mast, and the squad of Filipino soldiers stood ready to fire a salute with their rifles. White had completely forgotten the honor guard when suddenly all six fired a volley into the air.

White was instantly sober. Again, he saw everything so clearly. He knew he must cross the hedges. They, and the trees and grave markers beyond, were cover. But Maria just stood there. She seemed stupid. She seemed deaf. He couldn't wait, but he just couldn't leave her. So he grabbed her by the collar, yanked her off of her feet, and threw her through the hedge.

He saw her shocked face as she flew through the leaves and branches. He saw her clothes being ripped and torn. He saw the perfect hole she made going through the hedge and knew this was his hole to follow.

But diving through, he looked back at Walker and Kelly. Walker had been watching White. He grabbed his Maria by the collar and flung her, too, through the hedge. Before the hole could close, he flew in behind her.

Kelly had seen it all, but he chose a different route. He left his Maria standing there, and he dove through the hedge alone.

White went flying through the hole. Maria was already out of the hedge and soaring across the ground. Then she hit the earth. She tumbled head-over-heels twice and then rolled sideways till she stopped. Her eyes were wide, looking up at the sky in shock.

Before he reached the outside of the hedge, White knew he had made a big mistake. He realized what the gunshots were and that they weren't meant for them. Just before touching ground, he looked to see as Walker's Maria, and then Walker, came flying through the hedge. White rolled when he hit the ground and, as he came up, saw Kelly burst through.

White was on his feet in a second. He ran to Maria, who still looked up blankly at the sky. He talked soothingly to her. He straightened her dress. He patted her hands and cheeks.

Then, as if awakening to see a monster, her eyes unclouded, and she looked to see White above her. She looked sideways to see Walker, tending, as best he could, his Maria. She looked to see Kelly sitting up, scratching his head.

The fury came. She sprang up like a gazelle, threw White on his back, and sat on his chest. Her face was white and twisted in rage while she yelled down at him. Walker's Maria followed suit and began poking Walker with a sharp finger.

Kelly's Maria came running from around the hedge. She looked down in wonder at the scene before her. She ran and knelt at Kelly's side and spoke cooingly at him. She looked with daggers in her eyes at White and Walker.

White grabbed Maria by her wrists. She couldn't understand the words, but when he pantomimed the guns and the bullets and explained that he was trying to save her, a sudden light seemed to still her angry face. She stopped struggling, stayed sitting on his chest in deep thought, and began to cry. She hugged him. She kissed his lips, his cheeks, and his eyes. She cooed at him in Tagalog. She hugged him again.

The other two Marias stared at White's Maria. She turned to them and in rapid Filipino explained what had happened. It struck Walker's Maria like lightning. She leaped on him and covered him in kisses.

Slower, almost calculating, the truth dawned on Kelly's Maria and everyone there. He had left her out there. He had saved his miserable skin and left her in the open. She pounced on him like a lioness. White chuckled as she poked him with her finger. He knew that she was insulting him with every foul word she knew. And Kelly lay there and took it all.

Then White's Maria, looking down at a thoroughly defeated Kelly, began to laugh. White and Walker and his Maria joined her. Soon, that part of the graveyard was alive to belly laughs of the first order.

All except Kelly and his Maria. Then she, too, looking down at the helpless killer, began to laugh. Only Kelly, like a sulking, rejected dog, remained quiet.

From far off, White saw the chauffeur's jaw drop. He stared at the three couples as if he couldn't believe his eyes. Five of the six came walking up, their clothes ripped and torn, their bodies scraped and scratched by the branches. All six were roaring with laughter. Kelly's Maria had forgiven him.

White lay in the darkened room staring at the ceiling. Dismal thoughts rushed through his mind. He knew that the life of a whore must sometimes be very dangerous. She could easily come upon a very mean customer. But just as dangerous must be meeting someone she liked. On White's last night, he spent most of it holding Maria as she cried. When she finally made him understand, it cut him to the bone. No one had ever saved her before.

CHAPTER XXIV

White, Kelly, and Walker sat in the dark as the bus rolled through downtown Manila toward the airport. The ride was very different now from when first coming to the city. It was quiet. No one moved or yelled what plans they had to gorge themselves on the pleasures of R&R.

White looked out of the windows to the cars and pedestrians. Sitting silently, he watched as the colored neon lights faded into the distance behind them. Up ahead were the bright white lights of the airport. Those same lights that had so shaken his nerves on arrival now meant nothing. This time the blazing lights didn't faze him.

He looked at the soldiers around him. They all looked like old men—old, tired men—unloading from the buses and walking to the terminal. White, Walker, and Kelly found seats together and sat with their backs to the wall. Neither had said a word since leaving the three Marias, nor could they look at each other.

They sat still as statues until a loudspeaker came on and a voice began calling out names. First, they looked up at the sound, and then they allowed themselves to look at each other. White's gut sank as Kelly's name came out of the speaker.

White had a sudden, desperate idea to get addresses from his new comrades. Something stopped him. It was wrong. Both were going back to the bush. Both had good chances of being killed.

He had known for some time why none of the veterans ever asked replacements their names. He understood now how bitter a chance it was to know too much about anyone and why hometowns, family and girls, were seldom talked about among the veterans. It was because there was too much to lose by knowing too much about a comrade, if he was killed.

Every fact known about a friend was a nail driven into your own coffin if he was killed.

It was better to know as little as possible about anyone new. Still, he chanced it. He strained as he looked at them, hoping to bring on that clarity which he sometimes got in the field. He tried to force himself to see some kind of sign that they would "make it". But he didn't see anything. He didn't feel anything but a helpless nothing. His mind raced. He needed to say something to them, but what words could he use? Nothing sounded right, so he just sat there staring at Kelly.

Kelly stood up. He looked one last time at White and Walker. He, too, seemed speechless. He turned, stretched himself straight, and walked to the door out onto the airfield.

A half hour passed before the loudspeakers came back on. Toward the end of the long list of names, White's was called. He stood up and looked at Walker. Then Walker, a confused look on his face, nodded his head goodbye. More seconds passed. White nodded back, turned, and walked to the door. There was just nothing to say.

Intense silence filled the cabin of the C-141. White sat behind the right wing, unconsciously choosing the safest place on the plane. When everyone had boarded, the lights went out. Now, instead of the feeling of security in the dark, he felt a loneliness that pressed him deeper into his seat. He withdrew into himself as the plane climbed. The higher they rose, the farther his spirit dropped.

Something struck him. He was again faced with a choice. Would he keep falling? Would he stay down, or would he pick himself up and go on? If he couldn't shake this depression, he was surely finished.

An image formed itself in his mind. Then he saw it clearly in the dark. It was Lopez's smiling face. "Don' t'ink 'bout dat now," he said. "Jus' keep on gon' an' you gon' be all right."

"Yes," thought White. "I can keep going." He began to relax until the dark became comfortable again. "And I'll see Lopez and the others soon. Then I'll be O.K."

He sank still deeper into his seat, not to escape now, but to sleep. In minutes he began to drift. Images of his comrades spread before him. Somewhere in the hazy shadows, he fell asleep.

A change in the roar of the engines woke him. The plane was

slowing and descending. Men began sitting up in their seats. The drone became softer. White's ears began popping. There was a loud squeal of the tires on tarmac and then a roar of the engines to slow the plane.

The plane coasted to a stop. When the doors opened, the humidity of the outside air swirled into the cabin. The rain had turned into a light drizzle, but the air seemed as watery as ever. The cold of monsoon swept into him. They were back.

The soldiers stood and began filing out the exits. The first thing White saw as he got to the door were the many Vietnamese civilians in rice hats and black pajamas, loading and unloading planes.

Several officers and sergeants waited outside. They shouted out numbers for buildings a hundred yards away. White ran with the rest, trying to stay relatively dry, to the number of the building called out.

At the door was a corporal. "Find any place to sack out for tonight," he said. "You're gonna process in the morning. Chow starts at five in building number five. Process starts at seven."

White found a bunk. He crawled into it with his wet clothes, covered himself up with the liner, and tried to sleep. He shivered at first but knew that by morning he would be dry again. Something passed before his closed eyes—it was Maria. She was crying. But then her image started to change, and somehow she became Zahn. She was laughing... and then she faded. He fell into a deep, contented sleep.

With the first streak of dawn, he sprang out of bed, feeling rested and rejuvenated. But it wasn't only a good night's sleep that brought him to sudden life. He awoke with the sudden realization that he would soon be with his friends. He chuckled softly because he knew now that everything would be good again.

He took a quick shower—cold water—and then went to breakfast. They had real eggs, not the powdered, watery slop that was usual at the base camps, but real eggs. And real bacon and biscuits, too.

He was enjoying his meal when a frightening thought flashed in his mind: his friends, his comrades. How were they? Were they O.K.? Where were they? Then the worst question: had any been killed?

He left his third biscuit untouched and made it to the processing area without getting wet. It took only minutes to get his traveling papers and process back into the country. Then he went to get his gun.

The same sergeant that had taken it from him now handed it back. Like magic, White had it open. His fingers flew. In a blur he inspected the rifle. Everything checked out. He looked down at the sergeant. The man looked at White. He seemed to have seen this many times but seemed still amazed at a grunt's first instinct to check his rifle. Also, he seemed amazed at how sure and fast White checked it, how it seemed a part of him. Almost impatiently he said, "Nexxxt."

White was in a hurry now to get back to the company. Fear pushed him on. He waited in a light drizzle for the C-130 to take him north. He was the first to board and the first to exit when they landed.

A helicopter brought him to the base where he could process back into the company. He was told that they were still out in the field but that they would be resupplied that day. He was to ride out with the supplies.

Afraid of the answer, but having to know, he asked, "Any replacements going out with me?"

The sergeant knew what he really wanted to know. "Naw," he said. "They've been lucky. Not even a scratch this time out."

That afternoon White climbed aboard the first of the two helicopters being loaded with supplies. The rain had stopped, but the helicopter crew had left the side doors closed. He sat in a canvas seat against the back wall and waited to take off. Now he was very anxious. It was all too slow. More than anything now, he wanted to see his comrades.

The miles went by as he looked out the window to the grey world below. The rain had stopped completely, but a fog hung over the rice paddies. The helicopters veered west. Almost immediately, the scrub hills appeared. In the far distance, partly shrouded by the fog, were the mountains. Their tops were almost completely covered in the dark, water-soaked clouds.

His heart pounded when they entered the space above the trees marking the beginning of the true jungle. He was almost there. All thoughts of alarm, of the guilt he had felt in wishing to escape monsoon at any cost, left him and were replaced with elation. He would soon be with them again, and they would all be there. Headquarters had said so. None had been hit the whole time he had been on R&R. This time, no matter what, he wouldn't think of abandoning them.

Far ahead, spiraling upward into the mist was the red-colored smoke of a marker grenade. White knew when he saw the smoke that the company could see them coming. His eyes strained to see a hole in the canopy below. No. Still too far away. But with each second the helicopter came nearer to the fading red marker.

Then he saw it. Surrounded by the grey-green haze below was an acre-sized clearing. White's insides shivered in anticipation, and his eyes bulged out, trying to see through the trees at the edge of the clearing.

Something moved. It was a man coming out of the trees. Even before he could see his face, White knew that it was Smith. Only he had such blonde hair, almost as white as his pale skin. Smith stood near the edge of the clearing, motioning the helicopters where to land.

Then White was able to see that unmistakable sneer which seemed branded on Smith's face. To White, it was beautiful. That sneer seemed remarkably truthful—honest beyond bullshit—soothing because it was so dependable.

Someone else in the trees moved. White recognized Hahn, squatting on the ground, waiting for the helicopters to land. His face, always seeming boyishly curious, watched the landing helicopters. Behind him was Hong. And behind him, in the darker light further from the clearing, was Louis.

White's heart leapt. He was back. He felt safe, away from the maddening uncertainty of the outside world. Clarity surged through him. There was no doubt here. He understood it all again. Everything was so simple.

When Smith saw White, a pleased look flashed across his face. Just as quickly, it was gone, and those icy-blue eyes again bored deeply into White. But White had seen that hesitant look of a comrade.

He threw open the door and jumped out, seeing the smiles of recognition as his friends moved toward the helicopters. Turning to start unloading supplies, he felt hand after hand touch him on the shoulder in greeting. Reaching inside the helicopter for boxes of supplies, he saw a box labeled 'medical supplies'. When he turned to hand it to someone, Cloud's serious expression seemed to welcome him back.

With the helicopter unloaded, the men melted back into the safety of the trees. They knelt on one knee, eyes closed, as the whirling blades threw wet leaves and sticks at their faces.

As he stood, White could hear his comrades.

"Welcome back to the real world," said Louis, his incredible smile flashing.

"Now you gon' hav' some good story' to tell us," said an equally smiling Lopez.

"We ain't got time for no fucking stories," said Smith. "Get this shit distributed, so we can get the fuck out of here."

"Grouchy mudda fucker," said Hong.

"Ver' happy to see you, sir," said Hahn.

Frowning at everyone around him, Smith said to White, "Get your shit. We're over there."

White followed him. From every direction he saw others in the company nod a welcome. They were all dry. Even the newest in the company were dry.

Now, something attacked White's senses. They all stank. A bad, unwashed human smell oozed from all of them. "How can that be?" thought White. Except for R&R, he had been with them for months, and he had never smelled them before.

He followed behind Smith, smelling the pungent odor coming from him. When they reached his squad's point on the perimeter, he saw Farver kneeling on the ground, separating boxes of rations. He looked up, recognized White, and smiled broadly.

"Pick any spot around here," said Smith. He came closer to White and sniffed around him. He wrinkled his nose as if smelling something bad and said, "You smell like a fucking pussy-boy."

As Smith walked off, Lopez sniffed at him, also. "Ess jus' soap," he said. "You gon' smell better *mañana.*" He looked at White's pack and sniffed it.

White knew that there was nothing Lopez would appreciate as much as what he had in his pack. "Sit down, Roberto," he said. "I've got something I think you'll like."

They sat on the dank leaves, and White began to open his pack. Before the top was completely opened, he saw Lopez's eyes open wide. "He smells it," thought White. Lopez's face lit up and broke into a smile.

White pulled out the five-pound package wrapped in brown waxed paper. Inside of the paper wrapping was another of aluminum foil.

"Ro'st," said Lopez as White started undoing the foil.

"Yeah," said White. "Beef roast. I bought it this morning from a guy on K.P. Think it's still good?"

"*Claro*," said Lopez. "We gon' cut it?"

"Right now," said White.

As he reached for his knife, the odor of the roasted meat assaulted his nose. Suddenly, he felt nauseated. He felt a taste of bile in his throat. He had been sweating since his arrival back in Nam, but now it poured out of him. The thick, humid air seemed even harder to breathe in than usual. He had a moment of dizziness and feared he would pass out.

"Ess O.K., Blanco," said Lopez. "You jus' got to sweat out all dat R&R. You drink plen'y champagne, huh?"

White could only nod.

"Take two, t'ree day to get back in shape," said Lopez.

Louis came walking up to them with a smile spread across his face. But it disappeared when he saw how sick White had become.

"Wow," he said. "You look bad. How many gallons of that stuff did you drink?"

"Too much," said White. He handed the knife to Louis and said, "Here. You guys have a chunk of roast."

One by one his friends came to say hello. After a few words and a taste of meat, they went back to their places. Only Farver hadn't come over. He was sitting alone, twenty feet from White. White called him over with a twitch of his head.

"Take a piece of meat," said White.

Farver looked at the wrapper as he sat. "There's only one piece left."

"Go ahead and eat it," said White. "I'm so fucking sick I don't even want to think about it."

White awoke the next morning feeling much better. He still couldn't think of food, but hot chocolate hit the spot. Also, it was easier to breathe again as he sat there smoking and sipping.

Word spread around the perimeter. "Get ready to move out."

He had another wave of dizziness as he swung on his pack. It passed, but he was suddenly awash with an alcohol-smelling sweat, and he was suffering enough just standing there.

Smith walked up to him. He looked him up and down. His sneer seemed happy—glad to see White suffering. "Now you've gotta pay, muddafucker," he said before walking to the next man in the squad.

The first few yards were unbelievable. Foul-smelling sweat gushed out of him. He was soon soaked in it. Before he made a hundred yards, his feet were sloshing in the sweat in his boots. His pack seemed to weigh a ton, and his heart beat as if it were trying to jump out of his chest.

It got darker as the already dim light got weaker still. Through breaks in the canopy, White watched as the black clouds descended in the sky. Then it started. The rain came down in what seemed a flood and washed the stink of his sweat into the mud at his feet.

He was back. Monsoon was back. The cold was back. It sent its icy fingers creeping into every square inch of his body.

"It's miserable out here," he thought. But that didn't matter. He was back with his comrades where he understood everything again. If they didn't make contact, it would be much better for him tomorrow. Another few days and he'd be normal again. Then he could tell them about R&R.

CHAPTER XXV

White had reached the point that for the grunt goes beyond restricting human laws and theories. He began to feel, without doubt, that there is something, some force, overriding the laws of physics and metaphysics. He could not have put it into words, but the idea racing through him seemed unmistakable.

He knew some people would disagree. They could conceive nothing beyond the chance of swirling atoms and the physical adjustments of an evolutionary universe. Others could envision a creating, controlling force but one limited to the same particular creeds in which they themselves put their faith.

But it was so plain to see now. Anyone who tried could see it. Because it is generally the less educated people of the world that fill the ranks of the grunts, few of them will have ever explored scientific laws and theories. For the same reason, few of them will go beyond memorized phrases in organized religious rituals. But, after a serious fight, when death seemed certain, if asked what religion they had been reborn into, the combat soldiers' reply would likely be, "All of them."

And because the grunt unconsciously knows so much about the physics of ballistics and the effect of velocity and impact of flying steel against meat and bones, he becomes an advanced student in the psychology of human terror. Because the zinging metal and sharpened bamboo stakes have so many times missed his own flesh, he feels there is something extraordinary beyond his own power and luck—something Divine—steering him through his human nature. And when a time comes that he must choose between logic and intuition, he does not hesitate to put all of his energy into a physical plunge, a willing leap, into that steering force.

White and the company had been flown to a base camp. They had been there five days. What a wonderful five days it was. They were dry. They wrapped themselves in their dry ponchos and liners, sitting or lying on cots. They listened while the rain pounded on the canvas roof of the huge tent. They walked in dry boots on wooden pallets lying on the dry, bare earth.

At meal times, they hesitated leaving the warm cocoon that wrapped them. But they knew they must store energy for later, so they reluctantly donned their ponchos and boots and ran to the mess tent. They stuffed themselves. They avoided anything cold but drank and ate anything hot. Then they ran back to their tents, climbed back into their blankets, smoked, and slept.

They didn't like to see a sergeant or officer come into the tent. They knew that soon someone would come to say they would be moving out. Then, on the afternoon of the fifth day, Smith walked into the tent with a sullen look to his face. White and the others knew what that meant.

"Tomorrow," he said. "Going out somewhere close to A Shau."

Only White's eyes moved at the sound of that word. They darted from one comrade to another as he fought the sudden depression. Before going to A Shau the first time, he had been ignorant of the reality of the valley. He had imagined a monster—a killing monster. But the reality had been worse. The company had lost Jackson, Cook, and several others. Boudreaux, too, was gone and hopefully now back in the States.

Now there was no wondering what lay ahead. He saw the same desperate look on his comrades' faces that he was sure was on his own. He waited to see if anyone would say anything.

"Chopper?" said Louis, a forlorn stare plastered on his face.

"Yeah," said Smith. "Too many guns in the valley. They'd shoot us out of the sky for sure. Gonna come in a couple of clicks away and walk the rest of the way in."

"We going in alone?" asked White, futility surging through him.

"The whole battalion's going in," said Smith.

"W'at it look like?" said Lopez.

"Deep shit," said Smith. "When is it ever anything but deep shit around the A Shau?"

"Maybe this time it won't be so bad," said Louis.

"Maybe fucking elephants fly," said Smith.

"Maybe we'll just be lucky," said White.

"Maybe you're fucking dreaming," said Smith.

Silence. No one moved. At supper, a grim company stared at the food before them. Then, one by one, the men began to force down what now seemed a repugnant mess, knowing they would need all their strength in the days ahead.

A Shau. Back to A Shau. Back to the Valley of Death.

That night as he lay awake, White knew that a stranger would have listened in vain for any sound from the company's tents. But he would have had to come early in the morning hours before he would have found anyone asleep. Anyone, that is, except Lopez. He had been asleep since that afternoon.

The fleet of helicopters headed west, toward the mountains and the A Shau. The rain had stopped, but the world was still a grey haze. Soon, they had passed all the villages, and only the lonely jungle yawned before them.

Sitting on the outside edge of the gun ships, White knew the danger. He watched the ground below for any puff of smoke streaking behind a Russian rocket, aimed at them. If they were hit at this height there would be no survivors.

Off in the distance were the mountains surrounding A Shau. He tried to shut off all thoughts but the ones needed to survive. But rushing in and out of his thinking were clear, uncalled-for messages that somehow seemed urgently important. He let his mind explore them as he looked at the peaks ahead.

The N.V.A. and their leaders were marvelous. White could now testify to the bravery and resourcefulness of the N.V.A. He and the other veterans had witnessed heroism in the first degree as they fought the determined Asians. They had never captured any N.V.A. alive. All charged gallantly, not stopping until killed. All fought to the death if they couldn't escape.

He knew that it was true the Americans had the best technology and equipment for war, better than any other country in the world. But the brilliant leadership of the North Vietnamese offset that. Their generals, backed by their politicians and their people, forced the American infantry in the northern part of South Viet Nam to fight in the mountain jungles, where American air power and artillery was almost useless. Above all, they seemed united in their goal.

But the Americans had heroic fighters, too. He and the grunts, however, were at a great disadvantage. From the news they received from the States, he knew that the American generals, politicians, and civilians were alienated from the grunt. Many civilian lives were far removed from the boonie rat. These people had their own careers and interests, and if they regarded the soldiers at all, it was mildly. And he knew some thought of the soldier only with contempt, while some thought of the soldier with deep hatred.

The grunts had one advantage few people ever have. Apart from their families, friends, and some civilians, the soldiers no longer had support from home. They had, however, something infinitely stronger. They had each other, and each had the knowledge of his worth within the company. They had reached a brotherhood that most people would never know and would be forever poor for not knowing.

Still, there was a terrible price to pay to gain that knowledge. The longer in the field, the more experience he gained, the more the grunt became alienated from what most people outside of their ranks would call "normal" thinking.

How could their thinking be normal when, in the best conditions in the sticks, a grunt was always at the point of physical collapse? How should he feel and think when he sometimes went days without food and water and his mind swirled in a dehydrated fog? How could he ever be considered normal when his thoughts took turns and led to what the "easy chair" patriots at home in front of their television sets would call treason?

It had been strange for him when he began to realize he had more in common with the enemy than he did with his own countrymen back in the world. In a hazy, abstract way he had begun to think of the enemy more like a comrade—a respectable, honorable comrade. But as the weeks passed, it was no longer strange. It seemed natural. The N.V.A. and V.C. were truly deserving of respect. They were, by the best standards of one soldier to another, honorable.

"Stop," he thought. He couldn't think of that now. He had to concentrate. But, as much as he tried, other thoughts flashed before him. How long had it been since R&R? It couldn't be more than a few days, but it seemed like weeks… months… He couldn't remember. A sudden guilt pounced on him that he should have worn the shirts his mother made for him more often.

Then the fast-approaching landing zones instantly brought everything into real focus. A Shau…He was back. What now? Who was next?

At the foot of the largest mountain surrounding the valley was a natural glade. Elephant grass six feet tall waved and swayed in the breeze. As one, the helicopters suddenly veered toward the glade. They dropped like rocks, toward the ground below. The soldiers gripped tightly to the doors and to each other.

Then, in a whirl, the skids touched down, and the soldiers tumbled out. The company scrambled for the safety of the trees. They formed a perimeter. When no attack came, they made final plans. Then they moved out, walking across and upward, entering again into the jungle-covered mountains.

There were N.V.A. signs everywhere. Everyone knew all the passes and accesses to the valley were guarded. Footpaths ran in every direction. Even large truck tire tracks appeared on the muddy trails. A quick thought went through White's mind. "How could they get a truck up here?" It was many miles of thick mountain jungle to the nearest road in the north. But he knew that they could do it. They could do anything.

Trails were almost always booby-trapped and always led to N.V.A. The only time the American soldiers used trails was when there was little choice. Or, like now, when the N.V.A.'s own fresh tire tracks showed there was little chance of mines.

There was another bad thing about coming out by helicopter. Now there was no hiding. Because they had come by chopper, every N.V.A. in the valley and surrounding mountains would know about where they were. The company hastened upward, walking in the tire tracks.

The trees above them blocked all view of the sky. That meant no close ground support. To the company's right, the mountains slanted upward. To their left, the mountain sloped downward, the bottom hidden by the trees and underbrush.

Soon now. Very soon. Suddenly, the veterans eyed each other. Nerves grew taut. The short hair at the back of White's neck stood up. It was coming. It was coming.

Then came the first explosions. Strings of bombs, like strings of firecrackers, exploded in the trees and on the ground all around them. Clumps of dirt and wood splinters flew in every direction, stinging their faces. Hot steel shredded everything it met. The zinging steel mowed down bushes, small trees, and men.

A quick thought went through White's mind. At that critical, deadly moment, and at all the other times of seemingly imminent death, he was not afraid. He acted.

Leaves, dirt, and tree bark exploded around him. Everything seemed to be happening so slowly. A fraction of a second before his body could respond, his mind had already found a spot. His slower body went for it as fast as it could while his eyes and mind raced to see everything around him.

Then a light puff of air from an escaping bullet parted the leaves on a bush twenty yards from him. In his wild dive for cover, he shifted his rifle toward the bush, letting out a burst at the hidden sniper.

From a corner of his eyes, he saw as Hahn was almost cut in half by an explosion. His right arm was completely ripped off, and the skin of his face nearly blasted from his skull by the concussion.

The same blast hurled Jimmy Hong many yards through the air. A chunk of hot metal ripped open his throat. Other pieces of steel went through him as he flew through the air and over the side of the mountain. Neither Hahn nor Hong had had a chance, nor knew what hit him.

Now, the air was filled with machine gun fire. More leaves and tree bark flew when bullets struck everywhere around the soldiers. But White and the veterans who had not been instantly killed were now in some kind of cover.

Small depressions in the earth, only inches deep, had been dived for and scrambled into. Rocks no bigger than cabbages had hidden, desperate men behind them. A bush that could barely hide a rabbit concealed a man, and each man with cover now looked around him for a better position.

Many had not made it unhurt. Scattered on the jungle floor were wounded men and pieces of men who had not been lucky. Most were new replacements, but some were old timers. Some were dead, some mortally wounded, some seriously wounded, and many lightly scratched.

Lying on the ground was Louis. He lay on his belly, his face pressed into the leaves. His pack had been blasted off, and he lay unmoving with a large patch of dark blood between his shoulders. White's gut twisted into a knot, and he vomited.

His first impulse was to run to Louis regardless of the instant fire he knew he'd draw. At almost the same instant, he knew that he couldn't. To move now was probably to be killed uselessly. So he strained his eyes, looking for any sign of movement—breathing—anything to show that Louis was alive. But he couldn't see any movement. "No use," he thought as he shoved his body deeper into the leaves.

He lay still behind the log. The machine guns had stopped. Now each man, only his eyes moving, looked for the hidden enemy. A wounded replacement would groan and move. Instantly, he was fired upon by hidden N.V.A. Telltale puffs of bullets moving leaves showed enemy locations to the grunts. Each man waited patiently for a chance to get to a better spot. When they saw a chance, they dove for better cover, firing at the hidden enemy as they went.

Every wild move brought a new string of explosions from the ground and trees. Any movement brought bullets zinging toward them. Recruits moaned in agony, clawing at the leaves on the jungle floor. Some cried, begging for help. But to move was almost certain death. White knew that. Everyone knew that.

And White knew, too, that Cloud knew what the chances were of his reaching the clawing, crying replacements. White and the other comrades eyed each other, desperately signaling Cloud to stay back. But Cloud was more than just a comrade. He was a medic and a human being. He knew his job and his duty.

As he leapt to his feet, rifle fire and machine guns opened up on him. Hidden American grunts that had been waiting to see flashes from hidden N.V.A. now fired, silencing many of them.

Bullets tore at Cloud's pack and clothes while he ran toward a wounded recruit. It was amazing that he had not been hit yet. But now, an N.V.A. who had been hidden behind a tree suddenly stood up and aimed a Russian R.P.G. (Rocket Propelled Grenade) at Cloud's back. The N.V.A. soldier was instantly fired upon and killed but not before he had fired the grenade launcher. With a great whoosh, the projectile went flying toward Cloud and, with a terrific boom, exploded against the medic pack on his back.

The blast broke Cloud's back at a dozen places, sending him hurling through the air. But Cloud never felt it because the back half of his skull had been wiped off and his brains blown out. He hit the ground like a rag doll, bounced, and tumbled lifelessly through the leaves.

If there had been time, the company would have mourned. But whatever time they had left, the men used to survive. Cloud's dash had exposed hidden fighters, and the company emptied rounds at those positions.

Suddenly, all firing stopped. White waited expectantly for something more. He turned to look toward the right and saw Lopez kneeling above a hidden machine gun nest. His rifle pointed down toward something on the ground.

White crawled to Lopez's side. There on Lopez's face was something White would have found hard to describe. On the ground was an N.V.A. soldier shot to pieces. But his eyes blazed with hate and defiance. He fought to reach his rifle, but he was paralyzed. His mind seemed to strain to try and will his hands to move, but it was useless. Only his eyes moved as he glared at Lopez, unconquered. He again struggled to fight but couldn't. Lopez looked down at the soldier. It was with an expression of incredible sadness that he shot the man once, through the heart.

Now, the fight moved to the right. White could see hidden bunkers in the trees. Smith was beside him, fearlessly scanning everything. Then, a sudden blast hurled White to the ground. The shock of the blast stunned him, and the violent crash to the ground knocked all the wind out of him.

He sat dazed and deaf, watching the scene before him. Smith turned quickly. He looked down at White and saw that he was whole. White then saw Smith turn toward a movement at the bunker.

White tried to move but couldn't. He sat and watched as everything about him moved in slow motion. There was no sound, only the incredibly slow motion of everyone he could see.

Smith should have fired immediately, but froze. Stooping to come out of the bunker was a girl. In that instant the great clarity descended on White. It was as if he could read Smith's mind and knew she was the most beautiful girl Smith had ever seen. Smith just stood there looking at her. He should have killed her then, but he couldn't. Something in his hard interior stopped him at the sight of her. And in White's dazed state he somehow knew that Smith loved her.

But she was a soldier, and in her beautiful face was a determination set on killing her enemies. She came out of the bunker with an A.K. ready in her hands. Her eyes darted back and forth, looking for a target.

Smith seemed ready to shoot her when her eyes turned to him. He looked into those dark, slanted eyes, and White instantly knew two things. He knew Smith would never kill her, and he knew that she would kill Smith.

Smith seemed to want to say something to her. His lips moved, and White could swear that he read, "No, I'll help you."

He seemed to want to say more as she raised the A.K. White wished he could see a spark of compassion on her face, some look of regret, before she killed him. But all he saw was a willing look, one that was content to do her duty...and die.

White was paralyzed. He saw as she aimed at Smith and let off a burst that sent Smith crumbling to the ground. He saw as she was riddled with bullets from other men in the company. She fell in slow motion, lifeless, beautiful even in death.

Now everything stopped. White could see a platoon medic in front of him. He saw the medic's mouth moving but heard and understood nothing. Then, like awakening from a dream, sound and sense came back to him.

"Try not to move," said the medic. "You're gonna be O.K., but you got to stay still."

White brushed him aside. To his left lay Smith and the girl. His head turned to the right and there, squatting on his haunches, looking at him, was Lopez.

"Ess O.K., Blanco," said Lopez. "You gon' be all right."

White got to his feet. Lopez supported him on one arm and

slowly walked him around the area. They saw dead Gooks and dead and wounded G.I.'s.

When they approached the place where the fight had first begun, White looked down to see Farver. His body had been riddled with bullets; his head and face were half gone.

Then the two comrades saw something that brought both a glimmer of hope. Kneeling on the ground, working feverishly, was a medic. His hands worked quickly, stopping Louis's oozing blood.

"He's alive," thought White as he and Lopez rushed to them.

"He might make it if we get him to a hospital," said the medic.

Now, the two comrades blazed back into life.

"What can we do?' asked White.

"Make a stretcher with his poncho," said the medic.

They built a litter and opened packs of bandages. They held a solution-filled bag whose tube dripped fluid to Louis's vein. White ran to the company area. Before he could say anything, the captain, knowing what he wanted and with great concern, said, "They're sending fast birds for the wounded and dead."

White went back and stood with Lopez. The minutes seemed like hours. "What's taking so long?" said White.

"'Dey fightin' all over 'de valley," said Lopez. "'Dey probab'y need choppers all over 'de place."

"What do you think, Roberto?" asked White, looking down at the still unconscious—but still breathing—Louis.

"He's tough," said Lopez. "Maybe he can make it."

CHAPTER XXVI

Five had been killed, seven critically wounded or permanently crippled, nineteen lightly wounded, and one missing; more than thirty percent casualties, all in a half hour.

The fighting had stopped, but White could still hear explosions and gunfire from the ridges and mountains around them. From every approach to the valley, they heard the pounding of helicopter guns and rockets, artillery, and jets slamming into the trees. Answering N.V.A. fire echoed through the explosions.

White and Lopez faced outward on the perimeter, waiting for the N.V.A. infantry they knew were sure to come. Without having to be told, the veterans prepared for the attack. Looking sick with fright, the newcomers copied as best they could whatever they saw the old-timers doing.

White could hear the captain as he talked on the radio with the rear areas. He couldn't make out what he was saying but could tell by his tone that the news from headquarters was not good. He had never seen the captain so shook up and knew that whatever it was that had so shaken him was sure to be something drastically wrong.

A squad from second platoon broke off the perimeter and began searching farther down the slope to find Jimmy Hong's body. But the blast that had sent him flying must have flung him very far, so the squad made their way lower, searching every inch of ground as they went.

White looked back to where the captain and the platoon lieutenants stood. The captain was shouting on the radio. "I can't do that. I'm not gonna leave a man out here."

Someone spoke on the other end.

"Yeah, he's dead," the captain answered. "But that don't matter. I can't leave a man out here."

There was a pause as headquarters answered back. Then the captain went on, "Yeah, that's easy for you to say. You're not the one that's got to do it."

A rough voice, not loud enough for White to distinguish the words, but loud enough to rattle the squelch on the radio, shouted out orders to the captain. His shoulders sagged as he answered back into the radio, "Yes, sir. I understand."

White and Lopez looked at each other and then at the approaching platoon leader. Lieutenant Zigler had taken Sir's place when he had been rotated out, safe and whole, a month before. Zigler's face showed extreme depression and anger. "Change of plans. They're sending birds to get us out of here. We'll be leaving as soon as they get here."

"W'at 'bout Hong?" said Lopez. "We can't jus' leave him."

"Got to," said Zigler. "Orders from the top. We got to get out now."

White knew Hong was dead and that he wasn't making any sense, but the only thing that came out was. "But we can't just leave him here all alone."

"No choice," said the Lieutenant, understanding completely what White meant.

"Listen," he went on. "There's a LRRP platoon not far from here. They'll be here some time tomorrow morning. They'll find Hong and bring him back in. But we gotta go now. If we don't leave now, we might not get out at all. Way too many N.V.A. *Beaucoup* new regiments from the North." He looked at the two soldiers and said, "Ah don't like it any more than you. And the captain don't like it, neither. But we got to go."

A worn-out expression, one that caused him to look old, appeared on his face. He searched for something better to say. He strained, almost choking, as he said, "Sorry".

He turned to go and give the word to the rest of the platoon. Before he took a step, he turned again and said, "I'm sorry. I'm sorry."

White and Lopez turned their backs to the center of the perimeter and stared out into the jungle. White had thought that things couldn't be worse, but they suddenly were. They would leave Jimmy Hong out there. How could such a thing be possible? Their comrade, their friend. It was worse than seeing him dead.

He saw the agony in Lopez's face as he turned toward him. They couldn't talk. They could scarcely look at each other because they could feel each other's guilt. A mad idea came to White to rush out and find Hong's body, but he stopped. He knew that would be crazy.

He heard a distant clop, clop clopping. The sound grew louder as the helicopter neared. White waited for the signal that would call his reduced platoon to their wave.

Then he was up and running for a helicopter. He could hear the sound of A.K.'s and the "pings" as the bullets hit the helicopter. An N.V.A., whether a survivor of the fight or a new arrival, was firing at the incoming bird. The door gunner on the chopper fired into the jungle below. He must have killed the last N.V.A. because shooting from the ground stopped. The bird landed without drawing further fire.

White and Lopez helped load the dead and wounded, then climbed aboard and sat on the canvas seats. They breathed a sigh of relief when they reached a height safe from small arms. But the relief was short. They looked down to the floor. Louis was still alive but barely breathing. Part of Farver's brain leaked to the floor of the helicopter. Worst of all, chilling their already frayed nerves, they saw the sneer on Smith's dead face.

Unbelievably, none of the helicopters bringing them to the rear were hit. The company was assigned a quiet area to recuperate. White and a depleted and depressed company huddled in their tents. He sat reading a half-finished letter to his mother. He concentrated, trying to think of something to write that wouldn't betray his growing anxiety. It had become harder to write as the weeks passed but lately had become almost impossible. If he wasn't careful, his mother would know that he was in great danger. But he stared down at the letter in his hands and was at a complete loss as to how to finish it.

Something new had slowly been entering his thoughts in the last few weeks. Now, after the latest fight in A Shau, his mind was flooded with these new ideas. Surviving the year in Nam was no longer his main concern. What was happening to him mentally, what was draining him, was the uncertainty of what he was becoming.

He was changing psychologically into something he was just beginning to understand. What he feared now more than anything was what would happen to him if he did make it out alive. Every day it seemed harder to remember life before Nam. Every black night brought twisted images of dead men.

He looked at the new men in the tent and knew what they were thinking. Three or four man groups of them, who a month before could not have conceived of anyone wanting to kill them, sat terrified in the harsh reality of what they now faced. Their fiery baptism had drained their energy and innocence, and they sat numb and dumb. They sat either staring at their boots or gazing out, unseeing, at the canvas walls of the tents, oblivious to the rain.

The company received word. The LRRP platoon had reached where the company had the fight. They had spent a half hour looking for Jimmy Hong's body. Then they were attacked by overwhelming N.V.A. forces and had to run for it. It was only because they were in such good condition and because N.V.A. infantry were a good stimulus to run, that the platoon managed to get away.

But they got away without Jimmy Hong. Now, no one would go back. The area was now covered with N.V.A., and White and his depressed comrades in the tents knew that the search was over.

Dismal thoughts passed through White's mind as he sat there. He understood why everyone had chosen certain places to sit. Soldiers with two or three months in country distanced themselves from the newcomers. Three or four would sit on bunks facing each other, able to look at each other but not able to talk. Their baptism had come earlier, but this last fight had been their grim confirmation.

From three to six months in country, the soldiers were considered seasoned. That middle group seemed to have accepted the inevitable. They, too, were more comfortable with others of their own rank and sat in small groups. Some lay on their cots, listening to their comrades or to the endless rain. Some would slip over to the mess tents to steal any kind of food or drink. Others sat on the edges of their cots, smoking.

Those with over six months on the line were the old timers. They were the enigmas of the company. They had escaped death many times, and White knew that, like him, they must wonder how they could have done it. They were the most practical of the company, eating and sleeping wherever they could. But there was something cold and closed about them that couldn't be breached except by another old-timer.

Then there were the few short timers. There was no enigma here. They were still alive because they were the best soldiers. Their reflexes, instincts, and luck had brought them to a plane where they stood above and separate from everyone else of the company. They looked out, through red eyes, into a world that to them must be either dying or already dead. Adding to the depression was the arrival of replacements, their frightened faces bringing White even further down.

White and Lopez sat on their cots, facing each other. Lopez was short, but it showed only to the old timers. Gun on his knees, wiping it constantly with a rag, his eyes were savage, desperate, and lost.

White searched for something to say that might help his friend. Unable to think of anything else, he said, "Maybe you won't have to come out this time, Roberto. Maybe you're too short."

Lopez answered with a light shrug of his shoulders and continued wiping his rifle.

Both veterans looked up quickly when the tent flaps opened. There in the open door way, poncho dripping, was Lieutenant Zigler. He looked around the tent, spied Lopez and White, and began walking to them. Both veterans knew at a glance that something was up and that they were involved. The officer stopped before them and sat on the cot with White. He paused, thinking of how best to say what he had come for. White now looked directly at him, but, since seeing the lieutenant, Lopez had never lifted his eyes from his rifle.

"Lopez," said Zigler, "I know you don't want it, but I want to make you squad leader."

Lopez never blinked. He neither looked up nor stopped wiping his rifle. The lieutenant understood he would get no answer. Then he tried again.

"Damn it, Lopez, we need you. Look at all those cherries," he said, jerking his thumb toward the green replacements.

"Not gonna be no squad leader," said Lopez, finally looking up to the lieutenant. "But I'm gonna help 'dem if I can." There was a long pause as Lopez's eyes pierced the lieutenant.

White knew that neither the lieutenant nor anyone else could change Lopez's mind, and it seemed the lieutenant knew it, too. With a look of resignation, the lieutenant turned to White and said, "O.K., White, you're now second squad leader. Lopez…" he went on, "they're real weak in second platoon. You're gonna be going out with them."

That got a response. Lopez looked to the lieutenant and then quickly to White. His bulging eyes bored more deeply into White than they had ever done before. But this time they didn't have the look of anger, warning, or emptiness, as they had when White had first known him. Neither did they have that sure, confident look nor that humane, humorous look that White had learned to rely on so heavily. Now they had the look of deep helplessness, as if his last life line was being cut, as if a slender thread holding him up was being snapped.

"Sorry, Lopez," said the lieutenant. "That's how it's gotta be."

"Sorry, too, Lopez," he went on, "that you can't wait here for your papers. We need you bad." He stood to go. Before turning for the tent door he said, "I'll try my best to keep you out of the shit."

But he said it to a blank face. Lopez had returned to wiping his gun. Then White asked, "Ain't it usual for a guy to make corporal before sergeant?"

The lieutenant frowned at the two veterans and said, "Not in this outfit." He then turned and walked to the tent flap, threw it open, and stepped out into the rain.

The company had been six days in the sticks, and for those six days the sun had not come out. Because they were not very high into the mountains, the temperature wasn't so cold. But they were wet and had been since leaving the base camp.

White knew they had been lucky to have not yet made contact. But for the last two days, they had come across craters and clearings made by air force bombers. That meant N.V.A. activity. Even if they weren't near A Shau, N.V.A. activity was never good. Tensions rose.

Drinking was no longer a problem for White and the company. Now their only problem with water was that there was too much of it. They ate, shit, and walked all day in the constant rain. At night they slept in it. White had learned how to keep a cigarette lit in it and deeply inhaled the warm smoke.

His biggest problem, besides the N.V.A., was food. Most were now completely out. Some of the old timers still had LRRPs of chili con carne.

That LRRP was still despised, but the old timers grudgingly ate it, having saved it for last, knowing it would warm them. But White had saved a LRRP of spaghetti for something special. He wouldn't eat that one yet.

The word reached White that they would stop at the next convenient clearing to be re-supplied. He made his way, one at a time, to each man in his squad. He passed the word to be prepared, when they stopped, to help in clearing the L.Z.

An hour later they came across a bomb blasted, acre-sized opening in the trees. The company formed perimeter with White and Lopez's platoons joined in the line. Both comrades were tense. Both were nervous for the same reason. Lopez was very short.

White looked into the taut, twisted face of his friend. He searched frantically for something to say that could help. Finally, he said, "Did you get any sleep last night?"

Lopez's bloodshot eyes spoke for themselves, but in a barely perceptible answer, he shook his head no.

White had saved the LRRP especially for this. "I'll make chow," he said as he began heating water on his and Lopez's stoves. "Just try to rest a little, Roberto."

"Can't res," said Lopez. "Got to keep goin."

"But you got to get some sleep," said White. "You can't go on like this."

"I know," said Lopez. "I try, but I jus' can't sleep."

White looked across at Lopez as the water began to boil. He had warmed a can of pork slices from a C-ration can and cut the meat into pieces to add to the LRRP spaghetti. He toasted crackers and cheese and opened a can of peaches. He searched for pound cake, but all he had left was prune cake. He hoped that it would do.

"O.K., Roberto," said White. "It's not as good as you make it, but try it out."

He watched as Lopez took a bite.

"Ess good," said Lopez. "Ah'm not hungry, but ess good."

White watched as Lopez slowly ate. He knew it was bad, very bad, when Lopez didn't want to eat. He watched as Lopez forced down what White knew was his favorite meal in the sticks.

"Not hungry," said Lopez, looking up.

"Try a little more," said White. "Not all if you can't, but a little more."

"O.K.," said Lopez. "I jus' don' feel like eatin'."

Lopez finished the meal. Now he sat back against the tree and sipped at the hot chocolate. His eyes bulged out, the whites in them a color of sickly yellow.

"Let me take your guard tonight," said White. Before Lopez could answer, both looked toward the command post and saw Lieutenant Zigler approaching.

White's heart leapt. His gut twisted, but Lopez only stared out into the forest. Then the lieutenant was before them. He squatted down and gently said to Lopez, "Get ready. Your replacement's on the bird."

All thoughts of food, monsoon, and even N.V.A., disappeared. A great void attacked every fiber of White's being. The two comrades sat there. Neither could move nor speak. They sat, zombie-like, in the wet mud.

White wanted to say something, anything that would ease the strain and tension. He looked into the bulging, bloodshot eyes of his first teacher. Finally, he forced something out. "It's all right now, Roberto. It's all right."

White was dragged out of the depressing mood by the sound of approaching helicopters. He jumped up and ordered two of the newcomers in his squad to help unload the bird. He then looked down on a still-dazed Lopez.

"Roberto," he said, as he stretched out his hand to help his comrade up. "Let's go."

Lopez took his hand and rose to his feet. No words were adequate. Both stared at each other. Then they turned and walked to the now landing helicopter.

The crew of the Huey shoved out boxes of food and supplies. Men hurriedly carried cases away from the bird. The blades whirled, the motor whined, and leaves and branches flew. But White and Lopez neither heard the noise nor felt the wind and rain.

Lopez sat in the helicopter door. White stood looking at him until he was forced back by the whirling blades.

Lopez could only sit there, looking out at White. White stood dumb—numb—in the blast of the wind. He wanted to say goodbye. He desperately searched for something to say, to yell, to scream. But no words came. No words... No words.

CHAPTER XXVII

Time seemed as blurred to White as the mist-covered mountain around him. It had taken the company five more days to make their way out of the sticks to a base camp in the flatlands. He went through the routine of shots, changing clothes, showers, and tent assignments. He received orders from his platoon leader and made the round of his squad, giving instructions of their duty for the following few days.

When done with all his duties, he left the company area and made his way to the main gate. It was easy to get a ride in a truck going toward Hué. None of the guards at the bunker near the gate got out into the rain even to check papers. Everything was easier now. Humping, monsoon, hunger–everything physical—was easier. But digging its claws into him was a depression that a few months before he would not have believed existed.

All of his close friends were gone. Hahn, Hong, Cook, Jackson, Cloud, Smith. Maybe Louis. All dead. Some of his other friends had been killed or wounded, ripped and blasted to pieces, splattered beyond recognition. One comrade from third platoon—he couldn't remember his name—had suddenly collapsed in a skirmish with N.V.A. They hadn't been able to find a wound on him until someone brushed the hair back from his ear. A tiny split in the skin of his scalp a quarter of an inch long, showed where a steel splinter had entered his brain. The life had been instantly snuffed out of him with that small wound. He hadn't even jerked in spasms. Not even a drop of blood.

Boudreaux should be home now. But he, too, could have been killed before leaving Nam. A part of White's mind said, "No. He made it." Another part, the one that knew that "fair" didn't exist, knew that

Boudreaux, too, could be dead.

Now Lopez was gone, mighty Lopez, on his way back to the world. But a doubt dug its claws into White's mind. Did Lopez make it back home safely? It wasn't only in the sticks that people got killed in Nam. He could have been killed as soon as the helicopter was out of sight.

The driver, not even pretending friendliness, didn't even look at White or talk to him. That suited White just fine. He wasn't sure that he could have answered back. He stared at the brush on the side of the road, for the moment not even caring that he was out of the rain. The truck swayed around another curve and entered the highway to Hué.

He was going to The Green Doors for the first time since Boudreaux went home. The truck let him out in the middle of town. He began walking, ankle deep in rainwater, through the mostly deserted streets. He passed restaurants that were empty of customers. The only movement in them was waiters sitting, playing cards. Inside some of the stores were shop keepers who used slow business time to inventory and stack their wares.

As he walked alone in the flooded streets, he thought about how he was going to tell Linh that Boudreaux had gone home. She knew he was short but now he was really gone. How would he make her understand? He spoke neither Vietnamese nor French, and she didn't speak any English.

How would she take the news, even if he could make her understand what he wanted to say? But he knew that telling her was the easy part. She would know as well as he what could happen to any of them at any time.

His uneasiness grew when, from a block away, he saw the open shutters of The Green Doors. It got worse when he saw a face appear at the window and knew that it was Linh. She saw him.

She opened the door and stared at him, her face a mask of questions and fear. He could read her silent questions. "Where is Boudreaux? Is he O.K.? Is he dead?"

Slowly, trying to make him understand, she asked him questions in French. White stepped out of the rain and shook his head no. With his palm facing down, he lifted his arm to show a plane taking off and said, "Pierre. 'La maison'."

A quick look of relief flooded her eyes. But, almost as quick, the pain was back in them. Suddenly, she seemed so old, so beaten. She knew that she would never see Boudreaux again. He remembered what Boudreaux had told him once about how he felt about Linh. It wasn't that kind of love, one of a lover to a beloved. It was different. It was a man-woman friendship, one that had set White an example to be remembered.

White wanted to hold her. He wanted to comfort her. But he just stood there, afraid to move, afraid to say anything more. Linh smiled weakly and led him to the dining table. Helping him to remove his poncho, she made him sit. She said something he didn't understand and walked into the closed in section of the kitchen.

White sat there dripping, eyes red as fire. For the first time he knew completely what Boudreaux had seen in her. Her humanity went far beyond what poor human eyes could see.

After a few minutes she returned from the kitchen with a bowl of steaming soup. She tried to smile, but it just wouldn't come. It was the most miserable-looking expression White had ever seen. She tried one more time; her eyes squinted into slits, but she still couldn't smile. When her lips began to quiver at the corners, she covered her face with her hands and ran out of the kitchen into one of the other rooms.

White sat there for a long time. Forcing himself, he began eating the soup. He had just finished when the door that Linh had gone into opened, and Zahn came out into the patio. Her face was twisted, drawn in worry. She pointed with her head to the door she had just left as she said something in Vietnamese.

The only word White understood was Linh, but he knew what she had said. He nodded his head "yes" as she came next to him. She stroked his hair as she talked, trying to make him understand. Then she sat on his wet lap and cooed at him, still stroking his hair.

It was too much for him to take. He gently pushed her off and stood up. When she saw him putting on his poncho, she went into a hysterical spouting of words. She pointed to the rain and his wet clothes. He understood. She wanted him at least to stay and get dry.

But he couldn't stay. He dug into his wallet and tried giving her all the money he had. She looked at him with a hurt face and eyes full of tears. She wouldn't take the money. She screamed when he tried to make her take it.

White walked to the door, Zahn following him. He stepped into the rain and stopped at the bottom of the stairs. He turned once more to look at her. She looked at him, said something in Vietnamese, and then, as if pulling the words out from the bottom of her soul, said, "I lovee you too much."

White turned around and walked out into the pouring rain.

The university, too, was flooded. White stood in a puddle of water under a mango tree, across the street from the main building. The rain kept falling. Dead, water-laden leaves blown by the wind clung to his helmet and clothes.

A few steps and he could be out of the rain. Still, he hesitated. He was afraid. How could he face the Professor? There was no hiding from someone like him. He would see White's inner soul.

Still, something tugged at him, and he knew he had to see the professor again. He crossed the street, climbed the stairs, and stood before his open door.

The wise old man seemed to know instantly that he was under great stress. He walked to White and extended his hand. "It is very good to see you," he said as they shook hands. "I hope you are well," he went on. "But I can see that something is troubling you greatly."

White stood looking at him. He didn't know how to tell of the storm raging in him. But he saw in the professor's face that he understood. He saw, too, a genuine concern for him, and he felt better just seeing that.

"I don't know, sir," said White, forcing himself to speak. "Everything's so bad. It's like everything's coming apart." He paused as a shiver of cold went through him. "Maybe I'm just not strong enough," he said. "Maybe it's just too much or nothing really matters."

"Is it Boudreaux?" asked the professor. "Is he dead?"

"No," said White. "He went home a few days ago."

"Thank God," said the Professor.

As he looked at White, he clearly saw the depression in the young American and knew he was suffering terribly. The professor knew he was desperate, reaching out for anything to keep afloat. He paused as if to choose his next words carefully.

"It is very difficult, sometimes, to be a human being," said the Professor. "But if we remember the things which have made living a magnificent experience, perhaps it will help us to accept the things that are most terrible."

"Tell me," he went on, "would it have been better for you never to have known Boudreaux or your other friends?"

White couldn't answer. He looked down at the professor as he went on.

"Are you richer or poorer for knowing them?"

White didn't understand all of it, but he knew that what the professor was saying was helping him, and he gave it all his attention.

He led White by his elbow to a wooden chair next to his desk. Then he sat and looked at him for almost a minute. White felt his tension ease as he looked into the understanding eyes of the professor. He saw tenderness in those old eyes that went beyond nationality, race… time. He saw an understanding that transcended intelligence.

"Do you think, Mr. White, that the world is an accident?" he said at last.

White sat as if in shock, trying to get control of his frayed nerves. Again, the professor sat silent. Then he stood and grasped White by the elbow again and lifted him up. In his strangely soothing accent he said, "Perhaps you could join me for lunch." Holding onto White's arm, he led him to the school's cafeteria.

The strong odor of *nuoc mam* from the kitchen drifted through the dining room. The professor chose a table, and the two men sat down. White's mind was so clear when he was with the professor. He was aware that everyone in the room knew of their presence. No one was looking at them, but he knew that they all had seen the professor, and all were paying him the honor of "not seeing him".

White saw himself slipping again. Now that sense of clarity, instead of relieving him, depressed him more. His thoughts drifted back into the jungle.

Each time in the field, the killing sank him deeper into despair. Every step he took in becoming a veteran took something else out of him. He felt that his personality, his own true self, was becoming as ragged as his torn boots. It was as if a new skill or idea could not be born without killing one that was previously there. He didn't want to lose precious memories of family and home, but every day he found them fading.

The professor was indeed a wise man. Some claimed he was clairvoyant, but White knew he wasn't. He knew, however, that the professor had a deep understanding of people. He looked at the young man across from him, thought carefully, and said, "Are you a Christian, Mr. White?"

His tone had changed. He tried to add inflections and mood in his usually bland, but precise, English. He did amazingly well, but sometimes the rises and falls of the sentence were at the wrong places. With anyone else, stresses at the wrong places would seem comical. But, with the professor, it was done in what could only be described as great dignity.

"Yes," said White. "I guess I am."

"There are many things that I admire about Christianity and many more things I admire about true Christians." He paused, taking a sip of tea. Then, as if measuring every word, said, "I myself am Buddhist, but I have studied the major, and even many of the minor, religions of the world."

"They all have certain things in common. Each considers they have exclusive revelations of the Divine. Each has lists of commandments, must and must not do's, and conformities to their 'true' religion. But behind the dogma in most is the solid foundation of love. All other things take their respective, orderly places if this one condition is met."

He waited while a waiter, with a slight bow, placed a half loaf of French bread and two bowls of noodle soup before them. Next to each bowl he placed a plastic spoon and a set of chopsticks.

"Do you mind if I ask you a somewhat obvious question?" said the professor when the waiter left.

"Ask me anything you want, Sir," said White.

"In the deep jungle, traversed continually by North Vietnamese and possible Chinese forces, do you sometimes come to trails?"

"Yes," said White.

"When finding these trails, do you follow them, knowing that walking on them is much easier than through the jungle itself?"

"No, Professor," said White. "There are usually traps near trails, and we always try to stay away from them."

"Are you familiar with the words in your Christian Bible that say, I cannot quote it, 'difficult is the road leading to salvation and easy the road that leads to doom'?"

"Yes, Professor," said White.

The elder leaned back in his chair and for a minute seemed lost, searching for something which would help the boy. Then he turned his attention once more to the soldier in front of him.

"It is very clear that the early Christians suffered greatly for their religion. Through both Christian and Roman histories come stories of atrocities inflicted on them. Every abuse was done to them, but one that stands out is that of the Romans sending them into the arena full of starving and raging lions."

He paused for a moment and then went on. "Knowing their fate, the Christians waited behind the wooden doors of the dungeons. Families clung together. Old people and lovers embraced. If any group saw someone alone, they would take them into their own group."

He stopped as he soaked a piece of bread into the soup. He swirled the bread in the bowl, hypnotically, then went on. "Surely, this must have been the depths of despair: to know that shortly your spouse and children would be ripped to death and eaten by lions. But in the midst of death surrounding them, hearing the roar of the lions and the more savage roar of the crowd, the Christians began to sing. When the doors opened, the soldiers had no need to prod them out with their spears. They walked out boldly, singing to the lions."

White sat in deep thought, looking intently at the glowing man opposite him. The professor began again.

"That is another great truth of every real religion. Sometimes it is the easy trail that is fatal to your soul and the difficult one that leads eventually to inner peace. If one is truly religious and has lived a life worthy of a human being, when the time comes to leave this world, he can step into the next singing to the lions."

CHAPTER XXVIII

Three months had passed since the monsoon began in the mountains. The rains had caused vast flooding that washed away huge chunks of earth from the bomb-blasted clearings in the face of the jungle. Boulders stood exposed, free of layers of dead leaves, with the constant washing by the rain. Giant trees lay hunched over or leaned against other trees. Their wide and shallow roots uncovered by the floods were no longer able to hold them up.

It had not rained in two days, but the thick, misty air covered the jungle with a bleak, cold fog. The drenched leaves at the higher levels of the standing trees dripped their contents to the already heavily laden leaves below them, causing large drops to fall. Some of these drops struck the poncho hooches on the jungle floor with a deep thud.

It was rare for the company to stay more than one night at any one place, but the humping had been hard and supplies were low. Chances were slim that they could be found by roving N.V.A. The captain had decided two days before to stop and wait for the birds.

They had set up perimeter in the trees surrounding a bomb-blasted clearing and were to be resupplied that morning with food, ammo, and replacements. White looked around him to the men in the company. A few of the soldiers were nearly dry and the soldiers could easily be ranked by the dryness of their clothes and boots.

Superficialities like rank, race, body size, family trees, educational backgrounds, and religion, no longer applied. Those things White now saw for what they really were. Those social standings were now too absurd to consider.

The greenest replacements, not having as yet learned how to stay relatively dry, shivered, still wet, inside of their ponchos and liners. The intermediates in the company were, except for soggy boots, dry. The old timers were completely dry under their high-sided shelter.

The men in White's squad, all new, sat on the cold, wet earth. They had wrapped themselves in their ponchos and liners, covering their heads. They pinched the sides of the ponchos at the eyes, leaving a gap to peek through. From that slit they nervously watched him, their grim, intense, squad leader.

White had set his hooch so high that he could have almost stood under it. He had piled branches, sticks, and leaves six inches thick on the earth under him. This had left him with a very lumpy bed, but his body would never have to touch the cold, muddy ground.

At his feet was a flat rock slab a foot wide and a foot across. On the top of the slab, he had a small fire going. When the flame seemed about to die, he tossed one-inch squares of C-4 into the burning embers. When it caught, the plastic explosives whooshed into a strong, brilliant blaze that warmed everything within a few feet.

He had stuck sticks into the ground. On one of them he dried one of his boots, bottom up near the blaze. The other he had on, already dried. Hanging behind him, his poncho liner acted as a wall, keeping the heat in. He sometimes added pencil-size sticks to the flame. In minutes the wet sticks were dry and would burn evenly.

He frequently scanned the trees and brush. When his head turned to each side, his eyes would fall on his men. They seemed so helpless. A few had made an attempt at a good hooch and tried to stay as dry as possible. But the newest replacements had merely made a clumsy roof and sat or lay on the ground, shaking.

White thought it was indeed a pitiful sight, but what dug deeper into his conscience was that he now felt very little sympathy for them. He was becoming as insensitive to pity as he was to compassion, love, hate, and any other feeling. His emotions, his humanism, were becoming as numb as a recruit's buttocks after sitting on the earth for too long. Every day he could see something inside of him, some ambition, and desire, or goal, die. Now his main concern, his ultimate reality, was dry socks and boots.

He waited in the oppressive mist, still reading the replacements.

He knew they wished feverishly, and some prayed, that the helicopters coming to re-supply them would take them from the cold, watery misery they were in. But he knew better. There was more humping ahead. More humping, more cold, more wetness; and maybe death.

That was the pattern, either hothouse heat or shivering, wet cold. Wet from sweat or wet from rain…always wet. Humping. Boils and cysts. Pleurisies. Killings and mutilations. Recruits in and out. In the sticks for maybe weeks, on stand-down for a few days.

The company was to go in soon. Only two small skirmishes this time out. Two killed, eighteen wounded. But it wasn't over yet. It could happen again at any time. Then more replacements—or maybe this time it would all be over for him.

He thought that maybe if some of his friends were there it would be different. Everything seemed so much easier to take, so much easier to endure, when he had had them around him. But they were all gone. In their place was an emptiness that was being slowly filled by something that he couldn't name—something that frightened him more than death. Gloom and doom was all he saw. Gloom, doom and wet boots.

They "made it in" and were set up in the center of a large base camp. When coming out of the bush, they were usually brought to an area where they could pull guard around a perimeter or gun battery while they rested. But this time they were set up near an administration area and had no duties. That was a bit of luck. They wouldn't spend their rest time sitting in a muddy hole in the rain, surrounding a perimeter.

The rear echelon soldiers stared at the grunts. They whispered to each other as they sat in small groups in the mess tent, eyeing the sullen infantrymen. Administration, mess, laundry, and motor pool officers winced outwardly when encountering grunts and getting neither salute, attention, nor notice.

E-7's, E-8's, and first sergeants, accustomed to quick obedience, frowned quietly as they passed idle grunts. They sometimes showed displeasure to the frightened newcomers but went quickly past the intense, hostile veterans. These sergeants knew how eighteen-and nineteen-year-olds got to be squad leaders and how twenty and twenty-one-year-olds got to be E-6, in the infantry.

The company's tents were set up next to the living quarters of rear echelon company clerks. White lay on his cot. What was left of his platoon were either sleeping, or quietly talking and writing letters by dim lights. It was dark outside. The rain had started again, and the gloom inside the tent was nearly as thick as the oppressive rain and air outside.

All of the replacements, and even some of the veterans, had been lulled into thinking that here, in the rear, there was no danger. They were safe in the center of a base camp. There was nothing to fear except the stares of the rear echelon soldiers around them.

Suddenly, the most experienced of the soldiers picked up their heads. White sprang to his feet and shouted at the top of his lungs. "Get to the bunkers."

In the scramble for the door flaps, above the sound of shuffling feet and flapping canvas, came the high pitched whistle of incoming rounds. The company ran for the protection of the bunkers, forty yards away. They raced in the dark as the shrill screech of the rocket came nearer.

Then White threw himself head first onto the ground. His squad followed his example and were soon all facedown in the mud. An explosion erupted a hundred yards past them. White looked up to see two rear echelon soldiers standing above him. Each reached down and grabbed one of his arms and helped him up.

"That one's way off, sarge," said one of the soldiers. "But there's sure to be more. Come with us."

The two clerks led the grunts in a quick sprint to the bunker and then inside. Everyone sat on the dry, dirt edge. White sat, plastered with wet mud, between the two soldiers that had lifted him up. He looked from one to the other to see them smiling –friendly—at him. He was struck dumb, numbed by the surprise of seeing rear echelon soldiers that didn't look at him like he was something strange—a murderer. Then another whistling sound came toward them. It came closer and closer. The grunts wanted to hug the bottom of the bunker but looked on in awe at the two calm rear echelon soldiers.

"Naw," said one of them. "Way to the right."

"Fuckers can't hit shit," said the other.

They were so calm that White and the other grunts began to feel more at ease. He felt instinctively that these two men knew exactly what they were saying. They were pros when it came to incoming. Still, the grunts were unused to rockets and mortars, and they stared admiringly at the two soldiers.

"Looks like they're trying for the ammo dump," said the first clerk.

Then a series of whistles began overhead. Explosion followed explosion as the rockets found the range and adjusted their fire toward the ammo dump.

Boonie rats trembled, their wild eyes shifting from each other to the unworried typists. Suddenly, the two soldiers looked anxious. One said, "This one will be close."

The whistle became louder and louder. White thought the rocket would land directly on them. His heart pounded frantically against his chest while hugging the earth, desperately trying to force his body deeper. Infantrymen who could stay cool under rifle fire and grenades looked with awe and admiration at the cool rear echelon soldiers.

An explosion twenty yards away shook the bunker. One of the men said, "That one fell short."

"Yeah," laughed the other. "Oh, well," he went on. "They say you'll never hear the one that gets you."

White looked at the two smiling men. For the first time in country he clearly recognized and could name one of the things he saw in the faces of the camp soldiers when they looked at a grunt. So plain, so evident to him now, he recognized the look as pity.

This jolted him into a new perspective. At the first chance to help a fellow soldier, these two had jumped at it. There had been no hesitation on their part. They had purposely delayed reaching the safety of the bunker to help him up.

Their calmness had taken off some of the strain. Their deliberate, patient manner had taught him more than just how to judge incoming rockets.

White fumbled in his mind for something to say. He searched for anything to say to show these two soldiers appreciation and a bond with him and the other grunts. Finally, in a slightly quivering voice, he asked, "Get hit like this a lot?"

"Almost every night," said one. "You get to know pretty much where they're gonna land after a while. Sons of bitches just won't let us get any sleep."

"Yeah," said the other. "But this ain't nothing compared with what you guys go through. It must be a real bitch living out in the boonies. I don't know how you guys can do it."

"Yeah," said the other. "This shit is bad enough. But you guys are always in the shit."

"This looks like deep enough shit to me," said a voice in the dark.

"Yeah," said another grunt. "You can keep this shit. I want back to the bush where I can at least sleep at night."

"Yeah," said the first. "At least in the bush they're only trying to kill you. Here, they wantta murder you."

"Fucking assholes," said a shaking voice in the rear of the bunker.

Later that night, lying on his cot staring into the dark, White balanced in his mind the new perspective. He had not been as frightened for months as he had been in the rocket attack. Sheer helplessness had come into him at the approaching whistles. There was no fighting back, no struggle, and no defense. There was only the deadly whistle of the incoming rounds as they came closer and louder. There was just the terrible waiting for the incoming rockets. While the numbers of killed and wounded in the infantry were much higher than for units in the rear, it became clear that there was really no safe place in Nam.

He had lost some of his feeling of safety at being in a base camp, but he had gained something. Maybe for some of the rear echelon soldiers, the grunts were some sort of animal. But for most, the grunts were to be pitied, and, if possible, helped. White had learned another valuable lesson. He knew now that what separated the grunts from rear echelon was chance–fate–luck of the draw. It could have gone the other way. He could've been the clerk and they the boonie rats. Something more important than mere safety had occurred in the bunker. He had gained a new respect for the rocket-eating veterans in the camps.

Five days passed. For every night of those five days, the camp had been rocketed or mortared, or both. The grunts couldn't sleep well at night, knowing that at any time they could be forced to run to the bunkers, so many began, instead of napping, sleeping during the day.

White made the rounds of his squad and knew that almost nothing he said would help. Only their own will could maybe save them. Their own instinct, luck, karma, or intelligence would help them, but their own will was what could bring them through the year. Without that, they were lost.

He became more depressed as he looked into some of their frightened eyes and saw a desperate hopelessness. Even worse were the ones he saw that had a glimmer of hope but nothing else. No luck, no chance.

Something shook him from his depression when he saw the face of Lieutenant Zigler. The lieutenant had spotted White immediately as he opened the tent flap. White could see in an instant that Zigler had good news. He could also see that whatever it was, it would affect him, too.

Zigler walked slowly to White's cot. He stood in deep thought for a moment and then said, "We've got replacements coming." His smile broadened even more, and he said, "They'll be here in an hour."

White stared up at him. Something was going on, and whatever it was had Zigler to the point that he was almost laughing out loud. White could see the restraint on the lieutenant's face as he said, "Better get ready for this."

White couldn't imagine that anything could pull him back from the slump he was in. Still, he felt he should say something, so he said, "How many do you think we'll get?"

"Four, I think," said Zigler. "But you only got to worry about two of them."

More mystery. But why should he even be concerned about replacements? A twitch of curiosity wormed inside him.

"Why should I worry, Lieutenant?" White asked.

"Worry's not really the right word," said Zigler. "Hold on to your ass is what I really mean."

Whatever news he had, it was obvious that Zigler wanted it to be a surprise. White knew not to ask any more. Zigler wouldn't tell him if he were dying. But whatever it was, it had to be something special to make the lieutenant so happy. Zigler grinned down on White and then turned and left the tent.

It had taken months of hardship and the stress of combat to bring White to such a morbid state. He didn't think anything could have relieved him of the heavy weight he had been carrying within himself. But now he felt a faint stirring. The lieutenant was not excited for nothing. Something grew inside him again. He had thought that it was dead. But there it was again, that strange enigma—that uplifting feeling which keeps people from falling over the edge. Like a mustard seed, hope grew until he again dared to care.

No child ever waited as expectantly for Christmas morning as he waited in the tent. New recruits stared at him suspiciously as he paced the tent. Minutes seemed like hours as he listened through the rain for footsteps. Seconds dragged by while he waited anxiously. More minutes passed. He made the rounds of his squad, trying again to reach the green recruits. When he had finished with the last man, he sat on his cot and waited.

Then he heard a pair of footsteps outside the tent. When the flap sprang open, his jaw dropped. He was lifted up. He soared to a great height. Tons were lifted from him as he stared agape at what he saw. Throwing back the hoods of their wet ponchos were Jackson and Sam Cook.

The flap had not closed before White was up and across the room. He stood dumb before his two grinning comrades. Except for a pale, tired look, they seemed the same. Both looked boyish, mischievous, like they were hatching some prank.

"Bet you never thought you'd see us again," said Jackson. He paused to look at the three stripes on White's sleeve. "Huh, Sarge?"

In the slang of the times, anyone with rank above Corporal was labeled "lifer". Their life, their living, was the army. They were expected to pull twenty or more years. Cook knew that White would not stay in, but he couldn't resist the jab. He, too, looked at the stripes on White's sleeve.

"Fuck all lifers," said Sam Cook with a grin.

CHAPTER XXIX

It was true that war was a time of misery and misfortune, but now White knew it was also a time of great happiness, hope, and miracles. There were endless records of men living after being shot across the chest with machine gun bullets, of men having had mortar shells explode a few feet from them and not getting a scratch, and of men riddled with hot iron and recovering to live a normal life.

He realized these scenarios were, of course, the exceptions. More usual were the examples of death or mutilation. But most of the survivors he knew of close combat had a story similar to Jackson's and Cook's to tell. And, as the two comrades told their stories, the fantastic odds against their surviving stunned White to his ragged boots. As they talked, his imagination colored their words and added to them until he seemed to see it clearly in his mind.

"I'd been holding my guts in," said Jackson. "Man. That's some scary shit. Seeing your guts wanting to come out."

Jackson's abdominal cavity had been ripped open by a shredded bit of flying steel. It had caught him below his right ribs and neatly sliced open a ten-inch slit in his side. The shrapnel had not entered the intestines, shredding it to pieces, but it did make a gap big enough that he had to hold in his guts to keep them from spilling onto the jungle floor.

They got him to a field hospital, cleaned his wound and intestines, filled him with antibiotics, and did all they could in the limited conditions.

Then, something happened that was the dream of every front line soldier. In the scuffle and shuffle and the constant, desperate attempt to catch up with the increasing numbers of wounded, Jackson's medical papers ended up in the wrong stack. Instead of the usual "in country" hospital where most of the less seriously injured went, Jackson was transferred to a hospital in Japan.

Teams of international doctors and nurses stitched and glued what they could onto the wounded from Southeast Asia. Some of the staff was reduced to hacking and sawing off limbs, trying to save the lives of the mangled. But Jackson's wounds were simple. After stitching, all that was left was to watch for infections.

On arrival he immediately fell in love with several Japanese nurses. He joked with them, giving each a chance to practice their English.

"Man," he said. "I couldn't believe those fine Japanese *baby-sans*. You should hear how they talk. They all sound like those British chicks you see in the movies."

He winked at White and said. "But I made up my mind I'd show them how to talk proper English."

"No, no," he said boyishly. "It's not, 'How do you do?' It's 'What's happening?' " The nurses would practice as he urged them on.

He sometimes sang to them the latest popular songs from the States.

"Now, try this," said Jackson. "Sunshine, blue skies, please go away," he sang.

"Oh yes," said a nurse. "Otis Ledding."

"Yes, yes," laughed the others.

"Zone shine, blau skies, pleezy go away," sang the boldest.

"Yeah," said Jackson. "Now you got it."

He never complained and always cooperated with everything that the nurses and doctors wanted. In turn, they liked his easy manner and humor. Their already humane characters found it difficult not to take a personal interest in the young soldier. Also, it was a relief to see and deal with someone that was not seriously hurt.

But even Jackson's skill at mischievous, playful deceptions could not hide the fact that he was not badly wounded. He was well-liked, but everyone on the staff knew there were many wounded, all more seriously than he, needing attention. So it was with a genuine liking for him that the nurses and doctors, one by one, came to say goodbye.

Sam Cook had also had his miracle. The bullet had struck him center through the sternum. This was usually good for an instant or almost instant kill. But again, by whatever it is which decides the million-to-one odds, the bullet neatly passed through the bone, went through Cook's body without touching heart, lungs, blood vessels, or nerves, and exited between his ribs—two inches from his spine.

"When I opened my eyes, I knew I'd been hit bad," he said.

The shock of the bullet, and the fear that he had been shot through either the heart or lungs, kept Cook quiet when he awoke in the helicopter. He expected to die at any moment. He suddenly remembered Jackson. He turned to the side and saw Jackson's eyes on him.

"I was really surprised to see us both alive," said Cook.

"How are you, bro?" asked Cook through clenched teeth.

"Don't talk, bro," said Jackson. "You gonna be all right and me, too. But you got to stay still."

Neither said another word until the helicopter landed. They stared at each other as medics pulled them out of the chopper. Jackson tried to turn to see as Cook was put into an ambulance. Then they were rushed to different parts of the field hospital.

The doctors couldn't believe that Cook was still alive. They were even more surprised when they saw that the bullet had missed all of his important internal organs. It had, in fact, gone through him with the least possible damage.

But here, close to the front, doctors, nurses, and medics could not spare time for awe. They had seen many miracles. They saw miracles every day, so they shook off the uniqueness of this newest one, shuffled papers, and after two days sent Cook to another hospital.

Off the coast, in a hospital ship safe from the reach of rockets, teams of medical personnel worked around the clock, caring for the wounded. Apart from pain, Cook's biggest discomfort had been a queasy stomach from being on the ship. But for him it was a vacation. No humping, all the food and water he wanted, a clean bed to lie in, and air conditioning. That was the kind of war he liked.

"Yeah, man," he said. "That's what I like. Laying around not doing nothing."

He liked his nurse, and he liked the personal attention. He fantasized about her. He knew she was old enough to be his mother, but that's not how he thought of her. Neither did he think of her as an aunt nor as an older cousin. He thought of her sexually, longingly, as she came to check on him. In his mind she became twenty years younger and twenty pounds lighter as she walked past him.

"Can ya stay and talk awhile?" asked Cook.

"Well," she said, "I guess I can stay for a little while. How are you feeling, Sam?"

"Fine, Mona," said Cook. He reddened as he went on. "I've been wanting to ask you. Are you married or something? If you're not, maybe we could do something. You know, maybe go to see a movie or something?"

A sad look came to his face, and he said, "She was really special. You could tell she was careful how she talked to any of the guys that had been hit."

She had learned not to show distress while working on the mutilated soldiers. She knew that one wrong look could hurt them as much as their wounds. Because of that, she was able not to show the shock she felt when she realized what Cook's questions were leading to. Her heart felt as if it was being torn from her chest as she smiled down warmly at Cook.

"I was married, Sam," she said. "But my husband died a year ago."

"Oh," said Cook, "I'm sorry."

Cook thought about it for a minute and then said, "Well, I guess you're still feeling bad about that, huh?"

"Yes, Sam," she said. "It's still very hard."

"Maybe it would help if you started dating again," said Cook.

"No, Sam," she said. "He was the only one for me. I'll never have that again."

"But maybe it would help you," said Cook.

"No, Sam," she said. "That's all over for me. But don't feel too bad. I've had what everyone wants but what few people ever find. I wouldn't have had it any other way."

"Oh," said Cook.

"Now, Sam," she said while smiling brightly at him. "You're keeping me from my work. I'll stop by later, and we can talk again. O.K.?"

"Sure," said Cook frowning. "I hope I didn't make you sad."

"No, Sam," she said. "You've made my day."

She beamed at him and held her smile until she turned the corner. As she turned, Cook saw her cover her eyes with both hands and cry like a baby.

Cook said that on the ship, too, the staff was always overworked. They, too, did not like to send the young boys back into the grinder, but they knew many more soldiers needed help. Sam healed quickly, and they knew it.

So, it was with an incredible smile that Mona walked to his bedside and said, "Well, Sam. We can't make you any better here."

"Got my papers, huh?" asked Cook.

"Yes. You're being transferred to a hospital in country," she said.

"Well, Mona," he said, "Thanks for everything. I hope you all the best."

"Thank you," she said. "But, Sam. You've got to take care of yourself out there. Please be careful, Sam."

"Oh, I will," said Cook. "I'm a pretty careful guy, you know."

Mona leaned over the bed and, as tenderly as she could, kissed him on the forehead. She tried valiantly but couldn't hide the tears. She fled across the hall, stopped at the entrance to the next ward, and fought for control. Finally, she got hold of herself, smiled brightly, and went into the ward. She walked to the bed of a young soldier who had lost a leg and an eye.

"I tell you, guys. That's the saddest shit I've ever seen."

To complete the two miracles, the comrades found themselves together again at the Cam Rahn Bay Hospital. That was the best medicine. Seeing each other was the best cure. They begged and complained to the head doctor until they were given beds next to each other.

They relived their experiences in the other hospitals. But in the telling of the stories, the Japanese nurses fought to see who would give Jackson his bath and Cook's nurse could have replaced Raquel Welch on the Bob Hope Christmas Tour.

Weeks went by. They plotted late into the night on how to stay in the hospital longer. They mischievously schemed against the staff, delaying decisions to send them back to the field. But they were so vibrant, so alive, that they could no longer fool anyone. They had to go. Still, the medical staff knew the youngsters were great friends and waited to send them off together to the staging areas.

Here they managed five more days of R&R by bribing every clerk in reach that shuffled papers and pounded a typewriter.

"Man," said Cook. "Those guys in the rear got it made. All they do all day is stay high."

"Yeah," said Jackson. "But me and bro know how to deal."

Ready-roll joints, quarts of Jack Daniels, and cases of Coca-Cola appeared as if by magic in the easily bribed clerks' lockers. Cartons of their favorite cigarettes, cases of beer, and cans of peaches and fruit cocktail mysteriously appeared under clerks' beds. Finally, the two were no longer able to escape the inevitable and were sent back to the company.

Whether to someone's great credit and foresight or to an unthinking accident of policy, most of the wounded soldiers who could be sent back to the field when recovered, were sent back to their original companies. The effect of it was twofold. On Cook and Jackson's part, if they had to go back, it was infinitely better to go back to where one would find old comrades. On White's part, an incredible weight seemed lifted from him as he was reunited with his friends. It felt to him that not only were his two comrades resurrected but that he, too, had been brought back from the near dead. So, long into the night, in voices lower than a whisper, the three comrades told their stories.

Second and third platoons had been thinned out of almost all their old timers, and the company needed to spread out its veterans. White would have liked to stay with Jackson and Cook, but an inner intuition, a warning, told him it was better that they split up. That way there was less chance all three would "get it" at the same time. Sam Cook went to second platoon and Jackson to third. Both went as squad leaders.

Joy had been pulled back into White's heart. Since Jackson and Cook's arrival, he seemed injected with new life. His face had lost that deep, depressed look and now almost shone with normal, rigid control.

He made his rounds to each man in his squad, trying to teach them. He showed them little tricks to help make the upcoming ordeal less painful for them. He checked their equipment, trimming down the extra weight. He spent extra time with the recon sergeant and R.T.O., learning more about maps and coordinates. He went about his duties almost cheerfully.

But behind the newfound hope was a dreadful wall that seemed impenetrable by anything. This hard wall he had unknowingly put up himself, stone by stone, day by day, month by month, until now it was an unbreakable barrier nothing could penetrate. It was colder and harder than steel. It was thicker than the walls of old city Hué. But there was a disturbing hairline crack on its front. Like the push of water on a dam, it threatened to burst.

Mercifully, only a well-hidden, unconscious part of White's mind knew about the wall. The rest of it went about his business with a conscious aloofness, always careful not to get personally involved with the newcomers.

Whenever they could, the three friends spent time together in one or the other's platoon tent. Mostly they just sat or lay back, silent, content in each other's company.

And then the dreaded day came. The new first sergeant stepped into the tent. The three comrades did not need to be told. They looked at the first shirt as one would look at Typhoid Mary. They knew what his presence meant. They knew before he opened his mouth that they were going back to A Shau.

Needing to confirm it, White looked at each of his comrades. He saw the same dread he felt as he asked, "A Shau?"

The pale, lean first shirt nodded as he said, "Tomorrow. Eight o'clock. We'll be going in with two battalions. Got Second Brigade on the way to the north end of the valley. They gonna be waiting for us to push the N.V.A. to them or stop any reinforcements from coming in."

"Don't those generals know yet that all their plans are bullshit?" said Jackson.

"Those mudda fuckers don't know shit," said Cook. "All they're good for is picking their asses."

"Not there," thought White. Just when he had begun to feel good again, when he had found his friends again, the valley loomed before him.

And now he knew why A Shau was so bad. Anywhere else, he and many more could be killed. But in the valley they could all be killed— wiped out to the last man. That seemed much worse. It shouldn't matter if he was already dead, but somehow it did. That possibility ate at him, and he was suddenly speechless.

The three friends sat quietly, unable to talk and barely able to look at each other. It was after midnight before the three comrades went to their cots, and even with the scant sleep White awoke well before sunup. He got up and walked to the mess tent, finding Jackson and Cook already there.

They sat, not talking, as they sipped coffee. White knew that Cook and Jackson must be thinking the same thing as he was. Helicopter assault into A Shau. Two battalions. That meant lots of helicopters and lots of targets for N.V.A. gunners. Lots of Russian and Chinese missiles and rockets trying to shoot them down. Lots of N.V.A. infantry waiting on the ground for the ships that made it through.

Too soon it was time to get their squads ready. Then it was to the muster station to wait and board their wave. White looked through the rain to see Jackson and Cook sitting in the mud as they, too, looked at him and to each other.

Soldiers from the two battalions were scattered over a wide area, waiting in the rain when the helicopters began arriving. There were enough choppers to move half a battalion at once. White's company was somewhere close to the middle of the wave and he could see ten or more choppers on his side as they flew in loose formation.

The first miles seemed routine, but as they approached the mountains the soldiers became tenser. Some began to shiver from fear instead of the cold, wet wind. Suddenly, streaks of smoke from the ground, tails left from Russian rockets, flashed by several of the helicopters. One of the birds was hit; but the pilot kept control, turned and headed back toward the base.

Another was hit but couldn't keep control. Swirling violently, it plunged downward in a whirlwind, toward the jungle below. White heard a whooshing sound as a grey streak flew past his helicopter.

Now the pilots showed what they could do. Diving and swerving, zigging and zagging, almost all were able to make a landing in the grassy glades outside the valley. The helicopters hadn't touched down before all of the soldiers had exited and were running for the safety of the trees. As they ran they could hear mortar rounds landing in the glades.

Inside the trees, out of breath and pulling for air, White was relieved to see both Cook and Jackson huddled with their squads. Following whatever orders the captain had been given, the company moved forward quickly to put distance between them and the mortar rounds that were beginning to land in the woods.

White's company and the two American battalions stumbled toward those defenses. They slipped and tripped, sometimes sliding back a foot for every foot forward in the slick, pale mud beneath the leaves.

The rain had changed from a dull, cold sprinkle to a violent downpour. The soldiers trudged on deeper and higher through the dense forest floor that constantly angled slowly upward toward the ridges and mountains that surrounded A Shau.

At noon the company stopped. Most of the soldiers sat shivering in the downpour, eating cold LRRPs, too exhausted to build a hooch and heat water. But White, Jackson, and Cook, always managing things so their squads were nearest to each other at breaks and at night, joined two ponchos and crawled under them.

"When is this shit going to stop?" said White, looking out into the rain.

"Maybe another month," said Jackson, shivering.

"It's gonna stop for me in two more months," said Cook.

"Lucky short muddafucker," said Jackson. "But I'll be pushing you when you go because I'll be almost gone, too."

"You guys are both lucky," said White. "I'm not even counting."

"Don't worry," said Jackson. "Your time will come."

"Yeah," said Cook. "Anybody that can put up with Smith's shit like you did gotta be a bad muther."

"He wasn't so bad," said White.

"What he needed was a little boom-boom," said Jackson.

"He'd of had to pay her State-side prices," said Cook.

"Yeah," said Jackson. "She'd have ta been crazy, too."

While their hands warmed near the blue flame, the conversation changed.

"I'm gonna look up this girl I know when I get back to the world," said Cook.

"I'm gonna try to get in with my sister's friend," said Jackson. "Couldn't when I was home. Too young. But she'll be ready for 'The Kid' when I get back."

"Yeah," said Cook. "Ready to take all your bread and steal your car."

"Fuck you," said Jackson. "What you know about women you can stuff up a mosquito's ass."

"What about you?" asked Cook turning to White. "You got any girl back home?"

"Not anymore," said White. "I had a girlfriend, but she went to college after graduation." He stopped and thought, then went on, "Maybe I'll look her up when I get back."

"You'll find her, all right," said Cook. "You gonna do all right, bro. Just gotta get this shit out of your head."

"Yeah. You got a lot better chance than bro' here," said Jackson, jerking a thumb at Cook.

"Fuck you," said Sam Cook.

As they sipped the hot cocoa, Cook dug into the top pocket of his soaked shirt and came out with a clear, plastic bag. The other two soldiers watched while Cook unfolded the bag. Dry and unbroken were three long, unfiltered Pall Mall cigarettes and a book of paper matches. They each lit a cigarette and inhaled the strong smoke. Jackson smiled as he exhaled and said, "Now, that's perfect."

He paused a moment and then went on. "Y'all know, it's my birthday today, and this sure is a nice present."

Cook and White looked up and saw the grin on Jackson's face. His white teeth gleamed against his chocolate colored skin. First Cook, and then White, lost for words that would tell Jackson what they fully wished for him, said, "Happy fucking birthday."

On that day, twenty years before, Jackson had entered the world.

CHAPTER XXX

After the noon break, the company moved on. The weather improved from a downpour to a hard rain. The terrain changed so that a decision had to be made. Intersecting the normal, thick brush on the forest floor was a growth of extremely thick bush. It seemed a solid wall of vegetation. Thorns and other snags were so thick that, if entering it, the company would slow down to a crawl.

It would be so difficult to go through, choosing it could maybe give the company a chance to elude the enemy and come out somewhere they didn't expect. It was so thick a sniper could not see a target beyond two or three feet, and so overgrown in thorns they figured American soldiers would more likely find it easier going another way.

Also, the heavy foliage, stunted tree growth, and vines absorbed much of the impact of any explosive trap N.V.A. could set, offsetting potential damage to American infantry. All of these were good reasons why the captain decided this was the way to go. A quick call to division headquarters, coordinating his movements with the other companies, confirmed his decision to take the hard way through the almost impenetrable brush. All of the old-timers felt good about the decision, but it would be exhausting, bloody work for the first men at the point. Every foot of jungle, every step taken, had to be hacked out of living jungle.

Three men with machetes led the way. The first man in line cleared just enough of the brush to be able to advance. The two men behind him, one on each side, cleared their sides and top until a tunnel was dug through the heavy growth.

Even with ponchos on, the merciless thorns tore at the soldiers.

They ripped the strong material of the ponchos to get to the cloth of the soldiers' jungle fatigues and then to the flesh of their arms and legs. Vines that had not been cut out by the men at point ripped the faces of the men further back, threatening to gouge out their eyes.

Every few minutes the three at the front were changed. They walked to the rear of their squad, scratched and bleeding, as rain washed the blood to the mud below. Three more men would take their place and begin hacking their way through.

When each squad in the platoon had taken a turn at the front, another platoon took its place. White looked at each man in third platoon as they squeezed by him on their way to the rear of the column.

As Jackson came up to White, he stopped. His face was scratched at a dozen places. His hands dripped blood onto his rifle. He looked exhausted as he looked at White and said, "Man. That's the worst shit I ever seen."

"It'll be better at the back," said White. "The ground'll be sloppy, but you won't have to fight the wait-a-minutes."

Rotation to the point continued until it was White's platoon's turn. He walked to point and took the machete from an exhausted Cook. "We'll take it now, bro," he said. "Let's get together tonight. Me, you, and Jackson. I've got extra chocolate and four cans of pound cake."

"O.K.," said Cook. "If we can swing it."

White took first turn on the machete at point. It was an unbelievable mass of plants. Every swing with the machete, every move in any direction, and he was snagged by thorns or cut by sharp-edged blades of jungle grass. His legs below the poncho were being scratched bloody. After twenty minutes he had enough. He handed the machete to the man behind him and moved to the back of the squad.

The humping was much easier eight men back from point. The hardest part of the tunnel had already been cleared, and now only a little trimming made a trail big enough that no one farther back was tormented by the thorns.

But the easier humping opened up unwelcome opportunities to think instead of constantly fighting the jungle. And in the forefront of White's thinking was what was waiting for them someplace ahead. Most of his friends were gone. Many he had lost in A Shau. Now Jackson and

Cook were back with him, but what would happen to him if he lost them again?

As long as they stayed in the thick brush, there was little chance they would run into enemy. But the thick brush would not last forever. Even now, it was thinning out a bit. They would soon be out of the relative safety of the thorns and into areas sure to be infested with booby traps and N.V.A.

By four o'clock that afternoon the point stepped out of the thick brush into a section of beautiful jungle. The psychological change in White and the veterans was as sudden as the physical change in the jungle. Extreme caution permeated White's being. Beautiful jungle was always dangerous.

The forward observer team came to the front, shooting angles with their compasses, verifying the company's position. Since it was late afternoon, the captain gave orders to set perimeter. Again, Jackson, White, and Cook managed to get their squads as near to each other as they could. They arranged their men and found their own locations for the night.

White sat on the wet earth facing out toward the jungle ahead of him. The rain had slowed to a light drizzle. He looked to his far right and saw Jackson waving at him. He had already set two ponchos together to make a hooch. On the ground in front of him, already heating on the stove, was a cup of water.

As he ducked under the poncho's roof, White saw, farther to the right, Cook walking toward them. White pushed a bunch of twigs and leaves together and sat next to Jackson. Seconds later Cook stooped down under the roof and sat with them.

"I've got a full cup going, but you guys get more ready," said Jackson as he added small sticks into the stove.

"I've got chocolate and pound cake for after chow," said White as he, too, set a canteen of water to heat.

"I got a bunch of cigarettes for after chow," said Cook. He reached over with his canteen cup and filled it three-quarters full from the rain water pouring off the poncho roof. He put the cup to heat and wrapped his hands around the cup to dry them. When they were completely dry, he reached into his shirt pocket and took out a pack of cigarettes wrapped in plastic.

"Marlboros," said Jackson.

"Yeah," said Cook. "Marlboros. Only the best for guys like us."

"Yeah," said White. "Now if we could only get a little rain, things would be perfect."

"Yeah," said Jackson. "That's what we need all right. A little fucking rain."

The three soldiers sat quietly. Every so often one would take his hands and rub his face, ears, and neck to warm them.

"If we're lucky," said White, "it might even snow."

"I don't like snow," said Jackson. "Too dry. What I like is a good, wet sleet."

"Yeah," said Cook. "That'd be fucking great. A little sleet. But if it snowed, maybe the captain might let us take the rest of the week off, and we could go skiing."

"Yeah," said Jackson. "We could invite the Gooks, too."

"Naw," said White, content to be with his friends. "The motha's can't ski, and I don't know how, either. There's nothing big enough to ski on where I'm from. But maybe we could make a snowman."

"Make a snow *baby-san*, instead," said Jackson. "She can't be any colder than 'bro' here, sister."

"Fuck you," said Cook. "The only thing that'll let you stick that fucking black mamba of yours in her would be a snow *baby-san*."

"Fuck you," said Jackson. "The only thing your 'pee wee' is good for is to piss with."

White didn't hear the "Fuck you" answer that Cook responded with. Only his eyes dared move. That clarity, the unmistakably clear warning sometimes coming to him, struck him like a truck. It smashed him low, falling on him like a mountain. It weighed him down so that he could not have raised a finger. Looking at them, he saw clearly, without doubt, that they were both dead men.

His mind fought against it. A desperate struggle raged in him as he tried to prove it was a lie. That clarity, premonition—whatever it was—was a lie. It couldn't be. It was wrong. He was wrong. All the other times had been his mind playing tricks on him. Or maybe it was all just coincidence.

Then, just as suddenly as it had appeared, it was gone. He saw Jackson's mouth move and heard the words. "Hey, bro, you all right?"

"Yeah," said White. "I guess I drifted off for a second."

"Hey, bro," said Cook. "You look like shit. You sure you're O.K.?"

"Yeah, I'm all right now," said White. "It must be the cold. Yeah. It's gone now."

"Man. You scared me," said Jackson. "You were looking at me, but you was a thousand miles away."

"Man," said Cook as he looked at Jackson. "You do that to everybody, bro."

"It's nothing," said White. "I was just remembering something that happened one winter at home. I guess I just drifted off."

"O.K.," said Cook. "Let's forget it. Look. The water's ready. Let's get some hot chow in us. Then we can bullshit all you two want."

They poured the hot water into the bags of dehydrated food, folded them so the water couldn't escape, and let them soak. Each man took out whatever he wanted from the rest of the LRRP ration and began eating.

It was gone now, but the shock of the last episode of clarity was still haunting White. But at least now he could hide it from his two comrades. He ate his meal, occasionally glancing at them. He knew he could never tell them what he had seen. Even if he did, they wouldn't believe him. They might even think he was crazy. No. It was better not saying anything. Anyway, they had to go on. There was only one way out of the sticks now.

And even if it was true that Jackson and Cook were dead men, it was also true for him. He, too, was a dead man. Even if he lasted longer than they did, his end, too, was sure. It was coming as sure as the coming of night.

He wanted to lighten the tension that his premonition had caused, so, as he took a bite, he said, "Man. This is some good shit."

"Yeah," said Jackson. "And that's the right word for it, too."

After they had finished, White pulled out three packs of cocoa and three tins of pound cake. He handed one of each to his friends.

"Now this here really is some good shit," said Cook as he took a bite of pound cake. He washed down each bite with a sip of hot chocolate.

"Not bad," said White.

"No," said Jackson. "Not bad at all."

By the time they finished, their hands were completely dry. Cook took out three more cigarettes and handed them to his comrades.

White cupped the cigarette in his hands, the burning paper and tobacco heating his insides. For extra warmth he pulled on the cigarette, making the red glow give out more heat. He rubbed his hands, spreading the warmth. The smoke he pulled deep into his lungs. It, too, seemed to warm his insides, keeping out the cold.

He remembered how he had begun smoking. Right after the monsoon started, Louis had shown him how the burning tip warmed his hands. He had nearly choked on his first draw.

"You don't have to inhale," Louis had said. "I don't. Just blow it out if you don't like it. Just pull enough to keep it going."

That's how it had started. But with each cigarette he tried pulling a little smoke into his lungs. With each try he found that inhaling the smoke seemed to warm his insides. It became easier with every try. Now he was smoking for real, taking deep tokes into his lungs, coughing silently into his hands. He knew smoking wasn't good, but now it was too late. He was hooked and he knew it.

He watched as Jackson and Cook, too, inhaled. They seemed contented, pleased with the company. But wanting to enter again into his thinking was the premonition he had felt earlier.

This time he was able to reject it, force it away from him. He relaxed, watching his friends as they watched each other and him. An hour passed, and the jungle began to darken. Cook began to rise and said, "I guess I'll go check on my guys. See you two shitheads in the morning."

"Yeah," said both White and Jackson as they went out into the rain to check on their own squads.

White didn't think that he would be able to sleep that night. Even the comfort of his wet but warm poncho and liner couldn't take away the anguish in his mind as he remembered those few seconds of clarity. No matter how hard he tried, he couldn't take away the image he had of his last two friends lying dead on the forest floor. But, sometime late that night, he fell asleep.

He awoke in a sweat. It was his first nightmare since he was a child. He had had many bad dreams since then but nothing like the one that had just shaken him awake.

He couldn't remember what it had been about but knew it was very bad. It had to have been, when, finding himself awakening to another cold, wet, dangerous day in the highland jungles of Viet Nam, he felt an acute relief.

As he sat up and looked around, his relief was shattered by what he saw. Sitting together, drinking hot chocolate, were Cook and Jackson. They were looking at him, smiling. Jackson waved to him.

He didn't remember it all, but at seeing them together, White knew the dream had been about them. Trying to hide the apprehension, he waved back at Jackson. Needing time to compose his thoughts, he slowly made breakfast.

Finished eating, he walked, taking sips from his cup, to Cook and Jackson. The rain had stopped almost completely, making it easy to keep his cigarette lit. He ducked under the poncho and said, "What's the word?"

"Heading out later to join with C Company. Gonna climb that ridge to the south and come into A Shau," said Jackson.

They sat there, not able to say anything. White saw, from the center of the perimeter, second platoon's lieutenant coming toward them. He squatted down and looked at them and said, "Moving out in 'bout twenty minutes. Get your squads together. Be going in three columns. First platoon on the left. Second in the middle. Third on the right."

He looked at each of the three veterans and said, "I don't have to tell you about where we're going. You've been there before. I just want to say good luck and thanks for what you guys have already done for the company."

The march began, and with it came the rain. They walked on for an hour until the company joined with "Charlie" company. Charlie, too, had been divided into three columns. Together, the two companies began the climb up the last ridge before entering A Shau.

Another hour passed. The rain began to beat down heavily, obscuring whatever lay beyond a few feet to their front. Suddenly White knew. It had been building in him, but now his stomach twisted into a knot, and he knew. It…was…here.

Through the haze of falling water and the pounding of the drops on his helmet, he saw, then heard, the first explosions.

Like the first time, he was thrown many feet by the concussion, bounced violently off a tree, and was again knocked senseless. When images began to focus again, what he saw paralyzed him even more.

Cook lay face down in a bloody puddle of mud and leaves. A hole the size of a softball had been punched through his chest and back. He vainly tried to crawl but was so hurt that only his hands clawed at the leaves on the forest floor. The fingers stopped moving, there was a slight tremble of his body, and then he lay still.

White saw Jackson's tortured face as he left cover. He could see Jackson was yelling something, but all sound had left him. He could hear neither the explosions and gunshots that followed Jackson's dash to reach Cook, nor the screaming of the green guys while they bled, clutching their bodies. He couldn't hear his own scream of anguish.

He could only stare in paralyzed shock, watching Jackson near Cook. He saw as the bullets struck Jackson in the chest and legs. Unmoving, he stared as the next bullet struck Jackson on the cheek, tearing out the back of his skull as it exited.

Then he heard his first sound. It was a continuous, loud, high-pitched buzz. It was a sound that threatened to burst open the crack in the wall of his unconscious and let out a flood. It was a noise that drowned out all other sound. In a strange way, he wanted not to laugh, but to giggle.

Somewhere in the tangled mess of his shocked mind he remembered that he had once had an idea about youth being elastic. "Yes," he thought. "Youth is elastic and wants to spring back." But what he now feared more than anything was that sometimes elastic is stretched too hard and will not spring back. Sometimes it is stretched to a point where it will snap.

CHAPTER XXXI

White was in a state of severe shock. The physical effect of the bomb that had thrown him down and nearly killed him was nothing—less than nothing. It was the other shock, the one that shook his soul, that left him temporarily crippled, temporarily crazy.

The medic hovered over him. "Sarge. Sarge," he yelled. "Come on, snap out of it. You're gonna be all right." His face was inches from White's own as he stared into his eyes. When White began to focus the medic said, "O.K., Sarge. You gonna be O.K. now, Sarge." He stuck out two fingers of his right hand and said, "How many fingers do you see?"

"Two," said White.

"Yeah," said the medic. He turned to Lieutenant Zigler standing next to them and said, "I think he's gonna be all right, sir."

"Good," said Zigler. "Go check out somebody else."

Ziegler knelt next to White and could see the shock wearing off.

"Got to get you moving," he said as he helped White to his feet.

"We're forming perimeter. Our platoon's over there," he said, leading White to the far left. "Gotta be ready. They're coming for sure. Find yourself a good place and try to shake it off. Your squad is in the center, so try to get your strongest on each end, you in the middle. They'll be here any minute, so dig in the best you can and get ready for them."

Zigler stopped and looked at White. He held his shoulders in his hands as he said, "Sorry, White. I know they were your friends. But now we got to think about what's coming. I'd like to tell you to rest, but we don't have time to rest."

As he turned to go, he looked once more at White and the others around him. His eyes searched every man as he said, "You all know what the score is here. I already know what I'm gonna do. They're not gonna take me alive."

White sat behind a bush and faced outward. With every minute that passed, his head cleared, and he was able to think more clearly. But, as things came into focus, he remembered what had been running through his mind as the fight went on. He knew now. There wasn't any doubt left. He was really crazy, now. Not just mixed up, but crazy—fucking insane.

Why else had he wanted to giggle? He remembered that he wanted to laugh. The whole world was dying, and he wanted to laugh. Something had snapped and the whole fucking world–not just him—was crazy. There wasn't any escape or denying it. He was over the edge. That was the only sane explanation left.

But the longer he sat there, the more he came back to what he was before the explosion. Rational ideas, defensive ideas, asserted themselves into his thinking. The more he strained to think about what defense he could set up, the quicker his head cleared.

And the more he came back, the less funny everything was. Now he remembered what he must do. He had to get ready. They were coming, and he had to be ready for them.

All of the companies in the two battalions had sustained casualties. There would be full regiments of N.V.A. in the mountains and the valley. And they would soon surround the depleted American forces. The N.V.A. that were there stayed close to the American lines, knowing the soldiers would hesitate to call for artillery for fear of blowing themselves up.

White could hear them preparing for the rush. He knew that many had stripped to nothing but a loin cloth. They would be ready to tighten the tourniquets they had wrapped around their arms and legs. Those would be the first to come. Just before the charge, they would tighten all tourniquets and then come straight for the perimeter, throwing satchel charges as they ran.

Even blowing off an arm or leg wouldn't stop them. The tight tourniquets would keep them from bleeding long enough to make the last yards to the American lines. Then they would hurl themselves in a sure-death plunge into the perimeter.

Right behind them would be the regular N.V.A. They, too, would charge at full speed. But, unlike the first group with satchel charges, they would come firing A.K.'s. And even without tourniquets they would be hard to kill.

They were coming. It was starting…They were here. For the next few minutes White's mind went to automatic. He couldn't think. He couldn't feel. He could only react. From every side of the perimeter came N.V.A. They screamed out in Vietnamese as they came.

For five minutes that seemed an eternity, the fight raged on in front of and inside the perimeter. Then, as suddenly as it began, the fighting stopped. The entire first and second waves of N.V.A. were killed. The cost of attacking during daylight had proved too dear. They now knew the companies they attacked still had many veterans in them and that if they could win the battle, it would prove a pyrrhic victory.

Cautiously, they came toward the American lines. Inch by inch they crawled, conscious of every fold in the earth, every rock or log, every clump of brush that could conceal them from American bullets and bombs. Sometimes, one would make a mistake. He moved a bush, or a hole in the brush revealed an ear, and grenades were hurled at him— killing him.

The others came slowly on. When the whole force had drawn close enough to draw fire, they backed off a few yards. The hill was completely surrounded. Now the N.V.A. lay without moving, waiting for the word to charge the hill again and kill everyone at the top.

But for a reason White couldn't understand, they didn't rush the company. As the afternoon wore on and twilight approached, White knew that each man on both sides had to steel himself for what would come next. Even the most seasoned soldiers feared what they knew would now happen. Almost incomparable to anything, in a different category, was the horror of night fighting, the mortal struggle while blind.

White had somewhat shaken off the shock of the concussion and of losing his last two friends, but the last N.V.A. charge had severely shaken his nerves. He crouched as low as he could get behind the bush. He could see through the leaves several dead N.V.A. lying sprawled grotesquely around his front of the perimeter. Inside it was more dead enemy. He memorized every tree, rock, and shrub around him. He knew that with the dark they would come again. He had to be ready. He laid all of his grenades in front of him. He knew he must fire his rifle only if unavoidable. If he shot, the muzzle flash would tell every N.V.A. in sight where he was.

Most of the fighting would be done with grenades. They flew silently through the air and didn't give away one's position. Their blast would give a brief flash of light, giving the soldiers a moment of sight. But White knew he must know where everything was. To toss a grenade, hit a tree, and have it bounce back into your lap was killing yourself.

His nerves grew tighter with the advancing shadows. Poor plans for defense or escape raced through his mind. Images of his dead comrades ran through his thoughts. He remembered the last movie he had seen before coming to Nam, "The Alamo". That was fitting. Perfect. And that was what this was. His stomach tightened. He gagged until the taste of vomit filled his mouth.

The light grew dimmer...and then it was dark. The coal-black jungle night was upon them. His heart pounded furiously against the earth. Then, like a lighthouse to a floundering ship, he was saved. He was jolted by the sudden realization that he had a great advantage over the enemy. He could lie still, soundless, but the enemy must move to attack. When they moved, he would hear. He would pull the pin, wait two seconds, and then lob the grenade toward the sound. He would kill as many as he could before he, himself, was killed. It was the Alamo, his Alamo, and he was determined to make it a memorable one for anybody who got out alive. He'd give any N.V.A. that survived something to tell their grandkids.

Now his breathing and heartbeat became steady. "Yes," he thought. "That's the way." The ones that survived would always remember it... and they would remember him. They would know that he was a true soldier—a comrade. And he would live in their memory. That was the only comfort he had left. But it was enough. It would serve.

Then he remembered something else. In his first action against the N.V.A. he had thought of the bravery of the soldier that had come alone to attack the company... and die. He had felt his stomach turn as he had realized the extreme desperate loneliness of the last few minutes of the enemy's life. But then he knew. The N.V.A. hadn't come to die alone. He had come to die with them...he and the company, his fellow soldiers. And in a way it seemed to White that now, too, was a fine end for him if it was, indeed, the end. Yes. He would die in fit company among his friends and among his other comrades…the enemy.

He sat upright, knowing he couldn't be seen. He listened as he had never listened before. They were coming. He was sure of it. Suddenly, at the other side of the perimeter was an explosion. He waited for the charge. He sat unmoving, straigning his ears, listening for anything. But there was nothing more.

Then another explosion, closer this time, broke the silence. They were probing the perimeter. More waiting. An hour passed. He heard a click, a breaking twig, five yards to his front. He pulled the pin on a grenade, catching the lever when it sprang off. He lobbed the grenade into the black space before him, toward the enemy.

In the flash of the explosion, he could see two more N.V.A. They were charging the perimeter five yards to his right. One had a bag of Chinese satchel charges hanging at his side. He carried an A.K. and charged fearlessly. The other didn't carry a gun. He ran side by side with the other, grabbing and hurling grenades from the bag.

More exploding bombs illuminated the pair. Then, one of the company's new recruits, unable to restrain himself, fired his rifle at the two. One of the bullets struck the bag the leading N.V.A. carried. There was a great flash when the bag of explosives blew up.

In that instant a picture was branded in White's brain. In the brief light he saw the disintegrating head and torso of the one who had been tossing the grenades. The other, cut in half by the blast—intestines, legs, and feet atomized—flew through the air. His eyes were open. He strained to twist what was left of his body sideways, to look accusingly at White. His finger still pulled on the trigger, trying to bring his gun sights to bear on White. A look of defiance, unconquerable, haunted his face. He disappeared, rifle firing wildly, already dead, into the dark of the jungle.

Then it was quiet. Nothing moved. Intense, total quiet, except for the aircraft overhead. Jets and helicopters flew above them, waiting for word to fire down into the company as it was being overrun. But the big charge, the one that would send too many N.V.A. across the perimeter to wipe them out, never came.

No one slept. A faint light began to filter through the leaves. A half hour later White could see the trees ahead of him. Behind him, in the center of the perimeter, was the captain on the radio. When he finished talking, he turned to his platoon leaders with orders from headquarters.

Zigler crawled up to White. "How ya feeling?" he asked.

"I'm O.K. sir."

"Looks like they might have pulled out before first light," said Zigler. "Intelligence says there's a lot of new N.V.A. regiments fresh from the north, and they're all in this area. Gotta try to get out if we can. They'll try to get us out by chopper, but I don't think we'll be able to. Too many N.V.A. too close by. But be ready, anyway. If we can't get out by chopper, we probably gonna walk out."

"Yes, sir," said White. "I understand. What we're gonna do with the dead and wounded if we gotta walk?"

"Take them with us until we can get choppers," said Zigler.

Thirty yards beyond White's left front was a bomb-blasted clearing where the helicopters were supposed to land. A squad from second platoon probed beyond the perimeter to the clearing. Amazingly, the N.V.A. were all gone.

The company waited, the quiet almost as bad as the bombs. Then, far in the distance, they heard it. Fleets of helicopters headed for different areas in the mountains.

One of them exploded in mid-air. The delayed sound of the explosion reached the company some seconds later. Another helicopter exploded – and another. Others got hit but managed to keep flying. It was too much. Too many N.V.A. The fleets turned and headed back toward the base camps.

Zigler came back to White. "Get ready. We'll be moving out any minute."

"What about those helicopters?" asked White? "There could be somebody still alive."

"The closest ground pounders to them will check it out."

Poncho stretchers for the dead and severely wounded were made, a grunt on each corner. They moved out fast, hoping to put as much distance as possible between themselves and the superior numbers of N.V.A.

All that morning they fled eastward, expecting at any moment to be overtaken and surrounded. At noon they found out why they hadn't been attacked that morning, or followed. Instead of dividing their forces too thinly by pursuing each of the companies in the two American battalions, the N.V.A. had concentrated on only two companies.

Everyone with a radio or near one heard what was happening. White heard it on Zigler's R.T.O.'s radio. Man by man, the two companies were being wiped out. The last message from each of the companies was to call in all artillery, jets and helicopter strikes, onto their own position.

White went up to Zigler and asked, "Ain't we gonna try to help those two companies?"

"Three fresh battalions and a couple of Marine companies are on their way here now," said Zigler. "We're whittled down too much and got all those dead and wounded."

An hour after the final attacks began, a deadly quiet echoed throughout the mountains. That spurred the company on. They didn't stop for break. Instead, they increased their speed until everyone was on the verge of collapse.

White had been watching a soldier from third platoon. Every old timer could see that the man was getting mentally worse every day. But this last fight had really hurt him. White could see in his eyes–crazy eyes—that he was slipping fast.

At mid-afternoon they came to a river. It was wider and deeper than most. Thirty yards across with rushing white water, it roared before them.

Second platoon had been walking point. Two soldiers stepped out into the swirling current. It was only three feet deep in the middle, but the white water pulled at the soldiers' legs.

They made it to the other side. Others began to cross, some carrying a poncho with either a dead or wounded man. Now second platoon were all across, and third platoon began to go over.

White watched as the crazy soldier started across. His eyes were so crazy, so sick. Before he reached the middle of the stream, he slipped and fell. Splashing and fighting, he came up and stood there for a moment.

White couldn't believe the man's face. Wild eyes, desperate beyond measure, seemed to see something beyond what White and the others in the company could see. And whatever it was that he was seeing was terrible beyond description. The man was surely crazy. Then he took another step and slipped again. He struggled to regain his feet but fell back into the current. Thrashing around wildly, he got his head and shoulders out of the water. Before he could gain his feet, he fell again.

Once more he tried getting up, fumbling in place, straining to rise. But suddenly his eyes turned in their sockets, and he shouted out. "Fuck it." He slipped farther down and screamed out once again, "Fuck it." Then he went down.

He never came back up. Grunt eyes strained, looking to see where his body would rise. But as far as they could see down the river, it never did.

Another nail was driven into the coffins of White and every man there that had seen the soldier drown. A terrible new fear rammed itself into his tired mind. How close had he been to being like that? Could it still happen? Had it already happened? That giggling. He remembered giggling.

He crossed the river. Even the old timers wouldn't look at each other. White grabbed hold of an end of the poncho that carried Jackson's body, relieving a replacement.

Jackson's dead eyes stared at him from the poncho. In the back of his skull was a hole big enough to run a fist through.

"I'll never make it," White thought. "I'll never make it."

CHAPTER XXXII

The crazy soldier's drowning himself at the river crossing had shown White the invisible boundary between sane and insane. He had seen it coming for a long while. He had suspected it before, but then he remembered the euphoric freedom he felt when his last two friends had been killed. He almost giggled. And how far was it from an almost giggle to a hysterical laugh?

He knew at the river he had seen the boundary again, but had he crossed it? He hoped that he had not crossed over. Or even if he had temporarily crossed, had he come back into the normal? He hadn't wanted to laugh or giggle any more.

Was "not normal", discounting a physical imbalance or injury, anything more than an attempt to modify or completely escape something unendurable?

And extreme physical conditions were what he and the others had to deal with every day—an extreme place where they will probably be killed—and stages of dehydration, malnutrition, and exhaustion are normal.

But how normal was it when he had had thoughts leading him to the border of that "other place", ideas so terrible that a step beyond seemed like safety from those thoughts? Was it craziness, numbness, or simply becoming used to it that now left him cold when human bodies blown to pieces, intestines hanging in the brush like decorations on a Christmas tree, no longer have the same meaning to him?

When the "nothing" he felt at seeing torn, dead bodies first came to him, he questioned it. He thought, "How can it be that I don't feel anything? Shouldn't I feel at least something?"

But as more weeks went by, it had gone beyond questioning. Somewhere he had lost something holding him, limiting him to what he now knew was a half reality. Now he passed by mutilated countrymen and enemy alike without interest. He no longer asked himself if he had crossed the boundary. It didn't really matter. He knew that wherever he was, was the real world. This is what really was and what he really was.

He no longer regretted that he had become something beyond the normal. There were no more boundaries, no fantasies. There was no past and no future. But one thing became very clear. Without doubt was that he was turning into something vastly different from what he was even a few weeks before. He was becoming…his true self.

White and first platoon were at the rear of the column of march. It still rained every day, but now it was mostly showers. Everything at ground level was still wet, and the earth remained slippery and hard to walk on. Still, White liked the extra physical effort. He welcomed anything that kept his mind from some of the things creeping through it.

This was the second time out since the fight at A Shau. Last time out they had lost more men, both new recruits and old timers. In two different fights they had been whittled down to a dangerously low level.

Now, after a week at a base camp, they were again in the field. They had been re-supplied with equipment and recruits. There were so many new faces. White looked at them as they suffered along the march and felt little for them.

They hadn't made contact yet this time out. He fought for exhaustion, pacing up and down along the line, checking on his squad, until he felt his physical limits were near.

But even the extreme tiredness from humping didn't take away all of his bad thoughts amidst his struggle to concentrate on the terrain, listening for any unusual sounds, trying to be aware of anything with a different smell, and instinctively feeling for the enemy. Between these thoughts, jabbing his self image, darted flashes of what he had become.

He remembered seeing his first dead Gook. He had felt something tugging at his deepest self on seeing the dead teenager. But with each new mutilated corpse he was changing how he felt about them. Seeing dead Gooks went from an experience of compassionate sympathy for dead enemy to a curious, almost scientific interest in seeing exposed internal body parts. So interesting how those parts worked. Interesting, too, was how they could so suddenly become dead tissue. But dead, organic tissue is what nurtures the jungle. It was a cycle. The whole thing was a cycle.

He knew that something had changed when he no longer found terror or interest at decomposing, dead N.V.A. They now had no more meaning than seeing a dead dog or cat on the highway. The only thing still bothering him now about corpses was the smell. Nothing seemed to stink as much as rotting humans.

He wondered what was next. He didn't worry anymore about his callous feelings about dead N.V.A. But now even dead American G.I.'s didn't mean as much as they did just days before. Somehow, they were becoming as faceless and uninteresting as dead enemies.

Then the images of a dead friend would pass before his eyes, and he knew he still felt something. Smith's pathetic grin. Jackson's ash-colored face. Cloud's sudden lack of the back third of his skull. Farver's remaining dead eye staring up at nothing.

He still felt, but he didn't want to feel or think about his dead friends anymore. If he could just forget—erase them—he would feel better, maybe normal, again. Still, it was good to feel something, to hold, for a while at least, that bit of emotion that keeps one human.

Quicker than thought, he threw himself to the earth. His instincts had hurled him behind a foot-high log. His eyes searched around him for the enemy.

But there was only that first burst of M-16, then a deadly quiet. No follow up of A.K.-47, no grenades, no more M-16. Only that first burst coming from the front of the column.

Company radios spread the word. The point had killed three N.V.A. as the company had intersected a trail. Orders came from battalion headquarters to follow the trail west to see what it led to. The company began moving forward. As White reached the trail, he looked down to see the dead N.V.A. He was happy that he felt a tinge of interest in them.

He saw how young two of them were. The other was a little older, not a teenager any more. Maybe a husband. Maybe a father. And even if White was glad they were dead, he was only happy because now they couldn't kill him. More important, he was happy because somewhere inside him he felt a dim sadness at their deaths. He looked at them one last time, smiled, almost laughed, and moved on.

The company followed the trail for a mile without finding an N.V.A. camp or side trails leading to one. It was late afternoon. Third platoon was assigned to leave a squad near the trail to set up for night ambush. The rest of the platoon followed the company, a hundred yards into the jungle.

The next morning the ambush squad re-joined the company. New orders had come from headquarters. They were to travel cross-country and try to intersect the trail farther on, searching for enemy as they went.

By the second day after leaving the trail, White was out of food. By the third he was out of water. A week before it would not have been a problem because it rained every day. Knowing that, he kept only one canteen filled. The other five he left empty, making a lighter pack. But now it had been three days without rain. They hadn't passed any streams. They hadn't even passed slime-filled bomb craters.

At noon break he sat cross-legged on the ground. He had found a shaft of light through the trees that reached the forest floor. He adjusted himself so the light hit him directly on his face.

The hunger pangs had passed the day before. The gnawing, the craving for food, the desperation for any nourishment, had passed. Now he sat and breathed. He felt so light, so fast, like he could almost fly. Somehow, in his emptiness he felt full—as if he lacked nothing—complete.

His own sweat had washed him. His insides were empty. He suddenly had a word for what he felt: clean. He was clean inside and out.

He regretted that he had to eat to stay alive. He was clean now. If he ate, it would dirty him and make him heavy. The thought of food made him nauseated. Maybe if he…

Something stopped him. Not eat again? There was only one word for that: crazy. Or maybe not crazy. Maybe it was some kind of mind trick, like when high or drunk, that almost convinced him that he didn't need food anymore. But it seemed so real. Whatever it was almost convincing him he didn't need to eat seemed so real.

Hunger for food was gone, but a great thirst attacked him to his bones. Complete? He wasn't complete. Water! Nothing was complete without water.

He controlled his breathing, taking in air and letting it out slowly—controlled. He tried to will away the thirst. He dug deeper into himself, trying to overcome it.

But it never went away. He got to a point that he knew he could endure the thirst until he died, but he couldn't will away the thirst itself. He couldn't will away the throbbing ache in his head or the parched, raw feeling in his throat and mouth.

Word came down: saddle up. They started north, trying to intersect the trail. When they found it, they were to follow it east, covering ground fast, to reach an area where they could be re-supplied.

They walked hard and fast until, in late afternoon, they found the trail. Now, they walked even faster, covering four more miles. It was easy walking, no thorns, no brush, no N.V.A. Easy going.

It was almost dark when they stopped. They found a level spot near the trail. Ambush squads were set, up and down the trail, fifty yards from the main body of the company.

White's squad was on ambush on the eastern side. Guard schedule given out, the squad melted into their positions. The last thing White saw before the dark set in was the befuddled, drained faces of the newest recruits. He knew they were suffering--more than him. He was glad to realize that he felt a mild sympathy.

Before he fell asleep, he had a soothing thought. Maybe the worst of all those crazy ideas he had been having were just hallucinations. The lack of water was making it worse than it really was. It could be just some kind of mirage.

No. He couldn't fool himself. What was happening to him was real. He checked each man in his squad. They were all real, too. His mind drifted. Somewhere between the phantoms, he fell asleep.

Then, just before midnight, it began to rain. Soldiers that had cursed the rain a week before now felt blessed. They were saved. White welcomed the hurt in his throat as he gulped down cup after cup. He became dizzy as he hydrated himself to near bursting. He wallowed on the wet leaves.

At first light they were walking again on the trail, heading east. Refreshed now, all canteens filled, the old-timers that were left in the company still didn't like walking on the trail. They wanted the safety of the bush, away from possible N.V.A. But the captain, following orders, gave instructions to continue as long as it led east.

The rain stopped. White's squad was walking point. Suddenly, he smelled it. Drifting in the air, sometimes suspended, repulsive beyond description, was the horrid odor of decomposing flesh. They were back to where the three N.V.A. had been killed. The company had left them purposely in the open for their comrades to find.

Still thirty yards away, White saw something on the ground. He stopped. It was a shoe. Something on the ground near the dead soldiers moved. He motioned to his squad to stay put. He inched ahead, ready to fire. As he got closer, he saw more movement. Then he knew. Rats. Big, sharp-toothed, old ivory-colored jungle rats.

And they were eating. Even as the company moved up, they refused to leave the feast of the dead N.V.A. Two fought over the rotting, sickly pale cheeks of the N.V.A. nearest the trail. Others gnawed at his neck and arms. They snarled at the approaching soldiers, showing dirty teeth.

When White was nearly even with them, they ran off, squealing, into the brush. They didn't go far, only enough away to partially hide behind thorns and rotten twigs.

The odor was horrid. White blew out his nostrils, trying to get rid of the smell. It didn't work. Holding his breath didn't work, either. He tried breathing through his mouth, hating that he had to take such foul air into his body.

He noticed that the man who had been walking point was gagging.

He was new, only a month in country. White looked at him and, very calmly, as if he was talking to a child about an ugly cat, said, "Not too pretty, is it?"

The point couldn't answer. He stared at White as if he were insane. Still looking at him, angry at the point's naiveté, White said, "You better hope this is the worse shit you'll ever see." His eyes went back to the rats, and he said, "Well, at least they've got something to eat. That's more than we got." Unable to see the humor—but fearing White's stare—the point looked away.

The captain who had been through so much with the company, the one that White first knew, had been rotated out. The new captain, fortunately, understood he was green and had a lot to learn. That he relied on the companies' veterans showed them he was worth looking after—a keeper. White saw him coming, trying not to breathe in the foul-smelling air.

"See any sign of N.V.A.?" he asked.

"No, sir," said White. "Not a sign. Doesn't look like there's been anybody around since we were here. What you want to do now, captain?"

"Keep going," he said. "As long as the trail goes east, we follow it. Let's get out of this fucking stink."

White assigned another in the squad to walk point. He looked at each of his men, all newcomers, as they walked past the bodies and the rats. Horror and aversion was plastered on each face as they went by. One vomited; all gagged.

White understood. He could reason why but was puzzled by something else. The dead N.V.A. just didn't have much meaning for him. His only discomfort with the whole thing was the disgusting smell of the rotting corpses. The rats didn't mean anything. In a way he was even glad. Two days before, he had seen himself slipping, wanting never to eat again. Now he knew he was O.K. again. He would eat again. Everything had to. Even the rats had to eat.

CHAPTER XXXIII

Weeks passed, the monsoon ended, and the sun beat down heavily on the foliage at the top of the second canopy. Steam radiated from the leaves while they lost their moisture to the onslaught of the rays. They exhaled their poisonous oxygen which donated life to the other living creatures below. Giant vines wrapped themselves against trees, strangling their way toward the sun.

White knew that for someone with the right reception, screams of dying insects could be heard when a monkey, bird, snake, or another insect attacked and devoured them. Ants battled unthinkingly, killing anything they could to protect and feed the horde.

Birds and monkeys, perhaps slightly more intelligent than the insects, fought, instinctively mated, and died in an endless grim cycle. They lived their brief span unsuspecting of, and oblivious to, anything beyond their immediate reach.

He sat on the jungle floor only inches higher than the worms, clutched in the cycle of his thoughts. He didn't care about anything, anymore. Six months before, he would have been alarmed if he did not feel. But now, he was no longer alarmed. He no longer cared that he didn't care.

He was the company's old-timer. He had reached a plateau where he stood alone. There was no one to meet him, no one to greet him, and he just didn't care. To kill or not to kill was the question, but not to care was the answer.

He heard the faint click of a small branch being broken. His quick, dreadful gaze landed on a green recruit who had just snapped a pencil-sized twig to add to his stove. His face showed fear when he looked up to see the warning eyes of his platoon sergeant, White.

The replacement's body shook as he locked eyes with White. It was neither mercy for the ignorant nor sympathy for the recruit that caused White to look away, releasing the tortured green dude. He just didn't care. He would go on. He would do his job, but he just didn't care anymore.

He ate and drank because his body needed it. He shit to expel the waste, just like he had expelled feelings. The enemy's bravery no longer impressed him. Their comradeship for each other, their devotion to the cause, their zeal to kill him meant nothing any more. Nothing impressed him anymore.

He rutted at the whorehouses when he was in. He no longer drank or smoked dope, but he chain-smoked cigarettes. He was now at the point where he would prefer to run out of food, and even water, than run out of cigarettes.

Lieutenant Zigler had been wounded badly enough to be sent back to the world, and the new platoon lieutenant, green as grass, feared him. The new captain, too, feared him. They all feared him. He had no friends or even comrades. No one ever talked to him unless it was an officer or the first shirt with something about operations. No one else. That was good. He didn't want anyone or anything else.

Even the weight of a full pack didn't faze him anymore. No amount of humping tired him. He looked down at a fallen replacement, feeling neither pity for him nor impatience. But one look into those dead eyes and a recruit would not stumble again.

He had not written home in the weeks since Cook and Jackson had been killed. His parents got word to the company commander by way of the Red Cross that they had not heard from him. The captain started to order him to write, but one look into White's dreadful face, and the captain knew not to push. He gently said, "Try at least to write and let them know that you're alive."

But was he alive? Was he alive, or had he been killed as surely as Hahn, Hong, Smith, and the others? Had he been mutilated like Louis? The answer to those questions seemed meaningless. He felt as dead and crippled as anyone, and he didn't care.

That's what saved him. He knew when Jackson and Cook were killed that he was on the edge of total collapse. When the soldier from third platoon drowned himself, it made things much worse. Now, he just didn't care.

He was faced with something more urgent than life or death. That was no longer important. He was going to die. Just a matter of when. But he didn't have to go crazy. It was his choice. He could say if he'd go crazy or not. And the way not to go crazy was not to care about anything. Now he understood clearly what the slang phrase, "It don't mean nothing," meant. Nothing is worth going crazy over. Nothing means anything if you don't care.

But even as he told himself these things, something twisted itself—screwed itself—into his brain. Was it enough? Was he strong enough not to care about anything? Did he really have that choice? Something tugged at him—something dangerous—from below the surface of his conscious mind. It was something to do with feelings. But he willed it away, threw it to the side, because he didn't care.

White sat at the dilapidated table under the shade of the tree. His feet lightly pounded a nervous rhythm on the sidewalk. His rifle lay on the table an inch from his drumming fingers.

The waiter, too, seemed nervous. White knew why he made him jumpy. White just sat there drumming his fingers on the table top, looking intently toward the university fifty yards away. The waiter put the second can of warm coca-cola on the table in front of White and quickly retreated into the interior of the sidewalk café.

White's eyes were focused on the main building. Occasionally, he scanned the campus, but mostly he watched the administration building's entrance to the second floor. He had been trying for an hour to get the courage to cross the street. But the thought of facing the professor had stalled him at the café.

He hadn't seen the professor yet. Part of him wished that he wouldn't see him. That was his last qualm. What would the professor say—think—when he stood before him? The professor would know, maybe better than he, what he now was. He was worse than any animal. He was lower than the lowest worm. He was the foulest creature ever born.

Then, he saw the professor walking out of the building into the shade of the trees in the courtyard. He seemed to float across the walkway that meandered between the trees. Suddenly, he stopped. White watched as he slowly turned to look around him, searching his surroundings. "He knows," thought White. "He knows someone's watching him."

The professor turned until he faced the street. He looked from one end of the boulevard to the other. His eyes were too old. He couldn't see White sitting at the table. At that distance everything was a blur. Still, he stood, staring toward the street, waiting. White was not surprised. A year before he would have thought it impossible. Now he knew there were things that couldn't be explained with words. He couldn't even explain it without words. But he knew that the professor knew someone was there.

White stood. He saw as the old man's head turned toward him. He put a dollar on the table, and, not waiting for his change, began walking toward the university. He crossed the street, never having lost eye contact with the professor.

He was standing before him. He stood there naked, brutal, baring himself before the tiny man in front of him. His face twitched as he stood in the vacuum of the professor's eyes. He stood there guilty, a failure at being a man.

He saw in those ancient eyes a deep compassion, and White knew that the compassion extended out to him. But now, somehow, more than ever, he didn't care. He wanted to. He desperately wanted to care about something, even if only to show to the professor. But he was empty.

He stopped shaking and began breathing calmly. He lost himself in the professor's gaze. Then something in the professor's expression changed. White couldn't read that new look. It was like nothing he had ever seen before.

He knew that the professor saw it all. Those eyes that couldn't see clearly across the street peered into the deepest depth of his being. And he understood it all, too. He understood everything that White was feeling. The professor knew, perhaps better than he did himself, what horrors he had seen and endured in the war. And he understood what changes in a person those horrors could produce.

White looked into those slanted eyes and felt a sudden relief. He saw that the professor didn't hate him. He saw that neither did he condemn him nor feel disgusted with him. He knew that whatever else the professor thought of him, it was not as a murderer.

The professor walked up to within two feet of him. White stood still, unable to move under the professor's hypnotic eyes. He looked up at White, and, for a moment, all of the young man's pain was gone. Then the professor's face changed. Deeper than any passion was the serenity now on it.

White saw in it an acceptance of not only him but of whatever else the world could offer. But he saw something else that freed him from the last of his fear at seeing the professor. He saw in his eyes a total satisfaction for what he, the soldier, the human being, had become and was becoming. His eyes gleamed, and his skin seemed to glow as he said, "It is all right now, my son. Everything is all right now."

Looking down into those hypnotic eyes, willing to be hypnotized, White had somehow gone beyond sorrow. He had gone beyond terror. Staring down at the professor, he had become free of sentiment. "Yes," he thought. "Everything's all right now."

He slowly nodded his head yes and then hung it down low in a final bow of "goodbye". He turned and walked to the street. He stopped a rickshaw and got in. As the rickshaw left, he turned one last time. The professor stood where he had left him. His hands met at his waist, hidden in the sleeves of his black shirt. He looked out—tranquilly—into the world.

More weeks had passed, and the company was on stand down again. Some inner warning kept White from going to Hué. A gnawing, grinding, emptiness churned in his mind when he thought of the professor and the University. The same grinding kept him from The Green Doors. Whenever he thought of either, he experienced something he thought he had lost. Any memory of them and he became awash with a powerful apprehension that became so real he wouldn't think about it. Whatever else happened to him, he knew he could never again go to Hué.

But near the compound was the city of Phu Bai. It held no strings or attachments for him. Phu Bai was safe for him in a way Hué could no longer be.

Like many months before when he had been reborn to a new world of senses, something inside of him had been jolted into being at the death of his last two comrades. Later, he couldn't remember when, some force had sealed a door to his mind and his heart and would no longer admit anything to disturb it. Something else besides the "not caring" had shaken him to his roots.

But what was that eerie, tingling ghost that made him shudder when he thought about the professor and the girls at The Green Doors and those strange, raking talons clawing and scratching at the sealed door? What terrible thing was it making him tremble at the thought of Zahn?

Whatever it was keeping him from Hué also made him immune to any thought of fear in anything else. The streets of Phu Bai could have been filled with hard-core N.V.A. V.C. could be crouched, waiting in every building, and it would not have disturbed him as much as the thought of looking into the eyes of the professor.

N.V.A. and V.C. could only rip him in half with bullets. They could only blow his limbs off and splatter his brains and guts onto the town's buildings with their bombs. They could slash his flesh and stab him through the chest and neck with their bayonets, but they could not reach him as could the tearing image of Linh when she realized she would never see Boudreaux again.

He rejected the haunting, torturing image of all his comrades. Only when they peered at him, uncalled for, from the corner of his mind, did he feel and dread. Now, at the first sign of their presence, he erased them, cancelled them out, wiped them from his conscious mind. Or tried to.

He walked on, like a well-oiled, highly flexible machine. He glided smoothly, unconsciously, index finger on the trigger, thumb on the selector, past the guards at the main gate. He no longer tried sneaking through by riding shotgun for someone. He was going out, and, if anybody tried stopping him, it would be their problem.

He saw the guards as they watched him from the slit in the bunker's wall. They looked at each other and then back to him, and he knew that they knew what passed before their bunker was an old-timer grunt. After all, they were veterans, too.

It was their job to stop anyone from leaving the compound. They were supposed to check papers, passes, anything unusual, but the three guards remained motionless. Only their eyes moved, following him as he walked out of the compound.

White knew what the guards were thinking. He could sense their tension as he passed. He knew that he and others like him made people uneasy, but he didn't care.

It was a half-mile walk along the highway from the camp to the city. He walked past a farmer and his water buffalo, plowing in the paddy. The farmer stopped when he saw what approached on the highway. He remained motionless as his eyes followed the soldier's every move. His nerves eased up as White walked past. It was so easy to see—to understand. White could see the farmer in his mind. The farmer knew that even though the grunt had never glanced his way, he had seen everything.

White could see a faint figure far ahead of him. It was coming toward him. Then he recognized it for what it was. An old woman, all in black and in a rice hat, shuffled his way.

She toted a stout bamboo carrying brace across her bony shoulder. At the tip of each end of the brace hung a wooden bucket. Her job was to collect human and animal waste in the village and carry it to the rice fields for fertilizer. The spring action of the brace with the weight of the full buckets, and the movement of the moving woman, had to be timed perfectly. She loped, in a rice paddy shuffle, toward White.

Her old eyes had not yet focused on the thing ahead of her. She strained to see better, but White knew it was still too far for her. She continued on, her stride in perfect rhythm to the bouncing weight of the buckets.

When she got closer, she recognized that it was a man and that he was an American. So easy for him to recognize it on her face. Still, she shuffled, not missing a beat, toward the fields. But as she came still closer, her eyes focused and her pulse, as well as her feet, skipped a beat. He could almost hear her heart pounding like the beating of her tire-soled sandals on the asphalt, as she rushed past the zombie-like thing next to her.

White walked on. He came to the edge of town. Under a tree, sitting at a dilapidated wooden table, were two old men. They cackled to each other and grinned toothless smiles, looking like boys as they played with an ancient deck of cards. Both stopped abruptly when White walked by. Both heads turned as their eyes followed the soldier.

On the next corner was a middle-aged woman. She sold soup on the sidewalk from her homemade pushcart. The soup simmered on the hand-made stove, the odor of *nuoc mam* enveloping and overpowering all other smells.

Her eyes widened as much as they could when she saw what approached. She stared, hands unmoving, while White walked up to her and signaled for a bowl of soup. Her eyes never left him as he shoveled the noodles into his mouth with the chopsticks. When the noodles were gone, he drank the hot soup left in the bowl. She looked up into his stone face as he paid her and waited for the few cents change. He remembered again. He only paid Gook prices, and he always got the change.

Farther up the street was a parked American deuce-and-a-half. Standing next to the empty truck were two American soldiers, green to Viet Nam. They were surrounded by a horde of jumping, screaming kids. The children yelled out, their arms and hands stretched out toward the Americans. "You give me *beaucoup* chop-chop (food). You give me *beaucoup* chop-chop." In the Amerfranconese of the times, that phrase meant to give them something. Candy was what they really wanted, but they would take food, too. Actually, they would take anything.

The soldiers held up packets of C-rations, candy bars, and bubble gum, anything they could find, and pressed them into the frantic, small hands around them.

Then one of the shouting kids, a boy of about seven, turned and saw White approaching. His smile disappeared instantly. He gave the boy next to him a sharp elbow to the ribs. The other boy turned and saw White.

Elbows, pushes, and jerks had soon turned the entire mob toward White. All jumping had stopped. Even the two truck drivers seemed frozen in place, hands clutching boxes of C-rations above their heads.

The kids nearest the sidewalk pushed away, leaving an empty space for White to walk. The green soldiers did not fully understand what walked past them, but the kids did. White was a few yards farther into town when he heard the oldest of them turn back to the truck drivers and, with an arrogant, testy voice, said, "O.K. Now you give me chop-chop."

White came to a whorehouse. The girl on the front steps knew, too, what she was looking at. White saw her tremble inside, but she tried not to show any fear to the poor, lost creature in front of her. She forced a smile and, with a voice that quivered like her gut, said, "You number one G.I. I number one boom-boom girl. You come?"

White looked at the frightened girl. He wanted to reassure her, to make her feel safe, but he just couldn't smile. He took a deep breath and, as he let it out, barely nodded his head yes.

CHAPTER XXXIV

White had been secretly waiting, never daring to hope out loud, for the day that he had one month more. Today, he had thirty days left. He was, after eleven full months of shutting out the idea, short.

He sat cross-legged in the dust of a small molehill. There was not a blade of grass within a hundred yards in any direction. In front of him was a trench ten feet deep. It had been bulldozed into the camp dump. Other trenches, thirty yards long, scarred the earth around him.

Women and children rummaged throughout the smoking garbage. They no longer paid any attention to him as he sat motionless on the lump of dust above them. White watched while they scrounged, finding what to them was almost treasure. He could not help but admire the ingenuity of the Vietnamese. What to the Americans was junk, trash to be burned, was to them almost all useful. Pieces of plastic, cardboard boxes, rope, twine, bits of wood, and rubber tires were all useful to the peasants.

He sat and thought, occasionally getting a whiff of the smoking embers of burning trash. He liked the stink, the odor of civilization, the strong odor of anything that overcame the memory of the smell of rotting flesh.

His mind raced. His nerves twitched under his skin. His stomach twisted and knotted, remembering he was short. He knew fear again. It fell back on him, heavier than it had ever been. It had started again when he realized that he was short. He thought it was gone, never to return. But he was wrong. Dead wrong. Here it was again and more powerful than ever.

Still, it was different. Now it was a fear of what was to come if he made it home. What would happen when he saw his father? How could he even look at his brothers? Worst of all, how could he face his mother?

They would all see him and know what he had become. Everyone at home would know. How could they not know when they would see that any noise, any surprise move, sent him flying for cover? Would he be able to hide from them the fear he faced in his every waking hour? Everyone—everything—was dead to him. And he was numb to everything he had thought worthwhile when he had been home. Wouldn't they see that he had reached a level where he could possibly be crazy? Wouldn't they know that he was no longer like them?

But there was always a tiny spark, a dim light of hope that kept him from a final fall. It flashed weakly in a corner of his mind. It might be O.K. They could accept him, crazy or not; or at least let him be. They could never understand, but maybe they'd try.

He knew he could never be like he was before the war; but maybe he could be alive again, one day even happy again. Yes. If he tried really hard, he might look normal. Maybe he could do it. If he stayed away from anything that made him think too much, he could fool them. He might pull it off.

But those hopeful thoughts struggled against a powerful reality. He had four more weeks, one or two more trips to the sticks, before it ended. And these would be the longest weeks.

He remembered when Boudreaux and Lopez were short. They couldn't sleep. They couldn't eat. They had stared out bug-eyed—lost—into the jungle.

That had been a bad time for him, too. But now it was much worse. He was alone. There was no one left for him. They were all gone, and no one could help him now.

A movement caught his attention. He looked out to the next trench over and saw the guard. If a grunt was lucky, they sometimes sent him to the rear areas two weeks before leaving Nam. They sent him as a guard somewhere, watching over a section of the camp's perimeter that especially needed security. His duty was to stay at that position, sometimes all day long, and watch for any V.C. movements.

Keeping the grunt away from others was very smart policy. That way the nervous grunt would not be exposed to rear area politics. Green lieutenants would not accost him, demanding attention and salutes. Rear area officials wouldn't have to worry about rear area "bad boys" getting killed from having pushed a grunt's wrong button.

White knew in an instant that the other American, too, was a grunt. He also knew that the veteran had recognized him for what he was. He felt a spark, a grain of hope, as the gliding motion brought the guard next to him. They looked at each other for half a minute. How comfortable it was for White to stare into the black face of the grunt. How easy to read his history in every move he made, every blink of his piercing black eyes. So easy to understand.

He felt the tension and strain of the last few minutes go out of him. The other grunt, too, looked pleased. He looked down at White and said, "Short?" Nothing else he could have said would have confirmed his status as did that simple word.

After a moment White said, "Yeah. You?"

"Yeah," answered the guard. "I'm so fucking short I have to reach up to touch bottom". White looked at the stone-faced guard and almost smiled.

Two more weeks passed. The company had been resupplied that morning. Water, food, ammo, and replacements had been choppered in. White had set his platoon on perimeter. He had assigned guard for the night, and had eaten a light supper of pound cake and hot cocoa. That's all he could eat, his stomach refused anything else. It churned inside of him because tomorrow they would be nearing the approaches to A Shau.

The sun went low, and the darkness came. Then the pitch black came. He lay on the ground, wrapped in his poncho liner, his right hand clutching the rifle at his side. He had loosened the laces, but his boots now never came off. He was unbelievably tired. His body was near exhaustion, and his soul ached.

He had not slept more than a few hours in the last two weeks. Catnaps were the most he could get—quick, nervous catnaps, over at the least sound or suspicion. They helped only a little to ease his numb brain. "This is the last time," he thought in the darkness. This time A Shau would get him. It was finally his turn.

He was too short to sleep. Adrenalin pumped him up and kept him going. Everyone, even the others in the company who were now considered veterans, kept away from him. No one else was short. For him, only two weeks. Two weeks and a final hump into A Shau.

Green soldiers, their senses dead, slept around him or sat looking out into the black of the jungle, blind to what lay ahead for them. "They're babies," thought White, caring against his will. "What more can I do? They don't understand anything." He made almost constant rounds of his men, checking on them.

When he grew too tired, he went to his position and lay down. Now he was alone except for the phantoms swimming before his eyes. Dead and crippled comrades gathered around him. He tried to erase them, shut them off, so he could sleep. He tried to will himself to rest.

Sometimes his eyes closed and he dreamed. Images of N.V.A. waited for him in A Shau. They somehow knew he was short, and they were coming to get him. His body twitched and jerked as the bullets struck him, but still he tried to get away. He shot at them but always missed. They laughed at him when he turned to run. They followed him, chasing him down. He was shot to pieces but not dead. Now they came around him with their bayonets. They struck and stuck him, but he wouldn't die. An N.V.A. put a revolver to White's head, but before he shot, White would awaken in a cold sweat.

Then he would listen again to the frantic beating of his heart. He would see again the swirling ghosts in the dark. From somewhere far off he could hear someone calling. It was Zahn. But just as he reached her, N.V.A. appeared. Then he was shot and stabbed again.

After a long night, daylight began to penetrate through the canopy. White sat before his stove, eyes so red they could be seen from far away. He had checked his men on guard and now sat back to smoke and drink chocolate.

He was surprised to see, far to his left, a recruit eating a LRRP. Most were so exhausted after humping the day before that they had not yet stirred.

But here was this dark-haired, dark-eyed Mexican recruit, hungrily eating a LRRP of chili con carne. Then the youngster looked up and saw the death-like face of his platoon sergeant, White, looking at him. Apprehension and fear showed in his eyes, but there was something else, too.

White wanted to shut it off. He didn't want to feel anything. He didn't want to get involved with anyone again. Everyone he had gotten involved with was either dead or gone.

Now, something very strange began to happen to him. Images that he knew were not dreams swam before him. Memories jolted him, but these were happy images. Soothing pictures, acting like a balm, eased the bleeding sores in his soul.

Standing above him, looking down at him, was Boudreaux. Those frank, green eyes pierced him. That smooth, olive-colored face looked at him and took a heavy load from his tired mind. He gave White the two-fingered peace sign.

As Boudreaux's image floated away, another gracefully walked toward him. Lopez's light step brought him to White's side. His huge, bulging eyes pierced White with an understanding that left him transfixed. As he had done many months before, Lopez smiled such a pleased smile that White felt a stirring of hope.

Then it was Louis. His black face glowed with goodness, his black eyes shining with kindness. His muscles bulged like a true knight in armor, filled with chivalry. His white teeth gleamed with a cleanness that matched his nature.

In succession, images of the dead now came before him. But he now saw them as they were when alive. Cloud appeared with a closed-mouth grin. His medic pack bulged as if he would have liked to cure the world. He raised his hand in farewell, and, like his best forefathers, continued on the path of a true human being.

Hahn and Hong came together. They held hands while walking toward him. Hahn's baby face teased Jimmy Hong's Californian character. Looking down on him they smiled. They left together as they had come, brothers beyond blood.

Sam Cook and Jackson came together, too. They joked, jabbing each other, seeming to be planning some prank. Then Jackson turned to Cook. He teased him, but White couldn't understand the words. As always, Sam Cook could not sing for shit, but they both had a lot of soul.

Others swayed before him. Linh and Zahn, whores, cooks, black-toothed, smiling old ladies, and many more. The last to come, glowing like holy fire, was Professor Nguyen. His long, white wisp of a beard moved gently in the wind. His old, boy-like face wrinkled at the eyes as he smiled. Then his smile was gone, and, with a very solemn, perfectly toned voice, he said, "Do you remember about the lions, Mr. White?"

He, too, faded away. As he left, White felt very light. He felt safe. He felt like laughing.

He suddenly realized he had been staring all this while at the recruit. The boy seemed ready to burst with fear, and White realized why. Apart from the natural agony of humping and severe mental strain of the great possibility of being killed, his platoon sergeant had just stared at him like he was seeing a ghost.

White finished his chocolate and lit another cigarette. He disappeared into the thick brush to relieve himself. Then he went to the center of the perimeter and talked with the officers about the plan of march for that day. He gathered his squad leaders and went through the maps, marking target areas.

The march began. It was no longer hard for him. He felt light and rested. He was strong. The jungle unfolded before him, providing an easy path, and he was not afraid. The heavy air filled his lungs, and he was glad he could breathe again. Humping was easy around A Shau. It was going very well. It was beautiful. The jungle around A Shau was beautiful.

At mid-morning he began moving up and down the line, checking on the different men in his platoon. Some of the older men in the company were coming along, but the newest recruits struggled for every step. They fell, scratching their faces and arms on the wait-a-minutes. He tried to tell them about where they were going to get them ready, but they just didn't understand.

He came up behind the young Mexican he had stared at that morning. The boy struggled valiantly against the merciless thorns and brushes. White could see his concentration as he strained, trying to make out any kind of pattern in the thick underbrush. His frantic eyes searched high and low and side to side for any sign that could save him.

White liked him. He was trying so hard, fighting to get control. White had a sudden idea to help him out, but a quick warning stopped him. He was afraid but not for the recruit. He was afraid that he would be destroyed if something happened to the boy. He was pulled two ways. One pull was the distinct possibility that the boy would be killed later that day. The other pull was the memory of Smith. Only Smith had not come to him as a vision.

But now the meaning of his squad leader's sacrifice fully dawned on him. Smith maybe could have killed the girl to save someone else's life but not to save his own. White remembered that helpless, forlorn look replacing the sneer on Smith's face as he looked at the girl. Still, when Smith died, it might have been with a heavy heart, but it was with a clean conscience.

Even in death, White found that his comrades were still looking out for him, and he knew they always would. He came up from behind the young Mexican and matched his pace. The Mexican turned toward him, frightened.

In an instant, clarity entered White's mind. He became acutely aware of what had been digging its way into his consciousness for the last few months. Just to survive his tour of Nam was not enough. More important, imperative, was for his soul to survive. That was what was essential, no matter how long he lived...even if he died today.

Another thought brought the image of the last time he had seen the professor. He remembered that piercing, pleased expression as the professor had looked at him and said, "It is all right now, my son. Everything is all right now."

The professor was right. Everything—the jungle, the world, life, was just as it should be. Finally, after months of inner struggle, everything was all right and would always be as it should.

White looked at the Mexican recruit for a moment more and then smiled. He smiled as wide as he could. And the harder he smiled, the easier it became to smile. When the fear left the boy's face, White said, "You're doing fine, *amigo*." After a pause he went on. "After lunch, I'll show you how to set up your pack a little better."